Critical Acclaim for
Susan Wiggs

"In an authentically depicted historical landscape, Wiggs' complex characters confront situations that test their love, honor, and loyalty ... this work is definitely a cut above many historical romances."

—*Publishers Weekly* on *The Lily and the Leopard*

"Compelling, powerful, touching, this book has it all. A super read."

—Anne Stuart, author of *Saints Alive* on *Lord of the Night*

"Susan Wiggs [is] one of the romance genre's most shining stars ... who always create[s] a unique enthralling novel."

—*Affaire de Coeur*

"Susan Wiggs is truly magical."

—Laura Kinsale, author of *Flowers from the Storm*

"Heart-stopping duels, high seas adventure, and lush scenes of seduction abound. [Wiggs] spins a tale of love lost and reborn, of battles fought and races won. *The Mist and the Magic* is a must-read."

—*Happily Ever After*

"Enthralling; a marvelous mixture of fact and fiction. Susan Wiggs is a superb storyteller who has filled the pages of her novel with fascinating portraits. This powerful love story will move you to tears."

—*Romantic Times* on *The Raven and the Rose*

Tor books by Susan Wiggs

Jewel of the Sea
Kingdom of Gold
October Wind

Other titles:

Embrace the Day
The Lily and the Leopard
Lord of the Night
The Mist and the Magic
The Raven and the Rose

"Wiggs works on a huge canvas and with skill and creativity breathes life and feeling into a turbulent period of history. The action and adventure will capture your imagination. *October Wind* is a fabulous tale." —*Romantic Times*

"Susan Wiggs' *Kingdom of Gold* IS pure gold... the 24-carat variety. A tale of adventure and romance that lingers in the memory long after the last page is turned." —Ciji Ware, author of *Island of the Swans*

KINGDOM
OF
GOLD

SUSAN
WIGGS

TOR

A TOM DOHERTY ASSOCIATES BOOK
NEW YORK

KINGDOM OF GOLD

Cover art by George Bush

A Tor Book
Published by Tom Doherty Associates, Inc.
175 Fifth Avenue
New York, N.Y. 10010

Tor® is a registered trademark of Tom Doherty Associates, Inc.

ISBN: 0-812-55006-4

First Tor edition: June 1994

Printed in the United States of America

0 9 8 7 6 5 4 3 2 1

To my good friend and editor, A. Heather Wood

ACKNOWLEDGMENTS

For their constant help and support during the writing of this book, I wish to thank Barbara Dawson Smith, Arnette Lamb, Alice Borchardt, and Joyce Bell.

Suzanne Rickles and Pat Jones of the Houston Public Library and the Fondren Library of Rice University have, as always, provided immeasurable assistance with my research.

A special thank-you to Sharon Kay Penman for providing some delightful correspondence and much-needed research materials.

Many thanks to Kathryn van der Pol for her proofreading skills.

He that for virtue's sake will venture far and near,
Whose zeal is strong, whose practice true, whose faith is void of
      fear;
If any such there be, inflamed with holy care,
Here may he find a ready means his purpose to declare;
So that for each degree this treatise doth unfold,
The path to fame, the proof of seal, and way to purchase gold.

—Sir Francis Drake

PROLOGUE

London
Spring, 1572

"Bring me the child!"

Stunned silence greeted the queen's command. Her words filled the candlelit Royal Bedchamber, moving insidiously into the astonished minds of the listeners.

"Well, gentlemen?" Elizabeth Tudor closed her ivory-ribbed fan with a decisive snap. "What say you? Can you do it?"

Evan Carew felt a flash of shock and fear. He slid a secretive glance at Francis, hoping to catch his friend's eye.

But Francis Drake was staring at the bedridden queen, his gaze attracted to hers like steel drawn to a lodestone.

Even in the grip of illness, Queen Elizabeth was a daunting presence. Her vivid red hair was twisted and bejeweled into some fantastical arrangement. She wore layer upon layer of rich robes. Her outer garment of dazzling cloth of gold spilled as if molten over the burgundy counterpane.

Her long-fingered hands, as pale as her painted face, held the fan. She slapped it rhythmically upon one palm. Her face, stamped with an implacable character far more potent than mere beauty, showed the tautness of both impatience and physical pain.

Drake cleared his throat. Three years older than Evan, he had a bold tongue and plenty to say for himself. "If it please Your Majesty, this is a most singular request."

"I know it's 'singular,' damn your eyes. I—" A fit of coughing seized her. The fan dropped from her fingers. The jewels adorning her hair sparkled with each spasm.

As Drake and Evan watched in helpless alarm, a shadow moved into the circle of light surrounding the royal bed. An arras hanging rippled briefly with the movement.

The sight of the newcomer sent another jolt of shock through Evan. And on the heels of shock, a sharp sense of betrayal.

André Scalia, the most mysterious of the queen's intimates, held a glass goblet to her lips. She managed to swallow a little, then settled back on her brocade cushions.

"Thank you, André."

Evan stood chilled at the sight of André Scalia. The older man was tall and cloaked like a sorcerer, his face an exotic sculpture of harsh angles, his eyes dark and restless. Evan and Drake owed their every success on the high seas to the enigmatic man. In return for his secret support, André held a noose around their necks.

Elizabeth must have read the chagrin on the faces of her guests. "I shall not apologize for André's presence," she stated, her voice thinner after the coughing spell. "However, I assure you, no others are here tonight, listening to our secrets."

For some reason, Evan believed her. Believed the woman who had, in the fourteen years of her reign, raised simple verbal deception to a high art.

He took a deep breath. The smells of camphor and lavender barely masked the stale odor of sickness. "If it please Your Grace." His icy fingers dug into the brim of his hat, which he held in front of him. "We were born to serve you, of course, but we must know more about this mission to find the child you seek."

Her eyes gleamed like rain-washed stones. "Tell them, André."

André touched his gray, V-shaped beard. "Surely they needn't know more, Highness." His voice was soft, subtly accented, and cultured. "This is a matter of—"

"I know, André," she cut in. "Tell them."

André swept his black cloak over one shoulder. His chain of office glittered in the candlelight, and Evan caught a glimpse of his silver badge. "Gentlemen." His inflection implied that he thought just the opposite of Francis Drake, the young Devon sea captain, and Evan Carew, the swarthy Welsh mariner. "The queen has in her possession the journals of the late adventurer Sebastian Cabot."

A spark of interest flickered inside Evan. Cabot had served under five different monarchs, taken credit for innumerable acts of conquest, and had died at the venerable age of ninety.

"According to Cabot," André went on, "King Henry, eighth of that name, sired a child on a Spanish gentlewoman who was in the service of Catherine of Aragon. This lady, who was called Doña Gabriella, did flee England and bore a son in secrecy."

Drake caught his breath. "Whose word besides Cabot's do you have?"

André's thin eyebrows lifted. "Cease your questions. The whole reason for this venture is to find out the truth." Idly, he reached up and fingered his badge.

"Cabot encountered Doña Gabriella on Hispaniola in the Caribbean," André continued. "She had wed a man of obscure lineage. She called her only son—a strapping, fair boy—Phillip."

Evan and Drake stood very still, listening. Both had heard of King Henry's legendary appetite for women and his desperate quest for a son. But a child born in secret? No wonder the queen had demanded privacy for this meeting.

"Phillip married very late in life," said André. "His bride was a lady of distinction, descended of an English peer who had gone to Spain to fight the Moors."

André placed one hand on his hip and began to pace. His

slim Toledo dress sword slapped against his thigh. "The final details are uncertain. This lady died in childbirth some fifteen years ago. Her husband, Phillip, was ailing and expected to die."

Phillip. A vague, ominous buzzing started in Evan's ears. He felt himself on the edge of awareness, needing only the slightest push to propel him into the murky, perilous depths of intrigue.

"Somewhere lives a child of mine own blood," said Elizabeth. "A nephew."

"Madam," said Drake, round-eyed and solemn, "it is wonderful."

"He could be the salvation of England and the New Faith. If I could claim him early enough, before he . . ." Her voice trailed off.

Evan forced himself to speak. "Madam, will your people accept a . . . an heir of such uncertain lineage?"

A rattly laugh escaped the queen, and her fingers plucked at the bedclothes. "Accept a bastard's get, you mean? Young man, I am the daughter of Anne Boleyn, whom all of England called the Great Whore. Her marriage to my father was annulled and I declared a bastard." She opened her arms wide so that her great sleeves spread like a pair of golden wings. "Yet here I sit." With a voice as cold and hard as glass, she said, "If this child proves worthy to be king after me, then I shall make it so."

Not for an instant did anyone dare to doubt her. She had made herself the most powerful ruler in the Christian world, and her will was law.

Evan studied the floor, strewn with rushes and dried sweet bergamot. The buzzing sound grew louder in his ears, a chorus of accusing voices rising up to jeer at him.

He avoided the queen's eyes. They had the power to see into a man's mind, to smash through barriers and ferret out the truth. He must, at any cost, conceal his thoughts now, for he hid a terrible secret.

Evan Carew knew, already, where to find the missing heir to the throne of England.

CHAPTER 1

The Caribbean
17 September 1568

"Sail fine on the bow!"

The call from the foretop brought Annie Blythe rushing to the prow of the great Spanish galleon. On the slippery deck, she skidded to a halt, gripped the thick rail, and squinted at the horizon.

The sunset pierced her eyes. She saw only a dazzling, V-shaped shimmer of liquid gold racing across the water toward her.

"I can't see anything," she called out to no one in particular. Any number of ship's boys or common seamen might have heard her, but none responded.

Annie pressed her lips together in frustration. It was most vexing, this business of being a highborn lady. So many perfectly interesting people were afraid to talk to her for fear of breaching propriety.

"Patience, little one."

Even before she turned, Annie recognized the ever-present scent of cigar smoke and the oil-smooth voice of Don Iago Orozco, chief secretary to Don Martin Enriquez, the new viceroy of Mexico. Don Martin was aboard, eager to reach the mainland and take up the reins of power. Throughout the voyage, Don Iago had behaved as if his master were a second king.

With a polite smile, Annie faced Don Iago. As straight and spare as a lance, he was the picture of the Spanish cultural elite. His finely honed features bespoke generations of good breeding. Yet his hard eyes and thin, cruel mouth clamped around his cigar, so typical of gentlemen of the West Indies, disturbed Annie.

"The sun's too bright," she said. "I can't make out what the lookout has seen."

"And it's so important to do so, is it not?" Don Iago inquired, lifting one eyebrow.

Annie frowned. He often spoke in riddles that made her think his words held hidden meanings. "Important to do what, my lord?"

"Why, to see that which is unknown."

She wanted to hide from his penetrating stare. His shrewd, weighty stare. Sweet Virgin Mary, could he know her secret?

No, she told herself firmly. Impossible. Who her father was and, even more important, who her grandfather had been, were secrets kept well for more than fifty years. Don Iago was merely groping in the dark. He enjoyed baiting her because he hated her half-English father. In a world where injustice abounded, Phillip Blythe was the lone voice crying out for humanity toward the natives the Spaniards had conquered.

"Don't you have some papers to shuffle, my lord?"

Annie and Don Iago both turned to see Rodrigo Viscaino striding across the decks toward them. Her spirits lifted instantly, for Rodrigo was her father's best friend and she loved him well. Although he was nearing forty, he moved with the confident, athletic swagger of a much younger man. Eschewing the stiff doublet and billowing pantaloons so favored by Spanish gentlemen, he wore a loose green shirt, unlaced to the middle of his chest, and close-fitting black leather leggings. His simple garb, coupled with his flowing black hair and insouciant smile, gave him the look of a pirate.

Rodrigo Viscaino had a most unusual and intriguing background. He was part gypsy, part Indian, part Spanish—and all wild, passionate man. If, that is, the whispers of the viceroy's wife and her ladies were to be believed.

"As a matter of fact," Don Iago said stuffily, "I was just about to explain to our young friend the importance of this port."

Rodrigo drew her easily into the crook of his arm. "Lucky girl."

Annie flushed. She caught the sarcastic inflection in Rodrigo's voice; she saw the infinitesimal tightening of Don Iago's jaw.

"I should find your discourse most fascinating," she said courteously.

Don Iago flicked the stub of his cigar overboard. "Vitally important," he said, his close-cropped mustache twitching. "From San Juan de Ulua, we embark gold and silver for shipment to Spain. I'll show you the treasure house as soon as we land."

"Thank you, my lord," Annie said demurely.

Rodrigo took out his spyglass and aimed it at the horizon. *"Demonios!"* The word hissed from him, and his hand faltered.

Annie shaded her eyes and looked westward. The sun had lowered a notch, and now she could make out a sea-swept island that stood at the entrance to the harbor. Several squat, blocky buildings rose from the island. A fort, she realized, recognizing the black openings in the walls as gunports. Close to the island, the profiles of several ships bobbed against the sun-gilded sea. A lone ship's boat was rowing madly toward the mainland.

"What's the matter?" she asked Rodrigo.

He snapped the glass shut and thrust it into his belt. "It's incredible."

"What?" Don Iago demanded. "I command you to tell me at once."

"Those ships," said Rodrigo. "They're flying English colors."

Don Iago paled. His mouth worked like a fish's. At first no sound came out; then his shout sent every man aboard into a panic: *"The heretics are upon us!"*

Evan Carew fell to the deck of the English flagship *Jesus of Lubeck*, clutching his sides and writhing like a dying man. A few feet away, Francis Drake did likewise.

"Oh," gasped Evan, "oh, it's too much! I can't stand it!" Pulling himself up on his elbows, he wiped the tears of mirth from his eyes.

Drake's loud guffaws subsided to chuckles. "Did you see the lord treasurer's face? He was certain we were going to sprout horns and stick him with a pitchfork."

"Poor sod," said Evan. "They came all the way out in a ship's boat to greet us, thinking we were the fleet of some Spanish grandee." He drew himself to his feet and gazed at the island fort. "Admit it now," he said. "You did suffer a moment's worry when those guns went off."

"Nearly pissed myself," said Drake, combing his fingers through his dark red hair. "How was I to know it was blank shot?"

"My lord captain?" Charlie Moon, a thin, round-eyed ship's boy, approached hesitantly. In his cap, he sported his proudest possession—a long, green parrot feather. "Why did the Spaniards fire blank shot at us?"

"It was a salute, rodent," Drake said, patting the boy's cap.

"Why would they salute us?"

Evan grinned. "The treasurer and that other fellow—"

"The deputy governor of Veracruz," Drake said with certainty.

"—they thought we were the fleet of the viceroy of New Spain. That's why they came out to greet us." Evan planted his elbows on the rail and watched the Spaniards evacuating the island. The moment they had recognized the royal standard of England flying from the masthead of the *Jesus of Lubeck*, men had made the sign of the cross, jumped into the sea, and begun swimming for shore. Others had flung themselves into launches and rowed for the mainland as if the devil were at their heels.

"Idiots," Drake muttered good-naturedly, joining Evan at the rail. He waved at his comrades aboard the *Judith*, which he himself commanded and upon which Evan served as master.

"I see you've abandoned your ship, gentlemen," John Hawkins said, striding across the quarterdeck to join them.

Drake and Evan came instantly erect to face the captain general of the fleet of ten ships. "We must plan our next move, Cousin," said Drake.

Hawkins, as bluff and bearded as any common seaman, nodded. "I think it's clear. Whoever protects the low island holds the whole port of San Juan in his grasp. And by my reckoning, gentlemen, we do indeed hold the island. As well as Señor Delgadillo, who was kind enough to stay with us until we gain permission to make our repairs."

Evan braced his legs against the roll of the ship. They were anchored close enough to see the rough walls of the gun batteries and the black round muzzles of the cannon. A surge of excitement welled up in him. He had come to win a fortune; now success lay within reach. "By God's precious soul," he said, "we're in a perfect position to capture the treasure fleet of New Spain." Visions of gold and silver shimmered in his mind.

He would be rich.

Carew, the Welsh town that bore his family's ancient name, would be saved from the greed of its young lord, Owen Perrott, whose demands for taxes had beggared the common folk. Evan imagined children sitting down to a decent meal, women weaving thick, durable cloth for warm clothes. He envisioned his widowed father seated comfortably in front of a roaring fire, his larder filled with beef and butter instead of salt fish and seaweed.

Hawkins scowled at him. "You're too eager, my young master. I have no intention of attacking Spanish ships. Do

you have any idea, either of you, what would happen were
we to mount an attack?"

Drake and Evan exchanged a glance. They were both
young—Evan not quite twenty and Drake a few years older.

"War?" Drake ventured.

"Precisely," his elder cousin snapped. "This is Her Majesty's own ship. Do you doubt that this fact would escape the
Spanish?"

"We dare not risk it, then," Evan conceded, resigned from
his dreams for the moment.

"In any case," Hawkins went on, plucking at a fraying ratline, "we're in no condition to fight even a minor engage-
ment. Our hulls are leaking, the sails threadbare, our supplies
depleted."

"So what will we do?" Drake asked.

"We'll assure the lord treasurer that we come in peace, our
only intent to repair our storm-damaged fleet. We'll pay for
all store and supplies—"

"Sail there!"

The lookout's call held an edge of panic. "Thirteen great
ships, my lord captain! It's the fleet of Spain bearing hard
upon us!"

"God's teeth," Evan said as coldness formed in his gut.
"There'll be a thousand fighting men aboard."

"Gentlemen," Hawkins said, his hand clasping the hilt of
his sword, "we've just put our heads into the lion's mouth."

"How do you say 'treacherous, maggot-faced host eater' in
Spanish?" asked Drake.

Evan glowered at him. They were in a launch, sitting face-
to-face while four seamen rowed them out to the towering
Spanish flagship. The new fleet had anchored beyond the harbor, unable to pass the English ships at the island.

"For your own good," Evan said, "I'll not tell you. The
only Spanish you need teach yourself is how to say 'Yes, my
lord' and 'If it pleases my lord.' The last thing in the world
we need to do is to make the viceroy angry. Our task is to ne-
gotiate peaceable terms."

As they neared the great fleet, Evan felt a flutter of nervousness in his stomach. He hoped his knowledge of Spanish would suffice. He had been born with a sharp ear for languages, mastering his father's Welsh and the king's English as a child. He had come to speak fluent Spanish through circumstances he'd sooner forget.

At the moment, speaking Spanish was a skill he regretted having. The dirty white flag of truce fluttering from a pole in the boat seemed scant protection against the wrath of the proud, self-righteous Spanish viceroy.

The greeting they received when their launch came alongside the huge flagship did little to calm Evan's nerves. Fully a dozen muskets were aimed at his head.

"Lord, why me?" Evan muttered, grasping the rope ladder.

"Because you're the only one who can talk to these greasy devils," said Drake. "The question is, Why *me*?"

"Because you're the kinsman of Captain General Hawkins." Evan hauled himself up the ladder. The months at sea had toughened him, honed his muscles to taut sinews and burnished his skin to a deep red brown. He climbed with grace and ease, placed his hand on the gilt ship's rail, and vaulted over.

A man in a black doublet, a thin sword riding at his hip and silver buckles gleaming on his shoes, came forward as Drake joined Evan on deck.

"I am Don Iago Orozco," the man informed him. "Chief secretary to his lordship, the viceroy of New Spain."

Evan bowed and replied in Spanish. "We are at your service, sir. Er, your lordship. I am Evan Carew, master of the *Judith*, and this is Francis Drake, captain of the same and cousin to our captain general, John Hawkins."

Don Iago pursed his lips, obviously surprised at Evan's command of Spanish. "I trust you have some explanation for this atrocity." He jerked his head toward the ten English ships anchored close to the harbor island.

"We shall take that up with the viceroy, if you please."

"I don't please. You will state your business to me."

Evan nudged Drake and said in English, "He doesn't want to take us to the viceroy."

"Tell him he has no choice," Drake hissed. "Hawkins didn't send us here to parlay with underlings."

Evan took a deep breath. "With all due respect, my lord, it's the viceroy we came to see."

Don Iago's nostrils thinned as if assaulted by a bad smell. "Don Martin Enriquez does not deal with common Lutheran corsairs."

Evan felt his hackles rise. "See here—" He broke off as an extraordinary girl came to stand beside Don Iago.

Her small, dainty hand rested on the secretary's sleeve. She kept her eyes downcast and her voice low. "Please, my lord, my father and Don Rodrigo are waiting with the viceroy. What will it serve to delay these men?"

Soldiers shuffled their feet on the deck. Don Iago held himself completely still. Evan and Drake could do nothing but stare.

She couldn't have been more than thirteen, for her smooth pale cheeks still held a slight baby roundness. Freckles sprinkled the bridge of her nose. She had pale gray eyes and a glorious cascade of red-gold hair.

"Who the devil is that?" Drake whispered.

"An angel," Evan replied, blinking. "Perhaps they killed us, and we've gone to heaven."

Her grip tightened on Don Iago's sleeve. "My lord, please."

"Enough!" the secretary snapped, throwing off her hand with such force that she stumbled back against a man-at-arms. "I'll hear no mewling from you, you little whey-faced bitch."

Evan made no conscious decision to act. Yet he felt himself moving as if airborne, flying at Don Iago and flinging him to the deck. He straddled the fallen man, and his hands went around Don Iago's neck, crushing the starched ruff.

"Is this an example of Spanish honor?" he demanded, watching his opponent's face flush. "Is this how a Spaniard treats a child—"

He got no answer, for the soldiers recovered from their shock and dragged him off Don Iago. The secretary scrambled to his feet. "Kill him!" he sputtered. "Kill him now! The bastard tried to murder me!"

Evan shrugged out of his captors' grip, his rage gone now. "Don't worry, my lord. You'll live to insult womanhood another day." In truth, he was as dazed and surprised by his actions as everyone else. He had no idea what had prompted him to attack so swiftly, so violently, and so foolishly. He knew only that there was something about the girl that was so unassailably innocent and precious that he could tolerate no slur against her.

"They came under a flag of truce," she said, her face pale beneath the smattering of freckles. "You are honor bound to see to their safety, Don Iago."

Pure hatred flared in the secretary's eyes. The look was gone in an instant, replaced by harsh disapproval.

"I will take you to the viceroy," he said with obvious reluctance.

"God's holy wounds," Drake whispered as they followed the secretary to the viceroy's quarters high on the afterdeck. "Whatever prompted you to go for the bastard's throat?"

"I didn't like the way he spoke to that girl."

"Well, you picked the wrong time to indulge yourself in chivalry."

"He's taking us to the viceroy. Maybe it helped to put a brag countenance on our request."

They entered a luxurious stateroom. The viceroy of New Spain sat at a heavy, carved table, his back facing a wide bank of mullioned windows.

At first, Evan could not make out his features; he could see only the outline of a well-groomed head, a deep, stiff ruff, and shoulders exaggerated by a padded doublet. Then, as his eyes adjusted to the light, Evan made his bow.

And found himself staring into a pair of black eyes that made his blood run cold.

"This," said Don Martin, steepling his fingers, "this is what the heretics send as ambassadors?"

Evan showed no sign of his fear at the icy contempt in the viceroy's eyes. "I am but a humble messenger, my lord." Hastily he introduced Drake and himself.

"Why have you come here?"

"John Hawkins, captain general of the fleet, sends you greetings." As Evan launched into his prepared speech, he was aware of the viceroy's counselors drawing close and seating themselves at the table. Evan kept his eyes on Don Martin. It was like watching a snake; the viceroy had that same mesmeric fascination, charismatic yet deadly.

"With all respect to Your Excellency," Evan forced himself to go on, "before my master can suffer you to enter the port of San Juan, there should be some order of conditions."

"Conditions!" Don Martin held himself strangely immobile, yet his voice lashed like lightning. "Here I am, arriving as supreme ruler of New Spain, with a fleet and a vast military force, and you dare to speak to me of conditions? And to bar my way?"

"Sir, it is my master's earnest wish to safeguard his company and maintain the peace."

"What's going on?" Drake asked.

Evan hurriedly translated.

Drake fingered his red beard. "Can't say I blame him for being insulted. After all, the poor scab came all this way to find an English squadron in command of the gateway to his kingdom. It can't sit well with the oily bastard."

"Oh, do you mind your tongue." The voice, speaking perfect English, came from one of the men seated at the table.

Drake and Evan turned shocked expressions to the speaker. The girl's father, Evan realized. He had to be, for he had the same fine-boned regal looks, the same gray eyes. He was a great deal older than the girl, yet still handsome. Shades of yellow tinted his flesh and the whites of his eyes, evidence of bouts with tropical fever.

"Don Martin speaks no English," the man explained easily. "But if you persist in insulting him, I'm afraid I shall have to tell him to eject you on the instant."

Drake turned red to the tips of his ears.

"Speak the king's Castilian, Don Phillip!" Don Iago insisted, thumping the floor with his foot.

Evan cleared his throat and addressed the viceroy in Spanish again. "Sir, as to the conditions, we ask only—"

"No conditions," Don Martin exploded. "I am viceroy. I have a thousand men, and I'll enter my own port freely."

Evan felt a dangerous anger rising in him. "My lord, we represent our queen's own person, and therefore Captain General Hawkins is viceroy, too. Our powder and shot will take the better place to your Spanish soldiers."

His arrogance stunned the Spaniards. Don Phillip exchanged a glance with his companion, a dark, long-haired man who lounged in ungainly fashion on his stool.

"Jesu, Evan," Drake whispered, "what did you say to them?"

"I believe I just threatened them with pitched battle."

"Oh, well done," Drake muttered wryly.

The viceroy recovered first. "A corsair with backbone," he said. "Most unusual. Young master, you may tell your captain general that we will make a treaty with you."

Evan would have been gratified by the apparent concession. But the viceroy smiled at him. And it was the cold, confident smile of a duelist about to deliver the coup de grace.

"Amazing," Drake said, pressing the treaty and letters to his chest as they returned to the English fleet. "We've gotten an honorable agreement out of the sly chiselers."

"Have we?" Evan ran a hand through his salt-stiffened hair and remembered the viceroy's secretive expression. "I wonder."

"What's to wonder about?" Drake patted the documents. "It's all we could hope for. We'll be allowed to repair our ships and buy stores. We retain control of the island as a guarantee of our safety. No armed Spaniard may land on the island. We exchange ten hostages." With a satisfied smile, he leaned back against the gunwale of the launch. "For a crew with ten disabled ships, we managed to strike a fair bargain."

* * *

Evan slept badly that night, shifting in his hammock and coming awake at every creak of timber and rope. In the dark before the dawn, he abandoned his efforts to sleep and went abovedecks.

Both fleets lay at anchor. No more than twenty yards separated Spanish vessel from English. The water was calm and had the deep, impenetrable shade of ink. Evan cocked his head. He thought he heard the plash of an oar somewhere between the mainland and the island.

A fish jumping, he told himself.

But then he heard it again.

Followed by the unmistakable chink of arms and the rumble of muffled voices.

Evan leaned out over the rail and squinted into the darkness until his eyes ached. The shadow of a cloud glided toward the Spanish flagship. Then the shadow changed, resolved itself into a shape, and Evan's suspicions turned to hard certainty.

Cold sweat trickled down his neck as he went to rouse Hawkins.

"Sir," he whispered in the dark cabin, "I think they're boarding troops from the mainland."

Hawkins did not question Evan's suggestion. When dawn broke, he dispatched Robert Barnett of Saltash, the Spanish-speaking master of the *Jesus of Lubeck*, to voice an objection to the viceroy.

As Barnett departed in a launch, Evan was stung by the feeling that he would never see his comrade again. The day dragged on interminably as he waited. He did not even have Drake to pass the time with; his companion and a large group of seamen had gone to the island to guard the cannons. A number of Spanish mariners roamed the island, too. In accordance with the treaty, all were unarmed.

Hawkins placed extra guards on the Spanish hostages. He had only nine; the tenth had yet to arrive. No doubt the viceroy was having trouble finding men to volunteer, which further roused Evan's suspicions.

By sunset, Barnett had not returned, and Evan's nerves

were frayed to the breaking point. "I'm going to the island," he said to Hawkins. "Perhaps my knowledge of Spanish will help me discover what they're about." His hand fell to the dagger sheath at his belt.

"No," Hawkins said, frowning. "No arms. Not even an eating knife. We swore on our honor."

Evan did not argue. Hawkins was right. Whatever treachery the Spaniards might have planned, the English would keep their word. The notion of dying for the sake of honor held no appeal for Evan, but he liked even less the idea of living with the knowledge that he had broken faith. Leaving his dagger behind, he rowed a small ship's boat to the low island with its crude fort.

Salt water filled his boots, and as he stepped onto the pebbled shore, his feet made unpleasant squishing sounds as he walked through the evening mist.

The sight that greeted him filled him with hope. He saw no weapons on either Spaniard or Englishman. A group of men sat playing cards on an upturned barrel, the language barrier transcended by their avid interest in the game. Nearby, a lantern hung from a pole stuck in the sandy ground, and a string of fish smoked over a fire.

Drake sat cross-legged on the rocky ground, his hand of painted tin cards hugged to his chest.

"Evan, my master," he called out, "come join us. I've won a handful of these silver things from our hosts. In fact, I mean to wager it all on the next hand."

A Spaniard dealt, and Evan had to bite his tongue. From his vantage point, standing above and to the side of the players, he alone could see that the dealer was cheating.

CHAPTER 2

"Annie!" Phillip Blythe fixed her with a stare of angry consternation. "What the devil are you doing out here on the island? You're supposed to be on the mainland. You could be accosted—"

"I came back from the mainland in Don Iago's launch," she said without contrition. "Father, I had to see you. Don Iago said you're going aboard the English ship as the tenth hostage." She shivered, remembering Don Iago's unsettling smile, the thinly veiled malice in his eyes. "I don't want you to go." She took her father's hand and pressed it to her cheek. "It's too dangerous."

All around them, the island teemed with Englishmen and Spaniards, fraternizing with a familiarity Annie did not trust.

Phillip smiled gently. "I must go. The terms require it."

"But why you?"

"The viceroy had trouble finding volunteers. Besides, my dear one, half the blood in my veins is English."

She stared at the pebbles on the shore, heard them hiss with the motion of the incoming waves. "That blood will spill as freely as any other once the pirates realize they've been tricked."

His shoulders stiffened. "What makes you think some trick is afoot, Annie?"

She kept her gaze low. "I don't trust Don Martin and Don Iago."

Phillip sighed wearily. She looked up, and in that moment she could see how the years wore on him. Since her babyhood, he had suffered from tropical fever, and more than once he had lain near death. Besides illness, she saw plain, utter exhaustion, the fatigue of a good man who had spent a lifetime fighting a losing battle with greedy, unprincipled conquistadors. As a member of the Council of the Indies, he tried to ensure humane treatment for the natives. In return for his efforts, he had gained the enmity of scores of Spaniards who believed the natives no better than beasts of burden. He would have been removed from office long ago but for the influence of his late wife's family, the blue-blooded de Carvals.

"I must go," he said again. "I'm the only one who speaks decent English."

A burst of laughter came from a group of men near the battery. Glancing over, Annie recognized the dark, intense man who had attacked Don Iago.

In her defense. Ever since the incident she had wondered why he had leaped so madly upon the Spanish don, why he had risked death for her sake. But he was the enemy, and she would never have the chance to ask him.

She turned back to her father. "I speak English as well as you."

Phillip placed his hands firmly on her shoulders and drew her close. "Never, ever think of interfering in the politics of England or Spain, my willful girl." He drew back. "Look, I can delay no longer. I want you to take a launch back to the mainland."

"I will, Father." Even as she spoke, Annie knew she lied.

"Take these with you." Phillip gave her three items: an iron trefoil key on a large ring, a leather pouch containing an old embroidered handkerchief, and a ruby ring, which he twisted off his finger and suspended from a leather string around her neck.

A lump rose in her throat, and she spoke with difficulty. "Father, why are you giving me these?"

"For safekeeping. As I have told you, use them only if you have no choice. God was merciful, and in my lifetime I never had need of them. But if your back is to the wall, Annie, use them to prove your true identity. They will protect you."

Or damn me for all time, she thought, suddenly cold to the very tips of her fingers. "Father, please—"

"No more, Annie. You must be brave. If anything happens to me, Rodrigo will take you to my mother and stepfather on Hispaniola."

"Saints and angels, nothing will happen to you," she said fiercely. "You're not getting on that English ship."

He touched her beneath the chin. "Cease your arguing, sweetheart. I must go. Honor demands it. Now, get you back to the mainland and find Rodrigo. I believe he's collecting supplies for our English guests."

Through a sheen of tears, Annie managed a tremulous smile. "Rodrigo, protector of widows and orphans."

"He's a good man despite his wild ways." Phillip kissed her softly on each cheek, her brow, and then her lips. "Don't despair, little one. I'll be back before you know it." He propelled her toward a ship's boat manned by two Spanish seamen. "Now begone, Annie."

As she watched him walk down the beach to a different launch, she fastened the pouch and key to her stomacher. The ring around her neck felt as heavy as a millstone.

Phillip stood in the launch and raised his arm in farewell. She tried not to scream out her fears as the mariners took up the oars and struck out for the English flagship.

"Ah, the last hostage is on his way, then?" asked Don Iago, suddenly behind her.

She whirled around, a scowl on her face. She wished he had remained on the mainland like the coward he was. "Yes," she said, "over my protests."

"The plan's well in motion, then," he added, sliding one hand into his doublet.

Annie's stomach leaped in fear. "Plan, my lord?"

"Why, our plot to destroy every heretic in sight." He drew out a cigar and gestured absently at the men gathered near the gun batteries. "Every man of the true faith conceals a weapon. In a moment, a trumpet will sound, and the slaughter will begin."

"No." Her voice was a harsh whisper. She stumbled back, her gaze seeking out her father. Already he was just a short distance from the English ship, and too far away to hear her if she shouted a warning. "You sent him to be slaughtered!"

"You'd best make yourself scarce, girl," Don Iago said, "else you might get caught in the fray." His doublet gaped open, and a blade gleamed within.

"No!" This time, she screamed.

Don Iago's face reddened with fury. "Shut up, damn you, or you'll give us away!" He reached for her but she turned and ran, sobbing, her skirts hiked to her knees. She could hear his boots scrabbling over the rocky ground, his breath rasping as he gave chase.

Annie knew she must stop the slaughter. If the Spaniards' plan worked, she had no hope of ever seeing her father again.

Don Iago's hand clawed at her back and snagged in her coif. Terrified, she jerked free, and her hair flew out behind her. Don Iago stumbled and fell with a curse.

Seizing her advantage, Annie ran toward the dark-haired Englishman. He still stood near a group of men playing cards. When he had defended her from Don Iago, she had suspected him of decency. Now he was her only hope.

"Please," she said, panting, drawing him aside. The men looked up from their cards, regarding her as if she were mad. She ignored them. "Sir, I must speak with you."

His eyebrows winged upward in startlement, but he stepped aside and bent his head to listen. A curling lock of black hair fell over his brow. "Yes? What is it?"

"A trick," she gasped out. "They all have concealed weapons."

"Who?"

"The Spaniards," she hissed in fearful impatience.

"That's not possible. We have the viceroy's sworn word that his men remain unarmed."

"More fool you," she said, choking back tears. "I *know* Don Martin and Don Iago. They mean to—"

The blare of a trumpet split the air.

Annie watched a nightmare burst to life.

The Spaniards jumped to their feet. As if by magic, daggers and dirks appeared in their hands. In the blink of an eye she saw three throats slit. Blood spurted, showering the cards and coins that had lain as an innocent game between Spaniard and Englishman only moments earlier.

"Drake, run!" the dark-haired man shouted. "To the ships!"

"I'm coming, Evan!" From some twenty yards away, a stocky man with a red beard raced toward them. Fearsome rage flared in his pale eyes; then he turned to face an oncoming soldier. The Spaniard came on with dagger drawn and aimed at Drake's chest.

Annie held her breath in horror. Just as the Spanish blade kissed the front of Drake's shirt, his leg came up in a lightning bolt of movement. Even from a distance, Annie could hear the crunch of bone as Drake's foot smashed into the soldier's face.

The man called Evan let out a shaky breath. Drake raced out into the surf. "Make haste," he shouted. "The company of traitorous villains is bad for one's health."

Evan shook his head like a large dog coming awake. Then, instead of following his companion, he grabbed Annie's arm and dragged her into the shadow of the fort.

She fought and kicked. What a fool she had been to trust him and to stand amazed while their countrymen fought. If the English took the day, she might become their captive. They might subject her to the unspeakable acts whispered about by the viceroy's maids.

As he dragged her along, Evan seemed not to feel her

blows on his sinewy limbs. "Let go of me," she yelled. "My father—"

"Hush, and cry peace," he said through his teeth, shoving her against a stone wall between two sloping supports. "I'm just trying to get you out of the line of fire, if it comes to that."

She stopped struggling, realizing that the wall of the structure concealed her. "Why are you doing this?" she demanded.

His massive shoulders lifted. "Damned if I know. Perhaps because you tried to warn me."

"Evan!" Drake's shout held the ragged edge of desperation. "We can't wait any longer!"

Annie did not understand the word Evan uttered, though she guessed it was a curse. "Go," she said. "Save yourself."

He fixed her with a long look. Beneath the tumbling black locks of his hair, his clear, intelligent eyes were rich brown, the color of late summer honey, and set in a face that was rough but not cruel.

Evan said the curse word one more time, then dove into the desperate confusion around the nearest gun battery.

The fool, Annie thought as sick fear soured her stomach. He was going to try to take possession of the cannon.

She spared no more thought for the stranger called Evan. Her father was on his way to the English flagship. She must stop him, for the treachery of the Spaniards would cost the hostages their lives. Casting off Evan's warning to stay hidden, she ducked low and ran down to the beach.

Every available launch had been taken. They were crammed with terrified, betrayed English mariners, rowing like madmen to reach their ships.

Unhesitatingly, Annie tore at the laces of her bodice and skirt, then wrestled out of her cagelike farthingale. The iron key on its ring chimed as it hit the ground. In her shift, she dashed out into the stinging salt water in search of her father.

A swift undertow thwarted her efforts, hauling her two paces back for every one of headway she gained. Sobbing in frustration, she plunged on.

"Annie! Stay back!" Her father's faint voice broke through her panic. She stood in the waist-deep surf. Hope filled her chest. Phillip was still in the launch; he had not yet gone aboard the *Jesus of Lubeck*.

Cannon shot and musket fire spat in the air. Wincing at the sound, Annie shouted encouragement to her father and the two seamen at the oars of his launch. The English and Spanish fleets formed a menacing maze around the small, bobbing ship's boat.

"Hurry, Father!" she screamed. "Get away!"

One of the English ships blocked his escape to the island. Phillip's launch headed toward the Spanish galleon *Almirante*.

Clasping the ring he had given her, Annie watched in an agony of suspense. If he reached the *Almirante*, he would be safe.

Already the battle was falling to the Spanish. A ship, its deck crammed with soldiers, closed in on the English *Minion*. Grappling lines swung out like great threads of a spider's web and hauled the *Minion* close.

"Santiago!" The battle cry of Spain blazed across the waters.

"God and Saint George!" the English answered defiantly.

Annie kept her gaze fastened on her father. He was perhaps twenty oar strokes from the *Almirante* when she realized another of the English ships had moved in close.

Mariners manned the capstans, hauling the ships closer to their anchors, bringing one vessel broadside to the *Almirante*.

Torches smoked and flared on the English ship. Instantly, Annie knew what would happen.

"Father!" She struck out blindly for the launch. Salt water flooded her eyes and nose, and she came up choking.

At that moment, the English guns spoke.

Deafened by the roar, Annie dashed the water from her eyes. Some of the cannon shot bounced harmlessly off the oaken hull of the great Spanish ship. A few balls tore smoky holes in the sails and rigging. Sparks of orange leaped on the rail of the galleon.

"The magazines!" a Spaniard screamed. "If the gunpowder blows, we're all dead men!"

Annie's mouth formed a wordless O. Her father's launch veered in a different direction, but he was still dangerously close to the *Almirante*.

At first Annie saw only a few more sparks and began to hope that the shipboard magazine was safe from the bombardment. Then a muffled popping sound crescendoed to hellish thunder.

The explosion blinded her. Even from the island shore, she could feel the heat and force of the detonation. Yellowish smoke roiled across the water, shrouding the ghastly scene in a noxious sulfur smell.

Even before the smoke cleared, she knew her father was dead. No one, nothing, could have survived the blast.

All will to live left her, and she let the surf take her. Cool currents drifted through her wildly disarranged hair. Her face submerged, and she could feel herself losing consciousness.

A wave deposited her in shallow water. She came to her senses, choking and sputtering, her feet scraped by the rocky bottom. She would find no refuge in death now.

In a daze of shock and horror, she drew her knees to her chest and sat in the shifting surf. With numb indifference she watched the battle. Don Martin's flagship, that seemingly indestructible floating fortress, began to settle lower and lower in the water. The exploding magazine had torn a huge hole in the side, and water rushed in at a furious rate.

The English ships, cut from their cables and head ropes, attacked like a swarm of angry bees on a marauding bear. They sped in for the sting, then feinted back as their large, cumbersome prey lurched helplessly and began to sink.

Annie's discarded skirt washed up around her trembling legs. "Father," she whispered, clutching the ruby ring to her chest. The other treasures he had given her were gone, having floated off in the surf.

Panic shot through her, and she lurched to her feet. If anyone found them, guessed their significance, she would be hunted down by English and Spanish alike.

But she spared no more time searching, for a ship's boat emerged from the thick smoke that boiled across the water.

Moments later, she sat with her dead father's head in her lap, his blank eyes staring into eternity.

She lifted her tortured gaze to the seaman who had brought Phillip to her. "His soul has already taken flight," she said in a dazed whisper.

"No doubt to Paradise, miss. His last act was to throw himself upon me, to shield me from the explosion."

Annie forced herself to look at the innumerable bloody gashes in her father's back—mortal wounds he had taken for the man. She felt no surprise at her father's heroism, his sacrifice. Phillip Blythe had died as he had lived, as a man of honor.

Perhaps, then, it was fitting for him to die now, for Spanish honor was but an empty promise these days.

The sounds of battle at the gun batteries grew louder. Annie had never been in the thick of combat before. It bore no resemblance to the exciting narratives she heard in the taverns of Santo Domingo and Veracruz. Real battle was ugly and terrifying, the air full of inhuman screams, the sharp smell of blood, the stink of spilled entrails.

The man stood. "There's still a few Lutheran heretics about." Drawing a short dagger, he handed it to her. "Use this if you must," he said, then made the sign of the cross and ran up the beach.

With a dozen Spaniards in pursuit, Evan raced for the shore. Only he and two other Englishmen, a seaman named Dirk and a ship's carpenter called Denton, remained on the island.

They fought with weapons snatched from Spanish corpses. As they battled their way free, an explosion sounded at one of the gun batteries. The cloud of thick smoke smothered them, hiding them from their pursuers. Evan grabbed Dirk's arm and hauled him around the corner of the fortress. They leaned against the wall, sweating and trying to stifle their coughs and sneezes.

"There's a launch!" Denton whispered, pointing at the shore. "We'll take it."

"Best hurry, or our ships will abandon us!" Dirk looked right and left, then gestured with his hand. "After me."

Evan lowered his head and started to follow his companions. From the corner of his eye, he saw a flicker of bright green and slowed his steps. "Wait, Denton," he called.

No, he thought as he ran toward the vivid bit of color, which lay near a large, rounded rock. *Please God, no, please please please* ... His vain prayer ended on a curse, for his worst fears came true.

Charlie Moon, the ship's boy, lay dead, his green parrot feather still in his cap, his innocent face a mask of bewilderment. His throat had been slit to the bone.

"Evan, hurry," Dirk urged. "You can do nothing for the lad now! We'll be dead for sure if we're not gone by the time this smoke clears."

In a red haze of rage, Evan lifted up Charlie's limp body and followed his companions. The wind swept aside the curtain of smoke and gave him a view of the English line. Shot from the shore batteries ripped through the flotilla. The *Angel* had already begun to sink; the *Swallow* and *Gratia Dei* were foundering like harpooned fish. Worst of all, the *Jesus of Lubeck* was in its death throes, its masts and sails flying in pieces.

Even so, John Hawkins stood on deck, waving a silver tankard of beer in his hand as he directed the fight. His booming voice carried clearly across the water. "Stand lustily like men!" he exhorted the gunners. No sooner were the words out of his mouth than the cup was shot from his hand. "Hah!" Hawkins blustered. "God has preserved me! So shall he deliver us from these villains!"

Not soon enough, Evan thought darkly, gazing at the child in his arms. His boots crunched on the pebbled beach; then he stumbled into something soft and yielding.

Snapping to attention, he held the child in one arm and brandished his Spanish knife to defend himself. He froze in a combative stance, staring at the girl.

Wearing only a wet shift, she sat on her heels. Her damp hair, wild and vividly red, poured over her trembling shoulders like a mass of seaweed.

She held her father's bloodless hand and a short, pointed dagger.

The courtly man Evan recalled from the meeting aboard the flagship lay dead. Wood splinters and bits of metal had torn into his back.

Evan's gut roiled as he gently lay Charlie on the ground. "Miss . . ." He had no idea what to say to her. He heard his companions clambering into the abandoned launch, heard them calling his name in urgent voices.

He could not tear his eyes from the pale girl. He wanted to tell her he was sorry. He wanted to touch her, to take the wet, cold corpse away from her. Yes, that was it. She should not be burdened by this terrible death.

Bending, he reached for the body.

The girl uncoiled like a spring, coming to her feet so swiftly that Evan stepped back in surprise.

"Don't touch him," she said in English. "Don't you dare touch him."

Evan could only stare. How tall and lithe she was, her form boyish yet imposing, her face ablaze with grief and rage. Somehow she managed to appear more fierce and warlike than the hordes of Spanish soldiers.

"Miss." He cleared his throat. "Please, may I—"

"Saints and angels," she cried hoarsely, "have I not suffered enough?"

"Evan, damn your eyes!" Denton grabbed him roughly by the arm. "They're coming down from the gun batteries. Will you stay and let the cheating papists carve your heart out?"

As he spoke, Denton picked up Charlie Moon. Yanking at Evan's arm, he brought him to the launch and shoved him in. Dirk started rowing into the smoke-covered sea.

Evan took the body of the ship's boy into his lap. Resting his chin on the lad's cool, downy hair, he watched as the girl dropped to her knees beside her father.

Then she flung back her head and began to rock, the action so poignant that Evan's throat thickened.

"There," Denton said excitedly. "It's the *Judith*."

He stopped and looked at Evan, who was still squinting through the smoke at the island.

"Pity about the girl," said Denton.

Burning bright stars pierced the black canvas of the night. Watery moonglow made a sinuous path upon the water, disturbed by the wake of the *Judith*. A gromet played diffidently upon a hornpipe, blowing a mournful lay that set the mood of the crew to music. At Drake's orders, Evan had set a course to the north and east. Every inch of sail was stretched to its threadbare limits, for the Englishmen were in a hurry.

"Damn," said Drake, pacing the windward deck, raising his voice over the hiss and gurgle of water past the hull. "I would to God that I knew what's become of Captain Hawkins."

Evan nodded grimly. The exodus from the port of San Juan de Ulua had taken place in frantic confusion, and they had no idea how many of their countrymen had survived.

The *Angel* had been sunk by the guns of the shore batteries. The *Swallow* had foundered, and one of the caravels had simply disappeared. Like a pack of wolves on a dying bullock, the treacherous Spaniards had ripped into the wreck of the *Jesus of Lubeck*. All hands had been forced to abandon her. The last they'd seen of Hawkins, he had taken command of the *Minion*. Evan could imagine Hawkins's rage at losing the queen's investment in the trading mission.

He shared that rage. It was a hot, red thing, simmering in his brain like a pot brought to the boil. He had never known such treachery as they had suffered at the hands of the Spaniards. Don Martin had signed a treaty in good faith; he had sent personal letters assuring Hawkins that the English would be safe.

"We entered the port with ten ships," Evan said.

"Only two fought their way clear," said Drake. "I pray the *Minion* managed to elude capture."

Evan nodded. They had lost sight of Hawkins's ship, and a harsh northerly had begun to blow down the gulf. There was no question of going back to search for the *Minion*, especially in their state of disrepair and with heavy weather driving them out to sea. Drake had grappled with torn loyalties, ultimately deciding his duty as captain was to take his present company to safety and suffer Hawkins's wrath later.

"How many dead, I wonder?" Drake mused.

"Plenty, including the ten hostages we gave them in good faith. We won't know for certain until we find the *Minion*." Evan rubbed his hand over his weary face. "Francis . . ."

"Yes?"

"We lost Charlie Moon. Dirk, Denton, and I gave the lad a burial at sea just before we boarded the *Judith*." Anger and bitterness roughened his voice. "By my lady, they murder children!"

Drake made no response, but Evan saw his shoulders stiffen slightly. Evan sighed with a bone-deep fatigue that was slowly numbing his brain. Hatred, it seemed, was an exhausting business. "I shudder to think of those we left behind alive. The Inquisition will make their dying a long and terrible process."

Drake's fist struck the rail hard. "Why?" he demanded. "Are our countries at war? Hawkins behaved with dignity and restraint. He didn't lay a hand on the Spanish hostages."

"Even though he had every right to slaughter them the moment the Spanish dogs launched their attack," Evan added.

Drake began to pace in agitation. "My first mate is dead. I saw a Spanish soldier shove a sword clean through his body." His voice trembled. "What am I to say to his wife? They just had a baby. What of Orlando and Ribley and Collins—all of my crew who did not escape. And by the life of God, Evan! How am I to face Charlie Moon's mother? How will I answer to their families? Am I to say they died unarmed, because we were foolish enough to trust the word of a Spaniard?"

Evan drew a shuddering breath. "I have no answer to that,

Francis. I should have raised an objection when I saw them cheating at cards." He ground his teeth together. "It seemed a small matter at the time, but—"

"They betrayed their sworn oath." Drake drew a hissing breath. "And despoiled my reputation by making a disaster of my first command."

Something in Drake's voice caused Evan to turn and look at him. He saw the Francis Drake he had known since that day three years earlier, when Evan had walked into Plymouth with a pocketful of scraped-together coins and the dreams of a whole town resting invisibly on his shoulders. He saw a small, muscular man with dark red hair and beard, a strong face, and sharp eyes.

Yet something had changed. Lost was the bluff innocence of the adventurer. Drake's eyes had hardened. A chill slithered down Evan's spine, and he realized that Drake not only shared his murderous rage at the Spaniards; he intended to act upon it.

His hatred was as implacable as his faith. He would never forgive this injury.

"Why do you look at me so, Evan?" he asked in that same cold voice.

"I think," Evan said, "that Don Martin will live to regret this day. He's created a deadly enemy in you, Francis."

Drake touched his chest, where his loose doublet revealed a soiled shirt open at the throat. "Me, Evan? I'm no murderer."

"You won't avenge this day?"

"I came out here to learn the ways of the sea and to trade in this vast new empire. But now I'll have done with this contraband commerce." Drake drew a deep breath. "Our nations might not be at war, but *I* am, Evan. From the moment those contemptible bastards set upon us, I knew my destiny was the devastation of Spain."

"Sounds like a large undertaking for one man."

"One? You're not with me on this, Evan?"

"I didn't say that." Evan thought of the people of his village, the fishermen and crofters and laborers who had sacrificed to send him to sea and who depended on him to succeed. "I'll come back with you, Francis. Together, we'll ram ourselves into this empire." Evan had a fleeting image of the girl on the beach, half-crazed with rage and grief as she defended her father's body. The Spanish, it seemed, sacrificed even their own.

He pushed the image of the girl aside, saying, "And then, my good master, we'll extract a rightful payment."

CHAPTER 3

Hispaniola
November, 1568

In grim silence, Annie and Rodrigo rode a pair of mules up the trail from the port of Santo Domingo. A string of four silent retainers followed with the pack animals. Annie was too drained in body and spirit to give more than passing notice to the lush, green hills thick with vegetation, the peaceful clicking of insects, and the chittering of birds. She felt certain that she would never smile again, never wonder at the beauty of the aqua sea and the emerald islands, never let her heart warm to another human being.

Her father was dead, and the task of telling his parents fell to her.

Sticky sweat trickled down the back of her neck. Her grandmother, Doña Gabriella, had given birth to only one child—only Phillip. She had never seemed to regret the lack, for she clung to the steadfast love of William Blythe, the man who had taken both her and her illegitimate son into his heart.

Though Annie had not seen her grandparents in nearly two years, she remembered them clearly. She conjured an image of Gabriella, white-haired and dark-eyed, singing in the twilight, her voice ageless and utterably sweet. And Will, sturdy and devoted, proprietor of Gema del Mar, the most prosperous plantation on the island.

For the first time, an emotion other than stone-cold grief invaded Annie's heart. She loved her grandparents. She would sorrow with them, learn to feel again. In their arms, she would retreat into childhood one last time. Maybe then she would be able to face the future.

She glanced back at Rodrigo, who slouched upon his mule, a broad-brimmed native straw hat shadowing his sharp, handsome features. He tipped back his head to take a drink from his flask. She could just see his mouth, set in a straight line, and the stubble of a beard, dark against the pallor of his face. Since the battle at San Juan, Rodrigo had steeped his sorrows in fiery rum and bittersweet remembrances.

Resentment rose up in Annie; then she tempered her ill humor. He had lost his best friend. He had seen his countrymen betray their sworn word. She had lost the one she held dearest; why couldn't they comfort each other?

He saw her staring at him and pushed up the brim of his hat. The effects of hard drinking somehow enhanced his handsomeness. To her, he had always looked like a hero from a fireside tale: dark-haired, his skin bronzed, his features cleanly sculpted and intense.

"Are you all right, *muchacha*?" he asked.

"I was thinking about my grandparents, Rodrigo. What in God's name will I say to them?"

"You can but tell them the truth. That their son died as he lived. With courage. They'll endure. After your mother passed away and Phillip took sick, they expected him to die. And many times after that, the tropical fever laid him low, and they said their farewells."

"But to learn that he perished so violently, in such pain."

"He died quickly and honorably *muchacha*." The heat made him irritable. "He died a hero, sacrificing his own life for another. There are worse ways to go."

"Yes," she snapped. "Poisoning yourself with rum, for example."

He glared at her; then his expression softened. "Let's not fly at each other's throats. Not at such a time."

"I'm sorry." Her hand stole up to finger the ruby ring suspended around her neck. She wore it concealed inside her bodice. She had never managed to find the handkerchief and the key to her father's strongbox.

The loss worried her, for the large, heavy coffer contained the true story of Papa's lineage. But surely no one could know that. Besides, the coffer was safe at her grandparents' plantation, at Gema del Mar.

She rode on, trying not to remember other times she had traveled this path, when she and her father had sung seamen's ballads to pass the time. The road seemed more overgrown than she recalled, vines snaking across the track, branches hanging low so that thick, shiny leaves brushed her head and shoulders as she passed. Papácito Will had a competent overseer. Why wasn't the road clear?

The vegetation grew denser with each plodding step of the mules. As they neared the top of the hill, Annie had the eerie sensation that she was riding through a long, green tunnel. The darkness was strange, aglow with emerald light. She heard the liquid rush of a spring spilling over rocks and remembered that the natives considered it a sacred place of wood gods.

Sometimes the house servants would tell her stories that were all the sweeter for being forbidden to a Catholic girl. The tales held an edge of poignancy, too, for the people who had inhabited this island since time out of mind were nearly gone, succumbing to the diseases and murderous impulses of the Spanish conquerors.

She listened for the steady grinding sound of the *ingenio* that crushed the whitish liquid from the pulpy stalks of cane. She listened for the songs of the workers as they manned the apparatus. By now, she should be able to smell the burnt sweet aroma of boiling cane syrup.

Instead she heard only the whir of the jungle. She smelled only the heavy orchid scent of the plants.

She threw a glance over her shoulder at Rodrigo. He seemed to hold himself more stiffly upon his mule. His shoulders were tense, and he was craning his neck, trying to see past her.

"Something's different," she said.

"Yes."

They reached the pinnacle of the last hill on their journey to Gema del Mar. The mules brought them out into glaring sunshine, a sky of sailing clouds, and a vale of green-draped jungle.

"We're lost," Annie said, irritated.

Rodrigo maneuvered his mule into lead position. "No, we aren't. Annie . . ." Something in the harsh tone of his voice chilled her. "*Muchacha*, I want you to wait here with the bearers." He never took his eyes off the dark valley.

She stared in the same direction. Realization broke like a cold sweat over her. The vine-draped shapes far below were buildings. Her grandparents' villa—she could just see a bit of the red-tiled roof. And the outbuildings—servants' quarters, barns and huts and stables. They were all still there. But the jungle had reclaimed them.

"*No!*" The denial whispered past her knotted throat. Ignoring Rodrigo's protests, she kicked her mule and headed down into the valley.

Please God, let them be safe. . . . Disjointed prayers screamed through her mind. They must be all right. They couldn't have abandoned their home.

When she and Rodrigo reached the plantation, the last spark of hope was snuffed out. They had to wait for two of the servants to hack a path through the lawn where she had once played, to the veranda where her grandmother used to sing to her.

The once handsome house, with its plaster and tilework, its expensive glazed windows and wrought iron gates, had fallen to ruin. Slimy mildew crept over the lime-washed walls.

Jagged shards of glass framed the windows. The smell of stale smoke emanated from the blackened ceilings.

The door looked as if it had been wrenched from its hinges. His face somber, Rodrigo stepped inside. "Annie, stay—"

"No," she said simply, following him.

"Just watch your step."

As they made their way through the rooms and patios of the villa, Annie was seized by a terrible sense of violation. Someone had invaded the peace and prosperity of her grandparents' home. Someone had laid waste to a lifetime of building.

Broken furniture, smashed vessels, dry fountains, burned books in great piles. Charred heaps of clothing. Torn hangings and draperies, flies buzzing over spoiled food. Nothing had been left unharmed.

She and Rodrigo stood together in the central patio. The creeping growth had not yet claimed this spot. It was like standing in a bowl of sunshine, the light glinting off the *azulejo* tiles imported from Portugal, the shattered remains of a fountain crafted by a Moor called El Hakim. Annie saw herself as a child, toddling across the mosaic surface of the patio, her chubby arms stretched toward her laughing father while Papácito played a lively tune on a viol he had carved with his own hands.

She shut her eyes against the memories and whispered, "Who did this?"

"We'll have to make inquiries in Santo Domingo."

She opened her eyes and paced the ruined courtyard. "A native uprising?" she mused aloud, then answered her own question. "No, it couldn't have been. Papácito was the only man on the island who didn't keep slaves. The natives respected him for that." The words came in a flood. "Maybe a rebel tribe attacked from the other side of the island. I remember Papa telling me of—"

"Annie, stop." Rodrigo grasped her by the shoulders. His strong fingers dug into her. "Don't carry on like this. You'll make yourself crazy."

"Not knowing is what makes me crazy!" she yelled at him, the tears streaming down her cheeks. "I must know who did this."

"White demons," said a voice.

Rodrigo released Annie in surprise. She stumbled back to gape at the youth who stood there.

Although his blade nose and thin lips indicated Spanish blood, his straight black hair, glossy as a curtain of silk, and his painted, nearly naked body marked him as a native.

He strode forward, not flinching even when Rodrigo's sword snicked from its sheath.

"I mean no harm," the youth said in a musical patois, his native accent softening the Spanish words.

"Where did you come from?" Rodrigo demanded.

"I used to live here. Now I live in the forests beyond the hills."

"Where are Señor Blythe and his wife? Tell us all you know about this." Putting away his sword, Rodrigo encompassed the patio with a sweep of his arm.

"The white demons made a big fight here." He looked at Annie. "You, I remember. Doña Gabriella's granddaughter. Yes?"

"Remember me? How can you know me?"

"Paulo knows from looking." He pointed at his eye, which was surrounded by pasty white paint. "My mother was a housemaid. My father was a white demon."

As he spoke, Annie let her fascinated gaze travel over him. His chest was brown and hairless, streaked with ocher and black paint that made lightning bolts from his shoulders to his navel. A twisted string held a tiny woven cloth over his private parts. At each side of the scanty covering, his brown, muscular hips narrowed to long, sinewy, sun-browned legs. His near nudity awakened a strange curiosity in Annie.

Rodrigo stepped between her and Paulo. "Tell us what happened."

Paulo looked at Annie. His eyes pleaded with her to go. She braced herself, pressing her hands against the crumbling rim of the fountain basin. "Tell us both. Now. I want to know every detail."

"No, you don't, little mistress," said Paulo, and he began to speak.

". . . couldn't believe that it happened after all these years," Rodrigo was saying to his parents, Armando and Paloma Viscaino.

Annie was supposed to be resting on a chaise in the hall of the villa. Their frantic flight from Hispaniola, the turbulent crossing to San Augustine in Florida, had drained her. She wished she could retreat into a cocoon of slumber, but the events that had destroyed her grandparents and Gema del Mar held a sick, dreadful fascination for her.

"The native boy couldn't say how the Holy Office found out that William Blythe was a Jew," Rodrigo continued. "And I dared not inquire in town, for they might have seized Annie, too."

A chill eddied through her despite the sultry heat of the seacoast city. Armando, tall and straight despite his seventy-five years, shot a glance at her. "It's well that you escaped when you did. The Inquisition has a long arm." His voice faltered. He caught his breath, buried his face in his hands. "Will. Oh, God, Will."

A wealth of emotion infused his words. Half a century ago, Armando Viscaino and Will Shapiro had been hurled together by fate. The Spanish nobleman and the fugitive Jew had become unlikely allies in an adventure that had swept them across the world and entwined their lives irrevocably. Will had taken a new name, a beautiful Spanish wife, and had lived in a state of contentment and prosperity.

Until agents of the Inquisition had dug up his past and arrested him as a heretic.

Paloma, plump and serene as any matron, rested her hand on Armando's trembling shoulder. "*Calma*, beloved," she said in a husky voice. "He and his Gabriella are at peace now."

Armando took her hand and clung to it. To Annie it

seemed that a lifetime of devotion flowed across the bond. For a moment she wondered what it must be like to love so long and so fervently; then Rodrigo was speaking again, responding to a question his father had asked.

"The boy said the arrest was made at night. They took Will and Gabriella to the Holy House in Santo Domingo." He glanced at Annie. "I like to think they died a quick death."

"Don't mask the truth," she said, her toneless voice hiding a host of horrors. "Papa tried to shield me from knowing the inhuman cruelties of the Inquisition. But the pigs who call themselves priests and bishops make a spectacle of their savagery. By the time I was six years old, I had seen the victims, mangled by all manner of torture, dragged out to the *quemadero* to be burned alive. And I remember thinking that the burning was a mercy compared to what had gone before, within the walls of the Holy House."

Rodrigo sank to his knees in front of her, taking her by the shoulders. "Annie, stop. It does no good to think of such things now."

She wrenched herself from his grasp and stood to pace the long, plaster-walled room. "Then tell me, does it help to forget, Rodrigo? Shall I just put this obscenity from my mind so that it will all happen again?" She whirled to face Rodrigo and his parents. "I shall never, ever forget. And I will think of a way to fight this madness, to ask people if mass torture was what Lord Jesus Christ had in mind when he preached to his disciples."

Rodrigo grabbed her arm. With his other hand, he held her chin so that she was forced to look at him. "It's talk like that, *muchacha*, that will get you a place of your own at a Holy House. I understand the one here in San Augustine is quite well equipped."

His words cut like a blade, and she realized she was weeping, the tears burning her cheeks and searing her throat. With a muttered oath, Rodrigo gathered her into his arms and pressed her cheek against his chest.

"*Ay de mí,*" he whispered. "What have I said? I'm sorry, Annie. You scare me with your brash talk. I can't stand to think of what would happen if you, too, fell into the hands of the Inquisition."

She wept quietly as she had so often since her father had been struck dead in the harbor of San Juan. She thought about the key he had given her, and a familiar sense of guilt ate at her. At Gema del Mar, she had searched for hours through the rubble, looking for the strongbox that contained her father's secrets. The box was gone. Annie shuddered to think who might possess it now.

She had said nothing of her worries to Rodrigo, for he had troubles enough without the matter of the missing papers. At length, she pulled away from him and accepted a handkerchief from Paloma to dry her face.

"The anger eats at me," she confessed, nearly undone anew by the sympathy she saw in their faces. "I feel helpless. My grandparents were good people, loyal to Spain."

"There is no life without suffering," said Paloma, her eyes haunted by sadness. "We can but try our best to cope and to cherish the joys that come to us." Unconsciously she leaned against her husband's shoulder. The long years of tragedy and triumph seemed etched on her nut-brown face.

Rodrigo looked relieved by his mother's intervention. "I did not presume wrong, then," he said, "in bringing Annie here."

"Of course not," Armando said. "Annie, we want you to stay."

She stood stock-still as realization crashed over her. In the tumultuous weeks since the awful discovery at Gema del Mar, she had not paused to wonder about the future. Now all her tomorrows stared her in the face. She was to spend her life here, in this Spanish outpost, living amid Spanish dons who grew fat upon the sweat of native and African slaves, worshiping at the church that had tortured and murdered her grandparents.

She glanced at Armando and Paloma and basked for a moment in the gentle welcome that seemed to emanate from them. She was tempted to stay, to give herself unto their protection. But that would be cowardly, and the daughter of Phillip Blythe was no coward.

"No," she said, her eyes smarting again with tears she refused to shed. "Don Armando, I thank you for your kindness, but I cannot stay." She aimed a dark look at Rodrigo. "Had I known that your son meant to abandon me here, I never would have come."

"You can't mean that," Rodrigo said, equally angry. "What else would you have me do? I know it sounds cruel, but you don't have many alternatives. An orphaned girl needs protection, the security of a good home."

"How long would this place be secure if I stayed?" Annie swept her arm around the room. Its decor was a pleasant mixture of native and Spanish—mats woven of palmetto fronds, heavy carved furniture, oil paintings and wooden masks decked with feathers and shells. "My grandparents died as heretics. That damns me as well. You said yourself the Inquisition has a long arm and many eyes."

She went and knelt in front of Paloma and Armando. "I will not stay and endanger you as well."

Rodrigo drew her to her feet. The fury in his eyes glowed like live coals. "Have you a better idea, then?" he demanded. "Perhaps you should seek out the protection of your *other* family. The one in Windsor Castle."

His suggestion hit her like a slap in the face. "Damn you to hell, Rodrigo Viscaino," she said through her teeth. Lifting her skirts, she fled the room.

She found him hours later, strolling the wall walk that bordered the tiled roof of the villa. She had cried herself to sleep in her small, tidy guest chamber and had awakened to find herself strangely calm and resolute.

Because now she had a plan. She knew what she wanted to do. All that remained was to convince Rodrigo that she had chosen wisely.

Twilight purpled the horizon. A few pitch torches burned at intervals on the wall walk. From her vantage point, she could see lights winking in the harbor. She heard distant bursts of laughter and song from the rough wharf-side taverns. In the garden below, frogs and cicadas sang a welcome to the night.

Drawing a deep breath for courage, she tapped her foot. Rodrigo turned to her. In the indigo light of evening, the hair curling over his collar looked dark as ink.

"Annie?" He edged closer, yet kept his distance as if he feared what she would do. "Annie, I'm sorry about what I said before. I had no call. Sometimes you bring out the worst in me. Your father was wrong to charge me with caring for you. I'm just an unfit guardian for a girl like you."

His mouth was turned up in a charming half smile, yet his words disturbed her. She could not let him think so little of himself, not if she meant to convince him to go along with her plan.

"You're wrong, Rodrigo," she said. "You *have* taken care of me. If it weren't for you, I'm certain something dreadful would have happened to me by now. You did stop me from setting fire to the Holy House of Santo Domingo."

His shoulders relaxed with obvious relief. "I'm glad you see reason. You'll be happy here with my parents. My mother's father, Joseph, was a great scholar, and she is a learned lady. She'll train you well, and when the time comes, you'll make a proper wife to some very fortunate gentleman."

His vision of her future made her slightly nauseated. The bleakness of the life he described hardened her resolve. "Rodrigo, I'm not staying here. Even if it weren't for the danger of being found by the Inquisition, I wouldn't stay."

He drew a quick, hissing breath of impatience. "Annie, I fear you have no choice."

"I do." She held fast to the wrought-iron railing and glared at him. "The world is cruel to women, but I won't be a victim. I won't be dictated to by you or any other man."

He scowled. "God, when you speak like that, I really can believe you are your aunt's niece. They say she is a veritable she-wolf."

The mention of Annie's secret connection to a monarch thousands of miles away made her skin prickle. "Just listen to me, Rodrigo. I have a plan that will work, but I need you."

His expression turned skeptical—one eyebrow lifted, his mouth quirked in a half smile. "In what way?"

"I want to stay with you until I'm old enough to fend for myself. I want to go where you go, to be with you day and night."

A nearby torch flared with a sizzle of resin. His large, strong hands gripped the railing until his knuckles whitened. She could see his heart sink in his eyes. "That's crazy. Surely you don't expect me to act as your dueña. I'm a man of . . . hard ways. I like to drink and carouse and swive willing wenches. I like to howl at the moon from the deck of a ship."

"That's perfectly agreeable to me. I won't ask you to change your ways on my account."

Rodrigo began to pace like a wildcat in a cage. "You won't have to ask, because you're not staying with me."

Annie stood immobile, willing back the sting of childish tears, swallowing hard until she found her voice. "My father was your best friend, Rodrigo. What would he think if he knew you were abandoning me to a miserable life?"

He stopped, stiffening as if she had stuck a dagger in his back. "What would he think if he knew you were using his name as a weapon against me?"

She touched her hand to her throat, wishing she could soothe the ache of tears there. "Do you hate me, Rodrigo? Did you tolerate me only because of my father?"

"Damn it, you know better than that." His hand shot out. She winced in anticipation of his blow. Instead, he cradled her cheek in his palm. Somehow, the gentle touch hurt more than a slap. "You're a remarkable young lady, and you know it. You're brilliant and high-spirited, and I'm certain one day you'll be most dangerously beautiful."

She blinked, surprised by his words. "Then why—"

"Because it's not right." His hand dropped. "I'm an adventurer, Annie. Rootless, restless, with nothing and no one to hold me."

Annie feathered her fingers over the warm spot on her cheek where he had touched her. With her parents and grandparents dead, she wondered if anyone would ever caress her with affection again. "Don't you ever get lonely?"

"Drop it, Annie."

"No. I'm coming with you. I have it all figured out. I won't trouble you at all, Rodrigo. In fact, I'll help you. I'll be your scribe or page or ship's boy—"

"Ship's *boy*?"

"Yes." She smiled, pleased to have his interest at last. "I shall cut my hair and wear trousers and learn to spit and swear. I'll even learn what swiving is."

His jaw dropped. "Over my dead body," he growled.

"I certainly hope not. Please listen to reason," she hurried on before he could object. "The Holy Office will be looking for a girl. As a quiet boy, I'll surely elude them."

"You? Quiet? Since when?"

"Well, that's a virtue for me to work on."

"Annie, this idea is insane."

"The *world* is insane, Rodrigo. My father was killed because the viceroy of Mexico betrayed his word of honor. My grandparents were tortured and burned alive because of fear and ignorance in the church. What I propose is quite rational compared to that."

Cursing under his breath, he strode toward the stairs leading down to the patio.

"Rodrigo, please," she called after him.

"Begging ill becomes you, Annie," he said over his shoulder.

Very well, she thought, watching him leave the villa and stride toward the taverns in town. I won't beg. I'll *show* you that my plan will work.

Two hours later, Rodrigo sat in the roughest tavern in San Augustine. He had a bellyful of cheap wine, a cigar clamped between his teeth, and a willing wench at his side. It was the first time he had felt even vaguely happy since losing Phillip.

The thought of his slain friend dimmed his good cheer. Ah, Phillip. He'd been so much older than Rodrigo, but from the day Rodrigo was old enough to toddle after him on fishing ventures, they had felt the bond of brotherhood.

Even so, Rodrigo had never imagined the task of raising Annie would fall to him. He had always expected to die first, for he lived fast and recklessly. Phillip's demise had taken him by surprise, leaving an awkward, half-grown girl for Rodrigo to . . . He had no idea what to do with her. He didn't know the first thing about girls. Good girls, anyway.

"Where are you, *caro*?" the woman asked, her hand stealing up from his knee to his inner thigh. "You look a thousand leagues away."

Rodrigo shook off his thoughts and turned to her. Marina, that was her name. She was a convict transported to San Augustine to amuse the soldiers. Though unwashed and dressed in cheap homespun, she exuded an earthy charm that suited his mood.

He grinned and gave her bottom a gentle pinch. "No, love, I'd be a fool to stray from you."

The patrons of the cantina were mostly idle soldiers and seamen, with a few locals mixed in. A group of rag-clad ship's boys huddled under the rickety stairs, casting dice.

"Then what were you thinking?"

He shrugged, took a sip of the raw young wine in his cup, and opted for a safe answer. "I sail tomorrow for Nombre de Dios. I'm to take up duties as an officer of the treasury there."

"Ah." Marina pressed herself against him. Her small, pointed breasts stirred a reaction in his loins. "Then we must savor the night, no?"

"Yes." Under the table, his hand lifted her skirt and smoothed its way up her leg. "We must definitely savor—"

"I did *not* cheat!" said an outraged voice from under the stairs. "That was a seven I rolled, and if anyone says elsewise, he's a goddamned liar!"

Half-amused, Rodrigo stilled his questing hand to watch the little drama between the ship's boys.

"That wasn't no seven you rolled," another boy shouted. "I

saw it with my own eyes—a four and a three, and that makes eight."

The group of boys moved back. Rodrigo had a view of the two opponents. One was a compact, muscled youth of about twelve, the other a tall, wiry lad with spiky hair sticking out from under a knitted cap.

"Who taught you to count?" the tall one demanded. "I *did* roll a four and a three, and that makes seven."

"Eight!" the other shouted, giving the tall one a shove. "And I'm not a liar. You take that back!"

"Seven! And you're *not* a liar, you're just stupid!"

The boys came together in a tangle of flying fists and ear-singeing curses. Yelling words of encouragement, their companions fell back to give them room.

Rodrigo saw the tall one's head snap back as his opponent's fist caught him. Blood spurted from his nose, and his cap flew off, exposing a mop of crudely barbered, rust-colored hair.

Unfazed, the lad charged his opponent, butting him in the stomach, sending him sprawling, and diving onto him. The two rolled across the dirt floor, crashing into stools, tables, and a few patrons who were too slow to get out of the way.

"Demonios!" Marina whisked her skirts away from the fighting boys. "I've had enough of this, Rodrigo. Let's go."

Rodrigo barely heard. He rose and stalked across the tavern. What had begun as an amusing diversion had turned dangerous. He stared down at the taller youth, who was now straddling his opponent and pounding his face.

"Jesus Christ," Rodrigo muttered, grabbing at the frayed collar. He dragged his quarry off the stocky boy and made for the door, ignoring Marina's cries of dismay.

Once they were in the street, Rodrigo roared, "What the hell do you think you're doing?"

Annie dragged her sleeve across her face, smearing the blood that trickled from her nose. "Proving to you that I can be a boy."

He marched down the street, heading toward his parents' villa. "Of all the ill-considered, idiotic, insane—"

"Rodrigo!" She raced after him. "Everyone in that tavern was fooled. And you were, too, at first. My plan will work! You can't deny me."

For God's sake, Phillip, Rodrigo said silently. *What the devil do you want me to do with your daughter?*

He mulled over the possibilities. The Viscaino family had connections with the House of Trade in Seville. Annie could live among relatives who would bring her up as a lady. Or a convent, perhaps, then an early marriage . . .

They reached the villa. He stopped walking and looked deep into her face, which was painted by milky light from the moon and stars. How any girl could look both so stubborn and yet so vulnerable baffled him. Eyes that held such a world of hurt and tender appeal should be outlawed.

"Who said anything about denying you?" he snapped, pushing her through the gates of his parents' house and propelling her toward the water well. "Now, clean your face and get a good night's sleep. We sail to Nombre de Dios at dawn."

CHAPTER 4

London
1570

"Christ's bones!" The queen's voice rang through the Presence Chamber. As one, the members of her council flinched. "How dare they? How *dare* they rise against me, try to put my slut of a cousin on *my* throne?"

"Madam, your armies have crushed the rebellion in the north like a boot on an anthill," said William Cecil, her secretary of state. "You've no more to fear on the Scots Catholics' account."

"The leaders are being taken to the Tower as we speak," said Sir Christopher Hatton.

Elizabeth sent him a withering look; then she let her imperious stare rake like a set of talons over every man present. All stood tense, fearing her temper. All save one.

André Scalia, a foreign minister, lounged against a sideboard, watching like a bettor at a bear baiting. He knew that, in time, Elizabeth's temper would spend itself as it always did, leaving a wreckage of male pride in its wake.

"That's all well and good, my lords. But it seems none of you has seen fit to trouble himself about the expense."

André relished the bewilderment on the noble faces of the council. With the exception of Cecil, the blue bloods who surrounded the queen thought seldom of practical matters.

"The expense, madam?" the Earl of Bedford asked timidly.

She raised her hands, with fingers outspread, to heaven. "Give me strength," she said through her teeth. "Aye, the expense! For years I've calculated and contrived to keep the Crown's finances solvent. Now I'm obliged to pay for three separate bodies of troops. It will put me in debt for a year."

"Madam, could we not seize the assets of the rebels?" Cecil ventured.

"Aye, Lord Burghley's right." Robert Dudley, the Earl of Leicester, took her hand and kissed it enthusiastically. "The estates are worth a fortune . . ."

Bored by the debate, André took out a small knife and began to pare his nails. Let them talk. He would wait his turn, and then he would propose the only workable answer available to the queen. For the moment, he was content to let the others exhaust her temper with their uninspired, pedestrian solutions.

As he so often did, André retreated far into the past and contemplated the events that had brought him to Elizabeth.

To the one person in the world whose blade-sharp mind, shameless ambition, and unyielding will matched his own.

He had been born to luxury, the cosseted son of a Spanish nobleman living in the kingdom of Naples. Heir to the dukedom of Albuquerque, he had enjoyed every privilege from the finest tutors of Siena to the most skilled masters of the hunt and horse marshals of Andalucía.

Then, at the age of thirteen, he had lost his mother to a mysterious illness that, in later years, he realized had been poison. The duke's second wife appeared almost instantly, as if she had been waiting to step into her role. Before long, André understood why. Five months after the wedding, she gave the duke a second son.

André's young heart had rejoiced at the idea of a brother. His joy rendered him oblivious to the burning, malicious hatred of his stepmother. She was not content to let her child play the second son, the one who would be given to the church while André inherited a dukedom.

She had set about with a will to disinherit him. She wouldn't have blinked at poisoning him. But she found another way.

In a single stroke, she destroyed his future.

Since that day nearly fifty years before, André had carried inside him the memory of the boy he had been. A handsome youth whose heart had been full of love, his mind free of cares, his soul as light as spindrift.

That boy was as dead as a corpse in a crypt. André Scalia had devoted his life to fleeing the memory of the horror that had befallen him.

Shaking off the unwelcome remembrances, he watched with satisfaction as the queen dismissed her council. André waited until they departed, knowing he should go with them, knowing he would stay.

Unaware of his presence, Elizabeth sank to her carved chair at the head of the council table. Her slim white hands came up to cover her face.

Ah, Elizabeth, André thought, granting her a moment of solitude. He had met her in the springtime of her reign. Flush with victory and her newfound sense of power, she had set about surrounding herself with the greatest minds of the realm. André, then a member of the Venetian ambassador's entourage, had quickly come to the fore.

Something powerful and electric had passed between the ambitious Tudor queen and the sharp, graying André Scalia. They were kindred spirits, each devoted to a cause they put above love, above family, above God himself.

For a dozen years he had served her willingly, well, and with utmost discretion.

He moved forward, his velvet robes swishing as he approached the table and sank down on one knee before her.

She fixed him with a stormy gaze. "Do you practice lurking about in shadows, André, or have you a natural gift for skulkery?"

He took her chilly hand, brushed his lips across the knuckles, and stood. "Neither, madam, or perhaps both."

She planted her elbows on the table. "You'd best be away, then, for I'm in a bilious mood."

"Then I'd best stay, madam."

Her hand, so delicate and yet so strong, cracked down on the table. "Damn them all! How dare they try to placate me over this northern rebellion? How dare they wave balance sheets and census rolls in my face? How dare they speak of minting new coin and, God forbid, paper promissory notes to pay the Crown's debts?"

André waited patiently while she vented her spleen; then he smiled in anticipation of the discussion.

Her snapping eyes narrowed. "Hell's teeth," she exclaimed. "You're an old man, André. You've no right to be so comely."

He bowed. His severely handsome looks had always been a useful attribute. "Madam, I daresay the queen's grace would have little use for me were I ugly."

She lifted one eyebrow. "I like pretty men. Those with good minds are doubly pleasing to me. Now. What think you of this latest disaster?"

"I think the Crown needs revenues, and quickly."

"Quite so. Shall I seize the rebels' estates, then?"

"That might rankle certain powerful subjects unnecessarily. There is another possibility."

"And what might that be?"

"You could get the revenues you need from your most formidable enemy."

A dry bark of laughter escaped her. "Which one, André? Now that His Holiness has issued his Bull of Excommunication against me, I have all the Catholic nations of the world to choose from."

"Ah, but the greatest, and the richest, is Spain, madam." André savored every word, for he had a personal vendetta against Spain.

"True," said Elizabeth. "Are you proposing that we raid the Spanish ships bound for the Netherlands?"

"Channel piracy is a possibility, of course, but it's dubious. Some of the supply ships contain little more than victuals. I propose we cast our nets in richer waters."

Her eyebrows lifted. He loved her expression of unabashed greed. "The New World empire, you mean."

"Precisely. For years, our English sea dogs have moved about those waters. They engage, for the most part, in honest commerce. But I'd wager some of them are not above taking a treasure ship here and there. The fact that the booty is for the Crown would quell any misgivings about honor."

"It's dangerous," Elizabeth mused, drawing a lacquered nail along a groove in the tabletop. "We lack the resources for an all-out war with Spain."

"I'd never suggest war, madam. The world need never know you've sanctioned a few random acts of piracy. You'd be a silent shareholder in the enterprise—and a silent recipient of the dividends."

"You understand, André, that I cannot give my permission for piracy."

"Of course not. Then, if you'd rather . . ." Letting his voice trail off, he bowed and turned to go.

"I said," she called out, her voice lashing like a whip, "I could not give my permission. But neither can I govern the behavior of a few bluff adventurers."

André permitted himself a brief, tight smile before he turned. "Very true, madam. The sea dogs are an unruly lot, fiercely independent."

She cupped her chin in her hand. "But who would risk it, André? What man would plunge himself into the middle of a school of Spanish sharks and live to tell about it?"

"There you are, Evan!" Drake called across the crowded riverfront tavern. He gestured impatiently as Evan negotiated a path through the raucous throng of mariners, river pilots, lightermen, and fishwives. As he joined Drake at the rickety three-legged table, Evan inhaled the smells of stale beer, sweating bodies, and stewing cabbage. For a moment, he experienced a sudden sharp yearning for the fresh sea air of his native village on the Welsh coast.

But he knew he would not go there again—unless it was in triumph.

Drake took one look at his face and said, "You went home, didn't you? You went to Carew."

"I did." Evan laced his fingers on the table. "I had to, Francis. After the disaster at San Juan, my share of the enterprise was paltry enough, but it was more than my people earn in a season."

"Things are still bad there, then?"

"Aye, bad as can be. The Council of Wales is bound and determined to crush any sense we have of being Welshmen. Owen Perrott of Castle Carew is still squeezing the tenants dry in order to ingratiate himself with the Crown."

Drake scratched his head. "Ingratiate himself? Didn't the queen have his father put to death?"

"Aye. John Perrott was one of King Henry's by-blows and was a danger to the Crown. Owen seems determined not to test the queen's tolerance." The young lord vented his anger on the peasants, Evan thought bleakly. His demands grew more unreasonable with each passing season. "I feel so damned helpless, Francis. My people gave nearly everything they had so I could go to sea and bring home the rewards. They can't hold out much longer."

Drake signaled to a barmaid, who drew a flagon of barley ale and set it before Evan. Her bodice, tightly laced up the front, provided an ample view of her cleavage. While serving the ale, she bent down farther than was necessary and sent Evan a sly wink.

He pretended not to see, and she withdrew. Drake chuckled. "You're too pretty for your own good, Evan. Not interested, eh?"

Evan shrugged. "Babies come of dalliance. And the world is no place for babies."

"Don't say that." Drake took a long drink of his ale. "You're too young to be a pessimist."

Evan thumped his fist on the table. "Then give me a reason to hope, Francis!"

Drake's smile thinned to a grim line. "I wish I could. All of England was outraged at the treachery at San Juan, but no man is willing to risk sponsoring our reprisal and inciting war with Spain. The queen won't tolerate it."

Disappointment sank like lead in Evan's gut. "Not even Hawkins? He's your kinsman."

Drake's fingers combed through his ruddy beard. "He claims I deserted him in the escape from San Juan. His ship barely made it home."

Evan heard the note of hurt pride in Drake's voice. "He has to say so, for the failure's upon his head. After all, he lost the *Jesus of Lubeck*, the queen's own ship. But can he think, in his heart, that you left with no thought for him?" Evan punched Drake in the shoulder. "You have your faults, my friend, but cowardice is not among them. Hawkins knows this well."

"Aye, but he'll be a long time admitting it."

"He probably lacks the wherewithal to undertake another voyage."

Drake rocked back on his stool and hooked his ankles around the legs. "He and every other investor I've approached. Damn it, Evan! The Spanish insult still burns like a fresh brand. Yet we've no ships, no money, and no men to avenge it."

Evan watched his friend's agitated face. "You're getting as impatient as I."

Drake leaned forward, planting the legs of his stool back on the floor as he made a visible effort to calm himself.

"The matter's urgent," he admitted. "I'm about to be married."

"Married!" Evan stared in amazement. "You? Who's the girl?"

To Evan's surprise, a blush rose up out of Drake's beard. "Her name's Mary Newman. A Cornish girl. We . . . get on . . . agreeably."

Evan grinned. "I know of marriages based on less. Felicitations, Francis."

"What about you?" Drake asked, clearly ill at ease on the topic of Mary Newman. "Have you some Welsh lass waiting for you?"

"No." Evan's reply was swift and certain. He had no place in his life for a woman, no place in his heart for love. "I'll never shackle myself to a wife. I've nothing to offer save a life of poverty and uncertainty."

"Don't be so quick to say that, Evan. The world is full of women, and a few of them are most interesting."

For some reason, Evan caught himself thinking of the girl at San Juan, her face streaked by tears, her hair wet and tangled, her eyes full of grief and rage. If that fierce, vengeful sorrow was her nature as a girl, he did not wish to meet her as a woman.

"Gentlemen, may I join you?"

Startled out of his thoughts, Evan glanced up to see a black-cloaked stranger. Light from the parchment-paned windows fell upon a narrow, angular face, sleek, graying hair, a pointed beard.

And a neck chain and sword hilt dear enough to buy a frigate.

Like Evan, Drake had assessed the man's worth quickly. He donned a hearty seaman's smile, stood, and bowed. "Our pleasure, sir. I am—"

"I know who you are." The stranger made a gesture with his hand. As if by magic, a jar of wine appeared on the table. "Captain Drake." He nodded at Evan. "And Master Carew."

Drake's eyes narrowed. "Are you from the moneylender? Damn it, I told that frigging usurer I'd have the—"

"Here now, my friend." The stranger held up a hand, and his lips thinned. A sort of worn comeliness gave his face an interesting character. Evan supposed it was his attempt at a smile. "All of England has heard of the massacre at San Juan de Ulua. I assume you'd like to see justice done."

"Precisely, sir," Drake said, his gaze kindling with enthusiasm. "In fact, I—"

"Wait." Evan had heard something in the stranger's voice, a smooth, mellifluous note that prodded him with suspicion. The man was a foreigner, perhaps a Spanish agent. "Who are you, sir?" Evan asked.

"My name is André Scalia, late of Venice, but I have been a score of years in England."

A Venetian. In all the world, there were none so enterprising and so unscrupulous as Venetians. "What is our quarrel with Spain to you? And why do we interest you?" asked Evan.

"For God's sake, let the man speak," Drake said.

André smiled. "It's all right. I like your caution, Master Carew. It will serve you well should you decide to accept my offer."

"And just what is your offer, sir?" Drake held himself tense on his stool, his fingers gripping the edge of the table.

André took an unhurried sip of his wine. The light caught a badge that fastened his costly cloak at the throat. Some sort of heraldic device, Evan realized. A lion.

"Gentlemen," said André Scalia, "I wish to finance your next expedition to the Indies."

Evan slapped at a mosquito that had been feeding on his neck. He swore under his breath.

"The natives use an herb to repel insects," said Drake, who squatted across a smoldering cook fire.

"My sweat washes it all off."

"Endure, then." Drake impaled three large prawns on a green stick and shoved it into the coals. "You'll be living high in Nombre de Dios soon enough."

Evan fixed his stare on the glowing coals. Although he had come with the reconnaissance fleet all the way from Plymouth, his part in the adventure had not yet begun.

Port Pheasant, a deep bay fringed by dense jungle, was their hidden anchorage on the isthmus of Panama. The sheltered cove lay to the south of Nombre de Dios, the town from which the great treasure ships departed for Spain. They would use Port Pheasant as their base of operations; Nombre de Dios was their target.

Evan could hear the banging of lumber as the carpenters assembled small, swift pinnaces, which had been brought in pieces aboard the larger ships. The rasp of saws and the banging of wooden hammers sounded out of place in the jungle.

"I say we sail in and make the raid," Evan said, scratching his neck. "My thirst for revenge might well lessen if I wait much longer."

"I doubt that," Drake said affably. "You'll always be a hot-head, Evan. And I know what you see when you close your eyes to sleep. I know, because I have the same nightmare. You see Spanish daggers, slipping out of Spanish sleeves, slitting the throats of unarmed Englishmen."

Fresh as yesterday, the rage streaked through Evan. In a blaze of remembrance, he saw the massacre again, heard the screams and smelled sulfur and blood, felt the limp body of young Charlie Moon in his arms. As always, he saw the girl with the red-gold hair, defending her fallen father.

"You're right, Francis," he agreed, giving his stick a turn on the coals. "But when did you become such an advocate for caution?"

"When I saw where rashness got me," Drake said darkly.

"Is it Mary, then?" Evan asked, knowing it was.

Drake nodded, pushing his spitted prawns deeper into the embers. "I truly loved her, you know. But I married her in haste. I never paused to think she might object to my adventuring."

Evan chuckled. "I could have told you that, my man. Women. Once you marry one of them, she expects you to wander no farther than the dooryard, and then only to pluck a posy for her hair."

"Spoken like a man who's never been bitten by anything stronger than a mosquito."

"And never will be, thank you. For after love comes babies, and God knows what trouble they are." Evan's voice was bluff, his grin jaunty, but inside, he felt a deep sorrow dragging at him. Back in Carew there were many babies, brought into a world of travail and deprivation. Perhaps if this new enterprise succeeded, he might feel differently. Thus far, life had given him no reason to wish to procreate.

He drew his skewer of prawns from the fire and dipped them into a shallow bowl of salt water to cool and season them. "All right," he said, peeling the crisp shell off one of the prawns. "So we've concocted the perfect plan."

"Almost." With his eating knife, Drake drew lines in the hard-packed earth. "Here's Panama City on the west side of the isthmus, and Nombre de Dios here, on the east, forty miles away. It's just a slim neck of land."

"Slim enough for our few numbers to grasp and throttle," Evan mused.

Drake's lips peeled back in a wolfish grin. "Indeed. You'll have to go alone to spy out the town, of course, since you're the only one of us who can pass as a Spaniard."

Evan swallowed the prawn he was chewing and fingered the small, pointed beard he had been cultivating. The thing was a nuisance, getting in his way when he ate and drank. Besides, it gave him the bloodthirsty look of a Catholic.

"Very well," he said. "You'll need to know where all the landmarks are. The treasure repository, the gun emplacements, the governor's house. Scalia told me of a government official called Rodrigo Viscaino who seems to be well versed in the movement of the treasure trains."

Evan scowled. "Scalia. How does he come by his knowledge?"

"Like the making of blood pudding, 'tis best not to know." Drake adjusted his skewer over the coals. "I suspect he buys information, spies on the Spanish ambassador, conducts secret correspondence in cipher, that sort of thing."

"He committed a great deal of money to this enterprise. I wonder why he hates Spain so."

"It doesn't matter. We'll make the Spanish bastards sorry for every drop of English blood they ever spilled. And get rich in the process."

"And repay our investor," Evan reminded him.

"Of course." Drake set to work peeling his prawns. "Without the help of André Scalia, we'd still be searching for a sponsor."

"I don't trust him, Francis. Not from my first glimpse of him."

"He could be something of a hackster, I agree," said Drake. "But we needed his investment."

"I wonder who we're really sailing for," said Drake. "The Republic of Venice?"

"If so, it's to our advantage. Venice is one of the few places where the queen has not made enemies."

"Just give her time," Evan said, grinning. Then a thought struck him. "I wonder if the queen has any inkling of our doings here."

"Can you really think she wouldn't?"

"No. In fact, the investor behind André Scalia could be the Crown."

Drake's smile stiffened slightly. "Let's not question fortune, Evan. No good can come of it."

"Captain Drake!" Denton came up from the waterfront and approached the campfire. He was lugging a cloth sack in his wake. "Look what we found when we were out hunting wild pigs." With a flourish, Denton untied the neck of the bag and dumped the contents on the ground: a tarnished breastplate, the surface engraved with flourishes; a crested morion helm with a broken red feather and a dent in one side; a round buckler that matched the breastplate.

"Where did you get Spanish armor?" Drake asked.

A chill crept over Evan's skin. During the weeks of preparation, he had managed to forget that they were in enemy territory. Now he was reminded just how close they were to men who craved their deaths.

"Why, we got it off a dead Spaniard," Denton explained. "He wasn't a pretty sight, either. All rotted and maggoty."

"How did he die?" Evan forced himself to ask.

"It looked like a wound from a dart or arrow." Denton gazed hungrily at the roasted prawns. "If you'll excuse me, sir, I'd best be about getting my own supper."

Evan and Drake exchanged a long glance as the man

walked off, then they studied the armor lying on the ground. It had been rinsed in seawater, but the stink of death still clung to the pieces.

His appetite gone, Evan flung his prawns into the bushes. "Who murdered him?" he wondered aloud.

"Someone who hated him in particular, or Spaniards in general?" Drake ventured. "Perhaps there are Huguenot pirates about."

"A proper pirate would've taken the armor."

"Maybe he was wounded and staggered off to die where the pirates or the natives couldn't find him. Or perhaps he crawled off in search of a priest to give him absolution."

"I like it not," Evan muttered. "Maybe Port Pheasant isn't as secluded as we thought."

"Don't be so gloomy," Drake said. "The armor's a godsend. You'll have no trouble passing for a Spaniard in *that*."

"You want me to wear those things?" Evan snorted. "A true Welshman never wears steel armor. Boiled leather is sufficient protection. I'll look like a smithy's furnace."

Drake laughed. "Just so long as you don't look like a Welshman."

Evan caught another wave of the death smell from the armor, and his stomach roiled. Disquieting thoughts nagged him. Somewhere, not too far away from here, a murderer stalked.

A colorful string of Welsh curses painted the jungle air. Evan stood waist deep in water, holding his bundle high above his head as he slogged ashore.

From the start of his solitary voyage to Nombre de Dios, disaster had followed in his wake. His raft of native wood, complete with sunshade and canvas sail, had waterlogged not ten miles from Port Pheasant. He had barely reached the shallows before the crude, unwieldy thing had sunk, its porous logs grown as heavy as steel bars.

He stepped out of a tidal pool and onto spongy ground just as a long black snake slithered down into the water.

"Christ on a crutch," he muttered, skittering away from the

pool and untying his bundle. His bare feet suddenly felt vulnerable, and he craved his boots.

As he sat on the ground to draw them on, he remembered the man who had made them. Griffith, the cobbler of Carew, had traded his best sow to the tanner for the finest leather. When the tanner had heard the boots were for Evan Carew, he had given back the sow and offered the leather freely.

Evan turned down the bucket cuffs just below the knee. Like everyone else in the village, the cobbler and the tanner had placed their faith in Evan. Taxed and starved by their overlord, Owen Perrott, the people needed to believe that help lay in their future.

Their faith was both a blessing and a curse. A blessing, for their generosity had opened doors for Evan. A curse, for he was honor bound to succeed.

Wearily he climbed to his feet. The parcel containing his armor, food supplies, Spanish money, and weapons felt weighty as an anchor. He pondered a moment, then decided to don the breastplate and helm in order to lighten his load.

He made an awkward job of buckling on the pieces. It was nearly impossible to see even with the visor up, for the morion helm limited his field of vision. It was a wonder the Spaniards got any fighting done in this attire. Yet they did. The conquistadors made up one of the deadliest war machines in all the world.

Evan glanced at the sun, which was slowly descending over the treetops. Keeping it to his left, he headed north. By his reckoning, he had some thirty miles of jungle to cross before he reached Nombre de Dios.

As he left the coast behind, the foliage thickened. Before long, he had to take out his sword and use it like a machete to hack a trail through the jungle.

Sweat soaked his body beneath the armor. He began to understand why the natives of the New World eschewed clothing. His Welsh and Gaelic ancestors had gone half naked into battle, too, though in winter they sometimes greased their bodies to protect themselves from the chill.

Unlike his predecessors, Evan rarely went without a shirt.

In addition to the fine education he'd gotten alongside Owen Perrott at Castle Carew, he bore another token from those days, which he took pains to conceal.

Lost in past bitterness, he heard only the sound of his own breathing, the muffled thud of his footsteps, and the brush of leaves as he battled his way through the jungle.

When a dark shape jumped out at him, he was startled into a yelp.

He raised his sword, but the shape leaped upon him from behind, knocking him flat. The visor snapped shut with a metallic clang.

A panther? He had never seen one of the jungle cats, but knew from seamen's yarns that they were sleek, black, and deadly.

Then, through the bars of his visor, he saw his assailant. A man.

Sleek, black, and deadly. Bluish tattoos dotted his forehead. A bone of some sort hung from one ear.

An African? Evan thought wildly. Yet he had never seen an African quite like this. His attacker had a narrow nose, a sheen to the hair . . . and a stone dagger in his large hand.

The weapon descended toward Evan's throat just above the edge of his breastplate.

"Mercy!" he screamed in Spanish.

The blade stopped. "Mercy?" The man had a deep voice that resonated painfully in Evan's helm. "I thought I killed you once, Vargas. Now you ask me to take mercy on your ghost?"

Evan absorbed the words, spoken in a strangely melodic patois. The statement gave him a ray of hope.

"I'm not Vargas, whoever that is," he said quickly, in his best Spanish. "I . . . found this armor on a dead man."

A hand covered the visor and pushed it up. The tattooed face loomed close, inspecting Evan. "You are not Vargas?"

"Not Vargas," he repeated desperately. "Please, I mean you no harm."

"You are a round man," the stranger said stolidly, banging a meaty fist on Evan's armored chest. "You mean Rico and all his people harm." Rico stood. Grasping the armholes of the breastplate, he hauled Evan to his feet, lifting him as if he were a small child.

Evan wrenched off his helm. Rico was a full head taller than he, his limbs straight and shapely. He was naked save for a red silk neck cloth and a chamois loincloth.

Rico drew Evan's sword and tested the blade with his thumb. "This is good," he said, eyeing the sword appraisingly. "Toledo?"

Evan frowned. For a native, this stranger was surprisingly worldly. "Yes," he said. Drake had given him the sword, plunder from a minor caravel they had seized in the Leeward islands.

Rico stepped behind Evan and poked the tip of the blade at his back. "Walk," he ordered.

"Where are we going?"

"To my village."

"Why?"

"So my people can kill you."

CHAPTER 5

Evan argued his fate all during the hour-long walk through the wilderness. He talked until his throat grew dry, his tongue thick and clumsy. He told Rico everything he had dared to reveal: That he was English. That he was dedicated to the destruction of Spain. That he wished no harm to native or slave.

Rico kept the sword point in Evan's back. He said nothing, made no response at all. He remained a skeptical, ominous presence behind Evan, prodding him on and on.

They reached a spot where the path seemed more distinct, an avenue hacked out of the brush.

Rico let out a series of low whistles. To Evan's left and right, dark shapes melted down out of the trees and disappeared.

Sentries, he realized. Their destination was at hand.

His certainty grew as he smelled the scent of burning wood and roasting meat. Despite Rico's dire promise, Evan felt his stomach contract with hunger.

Moments later, he found himself standing in the middle of

a settlement, bamboo huts all around him, hard-packed red-dish earth beneath his feet. A ring of dark, spare faces peered at him. Some of the bolder men moved in close.

Feeling like an animal in a cage, Evan flung up his head and glared at them. Many of them shared Rico's unusual looks: the mahogany skin and smooth hair, the slender height and fine-boned features.

What race of people was this? he wondered. Neither African nor native, but a strangely handsome mingling of the two.

Rico spoke to the villagers in patois. Evan could catch only a few words, none of them encouraging: ". . . wandering about . . . armed like a round man soldier . . . argues in the devil's tongue . . ."

An older man, his face wizened as a walnut, said something in a guttural, commanding voice.

A half dozen men descended on Evan. He struggled, but they tore off his breastplate, caught his wrists, and wrapped them tightly with a length of rawhide cord. They tethered him to a T-shaped stake, his bound hands raised high, his feet nearly coming off the ground.

The men fell back to survey their handiwork. Evan looked into their faces, and his blood ran cold. Never had he seen such deadly hatred. Their loathing reached out to him like the tendrils of an invisible vine, choking him with their promise of vengeance. Women and children joined the men and added the sharpness of their own malice.

They aren't just going to kill me, Evan realized with a new jolt of terror. They were going to tear him apart by inches.

Slowly, he put out his tongue to moisten his dry lips. "Please," he said. "Please, will you listen to me?"

"No, round man devil," said Rico, pacing, his wide bare feet slapping the ground. An ankle bracelet of shells rattled with each step. "You listen to us. You hear the song of the Cimaroons' hatred."

"Cimaroons? I do not know the word."

"You lie, Spanish man."

"No. I wish to know who holds me captive, and why."

Evan hoped to get them talking. Perhaps it would dispel some of the steam of their rage. "Who are the Cimaroons?"

Rico opened his mouth to make an angry retort. Before he could speak, a woman stepped forward. Lithe as a willow in the wind, she appeared beside Rico.

For a moment, Evan forgot his fear and absorbed the vision. She wore a sheath of brightly woven cotton. She was dark-skinned and black-haired, with brown velvet eyes slightly uptilted at the corners. Generous lips and a narrow nose. And upon one beautiful burnished cheek, a livid scar in the shape of a cross. She had been branded like a cow . . . or a criminal.

"He asks who the Cimaroons are," she said in a deep, melodic voice. "He must be told. Even the evil one must know his enemies."

Evan expected one of the men to thrust her away, for surely a woman had no business joining in the affairs of tribal elders.

No one made a move to stop her or silence her. The beaded hem of her primitive shift rattled as she planted herself in front of him.

"We are all Cimaroons. Our grandfathers and grandmothers suffered at your hands. Some were brought in chains across the big water. They were made to work until they died . . . or escaped. Others are children of this earth. Your people brought us together. Our blood mingles and boils with our hatred for the Spanish and their holy men who pray with beads and water, and, in the name of the Christ god, do their killing."

Evan had to listen closely to her words, picking out the meaning from her unfamiliar rhythmic accent. Even if he missed some of what she said, he understood the fierce expression on her face and the impassioned tone of her voice. Apparently, the Cimaroons were a tribe of people descended of African slaves and natives of the New World.

They had double cause to hate the Spanish.

"I'm not one of them," he stated. "I'm not a Spanish round man."

Rico gave a snort of disbelief. He kicked at the armor lying on the ground. In the same moment, the woman reached out and tweaked Evan's beard.

"You wear the round man's steel shell," she said. "You have the devil's beard. You speak the Spanish tongue. You do not fool Casilda."

Casilda. Evan had the foolish urge to say her name aloud, to feel it ripple over his tongue, to taste its sweetness. Casilda. A name as lovely as its bearer, and yet as sibilant and dangerous as the hiss of a snake. A pity she wanted to kill him. He would have liked to know her better.

"We will treat you the way your people treat us," Rico said. "We will beat you until you are sick from the pain. Then we will slit you open, like so." He drew his finger down his breastbone to his belly.

"Then," said Casilda, "we pull out your insides and set fire to them. Sometimes the strong ones survive." She leaned close, her beautiful, scarred face a breath away from his, her hot, dark gaze burning him. "Are you strong?"

"For Christ's sake!" Evan burst out. He twisted his head to one side and spied the children. Some hid their faces in their mother's skirts. Others giggled nervously, while still others simply stared in horrified fascination.

"Will you listen to yourself? You say these things while your children listen. You teach them to hate without giving them a chance to know the stranger they despise."

"We must teach them the dangers of living in a world run by your kind," Casilda retorted. "My mother never taught me to hate Spanish soldiers and holy men. Then one day, I was out gathering berries, and I came upon a Spaniard." Her face flushed, and the scar stood out starker than ever. "I did not know I should fear him. I did not know to run and hide."

"Oh, God," said Evan, slumping back against the stake. He wanted to cover his ears but his hands were bound.

"You begin to understand," said Casilda. "He took me away to the big white village. For ten summers I lived in his white house. I cleaned up his filth and sewed his clothes. He didn't wait until I was old enough to bleed before he took me on my back. Then, when I was in my thirteenth summer, the babies started coming. One, two, three sons I bore him. He tore each one from my breast, gave them away as presents to his friends or sold them to the miners of Potosí."

Bitterness made her face as hard as carved wood. "I ran away once." She turned her cheek to him so that he could see the ugly brand. "This was my punishment. The second time I ran away, I vowed I would escape—or die." She leaned down and put her face very close to his. A wild, musky female smell emanated from her. "*That* is the price of protecting our children's innocence. *That* is what comes of shielding them from our hate. Are we wrong, then, to poison their young minds?"

"How can I answer that?" Evan said in a daze of horror and fear.

"You need not."

Three men came forward. Their shiny black onyx knives glinted in the harsh sunlight.

"Wait!" Evan said desperately. "Let me speak. I'm not a Spaniard, do you hear me? I am not a Spaniard!"

The men shook their heads.

Casilda held up a hand. "Let him entertain us with his lies."

"I do not lie," Evan said. "I look and talk like a Spaniard, but I belong to a different . . . tribe. We are called Englishmen." He knew he lacked the time to explain the differences between Welsh and English. "In my country, we are the enemies of Spain. The Spanish king, who is called Philip, tried to rule my land as he tries to rule yours. He wed our Queen Mary, brought his holy men, and they tortured and burned my people. Now we have a new queen, who is called Elizabeth. She hates the Spanish as you do. And I am in her service."

"In her service?" Rico scowled. "You wear the round man's shell. You carry his sword. How does this serve your she-king?"

"Our numbers here are few," Evan said. "We work in secret because we could not win against the Spanish by fighting openly. Our aim is to take the city of Nombre de Dios by surprise, to steal the treasure there, to leave the soldiers broken and bleeding so they can bring no more harm to anyone."

"Nombre de Dios?" Casilda asked, "The white city?"

Evan nodded. "If that is what you call it."

An argument broke out among the ranks of men. Though Evan could not understand their words, the suspicion in their eyes told him he had lost his bid for freedom.

Two men unbound him and turned him so that he faced the stake. Spreading his arms wide, they retied his wrists. Feeling as helpless and vulnerable as an accused heretic, Evan glanced over his shoulder.

A large man, flexing his bulky shoulders, came forward with a whip made of braided rawhide. He paused to speak in low tones to the other villagers.

The sight of the whip hurtled Evan into the past. For a moment, he was eight years old again, and Owen Perrott had been caught torturing one of the lurcher puppies in the barn. While Owen watched with an insolent smirk on his young face, the whipping boy of Carew was made to shed his tunic.

The great U-shaped stool, which lingered in nightmare memory even now, loomed before Evan. A nudge from behind sent him down on the stool, his sweaty hands clutching the curved sides of the whipping stool and his face staring down at the floor. He remembered the floor vividly, stone flags covered by rushes, tiny bugs skittering industriously through the mess.

Owen's master had used a horsewhip, the leather thin and supple. When applied correctly, it sliced into flesh like a hot blade into butter.

At first, Evan had tried to play the man, stifling his sobs, pretending he was made of stone. He quickly learned that Owen wouldn't cry peace until Evan was screaming for mercy.

And scream he did, pleading while his back and buttocks took fire and ran with blood. Owen waited. He had always liked Evan well enough, but seeing the whipping boy beaten in his place always held a sort of perverse satisfaction.

The sound of tearing fabric brought Evan back to the present. He was no longer a whipping boy in Castle Carew, but a condemned man in the middle of an uncharted jungle, surrounded by savage people who meant to kill him.

His loose shirt fell away from his back. Evan squeezed his eyes shut to block out the humiliation. He hated to reveal what had been done to him. Even now, in his last moments among the living, he had his pride.

Miserable seconds passed before he noticed that the Cimaroons had fallen silent. He looked over his shoulder to see all eyes fixed on his back.

The scars. Dozens of them slashed across his back, layer upon layer of shiny tissue from those countless beatings. The ridges and gullies, ranging from livid red to thick white, formed the horrible topography of his brutal youth.

Then the people began to whisper, pointing at his back and arguing. With a knife in her hand, Casilda strode forward, stood in front of him and peered into his face. Evidently, among the Cimaroons, there were no rules placing women secondary to men. "Who did this to you?" she demanded.

Evan pressed his brow against the stake and lied a glorious lie. "Spaniards."

Her black knife slashed out. The binding on his wrists gave way, and his hands dropped to his sides. He leaned heavily against the stake until Casilda grasped his arm. Her grip was firm though gentle as she led him away from the stake.

"Now what?" he muttered.

She thrust a hollowed-out gourd at him. "Drink. And then we talk. We want to hear more about your plans to kill the devils of the white city."

Rodrigo laid down his quill and pinched the bridge of his nose. His lamp burned low, for he had worked long into the night and had used up most of the oil. He lit a candle from the meager flame and scowled down at his ledger as if it were his sworn enemy.

Facts and figures. Bills of lading and balance sheets. Numbers that had to be reckoned down to the last peso.

He hated the work, hated his cramped office in Nombre de Dios. Phillip had always made it look so easy, figuring rapidly and accurately, then closing the book with a satisfied thump.

"Where the hell are you, Phillip?" Rodrigo said to the darkened corners of his office. "We need you now."

The lamp burned out, and the remaining candle made a dance of shadows on the walls. Rodrigo poured wine from a decanter into a silver goblet and took a long drink. His need for his gentle friend was real, had been real for the past two years.

When Annie had appeared before him, her slender body in rough boy's clothes and her beautiful hair raggedly shorn, he had expected the lightning bolt of Phillip's displeasure to strike him dead on the spot.

Yet Phillip's spirit had not risen from its eternal sleep. With Annie posing as his scribe, Rodrigo had taken ship. At Phillip's death, the *contador mayor* of the treasury had appointed Rodrigo in his place. He did not like the shuffling of papers and the balancing of books, but the treasury paid him princely sums, nourishing his appetite for fine food, good wine, and lusty women.

Even chained to a desk, he might have found a measure of contentment as an agent of the royal treasury, but for Annie.

"Annie," he muttered, rubbing his temples. "What in God's name am I going to do with you?" She was growing up with a speed that left Rodrigo breathless. At thirteen, naturally athletic and husky-voiced, she'd had a little trouble playing the boy. The trews and tunic had fit her sticklike figure better than girlish frills and farthingales.

Yet while a real boy grew thick-limbed and strong, his voice deepening and his face sprouting a beard, Annie simply grew . . . more Annie-like.

Sometime last year she had become rather secretive about her privy habits. Swept up in memories, Rodrigo saw himself standing outside her chamber door and listening to her sobs. She wept as if her heart were breaking.

Frightened, he had knocked on the door.

"Go away," she commanded, her voice muffled.

Rodrigo had gritted his teeth and entered the shuttered room. He remembered the pattern of sunlight on the floor, golden bars through the slats of the shutters.

He had sat on the edge of her bed and pulled her into his arms. How slim and taut her limbs were, though there was a new softness about her, a certain yielding of the flesh that was invisible to the eye, yet clearly discernible to the touch.

"Annie. Annie, what troubles you?"

In a shaking whisper, she said, "Rodrigo, I am dying."

Cold fear washed over him. She was an inconvenience, aye, and a pest at times, but he had grown attached to her irreverent humor and cheerful presence. "What? Are you ill? Annie, tell me!"

She moved away from him and drew the covers up to her chin. "I'm . . . bleeding. And it won't stop."

It had been like pulling teeth, but he'd managed to get her to admit that she was bleeding from *there*. Rodrigo would have laughed if it hadn't been so sad. Poor motherless girl, trapped in the guise of a boy, confused and terrified by the changes in her body. Guiltily, he knew he should have done something to prepare her for growing up.

As best he could, he explained what little he knew of the womanly matter. "It's a bit of a mystery to me, too, *muchacha*," he confessed. "As best I understand it, a woman bleeds at each turn of the moon if there is no baby to nourish."

She brushed at her tearstained cheeks. "What do you mean, no baby? How do I get a baby, anyway?"

Flames of color heated Rodrigo's face. "Well, you marry, and your husband gives you one."

"Then where does *he* get it?"

"He makes it grow inside you."

Her hand slipped down to cup her belly. "Only a husband can do it properly?"

"Properly, yes, but . . ." Rodrigo stood and paced the room.

"Damn, I wish I had known my grandmother Catalina better. I met her only a few times on trips to Spain when I was a boy." He skimmed his finger over Annie's damp cheek, catching a tear. "Ah, she was very wise. Very gentle. She was known throughout the south of Spain as a great healer of women's ailments. Even when she grew very old, she would go out in the middle of the night to help bring a baby into the world. One of her daughters, Clara, learned the arts of midwifery from her."

An idea hit him. "You know, Tia Clara still lives in Palos. I could take you to stay with—"

"Palos is in Spain, is it not?" Annie asked in a small, cold voice.

"Of course. It's a famous place, Annie. The home port of old Admiral Colón himself."

"Then I won't go there. I hate Spain. If it weren't for the Spanish government, my father would be alive. If not for the Spanish church, my grandparents would be alive. I owe no loyalty to Spain, and I refuse to go there."

Rodrigo had pressed the point, though he was not eager to visit Spain either. He remembered it from his boyhood—a place of high, dusty plains and huge houses with dark halls. His parents had taken him there in their fruitless search for Paloma's other son, tragically taken from her at birth many years before. Most vividly of all, Rodrigo remembered the clerics, scores of them in every town, preaching hysterically against Jews and Moors.

Ironic, he thought, that it was Annie who had to hide from the Holy Office. Annie, who had not a drop of Jewish blood.

Rodrigo, a respected man of trade, called *Don* by nobles and officials, had a Jewish grandfather. His name had been Joseph Sarmiento of Ribera, a mariner on the first great voyage with Colón and sole survivor of the disaster at La Navidad.

Here in New Spain, it was safer for men of Jewish blood. The hounds of the Holy Office had not fully refined their techniques of ferreting out heretics. Yet, judging by the disaster that had befallen Annie's grandparents, the zealots were ready to take on the New World. He shuddered, wondering how long William Blythe and Gabriella had suffered before the fires of intolerance had consumed them. Such a waste. They hid but one secret: the fact that Gabriella's son, Phillip, had been sired by Henry VIII. *Dios.* Had the torturers wrested the truth from Gabriella?

Troubled by his thoughts, Rodrigo licked his thumb and forefinger and pinched out his candle. He sat for a long time in the darkness, toying idly with the silver medallion he wore on a chain around his neck. He was not eager to go to his big, soft bed. His empty bed.

Since Annie had become his ward, he had been careful with his women, meeting them in taverns and brothels rather than entertaining them at home. It was an inconvenience he was growing to resent.

The sounds of the night surrounded him: the song of the cicadas, the hush of distant waves, the faint tramp of soldiers on watch, the whisper of a voice in the hallway. . . .

Rodrigo snapped to attention, all weariness leaving him. Moving soundlessly in the way of his mother's people, he rose from the table and went to the door. It stood perhaps a hand span ajar, giving him a view of the stone stairs leading to the upper level of the villa.

Pale moonlight slanted down on a pair of cloaked figures.

"Nearly there," he heard Annie whisper. "I thought Rodrigo would never put out his light and go to bed."

The pair mounted the stairs. Annie's door shut with a quiet click.

Disbelief rendered Rodrigo immobile. Then fury took hold and awakened his wooden limbs. He left his office and took the stairs two at a time. Bring a lover home, would she? The little slut. Sowing her oats with abandon while Rodrigo took every precaution to hide his own liaisons.

As he reached the door to Annie's chamber, his hand went automatically to his hip, where his sword usually rode. He was not wearing his sword. Still, he did not hesitate. In his present mood, he was capable of killing them both with his bare hands.

He put his shoulder to the door and shoved it open.

"Rodrigo!" Annie gasped.

Moonlight leaked through the slats of the window shutters. He could make out Annie's slim form and her cloaked lover beside the bed.

"Not wasting any time, are you?" he snarled. In two strides, he crossed the room and grabbed the visitor by the front of the shirt. "I'll show you how I welcome a man who comes sneaking into my house at night."

"Rodrigo, no!" Annie cried.

He ignored her. "You son of a bitch," he said, drawing back his fist. In the same moment, Annie's visitor swiftly brought up a foot. A hard knee drove into Rodrigo's groin.

He felt as if a shovel had been plunged into him. His lungs emptied. Stars performed an excruciating dance before his eyes. His grip on the shirt slackened, and then Rodrigo was falling. Down, down, down into a dizzying vortex of pain.

His chest slammed onto the floor. The flagstones were cool against his cheek. His opponent jammed a knee into his back and twisted his arm around behind him. A new pain tore at Rodrigo's shoulder.

He tried to summon the strength to throw off his opponent, but the fall had robbed him of breath.

"Did you hurt him?" Annie asked her visitor.

"I don't think so. Well, maybe just a little, but he asked for it."

Rodrigo decided that he had lost his mind. That was a woman's voice. *Dios*, had a woman beaten him into this unenviable position?

"Rodrigo," said Annie, "this is not what you think. Now, if she lets you up, will you promise you won't attack her again?"

He managed a grunt of assent. His arm was released. The weight left him. Slowly, his every movement adding to his pain, he grasped the bedpost and hauled himself up.

Annie lit a candle. His eyes adjusted to the dim glow. Behind the flame, Annie's face looked pale and infuriatingly uncontrite.

He studied her visitor. What he saw nearly sent him slithering back down to the floor.

She had thrown off her cloak to reveal a man's tunic. Bare legs and bare feet. A fat black braid hanging over one shoulder. And a face that arrested his breathing once again.

Rodrigo had never seen a queen in the flesh, but if he had, this is how she would have looked to him. Flawless skin. High cheekbones and a proud, narrow nose. Full lips, defined by a natural, vivid red. Eyes tilted ever so slightly at the corners.

Her exquisite beauty unsettled him in more ways than one. This was no Christian queen, but some exotic heathen, a tribal princess, a—

"Valeria." At last she spoke. "My name is Valeria, and I am a Jew." She stated this without fear, even though the words she uttered could mean death if they fell on the wrong ears.

"Damn." Rodrigo sank to the bed and tangled his fingers in his long black hair. A Jewess. He had a Jewess in his house. And she had nearly beaten him senseless.

Annie dropped to her knees beside him. "Rodrigo, don't be angry. She had nowhere else to go. We've got to help her."

He took a moment to study his ward. Grubby face, scruffy hair, and sheer, stubborn purpose shining out of her wide gray eyes. "Annie, you're driving me crazy," he muttered. "I should have sent you long ago to some convent that would turn you into a demure, unassuming female."

She must have heard the resignation in his voice, for she grinned. "Does such a place exist?"

"Probably not in the known world." He glanced up at Valeria. The shadows carved deep hollows in her gaunt cheeks. Feeling more weary than ever, he limped toward the door. "Come with me, both of you."

Annie planted herself protectively in front of Valeria. "What are you going to do?"

"I'm going to feed her before she starves to death."

* * *

He could not keep himself from watching her eat. She was—or had been—a true lady. He'd forgotten until now how dainty a lady was, how refined her manners could be.

She held the stem of her wine goblet by her fingertips and took tiny sips. She broke off bits of bread and dipped them in the wine. She nibbled sparingly at the large wedge of white cheese and ate small pieces of the banana and papaya Annie had brought in from the patio grove. The smoked loin she pushed away.

Rodrigo edged the platter toward her. "Eat some of the meat," he said gruffly. "You need to strengthen your blood."

She looked pointedly at the food. "Thank you, no."

Understanding broke unpleasantly over Rodrigo. "Christ on the cross," he muttered, sweeping the platter of pork away. He was but a marginal Catholic, only conversant enough with the faith to be convincing should he ever be questioned. His mother had taught him the Jewish ways of Joseph of Ribera, but it was too dangerous to practice the old customs. "I forgot."

Her mouth softened. It was not quite a smile, but it gave him hope. "The important thing, Don Rodrigo, is that *I* never forget."

Annie, who sat on a bench across from Rodrigo, gave a great yawn and cradled her head in her arms on the table. Within moments, her breathing evened out and she slept. A great tenderness welled up in Rodrigo, and he resisted the urge to reach across the table and stroke her tousled hair.

He waited until Valeria had eaten her fill. At last, she dipped her fingers into the bowl of lemon water and discreetly rinsed her hands. Her long, beautiful hands. Her strong, lethal hands. Then she began to speak as if she had read the questions in his mind.

"I come from Toledo," she said, "where my family lived for generations. When our faith was outlawed, many of my kinfolk left to seek a more tolerant homeland. For my grandparents, who could not conceive of any home except Toledo, there was no choice. They pretended to convert to Christianity. My parents did the same, and so did I. In secret, we kept our true faith alive. We became Marranos."

Rodrigo nodded. The derisive term described insincere converts who privately celebrated Jewish rites and holy days.

"I married last year, and my husband and I moved to a new quarter of town. It was only a matter of time, I suppose, before we were found out. It seems the church rewards nosy neighbors." Valeria sipped her wine. "After that, of course, it was all over. My husband confessed under torture and died a martyr to our faith."

"How did you get away?"

"I was helped by a network of sympathetic Christians. We got to Cádiz and—"

"We?" asked Rodrigo.

Valeria groaned as if someone had slipped a knife into her back. She pressed her hands to her bosom. A look of unspeakable pain crossed her face.

"Oh God," he said, feeling her grief and rage. "You had a baby."

"Yes." Her voice was husky with sorrow. "A son." She pushed the wine away. "He died. He caught a fever on the voyage to Hispaniola, and he died."

"Hispaniola? Then what are you doing here?"

"A ship is no place for privacy. I had to bury my son properly, bathing his poor little body in warm water and saying the *Shema Yisrael*, the Jewish prayer for the dead. Of course, I was observed. It couldn't be avoided."

"What happened?"

"I was put in chains. I was supposed to be taken to the Holy House at Santo Domingo for questioning."

"But you escaped," he said with a long sigh of relief.

Valeria grew fierce. "Chains were not enough to bind me when I wanted to be free. As soon as we made port, I stowed away on another boat."

"The boat that brought you here." Rousing herself, Annie got up on her knees and propped her elbows on the table. "It's a good thing I saw you stealing that loaf of bread. If it had been anyone else, they would've asked questions. You're safe with us. Rodrigo will know what to do."

Valeria slid a glance at Rodrigo. He nearly drowned in the black pools of her eyes. "Am I safe?" she asked.

He thought of all the dangers inherent in harboring a Jew. He wondered how he would explain her presence in his house. He asked himself why this thin, bedraggled, lovely woman touched his heart. Then he remembered Joseph of Ribera and said, "Yes. I may live to regret this, but you're safe here."

CHAPTER 6

"That is Nombre de Dios," Casilda said, parting the tall grasses and broad, fanlike leaves that grew along a high bank above the town. She pointed at the shoreline far below. "Our journey is over."

Evan stared down at the city that guarded the Spanish treasure. The late afternoon sun painted the scene in shades of pink and gold. A few unpaved streets meandered down to a harbor crammed with ships and smaller vessels. There were perhaps two hundred buildings and dwellings— whitewashed wooden houses with palm-thatched roofs, a blocky church with a square tower, and a cluster of warehouses facing the docks. Men on foot and on horseback moved through the main plaza, passing draped horse litters and natives with large baskets balanced on their heads. At one end of the city, a lightly armed garrison faced the sea. At the other end, a crude bulwark provided defense against pirates and Cimaroons.

"Christ Almighty," was all Evan could say.

"You are not pleased?" Casilda brushed a lock of silky

black hair from her face. The sea breeze caught it and lifted the strands. "This was your quest, was it not? To find the white city?"

"Yes, of course. I just didn't expect it to be so large. It's at least the size of Plymouth."

"Ply-mouth?" Her mouth puckered as she tried the unfamiliar word.

"It's a port city in England. Nombre de Dios looks to be as large. We're going to need more men and guns and ships than I thought if we're going to take it."

"You will find a way, Evan."

He glanced at her, startled to hear her call him by his Christian name. During the two days of their journey from the Cimaroon settlement, she had walked tirelessly, shown him how to harvest fruits and nuts and tubers from the jungle, and how to steer a course by the sun. But never before had she called him by his name.

Still, even before today, a bond had formed between them. From the moment Casilda had seen his scars, she had drawn him into her heart. Perhaps because she, too, was scarred. She had overridden the objections her people had raised regarding this journey. She knew the way to the white city, and the lay of the streets and buildings.

Evan studied her openly now, his gaze taking in her breeze-tossed hair, her large, exotic eyes, her brown, lovely face. In her, the traits of African and native came together in a unique and beautiful way. She held endless fascination for him; like a precious stone cut by a master, she had facets that glimmered with every move she made.

"Why do you stare, Evan?" she asked.

"I'm sorry." He looked at the toe of his boot. "In my country, a man who stares at a lady in a certain way would get his face slapped."

"Why?"

He marveled at her innocence. Even after the horrors she had suffered, she still managed to seem as bright and new as dawn in springtime.

"Because," he said, "when a man stares like that at a lady, it usually means he's entertaining lusty notions."

"Lusty notions?"

He was beginning to regret the turn their conversation had taken. "Never mind. We'd best not go to town until morning. Where shall we camp tonight?"

She lifted her bundle, which contained clothing and net hammocks. "This way. I know of a place the white demons have not found."

His ungovernable gaze stayed fixed on Casilda as he walked behind her. The doeskin shift swished from side to side, outlining her sleek, muscular buttocks.

"Why did your people let you come here alone with me?" he asked.

"Why not?" She tossed her head and blue highlights glinted in her hair.

"Well . . . you're a woman and I'm a man."

"That is one thing you do not have to explain to me, Evan." Laughter lightened her voice. "Your people must be like the Spaniards in this. You do not teach your women how to protect themselves. My people do."

He fell silent. She was right. She was armed like a warrior, from the bone-handled knife stuck in her hip sheath to the poison-dipped darts strapped to her ankle.

"Are you worried about going back to Nombre de Dios?" he asked.

. "If I was worried," she said, starting down a washed-out ravine, "I would not have come."

"Oh. What if someone in the city recognizes you?"

"No one will. My master kept me in his house at all times."

"What if *he* recognizes you?" Evan persisted.

"He will not." She held back a branch so he could step under it. Evan heard the roar of rushing water somewhere close by and surmised that they had reached a tributary of the river Chagres.

"How can you be so certain?" he asked.

"Because he is dead." Taking Evan's hand, Casilda led him to a green glade where a stream cascaded into a pool and thick-tongued flowers decked the banks in an explosion of color.

"Dead?" asked Evan. "Are you sure?"

"Yes." Casilda set down her bundle. "I killed him."

Evan lay in his hammock, his hat pulled down over his face. Twilight veiled the hidden glade, and frogs peeped a welcome to the night. He and Casilda had eaten a small meal of maize cakes, nuts, and berries. He was pretending to sleep. In truth, he was watching Casilda from beneath the brim of his hat and thinking about what she had said.

No emotion had flickered on her face when she had told him she'd killed her master. To her, taking a Spaniard's life was of no more consequence than wringing a pullet's neck.

Oblivious of his attention, she crouched on the bank and rummaged through her bundle.

She had killed, but did that make her a murderess? Some Englishmen believed natives and Africans soulless, capable only of blind tribal loyalty. Some said they mated without discretion and killed without remorse, that they lived in packs, with less sense of virtue than wolves on the prowl.

Evan knew better. He had seen a Cimaroon man holding his infant son and cooing a lullaby to the child. He had seen the bonds of love between man and wife. He had seen a hunter share his kill with an elderly woman.

Casilda came from a people to whom life had dealt harsh blows. But that did not make her less than human. In fact, perhaps she was more, for she had survived enslavement and the loss of her children, and her only visible scar was the brand on her cheek.

Still, the fact that she had killed lodged stubbornly in Evan's mind. And just as stubbornly, fascination grew in his heart.

She drew a garment from her bundle and shook it out. It was a tunic, roughly spun and ragged at the hem. A slave's garb, Evan realized with a sudden lurch of his stomach. Tomorrow she would pose as his slave when they entered Nombre de Dios.

She muttered an unfamiliar word under her breath, and he realized she shared his opinion of the garment. She slung it over a low bush and stretched her arms high. Her breasts thrust against her soft doeskin dress, and her throat was a silky brown column that made his mouth water. Evan grew hard, uncomfortable, and overly warm just looking at her.

Lowering her arms, she walked toward him. "I am going to bathe in the stream," she announced.

Evan pushed back his hat. "How did you know I was awake?"

She gazed pointedly at his erection straining against his breeches.

"Oh," he said, chagrined. He drew up one leg. "Why are you going to bathe? In my country, it's considered unhealthy."

"Bathing has not struck me dead yet," she said, turning away. "Join me if you wish."

"I don't wish," he called after her.

She turned back, her hands working at the front laces of her shift. "Why not?"

"Because I might have more of those lusty notions."

She shrugged, dropped her shift, and waded into the pool below the cascade. "Please yourself, then."

Evan nearly exploded at the sight of her with her head thrown back, her eyes closed, her nude body gleaming with clear spring water.

Moments later, he splashed out into the pool with her, moving awkwardly over the rocky bottom and feeling the delicious cleansing currents of the stream.

She opened her eyes. "I thought you were not coming."

"I had them anyway."

"Had what?"

"Lusty notions."

"*Ay de mí!* When will you tell me what lusty notions are?"

Evan dove into the water and surfaced in front of her. He caught her in his arms, marveling at her sleek, firm body, the startled O of her mouth, her wide, twinkling eyes.

"Better I show you, *cara*," he said, lowering his head to kiss her.

"I've not seen you in the city before, señor," Rodrigo said to the stranger. "I wonder why that is."

Yes, why? Annie's thoughts echoed Rodrigo's words. They sat in his public office on the ground floor of the villa. Thick-walled and cooled by sea breezes wafting through the open windows, the room served as a place of inquiry for men of all manner of business.

Seated at her small writing desk, Annie studied the new-comer. His clothes were threadbare but clean. Eschewing fashionable but fragile hose, he wore black leather breeches and tall boots. A blousy white tunic showed a pair of shoulders that had no need of padding to add breadth to his well-conditioned body.

Idly turning the brim of his hat in his hand, the man said, "I am new to Nombre de Dios, Don Rodrigo. My name is Arturo Reyes."

A common enough name, Annie thought. She dipped her quill to record it beside the date, watching her hand move with a curious detachment. Arturo Reyes. Arturo El Rey. King Arthur.

Smiling at the fanciful notion, she completed her entry and looked again at the visitor. His hair and beard were black, gleaming with blue highlights, and looked unusually clean. Annie hooked her bare feet around the legs of the stool and tried to remember the last time she had bathed. The answer eluded her.

Valeria bathed often. In secret, of course, for excessive cleanliness was suspect behavior among proper Spaniards. Annie had expected Rodrigo to object to Valeria's habits, but he seemed not to mind. Valeria, whom he had introduced as an old family friend from San Augustine, had no trouble pleasing Rodrigo.

"And who is your companion?" Rodrigo asked the man.

For the first time, Annie looked at the woman who stood in the shadows just inside the doorway. She kept her eyes downcast. Her hair fell forward, obscuring her face.

"That's Casilda," said Arturo Reyes. "She is my slave."

At the sound of her name, Casilda looked up, tossing back her hair. Annie stared at the thin, severe face. A livid burn mark marred one cheek. A slave.

Annie's esteem for the handsome Señor Reyes plummeted. "What is that mark upon her cheek?" she blurted out.

"Watch your tongue, boy," Rodrigo warned her.

"I'm truly curious. Were you trying to brand her, señor, and she had the bad grace to move, or did you simply maim her with a hot poker?"

Arturo Reyes made a hissing sound as if he himself had been burned. "Your questions are impertinent, rodent," he snapped.

Annie clamped her jaw against a reply. During the years of posing as Rodrigo's scribe, she had taught herself to tolerate all manner of abuse. Yet this stranger sorely tested her endurance.

Visibly conquering his temper, he turned to Rodrigo. "As a matter of fact, I've brought Casilda to be baptized. Can you tell me how I might accomplish this?"

"I don't usu—" Catching himself, Rodrigo amended, "My many duties force me to perform my devotions in my own private chapel."

He and Annie rarely spoke of what had happened at Gema del Mar two years before, but they never worshiped at a church unless it simply could not be avoided.

"When is mass celebrated?" Reyes asked. "What time of day, Don Rodrigo?"

"I'm not sure. You can check with Fray García at the chapter house. He's a better adviser than I in the matter of native baptisms."

Indeed he was, thought Annie nastily. Fray García sometimes went along on slave raids and conquests. The natives who proved intractable were tortured and put to death. Fray García, all compassion, baptized them first, saving their souls so that when the conquistadors murdered them, they would go to heaven.

"Well, perhaps you can help with a few other matters," said Reyes. His sharp, observant eyes seemed to take in every detail and commit it to memory. Annie wondered at his interest in Rodrigo's plate ewer and bowl in the corner, and in the frayed wall hanging that depicted the lion of Ribera, the symbol of Rodrigo's grandfather, Joseph Sarmiento.

Reyes laid a document on the table in front of Rodrigo. "This is a contract from the Council of the Indies in Seville. I've been granted permission to set up a supply post for the mule trains that bring the treasure from Panama."

Rodrigo perused the document and rubbed his finger over the waxen seal at the bottom. "This is a very lucrative contract, señor," he said. "Supplying the *recuas* has made more than one enterprising gentleman rich."

"That is my hope. I came across the Ocean Sea to serve God, of course, but also to get rich. Have you a schedule of the *recuas*? I shall have to know certain things—when the treasure from the mines of Peru is laden. When the train departs from Panama. How long it takes them to travel from Panama to Nombre de Dios. How many guards—"

"Guards?" Rodrigo asked. Leaning back in his chair, he crossed his arms and hooked his hands under them. "You ask a lot of questions, señor. Why would you need to know the number of guards?"

Reyes let out a huff of impatience. "Señor, this is a wine concession. I hope to number the soldiers among my customers."

"I see." Without looking around, he said to Annie, "Fetch this season's schedules."

Lately, Annie had grown prickly at his commands, even though she knew his brusque treatment of her was only pretense. But the curt orders had become second nature to Rodrigo. With each passing day, she grew more weary of enduring them.

She selected a key from her ring and opened Rodrigo's cabinet. She felt Reyes's eyes on her, watching her every move as she fetched the documents. He and Rodrigo made small talk as she sifted through the papers. A devil of impulse seized her, and she made a tiny mark with her quill, a mark that changed the date that the mule train would start out. Reyes was a crude entrepeneur, a slave owner. He wished to get rich, but he would do so without her help.

Unrepentant, she set the papers before him. For a moment his flinty gaze held her immobile, and she thought he might have seen through her disguise. No. He was just eager and greedy, same as any conquistador.

Reading the list of dates and events, Reyes scribbled the information with a graphite pencil on a scrap of parchment.

"Anything else, señor?" Rodrigo asked.

"No." Reyes gave him a tight, satisfied smile. "Thank you, Don Rodrigo. You've told me everything I need to know. Good day."

Turning sharply on his heel, he strode to the door. The slave girl cringed when she saw him approach. He grasped her arm. "Let's go, wench. Your heathen days are nearly at an end." He jerked her roughly out into the sunlight.

"Demonios!" Annie burst out. "That man is a son of a bitch."

Rodrigo scowled at her. "Watch your mouth, brat. You don't have to play the boy when no one's around."

Annie set her hands on her hips. "Well, what did you think of him?"

Rodrigo planted his elbows on the desk and looked outside, where Reyes was half dragging Casilda across the plaza.

"I thought he was a son of a bitch," he said.

"I hate this," Evan said through his teeth as he and Casilda crossed the plaza. "I truly hate treating you like this."

"You got the information you sought." Casilda pretended to stumble. "It is not so bad."

"Not so bad?" Evan turned down the street that led to the church. "Look at how I have to treat you. How can you stand being dragged, pushed, handled like a beast?"

They reached the church steps. "I can stand it," Casilda assured him, leaning back so that he was forced to push her.

He grasped her roughly by the shoulders, sickened by his own behavior, feigned or not. "Why, damn it?"

"Because I love you."

Her simple, direct statement snatched away the last of his control. "Casilda," he said. He hauled her into his arms and crushed his mouth down on hers.

Their kiss held echoes of the night they had shared. Evan loved her strength, her beauty, her fire. All night they had pleasured each other, the unexpected passion as hot and luminous as a greenwood fire. In the least likely of places, at the least convenient of times, Evan had found love. He had no idea where his heart would lead him, but he did not care. Loving her was as seductive and inevitable as the pull between the moon and the tide.

He held her and cherished her while his loins took fire and the blood thumped loudly in his ears.

A moment later, she stiffened and pulled back. Belatedly, Evan realized that the pounding he had heard was the tramp of boots on the dusty street.

Casilda wrenched herself from his arms. Evan turned to see a pair of soldiers striding toward them. One held the leash of a large gray deerhound. On the church steps, a tall, thin friar glared at Evan in disapproval.

One of the soldiers, decked in crusader's green and white, stopped in front of Evan. The deerhound sat on its haunches, its black lip lifting in a snarl. "What's this?" the soldier demanded. "You show too much favor to that heathen wench, sir."

"And in the sight of the house of God," the friar said.

Evan's throat dried. Unconsciously moving in front of Casilda, he tried to keep his eyes from the gleaming swords and daggers of the soldiers. "The wench is my property. I was just bringing her to be baptized."

"You have a strange way of preparing her for entry into the true faith," the soldier retorted. "We frown on familiarity with heathens."

"Aye," said the other. "Take them by force if you must, but for God's sake do it in private." His gaze slithered over Casilda. "Though I do admit, that's a handsome wench you have there."

Evan wondered if they could hear his heart hammering behind his breastplate. "If you'll excuse us, I'd like to have a word with the friar."

"Later. Come to the barracks first. We want you to share the goods."

Evan sent a frantic look to the cleric, expecting him to intervene. The friar simply looked on with mild interest. Catholics, thought Evan. Their church was a sewer, their religion an excuse to torment the innocent.

"Not now, I'm afraid," he said offhandedly. Secretly he measured the street, wondering if he and Casilda could outrun them.

"What's this?" the soldier asked. "An Indian lover, eh?"

"No, of course not. I have business to conduct and no time for the likes of you."

The soldiers exchanged a glance. "Then go, but leave her with us. We'll show you how a real man governs a slave. Step aside."

"Beat me." Casilda's whisper was a barely audible breath in Evan's ear.

Shocked, he pretended not to hear. "Gentlemen, it occurs to me that soldiers of the empire must have far more pressing matters to contend with."

"Do it," Casilda persisted.

While all of Evan's instincts rose up in heartbreaking denial, he spat, *"Puta!"* His arm streaked out, and he backhanded her. He hoped the soldiers had not seen him cushion the blow with his sleeve.

Casilda cringed, covering her mouth with her hand. Only Evan saw her bite down on her lip, causing it to bleed. "Again," she whispered. "Again."

"Stop that sniveling," Evan said, dragging the words out with reluctance. He slapped her. Casilda's head snapped to one side. Her pained expression looked so convincing that Evan wondered if he had actually hurt her.

"Stop!" The shrill call came from the end of the street. Fleetingly Evan saw Rodrigo Viscaino's assistant running toward them.

"Again," Casilda whispered, pretending to shrink from him.

Evan grabbed a handful of her hair. "Come, wench. These men have done enough interfering."

"Let go of her," said the scruffy boy, launching himself at Evan. "You bastard, what kind of swine are you?"

Evan found his arms filled with wiry limbs and pummeling fists. The lad was quick, and his righteous anger gave him strength.

"We'll take the wench in hand," one of the soldiers offered. He grasped her arm and cupped his hand around her breast.

Casilda looked sick. The boy pounded Evan's chest. "Saints and angels, run!" the boy yelled at Casilda.

Casilda's hand came up sharply. Her finger gouged the soldier in the eye. With a howled curse, he flung her away.

Even as he watched Casilda break from the startled soldiers, Evan felt a jolt of recognition. *Saints and angels* . . . Where had he heard that expression before?

Sparing no time to speculate, he dumped the boy unceremoniously on the ground. "Now see what you've done," he snapped.

"After her!" the soldier yelled. "Don't let the wench get away!" He unleashed the deerhound. The dog crouched low, ready to spring. The Viscaino scribe planted his foot on the end of the leash, and the dog reeled back.

Throwing a curse over his shoulder, the soldier and his companion gave chase. Furious, Evan followed. His legs pumped, and his breath came in short gasps. The sound of pounding boots and the howl of the straining dog echoed off the plaster walls of the buildings on each side of the street.

He kept his eyes fixed on Casilda and said a silent prayer for her safety. He refused to think of what would befall her if she were caught.

As they reached the main plaza, the possibility seemed less likely. His beautiful Casilda ran like a deer, dodging carts and crates and passersby with graceful ease. In comparison, the soldiers moved clumsily, their ungainly uniforms and gear impairing them.

"She's heading for the Panama Gate!" one of the soldiers bellowed. "Stop her!"

The gate was guarded by a fat sentry, who napped in the shade of a banana tree next to the tiny stone cubicle. Between his feet was a clay jar half full of wine or aqua vitae.

"Stop her, you fool," the soldier barked.

Startled, the fat man lurched to his feet. Casilda dashed past him and plunged down the dusty path leading out of town.

The guard cursed and snatched up a loaded crossbow. He sighted down the shaft, and his finger squeezed the trigger.

"No!" Evan screamed. He hurled himself at the guard, his hands outstretched to deflect the crossbow. His fingers were mere inches from the weapon when the bolt sprang forth. With a deadly whir, it sped toward Casilda.

Even from a distance, Evan heard the awful thud. And then a high, thin animal scream, the sound of a rabbit in the throes of death. Casilda stumbled, but she kept running.

"My God, the woman's possessed," said the sentry, making the sign of the cross.

"Go to hell," said Evan. He didn't remember drawing his sword, but suddenly it was in his hand, slicing toward the guard. The fat man jumped back. At the same moment, a soldier grabbed Evan's hand from behind, stopping the arc of his sword. "Sir, you are under arrest!" He turned to his companion. "Martinez, get the hound and go after the woman."

Evan wrenched free and faced the soldiers. If his brandished sword were not warning enough, the murderous expression on his face would have daunted the devil himself.

The soldiers backed off, but drew their swords. One of them raced back toward the church to get the dog. The guard snatched up his crossbow and another bolt. Evan thrust at the soldier with his sword. He had but little training in swordsmanship, and the blade carved clumsily at thin air.

The soldier laughed, clearly anticipating an easy contest. Frustrated, Evan dropped his sword, ducked under the swinging blade of the other, and drove his fist into the soldier's face. His knuckles split on impact. The soldier's nose caved in, and blood exploded in a great blossom radiating from the middle of his face.

Without slowing his movements, Evan lifted the wine jar and brought it down on the guard's head. The crossbow clattered to the ground, and the fat man sank, unconscious, on top of it.

Snatching up his sword, Evan left the city to find Casilda.

It seemed he had run a thousand miles. In a way, he was grateful for the utter fatigue of his body, for by nightfall his mind was numb to the rage and grief that had possessed him earlier.

Darting and feinting through the wilderness, Evan had made a sinuous trail to confuse the searchers. He had splashed through streams and salt marshes to confuse the dogs. Only when he was certain he had lost the hunters did he allow himself to seek out Casilda.

He knew where she had gone. In the dark of night, moving soundlessly as she had taught him, he made his way back to the glade where they had spent the night before.

The light of a few stars misted the clearing. Casilda lay beside the stream, one shoulder against the ground and her knees drawn up to her chest.

Evan rushed to her side and fell to his knees. "Casilda!" he whispered, touching her face with a trembling hand.

Her skin felt clammy to the touch. She gulped air, then said, "I knew you would come. Help me, Evan."

"I dare not light a fire, and I can't see what to do."

"Let your eyes see through the darkness, Evan."

He forced himself to study her dark shape until his eyes ached with strain. What he saw, even dimly, was a horror beyond bearing. The thick-shafted crossbow bolt was embedded deep in her right shoulder, just above the bony blade. The flesh around it was puffy and sticky with clotted blood.

"Pull it out," she whispered.

"I can't, Casilda, it would hurt you too much. Let me take you back to town, find a doctor."

"No. I would rather die here. Please, Evan. I beg you. Pull out the arrow of the white demon."

Evan released a heavy sigh of hopelessness. They had left most of their supplies here. Rummaging through a parcel, he found one of the wineskins and held it to her lips.

She took a few feeble swallows, then turned her head away.

"Drink more," he said, his voice rough with fear.

"I do not like the thunder water of the white demons."

"Drink, or I won't help you."

"That is a lie, but I will drink more anyway."

As she slowly drained the flask, the moon rose, shedding ghostly light on the clearing, silvering the stream and settling like a shroud over Casilda.

"Now," she whispered, forming the word carefully as if her tongue had thickened. "I am ready, Evan."

He prepared himself as best he could with a clean tunic to stanch the flow of blood and a bracing gulp of wine for his nerves. In his travels, he had watched ships' barbers treat all manner of wounds. Now he wished he had observed them more closely.

He lay her on her stomach, bending to kiss her ear. "I love you, Casilda."

"I know. Hurry, Evan."

Steeling his shaking hands, he took hold of the shaft where it protruded from her shoulder and pulled up gently.

Casilda lay still even as she hissed with pain. "No, Evan! You must be swift and strong."

Evan understood. Years earlier, he had suffered from an infected tooth. The barber showed no hesitancy, but simply clamped the iron jaws of the pliers around the tooth and twisted it from its socket.

Sweat beaded on his brow, and his lips firmed with determination. Placing one hand on Casilda and the other on the shaft, he tore the bolt free and flung it far away.

They both cried out at once. Blood oozed from the dark, deep wound. Evan pressed the folded tunic over the spot.

Wanting badly to weep, he stretched out next to her and tucked her beneath one arm and one leg. She made no sound but soon fell still, exhausted by her ordeal and senseless with pain.

Evan lay wakeful until dawn tinged the forest. He knew he would go back to the city, for he was more determined than ever to wreak havoc on the Spaniards.

But first, he had to take Casilda back to her people.

Three days later, Rico blocked the path in front of Evan. He stared in horror at the burden in Evan's arms.

"What happened?"

"It's a long story. I'll tell you while we walk to the village."

Evan had told his tale by the time they laid Casilda on a woven mat in the communal hut. Reaching down, he caressed her feverish cheek.

"The first two days, she insisted on walking," he said to Rico. "I watched her grow weaker. She had a raging thirst. This morning, she stumbled and could not get up."

"And so you carried her," said Rico, nodding at an older woman, who sat on her heels beside Casilda. She had brought a wooden bowl containing some gray, pasty matter and papaya leaves.

"Help her," said Evan. "I beg you, don't let her die."

The healer gave a noncommittal grunt and began removing

the bandage Evan had fashioned from the tunic and strips of cloth.

A foul smell filled the air. Evan forced himself to look at the wound. The flesh was swollen and discolored. Thin red lines scored Casilda's back.

"The wound is putrid," the healer said, her voice quavering. "Casilda burns with fever. The evil flows through her body. When it reaches her heart, she will die."

"No!" The ragged cry tore from Evan's throat. Self-loathing swamped him. What a fool he had been to let himself love her. To lose his hold on his emotions and kiss her in public. To shy from beating her so that the soldier's suspicions were roused. God. It was all his fault.

He forced himself to look at Rico. The dark man glared back, grim and accusing.

Evan bowed his head. "I take responsibility for this. I should have been more careful. It is right for you to punish me."

"It will be as you wish," Rico promised him.

The healer had begun spreading the gray paste on the wound. Casilda's eyes opened, and she whispered, "Rico."

He stroked her hair. "I am here. You are back with us, Casilda."

"Yes. Now you must help Evan."

"He did this to you," Rico snapped. "He must die."

"No. It was my choice to go with him. If you harm him, my angry spirit will devil your sleep every night for the rest of your life."

Rico moved back slightly. He held his hands in front of his face, palms out, to ward off evil. "Why do you urge us to befriend the white demon?"

"Because he is a man who can love as fiercely as he hates. His hatred for the Spaniards is strong. He is the enemy of your enemy. Help him, Rico."

Rico and the healer exchanged a glance. The older woman pursed her lips and gave a curt nod.

"If that is what you wish, Casilda," Rico said.

* * *

Evan stayed with her that night, holding her feverish body in the curve of his own. She slept fitfully, and each time she awoke, he gave her sips of water.

Never in his life had he felt so helpless. He was losing her, and nothing he or anyone could do would save her. He burned with rage and frustration. He wanted to beat his breast and tear at his hair. He wanted to curse God and howl at the stars.

For Casilda's sake, he lay still, murmuring words of his heartbroken love into her ear.

At dawn, a cock crowed. Casilda lifted her head weakly. "Hold me in your arms, Evan," she said. "Hold me."

He knew the embrace would disturb the poultice the healer had made, but his heart told him it didn't matter. He sat up and cradled her to his chest, cupping his hand around her head as if she were a fragile orchid.

"It is done, my love," she whispered. "I go on ... ahead of you. My babies. Perhaps my babies wait for me ..."

"No. Casilda, please—"

"Kiss me, Evan."

He pressed his trembling lips against her warm ones, and it was all he could do to stifle a sob. Even now, she was soft and sweet. When he could bear the pain no longer, he lifted his head and gazed down into her face. How beautiful she was, a child of the forest receding deeper and deeper into a darkness he could not penetrate.

"I cannot wait for you," she whispered.

She spoke no more. Evan felt the instant she died. The softest of sighs escaped her. Her eyes were open, and he watched the pupils leap wide as if something had startled her.

Perhaps, he thought, hearing only the dull rhythm of his own heart in his ears, death always came as a surprise.

Very gently, he closed the eyelids of his beloved and placed a kiss upon each one, and then one upon her mouth.

"Good-bye, my love," he said and silently commanded God to witness his vow. His hatred was sharper now, even more focused than it had been after the massacre at San Juan de Ulua. He would stop at nothing to take revenge on Spain. He owed it to Charlie Moon, to Casilda, and to all the innocents who had died at the hands of the conquistadors. He would not rest until the empire was soaked with Spanish blood.

CHAPTER 7

London
1571

Queen Elizabeth closed the small coffer with a snap. When she looked up at André, her eyes sparkled like stars, a bittersweet reminder of the dazzling young woman she had been. "It is wonderful," she said simply.

"It's only the beginning," André assured her. "Drake has only been off his leash for a year." With hooded eyes, he studied her as she sat in the great state bed, the cushions piled high at her back. Her cheeks glowed with fever, and beneath her gold silk robes, her frail chest rose and fell with her rapid, uneven breathing.

At the far end of the chamber, a musician strummed softly on a lute. The queen's ladies sat in the light streaming through a bank of diamond-paned windows and worked at their embroidery. From time to time, they cast worried glances toward the huge canopied bed with its alarmingly tiny occupant.

André tamped back the alarm that clutched at his throat. "Madam," he said, "this gold is but a foretaste of the treasure that can be had. The captain of the packet Drake sent reports that this was taken easily from a few Spanish ships. They haven't even attempted the assault on Nombre de Dios yet."

"What is the delay, then?"

"For once, madam, I cannot be certain. From the reports, I gather Nombre de Dios is a rather large town. Drake has only a handful of men. He must plan carefully."

She nodded. "Waiting is an activity in which I have much practice. But I have never learned to like it. I'm sure Captain Drake—" A fit of coughing seized her. Clutching an embroidered handkerchief, she covered her mouth.

A gaggle of ladies-in-waiting bustled forward and began fluttering about the queen. They offered sachets of herbs and drafts of medicine, and words of advice that the queen waved away with a thin, pale hand.

André stepped back and watched. The sight agonized him. Elizabeth's robe gaped open to reveal a shift of white lawn. Beneath the fabric, her collarbone and ribs stood out prominently. Her physician, Dr. Burcot, had grimly informed the council that the queen was off her food, and her strength was waning. Leicester and Hatton had joked nervously that she subsisted on air and power alone, but their chuckles had a morbid ring.

André's concern took on the keen edge of panic. Though the queen had survived a host of illnesses, each one had left her a little more frail, a little more brittle, and a little more ill-tempered. And while her marriage was a topic of debate for every crowned head of Europe, he had come to realize that she would never take a husband. She would go childless to her grave before she would hand the reins of power and the destiny of England to a man.

André shuddered to think what would happen in the event of her death. He had a well-thought-out plan to flee to Basel the moment Elizabeth breathed her last. For though he served her discreetly, he knew he had enemies, and his head would roll if he did not have the queen to stay the executioner's hand.

Unless ... His hand stole down to touch the large pouch

that hung from his belt. Unless the succession could be assured in a way not even Elizabeth had ever imagined.

As patient as a spider, André waited in the shadows until the queen's ladies withdrew with their possets and herbs and useless charms. Clucking like anxious hens, they retired to their corner of the vast bedchamber. Then he came forward again.

"Madam."

"Now what is it, André?" An unhealthy whiteness rimmed her thin lips. "If you're going to try to make me drink that foul stuff—"

"Nay, madam. I have something to show you."

She motioned with her hand. "You rarely disappoint me, André. Come, then."

André pulled a thick leather-bound volume from his pouch and placed the heavy book in her hands. Frowning slightly, she opened to a random page and looked up. "A manuscript?"

André nodded. "Those are the journals of the late adventurer Sebastian Cabot."

She browsed idly through the pages. "I met him once, when I was very small, and once again during my brother Edward's reign. A fat man, more full of wind than substance, as I recall."

"Quite so," said André. "He never did accomplish anything he set out to do."

"How did you come to possess his private journals?"

I stole them, he thought. With a slight shrug, he said, "Cabot died at the age of fourscore and ten. He outlived all his family. In the end, he had but a few friends. I was one of them."

"How opportune." Elizabeth pursed her lips. "You do choose the most convenient of friends, André."

"So do you, madam." He could not resist the jibe.

"You're an impudent knave, but I'll let it pass. Why do you bother me with a dead adventurer's scribblings now? Did he find the Northwest Passage to the Orient and die before he could claim the credit?"

André cleared his throat. "No, but ... Your Majesty, if there is a grain of truth in these journals, Cabot may yet do you a great service."

"Tell me." She smiled without humor. "I have been served by some unusual men, but never by a corpse."

"Do you not want to read the manuscript yourself?"

"My eyes are poor, André, and I've no patience with reading a braggart's musings."

Reaching forward, he opened to a page marked with a crimson ribbon. "This is the important part. It seems Cabot learned of a love affair between your father and a certain noblewoman."

Elizabeth laughed dryly. "This is news? My father is reputed to have bedded half the court."

"In this case, madam, a child came of the union."

She sniffed. "A common enough consequence of mating. But I thought I was rid of my father's by-blows. Wasn't John Perrott of Carew the last?" She curled the crimson ribbon around her finger. "Is it John's son, Owen, then? I thought we had the boy well in hand—and well out of the way at Castle Carew."

"The journals refer to another of your father's bloodline."

"What?" Her harsh whisper snapped like a bowstring.

"According to Cabot, the lady's name was Doña Gabriella. She was one of Catherine of Aragon's ladies."

Elizabeth scowled. "Catherine of Aragon surrounded herself with a flock of sanctimonious Catholic sheep. Am I to believe there was a black one in the lot?"

"Possibly. According to Cabot, Doña Gabriella fled England and was never heard from again. Years later, Cabot was adventuring in Hispaniola when he encountered her. She had a child."

Elizabeth caught her breath with a hiss. "Cabot believed the child was my father's get."

André tapped the book. "He claims the boy—she called him Phillip—was the very image of King Henry."

The queen let out an explosive sigh. "So are half the tinkers' brats in Devonshire, you fool. The Tudors do not have an exclusive claim to golden hair and apple cheeks."

"True, madam. But Cabot seemed quite convinced. It bears further investigation." Calmly, André explained what the journals told of Phillip Blythe: His marriage to a lady of Spanish and English nobility. The birth of their only child. The probability that Phillip had died, for when last Cabot saw him, he had been sickly.

"Cabot saw the child?"

"No, only the father, Phillip. The child's name is not mentioned. But Cabot heard reports—"

"In other words," Elizabeth said slowly, her slim, long-fingered hand traveling over the yellowed pages, "there is, somewhere in the world, an orphan of royal heritage."

"As unlikely as the story sounds, I believe it has the ring of truth."

Elizabeth slammed the book shut and glared at him. "Why do you show me this now? Why did you withhold it from me all these years, André?"

"Because, like the rest of the world, I believed you would marry and get an heir of your own and have no need of your father's by-blows."

"Ah. But now I'm dying, and you're worried about your own neck. Leave me in peace, you scheming knave. I don't wish to have you in my sight as I die."

André's temper flared. "Shall I have you measured for your tomb, then?" Behind him, he heard the ladies gasp at his boldness. "Aye," he said with a toss of his head, "die now and let England fall to the Catholic Scots queen. She's a proven breeder, after all—"

A sharp bark of laughter burst from Elizabeth, ending on a cough. "Blackguard. Do you think me fool enough to rise to your bait?"

Relieved at her show of spirit, André said, "My liege, if I thought you naive, I would swear that I have the best interests of England at heart. However, you know me too well. My neck—and the head attached to it—have always come first with me."

A wry gleam shone in her eyes. "I sometimes remember why I like you, André. You know when to lie, and when to tell the truth."

He bowed from the waist. "I consider that a compliment, Your Majesty."

"Let us assume I have a long-lost nephew on Hispaniola. A Spaniard, André." She shuddered. "Christ's teeth, are you saying I should give my crown to a Spaniard?"

"I'm saying you should investigate the claims made in the journal."

She settled back on her cushions, selected a bit of sweet marchpane from a bowl beside the bed, and chewed thoughtfully. "Tell me of these claims."

"The child was born in 1556. His father was Phillip Blythe—"

"An unusual name for a Spaniard."

André nodded. "Doña Gabriella wed an Englishman. He gave the boy his own name."

"Tell me of the child's mother."

André allowed his mouth to curve in a smile. "She is one of the reasons this orphan is so interesting. She was a de Carval, of the great Andalusian family. But her mother was a Woodville."

The queen's eyebrows shot up. Her own great-grandmother and namesake, Elizabeth Woodville, had ennobled her family a century ago when she had married Edward IV. "Truly?"

"Aye, of the branch of the family that went to Spain to help win the kingdom of Granada from the Moors."

"A most interesting lineage," said Elizabeth.

"I thought you'd like it." André leaned close; the scent of lavender and medicinal herbs was overpowering. "Madam," he whispered, "if you were to find this child, bring him to England . . ."

Cunning sharpened her gaze. "Unacknowledged, of course."

"Of course."

"Then I could train him after my own fashion. Always assuming, naturally, that this is not some wild fantasy of Cabot's."

"Naturally, madam."

"You've a plan for finding my young kinsman?"

André let his gaze drift to the coffer of Spanish gold and silver, which had been all but forgotten during the queen's attack of coughing.

"I see," she said, following the direction of his gaze. "Drake again."

"Indeed, my liege," André said. "If the heir is to be found, who but Drake to find him?"

Annie grasped the stiff bodice of the gown and adjusted it so that the square neckline framed her bosom. "Jesu," she whispered as sweat filmed her upper lip, "this is torture." She turned to pick up a mantilla from the chest. Her bell-shaped farthingale swept a box of hair combs to the floor.

"Damn!" she said through her teeth. She had nearly forgotten how to move within the cumbersome confines of a gown.

She was breathing hard by the time she finished. Urgency drove her to the mirror, for she did not want to get caught trying on Valeria's dress.

She felt silly, but this afternoon, she had been seized by the inescapable longing to set free the woman inside her. She knew what had triggered the notion.

Valeria. Ever since she had come into Rodrigo's household, subtle changes had taken place. Annie could not remember when she had first noticed it, but Rodrigo had begun to wear a clean shirt to supper each night. And polished boots. And a very affected gold ring on his little finger.

His conversation had become almost courtly. He offered no outright flattery, but his eyes spoke for him as his gaze followed every movement Valeria made. And he ignored Annie.

Valeria had moved into their lives by quiet, barely noticeable inches, and now Annie could not imagine *Casa de Viscaino* without her.

Yet her presence had awakened a longing in Annie—a need to drop her long-held pretenses and discover herself.

Who was she? The boy in the tunic who cursed like a sea-soned tar? Or a girl on the brink of womanhood? Today, while Valeria was out at market and Rodrigo down at the docks for the arrival of a fleet, she had slipped into Valeria's room.

She had meant only to study the fabric of Valeria's two dresses—both gifts from Rodrigo. She had meant only to fin-ger the mother-of-pearl hair combs and sniff the bottle of rose water.

But the beautiful, feminine things had touched something deep inside Annie, and she found herself sprinkling on the lovely scent, covering her head with a cobwebby lace man-tilla and fastening it with crested combs. The dress hung pleasantly heavy, the fine wine-colored silk slippery to the touch.

Feeling like a new person, Annie spun about and dipped a curtsy to an imaginary gentleman caller. Again and again she looked at herself in the narrow gilt-framed mirror, moving from side to side to take in her image from every angle.

How remarkable she looked, with her cropped hair hidden under the mantilla and her figure encased in a fashionable gown. She bore no resemblance to the thin, gawky boy she impersonated day after day.

She walked to the tall, narrow window and peered through the slits of the shutters. The street below was powdery gray, crowded with laborers and fishermen. A few stray dogs for-aged in the rubbish heaped up against the building across the way. A tradesman with a bamboo cage of chickens hurried to-ward the marketplace.

Annie felt curiously detached from the people of Nombre de Dios. Until lately, she had been content in her role as Rodrigo's scribe. Now she found herself inclined to strange, indefinable yearnings that clutched at her body in places a lady wasn't supposed to think about.

Rodrigo had warned her that a transformation might come. Bumbling over the words, he had tried, on that long ago af-ternoon when she had been thrown into a panic by the onset of her menses, to explain the changes that were taking place in her body. He had helped her that day. She wondered if he could help her now.

How could he, when even she did not understand what she was feeling, when she could not even articulate what she yearned for?

"Aha!" Strong hands grabbed her from behind.

Startled speechless, Annie felt a pair of arms slip around her waist. Soft, warm lips touched her neck, and a hot whisper came to her ear: "Back so soon, *querida*?"

Annie spared no time to think. She hammered her elbows into his ribs and spun around. "Rodrigo! What in God's name do you think you're doing?"

"Annie?" His face paled. He let go of her as if she were a live coal. "What the hell are you up to?"

Uncanny awareness washed over her. She pressed herself back against the louvered shutters. Annie felt hot and flushed and awkward. Her body tingled from his embrace. The feel of his lips lingered on her neck like a phantom kiss.

"I—I was just trying on one of Valeria's dresses," she said, reaching up to pluck the combs from her hair.

His response vacillating between horror and amusement, Rodrigo took the mantilla from her. Without it, she looked both heartbreakingly adorable and woefully absurd. Her badly barbered mop of hair made her neck and shoulders seem inordinately thin between the puffed sleeves of the gown. Her wide-eyed expression of shame and startlement touched him.

"It's all right, *muchacha*. You've done nothing wrong. It was I who should not have sneaked up on you."

"You thought I was Valeria."

"You had your back turned. You are in her room, wearing her clothes. What else should I have thought? I'm sorry, Annie."

But was he? When he had held her, he had experienced a jolt of sensation that lingered even after she had turned to face him. That lingered even now, God help him.

"You're lovers, aren't you?" Annie asked. "You and Valeria are lovers."

Not yet, thought Rodrigo. And not for want of desire on

his part. It was just that he had a niggling, misplaced sense of honor where Valeria was concerned. "You should not talk so," he said sternly. "It ill becomes a young lady of quality."

She laughed bitterly. "I? A young lady of quality? Tell me another joke, Rodrigo, for I find nothing amusing in that one."

Calming himself, he placed a finger beneath her chin and drew her gaze to his. "This masquerade was all your idea, Annie. You practically forced me to go along with your charade. Much to my amazement, it works. But no matter what you wear, you are a princess of the blood royal."

"You think I should take comfort in that?" she whispered. "Shall I cross the Ocean Sea and proclaim myself Queen Elizabeth's heir?"

"Don't be foolish. What's the matter, Annie?"

She blew out a sigh and made a habitual motion to stuff her hands in her pockets. Only the gown had no pockets. Her hands skimmed down the shiny silk. "I don't know. Sometimes I just feel such a terrible discontent, Rodrigo."

"Everyone does at your age. When I was fifteen, I was in a fury at the entire world."

She set her hands on her hips. Boyish gestures had become second nature to her by now.

Guiltily, Rodrigo wondered if he had done right by her, letting her run wild as a boy, having her do a man's work in the treasury. Perhaps it was time to stop the charade.

"You never answered my question," she said.

"What question?"

"Are you and Valeria lovers?"

"That is none of your affair."

"Then I assume that means yes."

"Don't you assume anything of the sort, Annie. And what do you know of love affairs, anyway?"

"Everything." The lie was etched all over her face, but Rodrigo decided not to challenge her. "Enough to know that you are keeping Valeria in a state of dishonor. You should marry her, Rodrigo."

"Marry her? Don't be ridiculous. I can't marry her."

"She's beautiful, mannerly, and educated."

"She's also a—" He clamped his mouth shut and chased his longings away.

"A Jew," Annie said in a low, accusing voice. "That's what you were going to say, weren't you, Rodrigo?"

"It's not what you think, Annie. And I won't answer to a saucy child."

Her finger jabbed at his chest. "You hypocrite! Your own mother has Jewish blood! Do you hold Doña Paloma's race in contempt? Why don't you just become a Soldier of Christ? Why don't you drag innocent people from their houses and burn them alive? I hear there's a good living to be made by informants."

Rodrigo's large hand streaked out and slapped her across the face. Her head snapped to one side and she gave a small, sobbing gasp.

Self-loathing sickened him as the imprint of his fingers bloomed on her pale cheek. His palm stung, though not as much as his sense of guilt.

"Jesus Christ," he said. "You shouldn't speak to me like that. I'm not responsible for my temper when you insult me."

Her eyes were bright, but with her typical stubbornness she refused to weep. "Am I to keep silent when I learn that you, my guardian and dearest friend, think and act like the fanatics who killed my grandparents?"

"I'm sorry," he said again. "I'm sorry I struck you. But my reasons for not marrying Valeria are mine alone." He trusted himself to touch her now, and he took both her hands in his. "Annie, how can you believe that I loathe the Jews?"

She extracted her hands from his. "Then why won't you marry Valeria?"

He intended to marry for life, but Valeria was a puzzle to him. Though she seemed to desire him, she didn't seem the kind to make so lasting a commitment.

"Let's drop it, Annie. We will always argue about this and never accomplish a thing."

"True." She turned to the window and leaned on the sill. "Did the fleet come in safe and sound?"

Rodrigo frowned. "Not quite. There was a skirmish with pirates in the vicinity of Guadeloupe Island. One of the caravels was plundered and scuttled."

"English pirates?" she asked with interest.

"The Spanish captain believes so, judging from their speed and skill. And . . . other things."

"What other things?"

Rodrigo combed his fingers through his hair. "They were thorough, taking everything of value down to the studs on a hatch cover. And they didn't harm their captives. The French and Portuguese always do."

Annie shrugged. "I suppose that's something."

"It's little comfort to the investors of the caravel."

"I wonder if Viceroy Martin realizes it's his fault."

Rodrigo cocked an eyebrow. "I don't follow you, *muchacha*."

"It's his fault the English plague our fleets. Two shiploads of survivors escaped San Juan de Ulua. The insult was an affront to all of England. Do you think they'll ever forgive Don Martin for violating his treaty?"

"No." Rodrigo knew Annie had a sharp mind. Still, she never failed to startle him. "I hear their queen has an insatiable appetite for Spanish gold." He reached out and playfully tweaked her nose. "Thank God you didn't inherit the Tudor greed."

Moving to a stool, he picked up her tunic and breeches and tossed them to her. "You'd best change clothes, *muchacha*. We're heaving a guest at supper."

"A guest?"

"I'm not sure you'd remember him. His name is Arturo Reyes. He was in last year with some inquiries."

"I remember him," Annie said in a low, furious voice. "He had that slave woman with the scarred face. I remember that bastard very well."

The bastard had changed. Annie tried to identify the difference as Rodrigo's steward conducted Reyes into the *sala*.

Taking her place at the long, carved table, she subjected him to a moment of covert study.

He still moved with his rolling pirate's swagger, his tall bucket-topped boots ringing upon the stone floor. He still had that mane of midnight hair, that pointed beard, that jaunty grin as he greeted Rodrigo with a firm handshake, then bent to brush a kiss on Valeria's proffered hand.

The change was subtle, yet evident to Annie when Reyes turned to face her. It was his eyes, she realized, nodding briefly. How empty they were, how lifeless, like a fire long cold.

"How do you do?" she said in a low voice.

"Well enough." He stared at her as if trying to remember something.

Rodrigo held out a chair. "Valeria?"

Responding to his prompt, Valeria smiled and took a seat. The other three followed suit. Rodrigo said grace quickly, mumbling the words. Annie peeked at Reyes from beneath her lashes. He crossed himself sketchily, and with a shock she saw him touch his right shoulder before his left. Servants came forward to fill wine goblets and lay out a feast of meat roasted with onions, a pudding of squash, fresh brown-bread rolls, and bowls heaped with native fruit.

Valeria plucked a wild muscadine grape, rolled it between her thumb and forefinger, and said to Reyes, "Sir, why do you stare at me so?"

Reyes seemed to shake himself. One side of his mouth slid upward in a self-deprecating grin. "You've caught me out, Doña Valeria. A man like me has few opportunities to meet a woman of such extraordinary grace and accomplished manners."

His usual female companions were slaves, Annie thought darkly.

"My dear guest has no weakness for flattery," said Rodrigo, stabbing his knife into a piece of meat.

Valeria smiled. "Believe me, Rodrigo, I can stomach a gentleman's compliments every now and then."

With her life as a fugitive behind her, Valeria had blossomed. To all the world, she appeared the perfect Spanish lady, with glossy black hair, milk white skin, and a lovely round figure. Like any woman, she enjoyed a man's flattery, and Rodrigo's quick flare of jealousy amused her.

Annie stifled a wistful sigh. Sometimes she yearned for pretty compliments, too. She grabbed a roll, dug her thumbs into the top of it, and tore it apart. "You've not brought your slave with you tonight, sir," she observed baldly. "You know, the one you were beating when we last met."

There it was again, the icy loathing in the depths of his eyes, the dangerous tensing of his shoulders. "The woman died," he stated, then grabbed his wine cup and drank it dry.

Annie opened her mouth to ask the obvious question, but Rodrigo cut her off with a question of his own. "How are your plans for the supply concession coming along?"

"Everything's taken much longer than I had estimated. I've secured the necessary permissions and licenses." He held out his cup for more wine. "I still have many questions. If you will indulge me a moment, Don Rodrigo. I must choose between placing my concession at Venta Cruz, a little to the north, or right here at Nombre de Dios."

"You'll want to stay away from Venta Cruz," Rodrigo said. "By comparison, it's poorly fortified and prone to attacks by the Cimaroons. They're a fierce lot, you know. Quick to fight and slow to surrender. Even their women are warriors."

"I know," Reyes muttered, lifting his cup again, draining it again. "I'll steer clear of Venta Cross, then."

Annie sat straight up in her chair. Venta *Cross*? Had she heard him correctly? Had he spoken an English word? Composing herself, she glanced at Valeria and Rodrigo. They were deep in conversation about the wine and had not noticed. Reyes, too, dug into his food, unaware of his slip. For it was indeed a slip and one that set Annie afire with questions.

Was he a Catholic Englishman who had fled his Protestant queen's realm? No, he'd crossed himself backward. A mercenary loyal only to his own quest for fortune? No, a single

man wouldn't be able to accomplish a great theft. A spy ferreting out the secrets of the Spanish treasure trains?

The last question answered itself. Of course! That was the
reason for his queries regarding the movement of the *recuas*.
Reyes—or whatever his true name was—planned to plunder
the riches that passed through Nombre de Dios en route to
Spain.

It was all Annie could do to keep from flinging down her
knife and pointing the finger of accusation at the pretender.
She forced herself to remain calm, to eat politely, and to discover a way to use the information to her own advantage.

Pride glowed inside her when she recalled that she had al-
tered the schedules of the mule train from Panama to Nombre
de Dios. The trick might not stop him, but it would slow him
down.

A sudden thought snuffed her pride. What was she protecting, anyway? What did she care if a pirate carried off Spanish
treasure? It was treasure gotten by the sweat of native slaves,
used to feed the appetite of the church she hated. Perhaps she
should applaud the efforts of Reyes rather than try to stop
him.

Evan felt the lad watching him. Those probing gray eyes
seemed to tear holes in his façade. Hoping to drown the disconcerting notion, he drank yet more wine.

His investigation was nearly complete. He had learned the
route of the treasure train and the timetable of its progress.
Thanks to the cooperative Don Rodrigo, he knew the weak-
nesses in the defense of the mule train. He itched to get back
to Port Pheasant and inform Drake.

Since Casilda's death, Evan had moved through life in a
fog of grief and rage. Their love was like an almost forgotten
dream. They'd had so little time together. The cruelty of
Spaniards had slain Casilda and snatched a piece from his
soul.

Her death had added an edge of ruthlessness to his resolve
to vanquish the Spaniards.

Evan sipped his wine, only to peer over the rim of his cup
to find those clear gray eyes still fixed on him.

Damn, what *was* it about the boy?

Donning an ironic smile, he tilted his cup toward the youth. *"Salud."*

The lad took a sip from his own goblet. There was something strange about him, thought Evan, studying the smooth cheeks, the slim wrists. How old was the boy? Twelve? Fourteen? He showed no signs of maturing, of his voice deepening. It was all most curious.

"Tell us what happened to the woman," the lad said suddenly.

Evan's chest still ached with memories. He wanted to grab the insolent whelp out of his chair and shout that his Casilda had been murdered by a Spanish crossbow bolt.

Instead, for the sake of a greater revenge, he lied. "She took sick. The natives have little resistance to certain agues and diseases. It seems they lack any immunity to smallpox."

"Smallpox. Is that what she died of, then?"

"If I'd troubled myself to heed such things, I'd say that was it."

The child's knife hit the table with a clatter. "Saints and angels! You didn't even care to discover what ailed her?"

Rodrigo leaped up. "That was uncalled for."

The boy slumped down in his chair. Through lowered eyes, he glared at Don Rodrigo.

With the lad's oddly familiar words ringing in his head, Evan held up his hand. "I take no offense. If you'll excuse me, I shall go out on the balcony to smoke my cigar."

"Of course." Rodrigo bowed and sat down again. "I'll join you shortly."

Evan moved outside and stood with his back and the sole of one boot pressed against the wall of the villa. The plaster still held the heat of the sun. Harbor lights winked in the distance. In the darkness, this might have been any port— Plymouth or Bristol or Calais. There was a universal sameness in the swing of a ship's stern lantern, in the shush of waves and the creak of old timber.

But the balmy heat and the heavy fragrance of flowers reminded Evan that he stood in the dragon's mouth.

This was a house of secrets. He was certain that Rodrigo's scribe and the girl he had seen so long ago at San Juan de Ulua were one and the same. The moment she had said "Saints and angels" he had remembered her on the beach, weeping over her dead father. Now he wondered why he had not made the connection sooner. The fragile features, the wide gray eyes, the red hair had lodged in his memory for longer than he wished.

She was pretending to be a boy. Why? What misfortunes had befallen her since the death of her father?

A light footstep drew his attention to the open double doors. Evan stubbed out his cigar and came away from the wall to face the girl.

"Rodrigo sent me out to apologize," she said. Evan knew now she took pains to speak in a husky voice. "And I do, sir. It was not my place to question your treatment of your property. You acted no differently from any other dutiful Catholic."

That was the trouble with New Spain, Evan thought bitterly, even as he sensed an ironic note in her words. No one questioned a man's cruelty so long as he acted in the name of King Philip or the Catholic church.

"There is a certain virtue in asking the right questions," he said.

She moved to the edge of the veranda and stared down at the small courtyard. A trellis, heavy with jasmine vines, snaked up to the rail. The moon shone on her fine features. Feminine features. Yes, he was certain of her identity now.

"Then is it right," she said without turning, "for me to ask what an Englishman is doing nosing around Nombre de Dios?"

Evan froze. He stopped breathing. He could have sworn his heart stopped beating.

She knew.

The jaws of the dragon started to close.

Battling a sense of panic, Evan forced out a short laugh. "What nonsense is this?"

She turned back, and light from inside glimmered in her

clear-eyed gaze. "You slipped," she said in English. "You said Venta Cross instead of Venta Cruz. And you crossed yourself wrong."

Damn! Evan said nothing, made no indication that he understood her excellent English.

"Don't worry," she went on. "I don't think Rodrigo or Valeria caught you out. I'm the only one who knows."

The months with the Cimaroons had taught Evan to move with a pantherlike swiftness. He crossed the veranda to the girl. In one lightning motion, he twisted her arm behind her and pulled it up, pressing her against the iron railing.

"You shouldn't have said that," he whispered, ignoring her gasp of fear. "For now I know I have only one wagging tongue to silence."

She opened her mouth to scream for help. Evan clapped his hand over her lips. So soft, and her skin had such a delicate texture. How in God's name had she kept up her guise for so long? And how far would she go to protect her secret?

She struggled, and her small breasts thrust against his chest. Her frightened eyes rolled back to view the gaping darkness of the courtyard far below.

"Aye," said Evan, "I could push you off and say you fell." He wondered if he could murder this girl, snap her neck and grind out her young life.

The death of Casilda had fueled his hatred of Spaniards, yet even now his rage did not burn hot enough to move him to murder a woman. Thank God he had an alternative.

"Were I like you Spanish," he whispered, "I would do just that. Fortunately for you, I am indeed English, or more precisely, Welsh. I balk at killing girls."

Her eyes widened in startlement.

Evan's mouth curved in a humorless grin. "You see, I caught you out, too." He eased his hand away from her mouth and cupped her breast. "I assume you'd like me to keep my counsel on the matter."

She slapped his hand away, and he caught her wrist before she struck his face. "In exchange for my silence in the matter of *your* deception," she said stonily.

"Tell me your name."

She hesitated for perhaps a heartbeat, then looked him in the eye and said, "Anne Maria Blythe de Carval. And yours?"

"Evan Carew of Wales. Do we have an understanding?"

"Yes."

He let go of her wrist.

An unfortunate misjudgment. She, too, moved fast. Her hand brought forth a small, sharp dagger, and the blade touched his inner thigh just below the groin. To wound? Or to warn?

Evan stood frozen, torn between anger at her defiance and admiration of her boldness.

"Yes, sir," she said softly. "It seems that we know each other well."

CHAPTER 8

Plymouth, England
24 May 1572

Sitting at the captain's table aboard the *Pasco*, Drake lifted his cup and saluted the six men assembled in his well-appointed quarters.

"Good Whitsun Eve to you all, my masters," he said. "And may our third venture to New Spain be the most bountiful yet."

John Drake, Francis's brother, pounded the table with his silver cup, a prize seized on a previous voyage. "Hear, hear!"

Evan and the other officers echoed the call and drank. A fair wind pulled the *Pasco* and her sister ship, the *Swan*, inexorably through the Sound of Plymouth toward the churning waters of the open sea.

With seventy-three men in two small sailing ships, they intended to capture a large town and carry off its treasure.

Unlike the others, Evan realized that the sack of Nombre de Dios was not even the most audacious part of the adventure.

Bring me the child.

As clear as a ship's bell, the queen's command still rang in his ears.

Bring me the child.

As terrible as a miracle, the answer lay within Evan's grasp. Though he had not known it at the time, he had seen the lost Tudor heir grieving over her slain father, working as a treasury scribe, urging a slave woman to flee. And at their last meeting, he had held a royal princess in his arms and threatened to kill her.

Even as he ate and drank with hearty appetite, he turned the problem over and over in his mind. Should he tell Francis what he knew?

John Drake jabbed Evan in the ribs. "Wool-gathering again, my friend?"

Evan dragged his thoughts from the incredible prospect that he knew the person sought so avidly by the queen. "I suppose I was."

"And you a seafaring man," Francis joined in and chuckled, but quickly sobered. "You went home to Carew again, didn't you?"

Evan nodded. "And a pleasure it was, this time. My share of the last expedition paid six seasons' rent for the farmers." He closed his eyes and savored again the looks of stunned joy on the faces of his father, their neighbors, the farmers and fishermen.

"This is only the beginning," he had told them, thinking of the treasure-laden mule trains lumbering, virtually unprotected, across the isthmus of Panama.

"You deserved that generous bonus," Francis said.

"Aye." Joseph, another Drake brother, nodded affably. "It can't have been easy, walking into the lion's den."

"And coming out with their secrets," John Oxenham added.

"Those secrets were ill guarded," Evan admitted. "The last thing the Spaniards fear is a raid on Nombre de Dios. They've reigned there for so long, they've become complacent."

"Good." Francis motioned to a ship's boy to refill the mugs all around. "It's best they don't expect a party of England's finest gentlemen of the sea."

Although it had been a shock to find André Scalia in the employ of the queen, Evan saw now that the association was useful. The ships were fully outfitted with victuals to last a year, had three unassembled pinnaces in the hold, and both the *Pasco* and the *Swan* were in fine repair.

In the sunny days that followed, not a single doubt shadowed the minds of the adventurers. They made a swift run across the Atlantic, flying before the trade winds, in only twenty-five days.

They called at the isle of Guadeloupe—unconquered and rimmed by glorious white-sand beaches. For three days they bathed in the crystalline waters and let the strong tropic sun brown their winter-white skin.

Then, with Drake's impatient commands bellowing down the decks, they set a course for the Gulf of Darien, the gateway to the Spanish empire.

The two ships knifed through the narrow inlet to Port Pheasant, and the conquerors landed.

"What's here?" Dirk called, standing by a huge tree. "I'm no reader, Admiral Drake, but someone's left a message."

Evan and Drake hurried over to find a plate of lead fastened to the tree trunk.

Drake read aloud: " 'Captain Drake, if you fortune to come into this port make haste away; for the Spaniards have betrayed this place and taken away all that you left here. I departed hence this present 7th July 1572. Your very loving friend, John Garret.' "

"My God," John Drake whispered. "We missed him by only five days."

Francis pounded his fist at the lead plate. "Betrayed!" he roared, throwing back his head. "This was the perfect anchorage. The perfect hideout. Betrayed!"

He began pacing back and forth, sandy earth flying in his wake. "Could it be one of my own people? By God, I'll find every last English rover in the area and torture the truth out of—"

"Francis." Evan spoke quietly, reluctantly. "Francis, I must speak to you. In private."

"Now?"

"Yes." Evan had only to glance at the plaque and Francis understood. They walked off together.

"You know who betrayed us?" Drake demanded.

Damn her, Evan thought. *Damn her to hell.* Seized by a fit of conscience, he had been prepared to guard the girl's secret even in defiance of his orders from the queen of England. But Anne Maria Blythe de Carval had dug her own grave. She had doubtless alerted the Spanish to Evan's masquerade, and the soldiers had searched until they found this place.

Evan stood scowling at the sheltered bay while he wrestled with his scruples. He and the girl had exchanged secrets; he had given his word he would not betray her.

"Well?" Drake asked.

Evan picked up a bit of driftwood and hurled it as far as he could. The girl's deception—and her heritage—changed everything. She had made the first move; he owed her no further loyalty.

"It's my fault. I should have killed her when I had the chance. But then again, it's a good job I didn't."

"What? Whose fault? Who should you have killed?" Drake jabbed his finger at Evan's chest. "Our harbor's been discovered, our cache of stores rifled, and you goad me with riddles about some woman."

Evan pushed Drake's finger aside. "Not some woman, Francis. A girl. I met her in Nombre de Dios." Evan shuffled his feet. "It seems my disguise slipped a little. I uttered an English word. She heard, and challenged me."

"You should have slit her throat. Girl or not, she's a treacherous Spaniard."

Anger snapped through Evan like a stiff wind through taut rigging. "If I had done that, Francis, I would be guilty of murdering the child Queen Elizabeth sent us to find."

Drake's eyes narrowed with keen interest. "Evan. My God, man, are you certain?"

"The girl's name is Anne Blythe de Carval. Anne *Blythe*. Her father, Phillip, was the English-speaking man who was with the viceroy at San Juan de Ulua. He died that day. His daughter has been living with a man called Rodrigo Viscaino. She poses as his ward and scribe."

Drake used his sleeve to wipe the sweat from his brow. "Heaven be praised," he said in a low voice full of wonderment. "Phillip Blythe's child. Jesu, how long have you known?"

Evan looked away. Never before had he kept secrets from Francis. But never before had he felt so torn over so vital an issue.

"I realized she was the one . . . on the very night we answered the queen's summons."

"You've known for months!" Drake grasped Evan by the front of the shirt. "Damn you, Evan! Why didn't you tell me?"

Evan wrenched free of Drake's grasp. "She's just a child, Francis! Do you think I'm eager to tear her from a life she knows and thrust her into the jaws of the English court?"

Drake shook his head. His shoulders relaxed as if the anger had drained out of him. "You're too soft by half, Evan. Why did you choose to tell me now?"

Evan had a sudden remembrance of large gray eyes, a vulnerable mouth, a small, freckle-dusted nose. Willfully, he banished the image and the sentiments it brought. "I believe it was she who betrayed this harbor."

Drake stroked his beard. "If she has such courage, then perhaps she's a match for Elizabeth after all." A short laugh escaped him. "Marry, a girl! And we all assumed the lost heir would be a boy." Drake began striding down the beach. "Our plunder of Nombre de Dios will yield more than silver and gold."

"Yes." Evan felt slightly queasy. What if he was wrong? What if the girl had not betrayed them? But it must have been she, bold baggage that she was, holding a knife on him and making a bargain she never intended to keep.

"Sail there! Stands right ahead!"

The call from the lookout startled Evan. A small, two-masted ship perched on the horizon, the profiles of its angled lugsails dark against the pale, hot sky. They ran to the shore, Drake shouting as he went. "Man the guns! Every man to his charge!"

The Englishmen bolted into action, gunners ramming charges into culverins, their assistants frantically fanning the fires to heat the irons.

A puff of smoke plumed from the approaching ship. High on the afterdeck, a signal lantern flashed.

"Blank shot," Evan said with relief. "And what's that signal?"

" 'Tis Jamie Rance!" Drake shouted. "God be praised, he's an old friend of mine." He ordered his own signalman to reply that it was safe to enter the harbor.

An hour later, Drake splashed out into the surf to welcome the Englishman. Evan studied Rance's wind-scarred face, his gap-toothed smile, and the hard glitter of piracy in his small eyes. Rance had served with Evan and Drake under Hawkins. He had an affinity for the slave trade that Evan disliked.

". . . decided to bring myself back to the Caribbean," Rance was saying as he and Drake waded ashore. He spied Evan, and his grin widened. "Evan Carew!" He clapped him on the back. "What cheer, my master. Is all well?"

"Aye," Evan said, wondering if he meant it. "Tell me, Jamie, how did you know to come here?"

Rance shook a finger at him. "You Welsh. Always so suspicious, with your short arms and your deep pockets." He shrugged. "Rightfully so, I suppose. This hideout is not so secret anymore. I learned of it from a French Huguenot. Where he learned of it, I know not."

He was too vague to be convincing. Evan felt a rush of doubt. He had been wrong about Anne Blythe, then. He had spoken too soon. It was too late now. Francis knew her identity.

The qualms continued to plague him through the next several days of toil. Drake had decided to ignore the danger posed by the Spaniards who knew about Port Pheasant. The natural harbor, so sheltered and so close to Nombre de Dios, was too well situated to abandon. Besides, finding another port might take weeks, and there was always a chance that it was even better known to the enemy.

Jamie Rance, with his captured Spanish shallop, became a partner in the enterprise. His men added their labor to the work of building a stockade, assembling the pinnaces, and plotting a course to their objective.

As the pinnaces were being rigged to sail within the hour, Evan took Drake aside. "We need a new anchorage," he said, keeping his voice low.

"We've no time, Evan. We must move swiftly and surprise the enemy."

"If you wish to surprise them, you'll heed me, Francis."

"More riddles?" Drake lifted one rusty eyebrow.

"Just don't be too quick to trust Jamie Rance. He came out of nowhere to this harbor. He could—" Evan broke off as a new thought struck him. "Francis, you won't tell him about the girl, will you?"

Drake threw back his head and hooted with laughter. "I'll always be a thickheaded Devonshire sea dog to you, won't I, Evan? Of course I won't tell Rance about the girl."

Together with the three ships, the pinnaces slipped out of Port Pheasant and coasted northward to the Isle of Pines. Here, the large ships anchored. The crews went ashore to assemble themselves for the final approach to Nombre de Dios.

Evan looked warily around the small, thickly wooded island. A few straight pine trees had been cut down. The pointed stumps thrust starkly toward the evening sky.

"What do you make of that?" Drake asked. "Some of these trees are as tall as mainmasts. Have the Spanish taken to building their ships here?"

"I doubt it," said Evan. "There's far more profit for them

in plundering treasure from natives or mining silver at Potosí."

"Aye. The trees were probably taken for firewood. Still, I'll caution Rance to stay on the alert."

"You're leaving Rance here?"

"With our three ships and thirty men. Thirty of *my* men." Drake slapped Evan on the back. "You see, the thickheaded Devonshire lad has a lick of sense after all. Jamie can't interfere with our enterprise while he's here. Our men will keep an eye on him."

"Have you picked the men who will accompany us?"

Drake nodded vigorously. "Aye, the young ones. They have the fortitude to fight for hours." He lowered his voice. "And may God forgive me, but they hold their lives less dear than their elders—"

"Captain Drake!" A mariner's voice rang with alarm.

A band of dark-skinned warriors moved out from under the thick canopy of trees. The English stared in horror at the forest of painted bodies and sharp spears.

"Savages!" screamed a seaman called Robbie Pike. "To arms! To arms!"

Drake opened his mouth to affirm the command, but Evan stopped him. "Don't panic, Francis. I know these men."

"What? But how—"

"I told them to meet us here."

Evan dropped his sword belt and jogged across the beach toward the warriors. He had never spoken of Casilda to Francis. He kept her memory locked in his heart, his private pain, his reason for revenge. Over the months he had kept in contact with her people, promising that the grievances they shared against Spain would be addressed by both Cimaroon and Englishman.

"It's me," he called, dragging his hand across his clean-shaven face. "It's Evan Carew."

A turmoil of emotions rushed through him as he approached Rico. The warrior stood tall and straight, the feathers on his spear blowing in the breeze. Evan's love for Casilda and his grief upon losing her had bound him to the

Cimaroons. In a strange, spiritual way, these feral men had become his brothers.

"My friends won't harm you," he assured them. "We are on our way to attack the white city."

Drake came to Evan's side and introduced himself in Spanish. His command of the language was still elemental, but it had improved over the months. Rico's teeth flashed in a smile. "You are the one the Spaniards called *El Draquez*."

Drake pulled himself up proudly. "I daresay they'll call me worse than dragon before this night is out."

"You attack tonight?" asked Rico. "It is good that you hurry, then." As the Englishmen came cautiously forward, Rico said, "We, too, attacked the white city to avenge the death of Casilda."

Evan did not have to look at Drake to know his friend's temper was rising. "Easy, Francis," he murmured. "The Cimaroons take their tribute in blood, not treasure."

"But now they'll be on full alert in the city." Drake rocked on his heels, agitation evident in the sawing of his jaw. "They'll have sent for reinforcements from Veracruz and Venta Cruz, maybe even Panama." Drake studied the warriors with intense curiosity—and a measure of distrust.

"Look, Francis," said Evan. "They're men, like any other men. Not slaves, not commodities to be traded like bolts of cloth. They share our dislike for the Spanish. They know this land—far better than we do."

Drake's indecision never lasted long. He gave a curt nod. "We are allies, then. Have the soldiers arrived yet?"

"Not yet," Rico admitted. "But they will."

A sense of urgency tingled inside Evan. "Let's launch the pinnaces, Francis. *Now.*"

By the watery light of the moon in its last quarter, English crews rowed the pinnaces into harbor at Nombre de Dios.

A huge Spanish ship, black against the night sky, blocked the final approach to the city.

A ship's boat dropped into the water, and its crew began rowing frantically for shore.

Evan didn't wait for Drake to give the order. "Out oars, give chase," he hissed at the crew. His boat surged forward, cut off the Spanish launch, and forced her ashore. The other pinnaces arrived moments later.

It was almost laughably easy to subdue the landing party. Evan looked on in grim satisfaction as his men captured and bound the Spaniards to stop them from getting to Nombre de Dios and sounding the alarm.

The minor victory heartened the men, who had been worried about Rico's warning of reinforcements.

"Well done, my masters," Drake said, spreading his arms as if to embrace them all. He jerked his head toward the earthworks that rose to the east of the town. "Now, to the gun platform."

Another bloodless victory. They found a lone soldier on watch. He took one look at the well-armed Englishmen and surrendered on his knees.

"We'll take those guns," Drake ordered, surveying the six pieces of heavy artillery. "Unmount them and take them back to the pinnaces."

Greed was his first mistake of the night. While the men fell upon the culverins, the watchman broke free and raced toward the town, screaming at the top of his lungs.

Within seconds, the bell in the church tower pealed, and drumbeats summoned the citizens from their beds.

Swearing and barking orders, Drake divided the men into three groups.

"John!" he called to his brother. "Take Oxenham and mount your attack from the far side of town."

"Aye, sir."

"Set your arrows aflame, and see that your trumpeter blows lustily. The more confusion we stir up, the better."

Drake's eyes burned with excitement as he faced Evan. "Stay with the main body as we march into the square. Then, break away and—"

"I know what to do, Francis," Evan cut in. He had rehearsed the tactic over and over in his mind. Working alone, he was to seize the Tudor princess.

The years of waiting and planning gave wings to the English sea rovers as they entered Nombre de Dios. They burst upon the town like a storm, trumpets blaring, drums beating, fire pikes flaming, and battle cries springing from their throats.

The plaza stretched before them, a vast deserted expanse in the moonlight. Drake turned to the trumpeter, a boy of just twelve. "The heart of the city!" he shouted. "Sound the advance, my little master. We'll take the governor's house first."

The boy lifted his trumpet. Before the first note had ended he lay dead, a hole torn in his chest by a musket ball.

"Goddamn it!" Drake threw back his head and bellowed at the sky. Tears streamed from his eyes and he neither flinched nor ducked as another volley of musket fire spat from the far corner of the square.

"Francis, take cover," Evan yelled, grabbing him by the sleeve. Denton scooped up the fallen lad and scurried into the shadows.

"No!" Drake roared, trying to twist from Evan's grip. "Let the cowards show themselves."

A third volley drowned his furious shout. He stumbled, and Evan took the full force of his captain's weight. He alone heard Drake's grunt of pain.

Cursing, he dragged Francis to the recessed stoop of a shop. Just as the shadows swallowed them, a group of Spanish soldiers poured into the square.

"You're hit," Evan whispered to Drake.

"No, I'm not." Drake tore off his sash and began binding his leg. A blast of musket fire briefly illuminated his face. His cheeks were pale, his brow soaked with sweat.

"Damn it, Francis, don't be stubborn," Evan hissed. "Get yourself to safety while I complete my mission."

"Evan, I don't think you heard me correctly." Drake enunciated each word like a drunk struggling to govern his tongue. "I said I was not hit." His voice dropped to a deadly whisper. He grabbed a fistful of Evan's shirt and put his face very close. The odor of sweat and blood rose from him. "So help me God, if you dare to tell the men otherwise, I'll slit your frigging throat."

Evan stared down at Drake's fist, clenched like a vise of iron into his shirt. Not for a second did Evan doubt the threat. Drake's vendetta was stronger than all their years spent together on the deck of a ship. In that moment, as they sat nose to nose, glaring at each other, it was as if their friendship had no more substance than dust.

Drake let go. Evan stood and began to edge away. The blood feud was changing them both, hardening them.

"Where the devil are you going?" Drake demanded.

"While you finish binding that nonexistent wound, I'm going to organize the men to give these bastards the best of ancient Welsh compliments."

"What's that?"

"A hail of arrows."

The mantle of command fell easily over Evan's shoulders. He brought the main body to the ramparts of the largest building of the square, still keeping to the shadows. With confidence instilled by hours of drill, the men nocked their arrows into their longbows. Crécy, Poitiers, and Agincourt had been captured by the lowly longbow; this crude Spanish city would feel its sting, too.

When Evan gave the signal, the archers loosed their arrows. The slim missiles buzzed like a swarm of bees into the midst of the Spanish contingent.

Screams of pain keened from enemy throats. Three more volleys of arrows scoured the plaza clean of live Spaniards. From the edge of town came faint sounds of fighting—screams and gunshot, and the vague drumroll of fear in every man's ears. Drake's brother and Oxenham must have found a fight at the Panama Gate.

"To the governor's house!" Drake bellowed. He was on his feet again, and not limping. He must have convinced even himself that he did not have a musket ball embedded in his leg.

Only Evan knew better. By the uncertain light of pitch arrows, he saw the small trail of shiny darkness Francis left in his wake. The bleeding was slow, but steady.

Evan knew he should seize the moment to find Anne Blythe. Instead, worried about his commander, he hurried after Drake to the governor's house.

They broke through the gates of the villa en masse. A large horse, saddled and rearing in panic, clawed the air in front of their faces.

"We came not a moment too soon," Evan said, crossing the patio and ducking through an open door. "The governor was about to depart without saying good-b—" He broke off, realizing that the others had fallen into awestruck silence.

He followed their rapt gazes to the object of their attention. There, stacked against the wall, was a vast treasure of silver bars.

Almost reverently, Drake picked up one of the bars. "This weighs at least forty pounds," he said. "My masters, we're looking at a million sterling!" He threw back his head and shouted with laughter. "Gentlemen, we stand here in the mouth of the treasury of the world! If we fail to gain it, we've none but ourselves to blame."

Rain began to pelt the tiled roof of the villa. Like a message of warning from on high, a gust of wind whipped the palm trees. Within moments, the rain intensified to a heavy tropical storm.

"Then let's take the silver and be gone, Francis," Evan said. "The Spaniards won't be able to fire their muskets in this rain."

"No," said Drake. "The silver's too heavy. We wouldn't be able to carry off more than a few bars. Let's break into those waterfront strong rooms. I want the gold, the pearls, the emeralds."

"Francis . . ." Evan looked pointedly at the blood-soaked sash on his friend's leg.

"I command that we open the Treasure House," Drake

shouted. "And you, Evan, have another errand. If you do not
leave at once, I'll bring you up on charges of insubordina-
tion."

The fanatic light in Francis's eyes made Evan's stomach
sink. "Aye, sir," Evan said. He turned on his heel and
marched out into the driving rain.

CHAPTER 9

In the gray half light of dawn, Annie and Valeria stood at the window of Rodrigo's villa. The storm lashed at the panes. The howling wind tore at the tops of the palm trees and ripped leaves from the large bushes of poinsettia.

"I wonder where Rodrigo is now," said Valeria. A livid fork of lightning split the sky, and she shivered.

Annie rubbed at the glass pane. They had both heard the alarm bell and then the shooting, had both watched Rodrigo arm himself and race from the house.

"It was agony watching the fight." Valeria chewed her lip. "I wonder who it is this time. The French? Or maybe the Dutch? Surely not the Cimaroons again so soon."

"No, the Cimaroons don't use firearms."

"Nor do the clerics." Valeria shivered again.

Annie put her hand on Valeria's arm. "The Inquisition doesn't lay siege to a town in the middle of the night."

Valeria nodded. She seemed calmer, but she flinched when she saw more sparks of musket fire and heard the screams of men and horses.

"Do you think he could be hurt?"

Annie squeezed Valeria's hand. "Rodrigo? Impossible."
She tried to sound reassuring, but doubts and guilt pricked at
her. Ever since she had confronted the English spy, she had
been torn between reporting his deception to Rodrigo and
honoring the promise he had wrested from her. In the end,
she had said nothing. Not even to Rodrigo.

This morning's battle was the price of her silence, she was
certain of it. The bitter taste of remorse scalded her throat. If
innocent people died in the exchange, the fault would be hers.

"I'll never forgive myself if Rodrigo gets wounded," she
whispered.

"You're not to blame." Valeria struck her fist against the
window embrasure. "I never should have let him go
before—" She stopped and squeezed her eyes shut.

"You love him, don't you?" Annie asked.

"Yes." The simple, direct answer spoke volumes. Valeria's
face held a look of such pained yearning that Annie's heart
lurched. She did not know what it was like to love so fiercely,
so hopelessly. Valeria's expression convinced Annie that being in love was not a state to which she should aspire.

"I'm going down to the pantry to get us something to eat,"
said Valeria. "And some Jerez wine to calm our nerves."

Annie stood with her brow pressed to the glass and listened
to the beat of the rain on the roof. She heard the pantry door
creak open in a distant part of the house and wondered about
Rodrigo.

The first peals of the church bell had brought the household awake. Sheer confusion had reigned. Rodrigo had hustled the three house servants, along with Annie and Valeria,
into hiding in the root cellar. Then, grim-faced and cursing,
he had gone out to help defend the city.

Unable to tolerate waiting in the darkness, Annie and
Valeria had left the cellar. She felt safe enough, for no treasure was kept in this house. The fighting seemed centered
around the main plaza and the Panama Gate on the other side
of town.

As Annie waited for Valeria to return, a runner raced past

the house, informing the residents that the attack was led by none other than *El Draquez*. Drake, the Devonshire Dragon. He had lurked about the area for the past two years, striking like lightning and then disappearing. Until now, his prey had been ships. Never had he made so bold a move as to enter a fortified town.

With a fresh, sickening wave of guilt, Annie remembered the Welshman. Of course! He was in alliance with Drake! What in God's name had she been thinking of, keeping his secret, endangering the whole town?

The crash of a door startled her. Rodrigo must have come home. Relieved, Annie turned from the window.

When she saw who had entered the room, a scream gathered in her throat. The dryness of shock choked off the sound.

He stood in the uncertain light of the rainy morning, his feet planted wide, a sword in his hand and a look of savage purpose on his face.

Rainwater streamed down his swarthy face and plastered a mass of midnight curls to his brow and neck. He was clean-shaven, and resolve hardened his square jaw and chin.

It was his eyes that kept her mute. They seemed deep and distant, filled with the most curious mixture of determination and pity she had ever seen.

"I'm glad you didn't scream," he said in English. "I was hoping you wouldn't."

Annie pressed her back against the window. Her hand stole down to the folds of her tunic and closed around her dagger. "What do you want?"

He took a step forward, his manner not threatening, but not yielding, either. "I'm afraid you'll have to come with me."

"Never," she shot back, feeling the first prickle of panic. Her eyes darted to the door beyond him. Damn it, where was Valeria?

"I had to lock her in the pantry. She's safe," he said, reading her thoughts. "Look, miss, I swear on my honor you won't be harmed."

"On your honor?" she asked bitterly. "You came to this

city—this house—under false pretenses, all the while planning murder and theft. Is that an example of English honor?"

"Not murder. I mean to take you alive. I am in the service of England," he stated simply. "I hold my honor sacred—unlike your viceroy, Don Martin Enriquez."

"He is not 'my' viceroy."

A soulless smile curved his mouth like a sickle. "I know."

The sharp bitterness in his voice prodded a memory awake. She was on the harbor island again, her father's head heavy in her lap, her heart breaking. She recalled the Englishman who had passed her—the one she had warned of the attack. His arms had been burdened with the body of a young boy, and somehow, in that brief moment, sorrow had brought them together.

"You were at San Juan de Ulua," she whispered.

"Ah. You remember."

"I lost my father that day. I'm not likely to forget."

The rain outside began to slacken. Evan Carew came forward and touched her elbow. Annie tried to duck away, but he closed his hand around her upper arm and held her still. Never had she felt such raw strength in a man's grip, such quickness in his responses. And yet, oddly, she knew he would not willingly inflict pain on her.

"You're one of Drake's henchmen, aren't you?" she asked.

One corner of his mouth lifted. "I suppose you could call me that."

"I don't care if you're Christopher Columbus," she burst out. "You have no right to intrude here."

She yanked the dagger from its hip sheath. Quicker by a fraction of a moment, he grabbed her wrist. One by one, he pried her fingers free and took possession of the dagger. He stepped closer, pinning her between the window and the broad wall of his chest. "Mistress Blythe," he said, "if you fight, I'll be obliged to bag you like a partridge. Now, there's no time to get your things. All will be provided for you."

"I need nothing but my freedom, and you're taking that away."

His face flushed a deeper shade of red. "It can't be helped, miss. I am bound to bring you with us."

"For the love of God, *why*?"

He sucked in his breath. "That's a question better left unanswered, miss."

His statement chilled her blood. It could mean any number of things: That he meant to hold her for ransom. That he was only acting under orders. That he knew everything, but thought her ignorant.

"I will come with you," she said, allowing him to take her arm and conduct her out of the house. "But I will make you regret this, Evan Carew."

A stitch pinched Evan's side as he raced back to town. He had left the girl aboard a pinnace, in the care of Denton and Dirk, his most trusted subordinates. The men had been puzzled by the capture of what they took to be a scruffy boy, but they had asked no questions.

A pounding sense of dread told Evan something had gone wrong in town. When he reached the main plaza, his worst fears were confirmed. Drake stood ranting like a madman, waving his arms and stamping his feet. The damp, sandy surface of the square beneath his feet had turned bright red with his blood.

"Get on with the work, damn your eyes," Drake bellowed to his men. "Never mind me! 'Tis a scratch, no more." Even as he spoke, he stumbled, threw up his arms, and pitched forward, landing with a thud on the ground.

Evan reached him first, pulling him up by the shoulders. "Damn it, Francis!" He slapped his friend's face. "You've performed the greatest raid yet in New Spain. Will you not stay awake to see it through?"

Drake sputtered and swore. Someone shoved a flask of cordial into his hand, and he drank until he choked. "Enough," he roared, gathering new strength. "We'll smash the gate to the king's Treasure House, by God, or die trying."

Musket fire pelted the square. Hovering over Drake, Evan

asked, "And if we die, Francis? Who will be left to take up the banner against Spain another day?"

Drake glowered at him. "I hate it when you're right. Must you Welshmen always be so reasonable? Did you get the girl?"

Evan's shoulders felt heavy with doubts and guilt. By what right did he rip a young girl from the only life she had ever known and thrust her into the maw of intrigue? By order of the queen, he reminded himself coldly.

"Aye," he said.

"She is more valuable than any treasure," Drake said, staggering to his feet. "Let's retreat for now and find something else to plunder."

Evan did not pause to ask him what he meant; that must wait for later. The final order of business was to beat a retreat without any further loss of life.

They reached the pinnaces in short order. Evan had left strict instructions that the prisoner was not to be goaded, questioned, or even touched. He had said nothing about telling bawdy jokes, which was exactly what he found Anne Blythe and the sentries engaged in.

He had expected to find her cowering in terror. Instead she sat atop a grate, her bound hands folded in her lap, her head thrown back as she laughed at something Dirk said.

Drake leaned heavily upon Evan. His breathing came in short, harsh gasps. "*That's* her?"

"Aye," he whispered. "The lost Tudor princess."

"God, that red hair. She looks like a—a hoyden from the meanest hovel in Southwark."

"All the better for her safety," Evan pointed out. "No need to distract the men with her feminine charms."

"What feminine charms?"

"Indeed," said Evan. "I fear she possesses few."

The three pinnaces caught the tide and cruised into the deep gulf. Evan sat beside Anne Blythe and studied her obliquely. "You're taking this very well."

She lifted one eyebrow. The sardonic look nearly coaxed a

smile from him. "I'm accustomed to rough men and sea voyages."

"But we're English adventurers. Doesn't that frighten you?"

She looked across at one of the other pinnaces. "Your leader—Drake, isn't it?—lies wounded. You've taken no treasure save the bit some of the men stuffed into their pockets. I've met fiercer pirates on poultry runs to the victualing islands."

That stung. They had planned this expedition for years. Casilda, Drake's trumpeter, Charlie Moon, and too many others had given their lives to this cause, only to have their goal thwarted.

Furious, Evan snapped out an order to the helmsman. "Make for that merchant ship yonder."

Although the helmsman obeyed instantly, the oarsmen and mariners raised their eyebrows. The ship was the same one that had spied them entering the port just hours before. No doubt her crew was on full alert.

Evan was too angry to ponder the consequences. It was simply unthinkable to leave this treasure-laden bay without a prize.

"I shouldn't bother if I were you," Anne said in her annoyingly precise English. "It's only a wine ship."

"Well, damn it, I've a thirst on me," said Evan.

As the pinnace came abreast of the great ship, Evan stood.

"You'll never be able to board her," said Annie.

"Watch me," he replied grimly.

Annie tilted her head up to see him toss a rope with a grappling hook over the rail. As he climbed, his arm muscles bulging and his feet swinging free, she half expected someone to sever the rope.

Instead, Evan Carew reached the rail and leaped over. Annie waited with the same breath-held anticipation as the men. Seconds later, casks of wine and crates of victuals splashed into the water around the pinnace.

The men hastened to bring the booty aboard, but Annie kept her gaze aloft. Surely some alert sentry would go after the thief. In fact, she should call out to someone. At the very least, the Spaniards might rescue her.

And yet something held her silent. She did not wish to fall into crueler hands.

Evan reappeared, slid calmly down the rope, and said, "Out oars."

Annie planted her elbows on her knees. It was annoying having her hands bound, but she concluded that it was the lot of captives. "Feel better now?" she asked.

Evan scowled at her. "I came here seeking a fortune in gold and pearls. Instead I come away with Canary wine, salt beef, and a smart-mouthed rodent. How do you think I feel?"

"Like an abject failure?"

His frown deepened. "You're an impudent youngster."

"Shiver me timbers!" Her mocking cry drew the attention of the men, and she pretended to shrink from him. "Are you going to torture me? Keelhaul me? Make me walk the plank?"

Several men nearby burst into laughter.

Annie smiled congenially at them. "I assume that means I'm not in any physical danger."

"Of course not," said Evan.

"Very well, then, I have nothing to fear, and nothing to gain by begging for mercy. I'll simply down a cup of wine with you jolly fellows and await the ransom money from my guardian."

Evan Carew regarded her strangely. "What makes you think I'll ransom you?"

"I have a very rich guardian, as you well know, since you insinuated yourself into his household. And you obviously crave wealth, although you're not very adept at gaining it. I should warn you, though. Rodrigo Viscaino has a mighty temper. He'll not take kindly to your antics."

Evan fell into angry silence. As the pinnaces made a landing at Bastimiento, a victualing island where the gardens of Nombre de Dios were located, Annie felt the first vague glimmer of doubt.

If her captors did not mean to ransom her, then what in God's name did they plan?

"Another expedition," said Drake, peeling an ear of coal-roasted maize.

Annie, who was pretending to be asleep in a tangle of blankets near the fire, strained to hear his low whisper. Night sounds lifted from the forested island, and waves swished upon the shore. By moving her head slightly, she had a clear view of the two adventurers, Evan Carew and Francis Drake. They exhibited an easy camaraderie, lounging side by side while they ate.

"This time we'll not waste months planning, only to be thwarted by bad weather ... or ill luck." Drake touched the thick bandage around his leg.

"Nombre de Dios is already crawling with reinforcements from Panama," said Evan. "We wouldn't stand a chance."

"I'm not talking about Nombre de Dios, my good master." Drake bit into an ear of hot corn and chewed slowly. "The Spanish bastards keep their treasure in more than one chest."

"What about the girl?"

"We keep her with us."

"We could be months at this, Francis."

"She seems a hardy lass."

"Don't be daft, Francis. Why should we drag her along with us? She could be killed or fall sick. Then how would we answer—"

"I said she stays with us!" Drake's voice held the keen edge of command.

Evan glared at him. "You want too much, Francis. Surely the fiasco at Nombre de Dios will be forgiven—"

"Enough!" Drake slashed the air with his hand. "There is no such thing in this life as wanting too much. The main flaw in most men is that they want too little. The girl stays, and that's final. You'll take great care of her, Evan."

"I?" Evan nearly choked on his food. "Damn it, Francis, I can't play the nursemaid while you attack the Spanish empire."

Nursemaid! Annie stifled a gasp. Just how old did they think she was, anyway? For that matter, how much did they know about her?

Her hand stole up to close around the ruby ring secreted inside her shirt. The corsairs had been sent from England to capture her. There could be only one reason for that. Someone, somehow, found out that she was the granddaughter of King Henry VIII and kin to Queen Elizabeth.

Her thoughts flew back to the day almost three years before, when she and Rodrigo had viewed the wreckage of Gema del Mar. The house had been plundered. Her father's cache of secret papers was nowhere to be found. Had some unscrupulous knave sold the secrets to the English?

And what of this pair of bold pirates? Did they know of her significance, or were they merely lackeys sent by someone higher up?

The thought made her shiver. Perhaps she should destroy the ring, with its large jewel and the words "*Dieu et mon droit*—Henry Rex" conscribed around it. Then again, she knew there was power in possessing this link to the monarchy of England. She might need it to secure her release.

Letting out the faintest of sighs, Annie started to fall asleep. As she drifted off, a curious thought struck her. Not for an instant had she felt afraid.

With his belly distended by the quantity of stolen Canary wine he had drunk, Jamie Rance sidled over to Evan and clapped him on the back.

"All in all, not a bad take," Rance said, as though he had actually been part of the raid. "Of course, it does fall far short of our ambitions." A group of men joined him. A few sported gold earrings or neck chains seized in the raid.

"That depends on what one's ambitions are," said Evan.

With a moan, Anne Blythe sat up, coming out of the rough blankets like a rabbit from its hole. She blinked at the early morning light. Her hair was tousled, her face soft with sleep.

"By God, what have you here, Mr. Carew?" Rance asked, bending low to peer at her. "Is it male or female?"

The men in his company chuckled and elbowed each other.

With a quickness that took everyone by surprise, Annie shot to her feet and shook her bound hands at him. "I might be the devil himself, you low backwater scum," she said.

Rance laughed. "It speaks English, too!" Before Evan could intervene, he groped at her chest. "Heaven be praised," he shouted. "It's a girl!"

Evan couldn't tell what made him more angry—the flames of humiliation in Annie's cheeks, or the frank lust in the eyes of the men. He shoved Rance aside. "The girl is my concern."

Rance planted his hands on his hips. "Are we not brethren, Evan? What of sharing the booty?"

Evan stepped very close to Rance, so close he could smell the wine and sweat and brine scent that clung to him. "Listen, Jamie. If you or any other man so much as think about touching her, I'll slit your throat and bleed you dry like the pig you are."

Rance muttered something indistinct and moved off. The others followed and went to uncork another barrel of wine.

Evan turned back to Anne. From the very start, she had shown no sign of fear. He did not know why her calm state irritated him. "Why couldn't you have stayed out of sight until he left?"

She shrugged and plopped back down. "I'm not accustomed to cowering under the blankets. I daresay I shall never get used to it."

"Pray God you won't have to."

"I don't suppose I will." Was it only a trick of the light, or did a teasing glint flash in her eyes for a moment? "I believe you've convinced them that I'm your woman."

"Don't be ridic—" Evan broke off as the usefulness of the idea dawned on him. "Perhaps I'll let them think that. But don't ever expect me to act the lover in private."

She shook back her short red curls. Her frank gaze disconcerted him. "Why not?" she asked.

"Because you're—" He shot her a look of contempt. "Why

in God's name would I take a lover who's more boy than girl, more child than woman?"

Her cheeks paled. "Where did you learn to be so cruel, Evan Carew?"

He closed his heart to the wounded look in her eyes. "From the finest nobility in New Spain," he replied and turned his back on her.

Within a week, Drake's fleet sailed into the harbor of Cartagena, capital of the Spanish Main. The Cimaroons had retired to the coastal village to await their next meeting with their English allies.

"Lord bless me, sir," said Dirk, eyeing the port city, its tower silvered by moonlight. "Is this not a great madness?"

With his feet planted wide to absorb a swell, Evan studied Cartagena. Green and white pennons flew from the ramparts of the castle. About thirty gunports pointed out to sea. Not far from the English fleet, a frigate of about two hundred tons rode at anchor.

Evan pondered Dirk's reservations. Rance, thinking the game not worth the candle, had resigned his role in the enterprise. Now they had only the two ships, three pinnaces, a hungry and dwindling crew of less than seventy . . . and one completely baffling young woman.

Evan glanced down the decks at her. Anne Blythe stood in the cockpit with the helmsman, chattering away like a magpie. She had endured the voyage through the Gulf of Darien without complaint. She had eaten the poor rations and drunk the brackish water as if she were accustomed to the fare. She behaved for all the world as if being captured by pirates was no more alarming than a tuna run.

"Sir?" Dirk prompted. "You've not answered me. Is it not madness to sail in here?"

A smile tugged at Evan's mouth. "Aye, Dirk. But a fine madness at that." He caught Drake's signal from the *Pasco*. The winking stern light gave the order he had anticipated.

"Out oars," he called to the crew of one of the pinnaces. "We're going to take that frigate."

The men obeyed. Dirk's face pinched into a dour expression. "She's twice the size of our biggest ship," he grumbled. "And just look at all those guns."

Evan threw back his head and laughed. "Aye, Dirk, look at them, and ask yourself—who triumphed in the end, David or Goliath?"

Dirk's spirits seemed to lift. He saluted Evan and hastened over the rail to the waiting pinnace. Within minutes, the tiny English fleet closed in on the frigate. A score of men boarded her.

Evan was the first to land on the quarterdeck. He crouched low, his sword drawn and his gaze seeking the men of the watch.

Silence greeted the raiders. Evan frowned. Denton scratched his head.

"Ahoy!" Evan called.

More silence. The raiders shuffled their feet and muttered amongst themselves.

"She's a ghost ship," someone whispered. "By God, I don't like the feel of this."

"Belay that superstitious nonsense," said Evan. "Her stores are a gift. Let's get to sacking her."

The men fell upon barrels and hatch covers. The ship had only recently been abandoned, for the food was fresh— oranges and eggs, a crate of live chickens. Other than the plate dinner service and desk set seized from the captain's quarters, they found little of value. Still, the ease of the raid imbued the men with new courage, a commodity far more precious than gold.

"Master Carew!"

Evan crossed the quarterdeck in answer to Denton's call. "What is it?"

"Look what I found, sir, crouched beneath a ship's boat." Denton hauled forth an elderly man with frightened eyes, a filthy beard, and hands that shook violently.

"Are you alone on this ship?" Evan asked in Spanish.

"I am. I was left to keep watch."

"He was left to keep watch," Evan translated.

Dirk and Denton hooted with laughter. "Then watch this, sir!" Dirk cried. He ripped down a Spanish pennon and set it aflame with a pitch torch. Guffaws rang down the decks.

The old mariner merely shrugged his shoulders. "I told them they should have left more on watch." He spat on the planks. "But no, they wouldn't listen to Paco. They all had to go ashore to witness the duel."

"What duel?"

"A fight to the death. Over a woman." Paco spat again.

Evan couldn't suppress a chuckle. "You Latins. Your weakness of the flesh will be the death of you." Seeing the old man blanch, he added quickly, "It's just a manner of speaking, *viejo*."

"You're not going to kill me?"

"That's what your kind would do." Evan propelled Paco back to the nest of sailcloth beneath the ship's boat. "Go back to your nap. We've taken all we can carry."

The mood of the Englishmen soared. Moving round the next point, they encountered an even larger ship—a merchantman.

Evan had boarded the *Pasco* to confer with Drake. "I wonder if they've all gone to watch the duel as well," Evan mused.

"That would be too lucky," Drake said. "But she's quiet. Perhaps the crew sleeps."

Evan glanced at the moon. "Who else but mad dogs and Englishmen would bestir themselves at this time of night?"

They boarded the merchantman in stealth. As Drake had predicted, the crew lay about, fast asleep. He fired a pistol into the air.

The startled Spaniards came awake, rubbing their eyes, cursing, fumbling for their weapons.

"Get below, all of you," Drake yelled, his imperfect Spanish accent thickening the words. "The first man to resist will be the first to die."

They regarded him in confusion.

"Is my Spanish not good enough?" Drake demanded.

Speaking in low tones and trying not to laugh, Evan said,

"I don't believe they've ever heard Spanish spoken with a Devonshire accent."

Drake scowled at the Spaniards. "If you do not understand my speech, then heed this," he cried, brandishing his sword. To his men, he shouted, "Get them below and lock them up."

They cut the cables of the merchantman and towed her, in full view of the fortified city, out into the sound. Alarm bells clanged wildly from the town, and the thunder of great ordnance exploded into the night.

The shots fell short of their mark. The jubilant raiders transshipped the cargo to the *Swan* and the *Pasco* while muffled Spanish curses sounded from the hold.

Trailing triumphal laughter in their wake, the raiders sailed out of the harbor. Drake allowed the prisoners to row themselves ashore in launches and ship's boats. As they watched the furious men take their leave, Denton appeared with a crumpled letter.

"Admiral Drake, look! We seized this from one of those small sailing vessels yonder."

Drake handed the dispatch to Evan, who took one look at the letter and began to laugh.

"What does it say?" Drake asked.

" '*El Draquez* has been at Nombre de Dios,' " Evan read, " 'and has taken it. Had it not been that he was wounded by a blessed shot, he would have sacked the town. Please be advised to carefully prepare for him.' "

A chorus of guffaws rang through the night. By the time the Spanish managed to mount a decent defense, the raiders had disappeared.

Annie had to admire Drake's resourcefulness. Within the next few weeks, he found a hidden anchorage at a low island off the coast of the isthmus, and his men had constructed a timber fort. Well-provisioned with purloined Spanish victuals, the small crew settled in for what appeared to be a long stay.

Annie came upon Evan, who was watching over a vat of bubbling pine tar.

"I'm bored," she stated. "I always imagined being captured

by pirates would be exciting. Or frightening at the very least. I've read the only two books available, and I've trodden upon every inch of this island. It's all gotten to be desperately tedious."

He shot her a dark look. Annie found herself wishing he wasn't so damned comely, that his shining eyes did not seem so filled with intriguing secrets.

"Entertaining you was never our intent," he said, giving the pot a stir.

"And just what is your intent?" she demanded for perhaps the hundredth time. "I wish you'd tell me."

"Would it ease your boredom if I did?"

She sniffed. The tar smelled thick and acrid. "Rodrigo is probably out of his mind worrying about me."

"As a matter of fact," said Evan, "he's practically tearing apart the empire searching for you."

"He is?"

"Aye. He's hired his own band of mercenaries."

Interest kindled inside her. "How do you know?"

"We have our sources."

"Oh." She recalled the visitors who came from time to time in canoes. "The Cimaroons, you mean."

"Aye." He kicked at a coal that had strayed from the fire.

"Most people are taught to fear them. Even in church, the priests warn that the Cimaroons are savages who cut out a man's heart with their stone knives."

Evan's head came up sharply. A terrible anger rushed like a storm cloud across his features. "The Cimaroons are a gentle, just people struggling to survive."

His furious passion stirred a memory in Annie. She remembered the first time she had seen him in Nombre de Dios. He had brought a native woman to town to be baptized. A Cimaroon.

"Tell me about the slave woman, the one you brought to Nombre de Dios. What was her name?"

"Her name was Casilda." Each word fell like a cold stone from his mouth. "And don't you dare ask me about her. Ever. Do you understand?"

His intensity took her by surprise. "You loved her, didn't you?"

"Damn it!" He picked up a stick and flung it far into the forest. "Did you not hear what I said? You are never to mention Casilda again."

She stepped back, feeling burned by the blast of his anger. "Your defensiveness explains much, Evan."

"Don't try to understand me, Annie, and I won't try to look into your heart, either."

She caught her breath. "You called me Annie."

"Is that not your name?"

"Yes, but ordinarily you address me as 'rodent.' I think you're growing to like me, Evan."

"I think the heat must be addling your head, rodent."

She watched him work until he seemed calmer. His bare arms rippled with muscled flesh as he stirred the caldron. At length she said, "Rodrigo will find me. When he does, he'll make you sorry you were born. He is a very determined man."

"So am I," Evan assured her.

"I don't doubt it. But you're tempting fate by staying in Spanish waters."

He sent her a mocking smile. "And when did you become an expert in piracy?"

"When I realized that stupidity is a deadly sin."

"Maybe you won't have that long to wait before we sail for friendlier shores."

"Maybe I will. If you think to attack the treasure train from Panama, you're in for a long wait."

Evan's shoulders stiffened. She could tell he struggled to conceal his surprise. "Who said anything about treasure trains? What in God's name gave you the idea that we'd attempt such a thing?"

A bitter laugh rose in her throat. "I have plenty of ideas for someone who's more boy than girl and more child than woman."

His shoulders relaxed, and the anger seemed to rush out of him. "I should never have said that. I apologize."

"Don't apologize for speaking your mind, Evan. I assure you, I never do."

One corner of his mouth lifted, but he stopped short of a smile. "At least you're honest."

She traced her bare toe in the sand. "You'll have to wait another four months at least," she said. "Oh, I know the schedule you gleaned from Rodrigo showed otherwise. I changed it with my own hand. Nothing can be done inland until the rains have passed."

She reveled in his attempt to keep the surprise from his face.

"You prate about nothing," he snapped.

"And you're a poor liar, Evan Carew."

"She's right," Rico said, gazing across the campfire that night at Evan and Drake. "Your young woman knows the ways of the Spaniards."

Evan glared into the glowing heart of the fire. "She's a devious little wench."

Drake's mouth twisted in a grim smile. "And clever, too. How could she be otherwise?"

Aye, thought Evan. Her Tudor blood showed itself more and more as he got to know her better. She had the bold spirit and physical courage of Henry VIII, the sharp tongue and killer instincts of Queen Elizabeth. Where she had gotten her own brand of maddeningly appealing whimsy was anyone's guess.

"I say we make a run back to England with her," he said. "We could give her to André Scalia and be back within ten weeks."

"Too risky," said Drake. "We've only the *Pasco* left."

Evan masked his disapproval. Lacking the men to sail two ships, Drake had burned every prize he had taken and had sunk his brother's vessel, the *Swan*. Only Evan and a tight-lipped ship's carpenter knew it had been no accident.

"Damn it, Francis, it's risky keeping her with us."

Drake laughed. "Risky for whom? Are you starting to have feelings for our young guest?"

"The only feelings I have for her are annoyance and plain anger."

"Ah," said Drake, and the expression on his face told Evan he didn't believe him for a moment. "Indeed. As for myself, I find her most interesting. Do you know, I believe she'd make an excellent Protestant. She doesn't seem obsessed with counting beads and muttering hocus pocus all the time."

"You mean hoc est corpus."

Drake waved a hand. "Whatever. I don't think she takes Catholic teachings too seriously. That should please the queen."

"If we ever get her to the queen."

Annie sat upon the long beach that rolled down to the shore and watched the clouds flying upon a balmy autumn breeze. In her lap she held the pages of her journal, a sheaf of old parchment upon which she recorded her thoughts. Each day was much like the last—hot and uneventful, some of the men lying ill with fever while others sailed out on raids in the Gulf of Darien, the hours marked by the clang of a bell calling the crew to meals. Hearing footsteps behind her, she turned.

Unsmiling, Evan Carew dropped a pile of wooden objects at her feet.

"What's this?" she asked, scrambling up and eyeing him suspiciously.

"A cure for your boredom." One by one, he began setting up the wooden objects. "These are ninepins. The object is to toss a ball at them and knock them down. Tomorrow I'll teach you quoits. You throw an iron hoop and try to get it round the neck of a ninepin. And then there's always skittles or bowls—"

"You're brainsick."

He shot her a wounded look. "What?"

"I don't want to learn to play games, Evan."

"Then what do you want, if I may be so foolish as to ask? To go back to Don Rodrigo? To live your life as a boy? To labor as a clerk for the rest of your days?"

She caught her breath. "I want to be free to choose."

"That's unfortunate," he said curtly. "Do you want to learn this game or not?"

For want of a better choice, she learned to play at ninepins, and then bowls, and then quoits. Within a month, she had mastered all three sports and beggared the mariners who challenged her.

"You put them all to shame," said Evan one day as she was counting the shells she had won from her opponents. They used the shells as markers for the booty they swore they would have one day.

Annie dropped her shells into a small cloth bag. "I have nothing but time to practice. I'm still bored."

Annoyance pulled down the corners of his mouth. "Again?"

"Aye."

Evan turned on his heel. "We'll see about that, Princess," he said and stalked off.

A chill swept through Annie as she watched him leave. *Princess.* He had called her Princess.

"My God," she whispered, pressing her hands to her chest, feeling her heart pound wildly. Her suspicions hardened into certainty. "He knows who I am."

CHAPTER 10

"Don't risk it, Evan," Drake said, watching the pair of ships that rode at anchor a few cables' lengths away. "We've already taken a coastal trader, a great shallop, and a frigate. We'd best get back to home port."

Evan bent his knees to absorb a storm-driven swell that lifted the pinnace. "Not yet."

"Christ, we've no need of more vessels. Our hold is packed with victuals, powder, and gear. What in God's name are you after?"

Evan felt sheepish as he muttered, "Books."

"Books!" Drake roared. "We're pirates, not scholars. Who among us has need of books?"

Evan clamped a dagger in his teeth and perched on the side of the pinnace. "Annie," he said and dove overboard.

As he swam toward the coastal frigates, he knew himself for a fool. Drake was right; this time out, they had found enough booty to keep the crew supplied for another month.

But they had found no books, and Annie was bored.

He wondered why he felt responsible for her, why it bothered him to see her in a state of ennui. Perhaps it was that challenging manner she possessed, the way she seemed to dare him to justify kidnapping her. Or perhaps it was the rare and lively hunger in her eyes. For all her annoying tendencies, she had a quick mind and a thirst for learning he admired.

As he stealthily boarded the nearer frigate, he became aware of an unnatural stillness. The wind had died down as it did each evening, and the water lay calm and flat. A faint trickling sound poured past the hull, and he noticed that the vessel was in bad repair, the seams splitting and some of the boards pocked with dry rot.

Even so, he should hear some sort of movement, a snatch of conversation, the snap of a cook fire or the call of the sandglass boy.

He hopped over the railing and onto the deck. An unearthly yowl nearby brought him out of his skin. He crouched low, dagger in hand, to find himself confronted with a skinny, moth-eaten ship's cat.

Evan swore. He hurriedly explored the frigate, ascertaining that it was not only abandoned, but sinking slowly.

Apprehension dogged his footsteps as he went above to signal to Drake that he was moving on to explore the companion vessel.

Looking east, he saw Drake's pinnace gliding toward him. Looking west, he saw two well-armed ships surging in from around a jutting, tree-covered point.

"It's a trap!" Evan bellowed, grabbing the rail and preparing to dive over.

Drake shook a fist. "Damn it, Evan, I told you not to risk this."

"And I should have listened." As Evan prepared to rejoin his fleet, Denton fired a flaming arrow at the frigate. The dry, worm-eaten wood caught quickly.

The least they could do was wait, Evan thought peevishly.

The cat yowled again as more arrows fired the decks and rigging. Evan cursed and snatched up the animal. The cat raked him with its claws, spitting and hissing as if possessed by the devil. Evan managed to stuff the animal into a sack. He lowered himself with a rope just as the Spanish guns spoke.

"For God's sake, hurry, Evan!" someone screamed from the pinnace.

He dropped into the hull. Founts of water erupted as cannonballs drove toward them. Drake yelled to the oarsmen. Using every inch of canvas and oar, the crew made for the coast. The shoal-draught pinnace could hug the shore, while the deep-keeled Spanish warships could not follow without the risk of running aground.

"Are you certain we'll be out of range?" Evan shouted over the furious noise of artillery.

"Nothing is ever certain in these waters," Drake yelled back. He grinned. "Except, of course, a Devonshire sea dog's luck."

Within minutes, they had run the pinnace aground. Some of the men jumped out into the surf, taunting the huge Spanish ships. The cannonballs dropped yards short of them.

Laughing, Drake poked at Evan's bundle, which rolled about the cockpit. "Find any books?"

"No, just a cat."

Savoring Drake's look of surprise, Evan joined the others on the shore. At a call from Drake, they all formed a line and turned their backs on the Spanish ships. As one, they dropped their breeches and bent over, giving their hosts a mocking English salute.

Annie was playing chess when she heard the lookout call that the pinnace had returned from its latest raid. Ignoring the leap of excitement in her chest, she forced herself to stare fixedly at the game. She used shells for chessmen, and the board was a sheet of bark inked with uneven squares.

She refused to acknowledge that the days of Evan's absence had seemed interminable. She refused to acknowledge the fact that she had missed him.

Her chess partner was herself. The others had long since ceased to challenge her, for she always won. In a way, it was fitting to play against her own wits. Ever since Evan had swept her away, she had been at war with herself.

She worried about Rodrigo. And yet the thought of going back to her old life in Nombre de Dios held little appeal. Rodrigo and Valeria were content, and Annie did not doubt that one day they would find their way into each other's hearts. Annie had a life of her own to live.

Frowning, she immersed herself in contemplating her next move. For a moment her vision swam and her forehead burned. She had not been feeling well, but the illness seemed minor compared to the awful fever that plagued many of the men. She took several deep breaths and sipped from a jar of fresh water. A short time later, a shadow fell over her. It took all her self-discipline not to look up.

But when Evan dropped a stack of leather-and-wood-bound books at her side, she couldn't stifle a cry of delight.

"I can't believe it," she said, picking a heavy tome and slowly paging through it. "Petrarch's sonnets." She gazed up into Evan's face.

When their eyes met, a jolt went through her. Princess. At their last meeting, he had called her Princess. As if that were not shocking enough, she felt a deep, visceral response at the mere sight of him.

The sun and wind had tanned his skin a rich brown color. His shirt parted at his throat to show black curls on his chest. His hair, long and windblown, was glossy and vigorous.

And the look in his eyes seemed, just for a moment, to hold the charm of boyish expectancy.

"Thank you, Evan," she said.

"Don't thank me yet." He swung a sack down from his shoulder. "There's more."

She reached for the bag, but he held it out of her reach. "Careful," he said. "You'd best let me."

He opened the neck of the bag. Annie heard a hiss, then saw a blur of gray as something streaked out of the bag and shot halfway up the trunk of the nearest piñon tree.

Annie jumped to her feet. "Is that a cat?"

"Of sorts. Don't get too close."

She studied it with avid interest. Its coat was dark gray, ribbed with paler gray, stretched over a skeletal frame. It clung with all four paws to the tree trunk.

"Why, it's starving," she said.

"I tried to feed it," Evan said. "All it seems willing to eat is small pieces of my flesh."

Indeed, his hands were covered in scratches, some fresh, others healing. With a sigh of resignation, he took a bit of salted fish from the sack and held it out to the cat. The cat flattened its ears, drew back its lips, and bared its teeth, but its nose twitched with interest.

"Sometimes she eats if I pretend I'm not watching," he said, glancing away from the animal.

"Tell me where you've been," Annie said, idly scratching a welt on her arm. The mosquitoes were bad here, hovering in hideous black clouds over the marshes of the island.

"Everywhere. We took on as much as we could carry in the way of provisions."

"I see." Hope sprang up. "Did you encounter Rodrigo?"

"No. Nor did we hear what he's about these days. It's been a long time, Annie."

Anger smoldered inside her. It was time to confront him. "And it's likely to be much longer, isn't it?"

The cat snapped at the bit of fish Evan held. He winced as small, sharp teeth sank into his finger, but he neither drew back his hand nor looked at the animal. "Aye," he said at last.

"How did you learn about me?" she asked.

His shoulders stiffened, but still he did not move. "It's not important."

"But you *do* know who I am."

"Aye, Princess," he said again. "Drake and I know, but we're the only ones. You'd be wise to guard your identity."

Annie bit her lip. Hearing him admit the truth made her worst fears seem even more awful. "Who sent you?"

"A . . . benefactor. No harm will come to you, I swear it."

"A benefactor," she echoed sarcastically. "Why did she send you, Evan? What does she want with me?"

He moved his hand slowly down the tree trunk. The cat followed, its claws scrabbling on the bark. "She?"

"You know who I mean."

"Aye." Evan blew out his breath. "At this point, I think she merely wants to see you. To know you."

"And you'll drag me to England to satisfy her curiosity? That seems a bit extreme, even for a corsair."

"Not for a queen. Aren't you curious, too, Annie?"

She thought for a moment. The fact that Queen Elizabeth was her aunt—or more accurately, half-aunt—had always seemed a nebulous concept. Yet now she found the idea intrigued her.

"Perhaps I am, but not curious enough to travel to a strange land to see her." Yet she didn't want to go home, either. Frustration nagged at her, for her choices were few and far from satisfactory.

Evan waved the bit of dried fish under the cat's nose. This time, the animal took some immediately. "The current succession is abhorrent to her," he said. "If there's any chance of a better alternative, the queen will seize it."

Annie laughed with humorless disbelief. "She'd actually consider me, of illegitimate bloodline, a woman raised as a Spaniard and a Catholic?"

"Stranger things have happened."

A flicker of panic blinded her for a moment. She shook her head and banished it. "It won't happen. However, if the impossible does come to pass, my first act will be to place you and Francis Drake under arrest and throw you in prison." She tapped her chin, considering. "No, I'll probably just have you executed outright. Drawn and quartered, of course, and your parts displayed in various corners of the realm."

One side of his mouth lifted. "Ah, you do have royal blood, Princess. Cold as ice." Then he turned away and inch by inch coaxed the cat to the ground. Soon he had it crouched over his hand, eating voraciously.

"Where did the books come from?" Annie asked.

"Our last exploit of the run. We were on our way back

when we encountered a packet. Your good friend, Don Iago Orozco, was aboard."

"He was never my friend."

"Then you won't feel guilty owning his private library."

In truth, she did feel a measure of dark satisfaction. She had always associated Don Iago with her father's death. She felt reluctant admiration for Evan and Drake as well. Their bold exploits along the coast were but a prelude to the greater havoc she knew they planned inland. Their activities at sea would divert attention from their true objective: the overland treasure trains from Panama.

Lowering her eyes so Evan would not see the knowledge there, she murmured, "Thank you."

"You're welcome."

Their civility felt strange and forced. Perhaps she simply did not understand the protocol that governed the behavior of captive and captor. She did not understand Evan Carew. Nor did she comprehend why she wanted so badly to know him.

The thought sparked her anger anew. "This is all very well and good, your efforts to appease me." Her raised voice frightened the cat, and it skittered away into the underbrush. "But the only thing I truly want is my freedom."

Evan stood and faced her. "I can't give you that, Annie."

"Why not?"

His knuckles grazed her cheek. The tenderness of his touch startled her. "You know why."

She jerked her hand away. "Ah, yes. You mean to drag me before the English queen so she can inspect my qualifications. Will she examine my teeth to see that they're all in place? Test me to see if I can recite the Protestant catechism?"

"You'll be treated as the most honored of guests."

She turned away. The subtle sting of a mosquito pierced her neck, and she slapped at it in annoyance. "I'll be a prisoner, and you know it."

With a trembling hand, Drake clutched at a length of hopsacking that covered the corpse of his brother Joseph.

The surgeon's assistant stood close by, tears streaming down his frightened young face.

"Honest, sir," he whispered, "I tried my best. With your brother . . ." His terrified gaze flickered to the array of crude graves that turned the tropical island into a burial ground. "With all of them, sir. The bleeding and purging just has no effect." His shoulders shook, and Evan touched him, silently urging the lad to stifle his sobs. Francis's silence was ominous, a weighty calm before a storm of grief.

Evan pitied the boy. The surgeon had died of the fever a few weeks before, and the lad was ill-equipped to contend with the epidemic.

"No effect," Drake said dully. With a swift movement, he snatched off the rough-spun shroud. Joseph's body lay before them, the yellow-tinged face serene, the lips rimmed with black.

Even as they gazed in horror at the dead man, another of the sick men gave a loud yelp. A fount of dark vomit soaked the sand beside his pallet. From the corner of his eye, Evan saw Annie duck beneath the shelter of plantain leaves, followed by Denton with a basin of water. Over the past weeks, she had been tireless in ministering to the sick, but for the most part her efforts—like those of the surgeon's assistant—came to naught.

"By God's sweet son," Drake whispered harshly. "A third of my men are dead of this fever, and more are dying. How can I fight a battle when I do not understand the enemy?"

Evan bent to replace the shroud. "Francis, let's honor your brother with a proper burial and ponder that later."

"Admiral Drake!" The call came from the plantain shelter. "'Tis the girl!"

Evan reached her first, sinking to his knees beside her where she lay on the sandy floor of the shelter. "What happened?" he demanded.

Denton wiped the sweat from his brow. "She just . . . fell. Dropped to the ground like she'd been shot. I fear—"

"No," Evan whispered. With shaking hands, he lifted her head into his lap. "She's just tired. A little rest will restore her." Yet even as he spoke, he knew her condition was much more serious. "Annie. Annie, can you hear me?" Her skin felt burning hot to the touch, and dry, without a drop of sweat. Gently, he used his thumb to lift one eyelid. With nightmare clarity, he saw the yellowish tinge.

Drake lowered himself beside Evan. "Is it the fever?"

"Aye."

"Oh, God. Not her. Please God, not her."

Drake's words echoed Evan's thoughts, but held a vastly different meaning. To Francis, Annie was a prize beyond price. She represented the security of his future. To Evan, she had been a brazen, sharp-tongued girl. Then, little by little, she had become something more—a woman of courage and bright wit who occupied his thoughts more frequently than he would have wished.

Denton arranged a pallet for her. Evan gathered her into his arms. She felt as light as a child and when he stood, her head lolled back, making her seem unbearably fragile. He laid her upon the pallet and squeezed his eyes shut for a moment. *Please God, not her. . . .*

The surgeon's boy came with his basin and thin-bladed knife. He took Annie's arm and drew the sliverlike blade across the inside of her elbow. Evan winced as the blood began to flow, a scarlet so vivid that his eyes hurt to look at it pooling in the basin. The blood of kings and queens, yet it appeared no different from the blood of a commoner.

Who would be next? Evan wondered. Himself? Drake? The thought welled up in him. All their plans had come to this—to a death-ridden isle where no one would know of their passing. The people of Carew would lose their champion. The Queen of England would have to bow to the superiority of Spain.

Suddenly he could bear it no longer. He snatched a damp cloth from a basin and pressed it to the wound on Annie's arm.

The surgeon's lad regarded him with a fearful eyes. "Sir! I must draw off the bad blood."

"I think not," Evan said sharply. "The Cimaroons have told us of an herbal cure. Why do we not try it?"

" 'Tis pagan!" the lad said.

"Let the boy do his work," Drake said. "Bleeding is one of the few skills he knows."

"Aye, he's an expert at it!" Evan's temper exploded. "Did the bleeding save Joseph's life?"

Francis's face drained to white. He caught his breath as if Evan had struck him. Without another word, he turned on his heel and stalked across the camp to where his dead brother lay.

Evan stayed with Annie. He bathed her forehead and neck with cool cloths. For the first time, he noticed how delicate her skin was, how soft. At her temples and eyelids he could see the dainty tracery of veins. How tender he felt toward her at this moment. She had infuriated him with her taunting, had made him laugh at her biting jokes, had stirred his emotions with her wide-eyed, wounded gaze. A feeling of helplessness wrested a curse from his throat.

"There, Evan, leave the lass to me a while," Dirk said. Evan had no idea how long he'd been standing nearby.

"All right," he said. "But no bleeding. No emetics or purgatives, either."

Dirk nodded and took the cloth from him. Evan left the shelter and nearly collided with the surgeon's boy. "Sir," he said, shifting his weight nervously from foot to foot. "Sir, you must stop him."

Evan scowled. "Stop him?"

"Admiral Drake." The lad pressed his hands together. "God helps us all, sir, but he's going to cut open his own brother to learn the nature of this disease."

Evan raced across the camp. Knife in hand, Drake knelt beside Joseph.

"Francis." Evan spoke past the bile building in his throat. "Francis, I beg you. Don't do this."

"Damn it, Evan! I must know what's happening to my men. Joseph would want me to find the enemy, to learn its nature. How else can I stop the dying?"

"I don't know, Francis. But not this way. Even if you detected some . . . some irregularity in Joseph's body, you'd still be powerless to find the remedy."

Drake sprang up, brandishing the knife like a weapon. An eerie light gleamed in his eyes. "I have to do *some*thing, Evan. If you lack the stomach for it, then begone!"

Sickened, Evan walked away. He glanced back once to see Drake summoning the surgeon's boy. The lad's mouth tightened as he watched the admiral press the keen blade to the torso of his dead brother.

Evan walked until his legs ached. He found himself on the leeward side of the island, brooding at the setting sun. When a party of Cimaroons arrived in a canoe, he lacked the heart to give them the usual exuberant greeting. He managed a nod when Rico approached.

"Drake's brother died today," Evan said. "The girl's been stricken, too." Thinking of the lives lost, the souls threatened, he picked up a handful of sand and let the grains spill between his fingers. "In God's name, Rico, what *is* this pestilence? Do your people not suffer from it?"

"Sometimes, but it does not kill us. And once a man survives the fever, he is immune forever after."

"Immortality be damned! We need a cure!"

Rico sat silent, contemplating the frothy surf.

"Can you help us?" Evan repeated, desperate. "Earlier, you spoke of some herb . . ."

"Our wisewomen use a plant. It sometimes lessens the fever. But maybe the magic does not work on Christians."

"We must try." Evan clutched the big man's arm. "Rico, I'm begging you."

The magical plant appeared to be some sort of common madder herb with whorled leaves and yellowish flowers. Ripening berries emerged from some of the blossoms. Rico boiled the whole plant and made a strong tea.

In the plantain shelter, by the light of a fire-pike, Evan took the clay cup from him. Annie and three other patients slept fitfully on pallets. The men of the night watch were unusually quiet. Drake's experiment on his brother's corpse had subdued the spirits of everyone. True to his word, Francis had studied Joseph's organs and found, predictably, nothing to aid his search for a cure. Shaken and weeping with remorse, he had laid his brother to rest a few hours before.

"You're sure it won't poison her?" Evan asked.

"I am sure of nothing. Christians are a mystery to me."

"Then I shall drink this draft first and wait a bit."

"As you wish."

The tea was rough and bitter, and Evan almost gagged. He could discern no reaction in his body save perhaps a subtle feeling of calmness. Or was the feeling hope?

"Help me, Rico," he said.

Rico held Annie's head and massaged her throat as Evan trickled the medicine into her mouth. They treated her and the other patients every two hours through the night and the next day.

On the second night, sheer exhaustion claimed Evan. He lay down beside Annie, tucking her into the lee of his shoulder. Her hair smelled faintly sweet, and his heart pounded with dread. Just before he fell into a fitful sleep, he pressed his lips to her temple. Her skin felt cool and pleasantly damp. He touched his lips to her brow and tasted the subtle essence of sweat.

"Thank God," he whispered, his eyes on fire with tears. "Thank God above, her fever's broken."

On Shrove Tuesday, the third of February, Drake announced that they would begin the move to plunder the treasure train.

Grief subdued the enthusiasm of the men. Only thirty adventurers had survived the tropical winter. Evan eyed the row of crude mounds on a distant point of the island. Drake's brother John, killed during an exploit, lay there. Beside him rested Joseph Drake, whose fate had caused the men to name the island Slaughter Isle.

They brought the *Pasco* and the pinnaces to a hidden anchorage on the mainland near the mouth of the river Chagres.

Drake chose seventeen adventurers to march overland with him. Rico led an eager group of thirty Cimaroon warriors.

His gear clanking, Evan found Annie in her cramped quarters aboard the *Pasco*. She lay in a hammock, the gray cat upon her stomach while she idly stroked its well-fed body. It was a marvel that she had managed to tame the recalcitrant little beast.

"We're off, then," he announced.

She sent him a sulky look. Fortune had favored her in the weeks following her recovery. She had grown brown and strong and more opinionated than ever. "Am I supposed to wish you godspeed and a safe return?"

"I'd not ask it of you, Annie. I want you to know, you'll be safe here. Denton and Dirk are trustworthy, and all the men have strict instructions to treat you with respect."

Setting the cat aside, she rose from her hammock and came to stand in front of him. "Should that make me feel better?"

Evan didn't answer; he merely looked at her. She was no child, he thought with a jolt of discomfort, but a woman grown, with high, rounded breasts that thrust against her shirt, gently flaring hips, and a ripe, full mouth.

Without even knowing what moved him, Evan touched her cheek. Her startled gaze mirrored his own feelings: Acknowledgment. Interest. Need. He took her in his arms and kissed her. At first their lips touched briefly, softly. Then he pressed hard, wanting to devour her. She was a petulant and difficult woman, but in his arms she became as pliant and responsive as a bride.

Untimely heat surged through his body, and it was all he could do to drag himself away from her. God above, he had kissed a princess of the blood royal.

She wore an expression of surprise. "Why did you do that?"

"I don't know."

She touched a finger to her moist lips. "I hope you aren't planning to do it again."

"I hope so, too," he admitted. "I'm sorry."

"Are you?"

"Are *you?*"

"Evan!" Drake's voice called from topside. "Enough of dallying! Make haste!"

Evan didn't wait for her answer. Ducking out of her quarters, he joined his companions in their assault upon the Spanish empire.

Rico proved a shrewd and able guide. Acutely aware of the need for stealth, he guided the party of raiders along the hidden forest and jungle paths, well out of sight of Spanish patrols. Brightly colored macaws darted among the high branches of the trees. Lizards sneaked amid the bony roots, and from time to time they heard the rustle of a wild pig foraging for food.

"No white man has ever walked this path," Rico said over his shoulder to Evan. "You are the first."

"We are honored," he said. Even as he spoke, his mind clung to his last vision of Annie—her soft lips, her startled eyes, and his body's own terrible reaction to her. What in God's name had he been thinking of? She was a Tudor princess, and he a lowly Welsh sea dog. She was both innocent and annoying, nothing like the aching memories of Casilda he kept secreted in his heart. He had absolutely no business kissing Annie Blythe.

Evan welcomed the ascent up the pine-forested hills of the Cordillera in the middle of the narrow isthmus. The humid air of the jungle gave way to crisp mountain sweetness. At night, the stars appeared sharp and innumerable, a band of milky light arching to infinity.

They reached the watershed of the Cordillera, and Cimaroons welcomed them to their tiny hillside village. Drake led his raiders inside the mud wall and regarded the people there. Men stood stiffly, defensively, in front of women and small children. Even when Rico announced that the strangers were their allies, the Cimaroons hung back.

"They surpass our numbers tenfold," whispered Robbie Pike, reaching for his dagger. "We'll never leave here alive.

These black devils have lured us away to murder us. I say we strike first and fight our way free."

Evan grasped Robbie's wrist and squeezed until Pike cried out in pain.

"That's enough, Robbie," Evan said through gritted teeth. "You make one threatening move against these people and I'll kill you myself."

"Well said, Evan." Drake strode forward, swept off his plumed hat, and bowed deeply before the villagers. They regarded him blankly as he recited a greeting in bad Spanish. But when he produced a fine stag-handled knife and presented it, hilt first, to one of the men, the wall of wariness started to crumble. Within a short while, Drake's ready smile broke through their timidity, and he had them talking excitedly. Many were eager to share their hatred of the Spanish. They showed brands and scars from wounds they had endured before making their escape into the wilderness.

Lifting his gourd full of guava nectar, Drake clapped Rico on the shoulder. "You and your people are the greatest friends a man could wish for."

"You treat us as brothers." Rico aimed a knowing look at Evan. "You respect our ways, and you earn our trust."

"Our alliance—God willing—shall mean death to the Spanish," Drake said.

"Come." Rico stood and motioned Drake and Evan to the edge of the village. "I want to show you something."

Drake and Evan exchanged a glance. From the avid look in Drake's eyes, Evan suspected that his friend anticipated a hidden cache of Spanish gold. Evan knew better. The Cimaroons had no use for gold, for it did not fill their bellies nor quiet their souls.

Rico brought them to a tree so huge that three men standing around it with hands linked would be hard-pressed to encircle its girth. Steps had been cut into the trunk. High in the dark, gnarled branches rested a platform of lashed-together poles. From that height, Evan realized, the Cimaroons could spy out the countryside for miles around.

Excitement built within him as he mounted the steps and clambered onto the platform with Drake and Rico.

The three of them stood, their hair stirred by cool mountain breezes, the broad green plains rolling down to the turquoise sea. So clear was the view that Evan imagined he could see the precise location of the *Pasco*. He wondered what Annie was doing now, what she was thinking of. Then he chastened himself for caring.

"Look this way," Rico moved to the edge of the platform that faced west and held aside a large branch.

Evan turned and caught his breath. Past the mountains, past the trees and plains, a misty blue vastness shimmered.

The Pacific.

It was as wide as infinity, so distant and immense that he could see the horizon begin to curve at the edges.

Evan felt a stirring inside him, as if the view held a lodestone that drew him closer and closer.

Hearing a hollow thump, he looked at Drake. He had fallen to his knees. He held his hands stretched toward the west, a look of stark wonderment in his eyes.

"Evan!" His voice was a harsh whisper. "It is the great south sea! The greatest of oceans!"

"Aye, Francis. We are the first Englishmen to see it."

Drake clenched his fist and thrust it into the sky. "Let God witness my vow. One day I will sail that ocean. Let this promise bind me until I succeed."

Evan, too, felt the passion for adventure rising through him. He clasped hands with Drake and held their fists aloft. "Unless you banish me from your company, Francis, by God's grace I will follow you."

The tree-covered mountains shaded the raiders during the two days of their descent to the plains of Panama. The open pampas rolled out, an empty sea of grass, which left the men dangerously exposed.

Evan's back and shoulders ached from his burden of supplies and weaponry, for like the others, he marched in a half-bent posture, ever watchful for Spanish troops on patrol. The men followed, complaining and swearing under their breath. Angry sunlight scorched the plain, and an incessant wind rattled the long, sere grass.

"I think we're lost," muttered Robbie Pike. "I see no golden city gleaming on the horizon." He took a long pull at his flask of aqua vitae. "These 'maroons be leading us astray, I think."

Evan scowled. "Best ease up on the drink, Mr. Pike. We're getting close. You'll need your wits about you."

"Close," grumbled Pike. "Tell me, when did you come to be such an expert on the Spanish empire?" A lewd grin curved his wet lips. "Ah, your little slut, eh? Did she whisper the secrets of the empire in your ear while you fucked her?"

Evan's fist shot out and smashed into Pike's jaw. Pike staggered, then crashed to the ground. The other men close by hung back, regarding the two combatants with keen interest.

Pike was in no condition for fisticuffs, and Evan in no mood for delay. Striding over to the fallen man, Evan jerked him up by the scruff of the neck.

"March," he ordered through gritted teeth, shoving Pike up over the crest of a hillock.

Pike moaned and cradled his jaw in both hands. "You've wounded me."

" 'Tis but a foretaste of what you'll get if you so much as think of the girl again."

Pike stumbled at the top of the hill and fell to his knees.

Evan grabbed a clump of his hair and yanked his head back. "Look, Mr. Pike. Does that satisfy you?"

Pike squinted across the rolling pampa. Watery shimmers of heat gleamed upon the ocean of grass. "Heaven be praised," he said in wonderment.

There, far in the distance, rose the glittering city of Panama. Evan released Pike and moved away to savor his first sight of the city. Spires and towers pierced the hard blue sky. The harbor teemed with ships that had brought the treasures from Peru.

"It's astounding," Drake said. "More bounteous than I ever dreamed. By God, Evan!" Drake clapped him on the shoulder. "We shall fill the coffers of England with more wealth than our queen can imagine."

"She can imagine a lot," said Evan.

Drake turned and motioned to Rico and the Cimaroons. "Someone must go into the city tonight. We must have the latest news on the treasure and the mule trains."

Silent looks of apprehension passed among the Cimaroons. A few of them spoke in rapid patois. Finally, Rico himself stepped forward. "I will go, Englishman."

"I'll join you," said Evan.

As they started down the hill toward Panama, Evan asked, "What were your men saying? Why did they hesitate to volunteer?"

Rico kept his dark gaze trained on the city. "Because going into Panama is suicide."

Rodrigo stood at the window of his chamber and stared out at the night. The city lay in silence; lampglow lit only a few windows of the buildings around the harbor, and the sterncastle lanterns of ships winked in the harbor.

Soon, Nombre de Dios would bustle with activity day and night, for the treasure trains from Panama were due to arrive.

Ordinarily, he would feel a pleasant surge of anticipation. But this year, he found himself thinking cynically of the Spaniards' plunder of the New World. They were like so many ants, digging treasure from the mines of Potosí in Peru, shipping whole mountains, bit by precious bit, to Panama. There, the treasure was rendered into bars. Priceless bricks wrested from the earth by the sweat of slaves and then transported in long, lumbering lines across the isthmus.

Aye, their toil had no more meaning than the work of ants.

Bleakness pressed at Rodrigo's heart. For half a year he had torn apart the coast, boarding ships, sending messages, putting his dagger to smugglers' throats to learn news of Annie. For his efforts, he had naught to show but a band of hired soldiers whose main purpose seemed to be filling their bellies with Rodrigo's food and wine.

"I'm sorry, Phillip," he whispered to the empty night. "I've lost her. You entrusted me with the welfare of your daughter, and I let her go."

He ground his fist against the window frame, loosing a light shower of plaster. It was as if Annie had been snatched from the face of the earth like a feather borne away on the wind.

The English pirates had seized her during the night of the raid. How could it be, he wondered feverishly, that they had found out who she was? He thought they had been so careful, hiding her identity, moving from port to port.

Yet someone, somehow, had discovered that she was kin to Elizabeth of England. The thought brought a chilling remembrance of the ransacked plantation, Gema del Mar, at Santo Domingo. Perhaps some clue had been found there and someone had fit the pieces of the puzzle together.

"Did you tell someone, Phillip?" Rodrigo wondered aloud. "It was never like you to be glib, especially with so deadly a secret, but I have no notion of how else they could have known."

Calling on his knowledge of diplomatic cipher, Rodrigo had dispatched messages to the Spanish ambassador in England. He prayed his missives would soon be answered, that he would hear news of a young flame-haired newcomer in England.

Cold fear clutched at his stomach. What if . . . he tried to will the fear away, but his mind clung to it. What if the English pirates had been sent to kill Annie?

Illegitimate heirs to the throne rarely fared well. He tortured himself with the thought. England had hardly flinched at the execution of Lady Jane Grey, despite the fact that she had been but sixteen, a pious girl maneuvered to the throne by her manipulative parents.

Annie could hope for even less sympathy. By now, her bones might be picked clean by scavengers and bleached white by the tropical sun.

Seized by the thought, Rodrigo picked up his wine goblet and hurled it at the far wall of his chamber. It dropped with a hollow, metallic clang. Every bit of his frustration echoed in the crash.

A few minutes later, the door pushed open. Clad in a light robe of unbleached cotton, Valeria stepped into the room.

Not now! Rodrigo wanted to yell at her. Not now, when I have nearly lost all control of myself. . . .

She glided across the room. With a movement as fluid as pouring water, she stooped and picked up the battered cup. Setting it carefully on the table, she said, "Talk to me, Rodrigo."

"I don't wish to talk."

She stiffened in anger and approached him. "*I* wish it. For months you've been cold and closed to me."

"Forgive me. I suppose I should accept Annie's absence with hearty good cheer."

She stepped into the pool of light streaming through the window. Her large, dark eyes were slightly puffy from sleep. Her thick, glossy hair tumbled down over her shoulders and breasts. Her aura of feminine mystery was slow torture to Rodrigo.

He glared at her and saw the woman he had been running from since he had first laid eyes on her.

"Damn it, Rodrigo," she burst out. "Do you think I'm not worried about her, too? I love her! I adore her lively wit and her sweetness. I ache with missing her."

"And you think whining about it will help?"

"No, but speaking in civil terms might make life bearable."

Life could never be bearable with Valeria. Rodrigo wanted her with a burning intensity that scorched his soul.

And yet he could not have her.

He suspected she would come willingly to his bed if he asked it of her. But he would never ask. Simply bedding her would not be enough. For the first time in his life, Rodrigo wanted more from a woman than a few hours of lively bedsport. He wanted intimacy, he wanted sharing, and he was scared to death that he wanted those things only with Valeria.

"Go back to bed," he commanded.

"Not until you tell me why you cannot talk to me anymore,

why you cannot even be near me. For pity's sake, you treat the servants with more civility."

"And what makes you think," he forced out, "that you are more than a servant in this house?"

In the pale moonlight, her cheeks drained to the color of milk. "Apparently I am less."

She turned very slowly. Before she took a single step toward the door, he spun her around and hauled her into his arms. Her body felt sinfully soft and dangerously yielding against his.

"*Ay, mujer,*" he whispered, breathing in the scent of her downy hair. "I can't pretend anymore, Valeria. I want you."

She pulled back and eyed him solemnly. "And that is the cause of your cruelty? Denial?"

He skimmed his hands over her shoulders, down her arms. "You make me crazy, Valeria."

A knowing smile curved her lips. "Believe me, that was never my intent, though I'll not deny it's an interesting notion."

He let her go as if her body had turned as hot as a brand. "Get out," he said hoarsely. "Go quickly, before I beg you to stay."

"And leave you wondering what my answer would be?"

He turned sharply to stare out the window. It pained his soul to look at her, to gaze into her wide, gentle eyes and see himself, with all his shortcomings, reflected there.

"Damn you," he muttered.

"Why?" she demanded. "Why do you damn me?"

"You're a woman of honor. If I so much as tasted your lips, I'd not stop at simply bedding you. I'd want you forever." Before he could stop himself, he blurted, "As my wife."

"And what makes you think," she asked in the softest of whispers, "that I would be averse to becoming your wife?"

He faced her, his jaw slack with incredulity. "You're a Jew."

She flung up her head. "I am also a woman, and though I love my faith, I know the sort of world I live in."

"You mean . . ." Rodrigo's throat went dry, and he swallowed audibly. "You mean you'd give up your faith to marry me?"

She gave him an ironic smile. "Not in this life."

He stood frozen while his mind caught fire. "Conditions, Valeria?"

"I wouldn't ask you to give up your faith. I think it's only fair you do the same. If you marry me, you'll be taking a Jew to wife." She placed her hand lightly on his sleeve. "I understand what a danger that would be to you, to our children. You'll have to want me very badly to risk your future."

Like a man in the grip of a silvery dream, he lifted her hand from his sleeve and carried it to his mouth. Pressing an intimate kiss to her palm, he heard himself say, "So be it."

"But Rodrigo—"

The rasp of iron hinges sounded somewhere in the house. Rodrigo stiffened and felt Valeria do the same. Tiny hairs lifted on the back of his neck.

"Stay here," he whispered. Drawing his dagger, he slipped out the door and down the shadowy steps.

It was probably one of the servants or soldiers, he reasoned, even as the blood thundered in his ears. Raiding the larder for a late night meal, or—

A light tread of footsteps sounded from the back of the house. Keeping to the dense shadows, Rodrigo made his way down a narrow, low-ceilinged hall. He passed the *zaguán* where he and Valeria had spent many a pleasant evening together, back when Annie had been with them and they had been easy with one another. He passed his office, where papers and letters lay in untidy piles, because Annie was not there to organize them.

Just inside the patio door, he spied the intruder, a cloaked black shape creeping toward the back stairs.

The stairs that led to Valeria's quarters.

Fear iced his veins. Had the Inquisition found her at last?

He held his dagger low to conceal its gleam. When the visitor reached the foot of the stairs, Rodrigo lunged. The two of them tumbled to the hard floor. The air rushed out of the stalker's lungs. A slim, wiry body twisted and bucked beneath Rodrigo.

A familiar curse burst from the criminal. "Saints and angels! Leave go!"

Stunned, Rodrigo leaped to his feet and yanked up the intruder by the shoulders. Fury, relief, joy, and finally amusement rose through him.

"Annie," he said.

CHAPTER 11

"It was too easy," Evan muttered to his companion. He glanced over his shoulder at the city of Panama, gilded now by the setting sun.

Rico made a sound of ironic amusement. "And you're complaining?"

"No, but I've learned never to trust unexpected good fortune. How is it that we were able to slip into Panama and win the information so freely? Then stroll right back out the city gates?"

"The Spanish are a boastful lot. Their pride takes the place of caution."

"I fear a trap," said Evan.

"We've set one of our own, *compadre*." Rico put his fingers to his mouth and whistled to signal the English scouts.

Drake met them with arms outspread and face alight with anticipation. "Well?" he demanded.

"Two mule trains are starting out this very night," Evan said.

"They travel in the dark to avoid the heat," Rico added.

"How convenient," said Drake.

"One of the travelers is the treasurer of Peru," Evan continued. "He and his daughter have a private train laden with precious stones and gold."

"Blessed Saint George," cried Robbie Pike, staggering into the midst of the group. "Let's attack now, without delay."

Evan glanced at him sharply. A poor recruit, that one. Pike had a weakness for drink and an impulsive streak ill-suited for raiding. But it was too late to voice his concern to Drake.

The adventurers peeled off their shirts and tied them around their waists so that in the dark they would be able to tell friend from foe. They moved to the Panama road and divided into two contingents, one on each side of the byway.

Evan lay alongside Drake, the dry grass tickling his chin. His ears strained for the sound of mule bells.

"Where's Pike?" he whispered.

"On the other side," said Drake.

"Damn! I wanted to stay hard by him. The man needs a leash."

"He'll behave right enough. The fortunes of England ride upon our success. And more, I owe it to the memory of my own two brothers, John and Joseph, who gave their lives to this enterprise, to see this through."

The pampas grass whispered on a ripple of wind. A light mist of dew settled over the land, bringing out the scent of the dusty road.

A faint chiming brought every man to rigid alertness. Evan cocked his head; the jingle seemed to come from the direction of Venta Cruz, not Panama. Across the way, a rustling sounded in the grass.

"Not yet," Evan whispered between his teeth.

"They wouldn't dare," Drake assured him as the *clip clop* of hooves drew nearer. "Everyone has strict orders to stay in his place until I sound the whistle. Besides, that's a horse's hooves, and a single set of them. Which one of us would be fool enough to mistake that for the mule train?"

Robbie Pike leaped onto the road, waving his arms. "Stop in the name of the queen!" he yelled.

Drake swore. A dark shape—Rico, Evan guessed—jumped out and hauled Pike down into the grass.

And the lone rider, his ears doubtless ringing with Pike's words, spurred his horse and galloped hard in the direction of Panama.

Curses and condemnations seared the air. Evan strode across the road and dragged Pike up by his hair. "You bloody fool," he spat, "you were to wait for the signal."

Pike jerked away and planted his feet wide. "I heard the approach. I feared he'd see us and ride off to alarm the town."

"Which is exactly what he's doing, thanks to you. By God, I'd thrash you to within an inch of your life if I thought you worth the effort."

"He's not. But still . . ." Drake's fist shot out of the darkness and smashed into Pike's face with a sickening crunch. Pike yelped in pain and slithered to the ground. Drake lifted his foot to kick the fool, but at the last instant he shot a pleading look at Evan.

"Jesu, Evan, stop me! Stop me before I do murder this night!"

"Easy, Francis." Full of respect for Drake's honesty, Evan put his hand on his friend's shoulder. Pike choked on the blood streaming from his nose.

Evan could feel Drake tremble and knew he suppressed a terrible rage. A rage Evan shared. They had waited for months, suffering the deaths of their comrades. They had traveled for miles, risking their necks with every step. Just like the raid on Nombre de Dios, triumph had dangled almost within reach, only to be snatched away by a fool's impulse.

Evan fixed Robbie Pike with a fiery stare. "I'll stay the admiral's hand for now, my master, but when we reach safe haven, by God, you'll wish you'd never been born."

Pike seized the moment to scramble away into the shadows.

In a hasty conference, the adventurers decided they had no

choice but to beat a swift retreat back over the mountains and into the safety of the jungle.

"Is that agreeable to you, sir?" Drake asked Rico.

"We can guide you back, if that is what you wish."

Evan noticed the hard glint in the Cimaroon's moon-silvered eyes. "Do you know of another alternative?"

Rico squared his shoulders. "We came to fight our Spanish tormentors. We are warriors. Will we give up so easily?"

The men who understood Spanish raised a chorus of denial. "He's right. The treasure's within our grasp."

"What can we do?" Drake asked.

Rico cleared his throat. "The first stop of the mule train is Venta Cruz, on the other side of the isthmus and north of Nombre de Dios. If we travel fast, we can reach the city before the alarm is raised there."

They covered the twenty-five miles in a matter of hours. Dawn tinged the horizon as they burst, howling, upon the city.

"*Qué gente?*" demanded the look-out guards at the city gate.

"Englishmen!" Drake roared. He drew his sword, the signal to begin the attack. The guards barely had time to be startled before their throats were slashed or their bodies pierced by arrows.

The Cimaroons killed with macabre glee. Evan had a dark understanding of their behavior. Were the roles reversed, a Spaniard would never offer a Cimaroon the mercy of a quick death.

Riding the tide of his stampeding comrades, Evan entered Venta Cruz through the city gates. They gathered in the dusty main plaza, weapons drawn and faces hot with blood lust.

"We'll sack the town." Drake's angry gaze swept the ranks of men. "Just to give them a taste of our power. You're not to lay hands on any woman, child, or unarmed man, is that understood?"

Men grumbled, even as they rushed off to break down doors or set fire to buildings.

Evan stood with Drake in the plaza. "They mislike your gallantry," said Evan.

"They'll respect it if they know what's good for them. Let's be after the pillaging."

Evan wanted to close his ears to the shrieks and prayers of the besieged townspeople. "No. The trains still have to make their way from Panama to Nombre de Dios. We'll have other chances."

Drake clenched his fist. "Will we? I wonder. All but the greatest of stubborn fools would cut their losses and run back to England. We do have no small amount of plunder from other raids, and the girl besides."

The thought of Annie gave Evan a jolt. He had kissed her, and she had cursed him. No doubt their failure would please her greatly. Pride and determination rose in him. "Francis," he said, "who's to say we're not the greatest of stubborn fools?"

Drake laughed. "Who indeed, my master? Aye, we'll—"

A chorus of female screams split the air, coming from a long, low building with its roof in flames.

"Let's go," Drake said.

Evan was already running. He ducked a charred swatch of thatching and battered at the door.

"It's locked from within," he said.

Drake hammered his fists on the stout pine door. "Open up! We've come to help you!"

"They're scared witless, Francis." Evan coughed as a wisp of smoke snaked into his lungs.

Drake nodded. "At the count of three."

Using their bare shoulders, they hurled themselves at the door. The hinges groaned. Timber splintered and plaster crumbled. The door gave way. His muscles knotted with exertion, Evan fell to his knees beside Drake.

Smoke stung his eyes. Squinting into the rectangular room, he saw a ward of women and babies. Low cots lined the walls on each side.

Drake blinked fast. "What is this place?"

A brown-robed nun snatched a large crucifix from the wall. Swinging it like a broadax, she came at the intruders.

Drake and Evan ducked.

Screaming invectives no nun should know, she renewed her attack. Evan jumped up and caught the wooden cross in mid-arc.

"Hold, Mother!" he yelled. "We've come to help." He wrenched the crucifix from her hands and flung it out the door. "If you wish for your friends to burn while you resist—"

"Prove your courage, Lutheran," the nun spat, "and get these women to safety." She ran to the first bed and snatched a swaddled babe from its mother's arms. "Lean on me, quickly," she said to the woman.

Drake and Evan hurried to help the others. "Is this a hospital?" Evan asked the woman he was helping.

"A—a birthing hospice," she gasped, swaying against him.

He grabbed the baby from her before she dropped it. The bundle felt impossibly tiny, yet fiercely alive, its elfin fists waving and screams pouring from its open mouth.

Evan, Drake, and the stout nun evacuated the women and infants, and a supply of foodstuffs besides. Behind them, the empty building burned.

The nun limped over to a toppled barrel that lay among the stores they had rescued. With an expert hand, she unbunged it, cupped her hands beneath the stream of wine, and drank deeply.

She looked up at Evan and Drake, motioning for them to partake. They eased their parched throats with the wine.

A gleam shone in the nun's eye. "That was communion wine."

"It's as wet as any I've tasted, Mother," said Evan.

"Blasphemer," she sneered, but her comment lacked the sharpness of a barb. She looked back at the burning hospice. "Why?" she asked.

Drake scowled. "Your country offends ours. We're honor bound to attack the cities of New Spain."

"That's not what I meant, pirate," she retorted. "Why did you risk yourselves to save us?"

Evan found it immeasurably sad that she expected nothing but cruelty from men.

Drake said, "An Englishman has no quarrel with women and children."

Evan saw a band of seamen heading for the food stores. "Leave that," he yelled, his implacable tone stopping them where they stood. "That's for the ladies."

The nun caught her breath. "Surely the Almighty never put life into two such tender pirates."

Drake and Evan exchanged a glance. "Us? Tender?" Drake asked. "Mother, you besmirch my reputation."

Just then, a shout came from the look-out tower. Rico waved his arms. "The reinforcements, three bow shots away."

"That's our signal to retreat," said Drake.

Evan bowed to the nun. Little richer, but with their spirits renewed by the triumph, the adventurers left Venta Cruz as quickly as they had entered it.

They traveled through the very heart of the Cimaroons' domain. No sane Spaniard would venture into these forests, where the very air seemed to seethe with hatred for the conquistadors. The raiders' pace quickened as they neared the spot where the *Pasco* and pinnaces rode at anchor in a hidden harbor.

"Ready for new work!" Francis declared.

His pronouncement had the hollow ring of failure.

Evan felt his strides lengthening, eating up the ground. He pretended he was not eager to see Annie, but the clamor in his heart mocked him.

A launch dropped from the *Pasco*. Dirk and Denton rowed it ashore. Evan took one look at their faces, and a heavy sense of dread began to roar in his ears.

"She's gone, isn't she?"

"How the devil did you manage to escape?" Rodrigo asked.

Annie selected an orange from the bowl on the table and

started to peel it. "As soon as the fleet moved from the island to the mainland, I made a plan. I waited until Drake and Carew took a band of men inland, and then I slipped into the water and swam away. My guards followed in a ship's boat, but I lost them easily in the dark."

Rodrigo emitted a thin whistle from between his teeth. He suspected that her matter-of-fact tone belied the terror she had felt, swimming through the shark-infested waters of the Gulf of Darien. "So Evan Carew is the man who called himself Arturo Reyes."

"Yes."

"And now he and his band of brigands are somewhere on the isthmus, plotting to attack and plunder the *recuas*."

"I believe that's their intent."

Rodrigo shook his head in disbelief. "They've got more nerve than common sense."

"Their lack of common sense has filled their holds with Spanish treasure," Annie reminded him. She chewed thoughtfully on a section of orange. "They're men of long memory."

"San Juan de Ulua, still?"

"Yes, still."

"There's a difference now."

The hardness in his voice seemed to startle her. She wiped her hands on a napkin. "What do you mean?"

"They know about you, Annie. I don't know how they found out, but they know you're blood kin to the Queen of England."

"Yes."

He reached across the table and took both her hands in his. "Annie, forgive me, but I must know. Did they . . . hurt you? In any way?"

She scowled; then understanding broke over her sunbrowned face. "Not in any way, Rodrigo. They may lack common sense, but they're not fools."

Relief left him weak. If they had raped her . . . Annie winced, and he realized his grip had tightened painfully on her hands. "I'm sorry. I had to ask. But why didn't they hasten straight to England with you?"

"Drake's pride, I think. He won't leave New Spain until he has the treasure he came for."

Rodrigo gazed across the table at his best friend's daughter. Losing Phillip had been hard, yet in some ways what Rodrigo was about to do was even more difficult. Ever since Annie had sneaked back into his life and told of her adventures as a captive of English pirates, he had known he must alter their lives forever. He must put away his own dreams and desires to protect Phillip's daughter the only way he knew.

"Annie."

"Yes?" She looked expectant. Candlelight flickered over her, and he saw how she had changed. Her hair had grown past her shoulders. The island sun had turned her skin a warm golden color. The last traces of baby softness had disappeared from her cheeks. He was startled to realize that she had become every inch a woman.

"We must do something to keep you from falling prey to English hunters again."

"We know they're about. We'll be more cautious now."

"No. That's not good enough. Carew had us all fooled for awhile. It could happen again. I'm speaking of something permanent and irrevocable."

A nervous laugh burst from her. "I don't like the sound of that. The only permanent, irrevocable state I know of is death."

Her macabre humor grated on his nerves and fed his anxiety. "Annie." He summoned the words from the hard, icy resolve that sat in his heart. "I'm speaking of marriage."

Her mouth dropped open. She snatched her hands away. "Marriage!"

"It's the one way to render you worthless to those who intrigue to use you. You must marry a Spaniard, someone who lacks even a drop of royal blood. That way, you'll be useless as an heir to the throne. The English never could abide Mary Tudor and her Spanish husband. They won't allow foreign influence to taint the monarchy again."

The natural glow had faded from her cheeks. "This is ridiculous. I have no wish to marry, and especially not for such a flimsy reason."

"I'm afraid your wishes have nothing to do with this. I'm your guardian. I have the power to force my will upon you if you resist."

She blinked fast, stubbornly refusing to weep, for which he was thankful. "You're a stranger to me, Rodrigo. I've known you all my life, and yet when you speak of forcing your will on me, I feel I don't know you at all."

"These are extraordinary circumstances. I'm compelled to take extraordinary measures."

Her widened eyes held a world of hurt and distrust. Rodrigo felt himself being hurled back into the past, remembering the day she had smiled her first smile, toddled her first steps, lost her first tooth. The day she had started her womanly courses, trying to be brave though she was convinced she was dying.

Then, she had regarded him with love and trust. Now, she stared at him as if he were a church inquisitor. He felt the loss of her esteem like a wound to the soul.

"Assume I agree to your outrageous plan," she said. "Assume I consent to marry a Spaniard to shield myself from the English. How will I explain to my husband that I wed him for those reasons?"

"You won't have to explain," Rodrigo said. "He already knows."

She slapped her palms on the table and stood. Rodrigo had never seen the Tudor queen, but in Annie he recognized the fierce pride and unbending will Elizabeth was reputed to possess. "You mean you've already found some hapless dupe to participate in this farce?"

"Yes."

She sank back into her chair. "Who?"

Rodrigo dragged in a deep breath. He thought of the woman asleep upstairs, the woman he loved, the woman he wanted to marry.

I'm sorry, Valeria.

"Well?" Annie prompted sharply. "I'm waiting. Who are you going to force me to marry?"

Rodrigo reached across the table and laid his hand upon hers. "Me."

Drake and his men had captured a Spanish supply ship and a frigate, enlarging their fleet as they increased their hopes for the new venture.

"We'll do it right this time," Drake vowed, jabbing a charred stick into the caulking of the frigate he had commandeered. "And if Pike moves so much as an eyebrow before the whistle sounds, I'll wring his neck. We'll hit the mule train just a mile to the north of Nombre de Dios."

"Sounds risky to me," said John Oxenham. "Why so close to the city?"

"They'll be off their guard," Evan said, enthusiasm pushing through the sense of loss that had plagued him since discovering the disappearance of Annie. He did not add the other reason he and Drake had chosen this course: After seizing the treasure, he would steal into the city and find her.

If she had managed to return. He ground his teeth together as he imagined her attacked by sharks, drowned, or made a captive of jungle outlaws. Damn! He should never have agreed to wait months before taking her to England.

Drake said, "We'll strike from a forest along the trail."

"We need more men," Oxenham said flatly. "Even counting the Cimaroons, our numbers are too few."

A whistle from the lookout brought them rushing to the rail.

"A sail," said Drake. "We'll make for it."

They closed in on the alien ship. A dozen white flags of truce flew from the masts.

"It's a trick," said Drake.

"Perhaps," said Evan. "There's only one way to find out."

Coming about, they presented their broadside to the ship and aimed all guns at it. A launch dropped from the foreign vessel and the rowers made for the frigate.

"I am Guillaume le Testu, in the service of France," a thin man bellowed from the ship's boat.

"A Frenchman?" Drake asked.

"A fellow privateer," Evan said. "Francis, he could be the answer to our prayers."

And he was. Le Testu, in command of seventy men who were hollow-eyed from lack of water and food, fell to his knees in thanks when Drake offered his stores.

The ravenous Frenchmen fell upon salt beef and fresh water. Though he staggered with weakness, their commander produced a gilt scimitar and presented it to Drake. "This belonged to Admiral Gaspard de Coligny. I would be honored if you would accept it."

"The honor is mine." Drake's eyes shone. Coligny was a famed Protestant whose convictions were known throughout England.

Drake and Evan waited while Le Testu ate. At last, he blotted his lips with incongruous delicacy. "I am a navigator and a pilot," he said. "I despise Spain and her church."

"You're a Huguenot?" Evan asked.

"I am." A dark look passed over the Frenchman's face. "You have not heard?"

"Heard what?"

"August last, on the feast of Saint Bartholomew, the French queen, that pox-ridden de Medici whore, arranged the assassination of Admiral de Coligny. Her henchmen botched the murder, but managed to create a panic among the Catholics." Le Testu drew a shuddering breath. "Thousands of Protestants were slaughtered. Men, women, babies. The streets ran with innocent blood."

The news hit the Englishmen like a round of heavy shot. Stares of horror and disbelief clung to Le Testu.

He nodded bleakly. "Spanish intolerance spreads like plague. Who knows where Protestants will be murdered next?"

"So you came to the New World to save yourselves," Drake said.

"And also to take revenge." Le Testu sighed. "I claimed a few prizes, but luck deserted us some weeks ago."

"It's found you again." Drake pulled back his lips in a fierce smile. "Join us, *mon capitaine*, and we'll teach you how an Englishman takes revenge."

Twenty picked Huguenots, fifteen Englishmen, and Rico with his Cimaroons set out on the mission. At the mouth of the *río* Francisco, they concealed their captured Spanish frigate in a sheltered cove and slipped upriver in a pair of shallow draught pinnaces.

Six men stayed with the boats, hiding along the reedy banks of the sluggish river.

"Give us four days," Drake said, ignoring the hissing rain that spattered the forest. Drenched to the skin, his red hair plastered to his head and his boots waterlogged, he raised his fist. "I swear we'll return a party of rich men."

Guided by the Cimaroons, they marched through the jungle toward the treasure route leading to the city. Before long, the clicking and buzzing of the wilderness and the rush of the river Campos yielded to human sounds: the thud of caulking hammers, the whine of ropes through pulleys, the grind of launching gear, the shouts of longshoremen.

At first light, the rain let up and Evan saw the distant dockyards of Nombre de Dios. "They're assembling the treasure fleet," he said to Drake.

"Aye, poor sods. After we're finished with them, they'll not be needing so much tonnage."

Rico dropped from the tall tree he had climbed in order to keep watch. "The mule train's coming from Venta Cruz. About two hundred animals, I'd say, and forty-five soldiers."

The news held the adventurers frozen for a moment. To a man, they were seized by the grip of imminent battle.

"No mistakes this time," Drake said. "We'll not have another incident like the one instigated by Robbie Pike."

Remembering how Pike had been vilified for his drunken bungling, the adventurers nodded vigorously.

"Prime the muskets," Drake said. "Ready the bows and arrows. And, by God, if you value your immortal soul, wait for the signal."

The wait seemed endless. Evan had chosen a longbow. Use of the weapon was as natural to a Welshman as breathing. Anticipation held him in its grip. His nerves stretched as taut as the string on his bow. He felt alive, his senses alert, his determination a pulsing force within him.

The mule train lumbered along slowly. Drake let the vanguard pass, and from his hiding place in the jungle Evan could see the plodding muleteers and their escort of soldiers. He knew they had walked all night. They were weary and eager to end their journey.

They would do so sooner than expected.

Drake put his whistle to his lips. Evan aimed at a tall, haughty-looking mounted soldier. The Cimaroons gripped spears and bows. The musketeers trained their sights on the heavily armed militia men.

"Now!" whispered Evan.

The shrill whistle split the air.

Evan released an arrow. The tall soldier clutched at his neck, a stunned expression on his face as he toppled from his stumbling horse. Muskets popped, and Cimaroons let fly their spears. The natives' warlike yips and howls made the hapless muleteers cringe or scurry for cover.

How does it feel, Evan wondered, nocking another arrow, to have your worst nightmare come true?

Soldiers and muleteers alike panicked. While their comrades dropped like felled stags around them, they fled.

Drake's whistle shrilled again, three short blasts.

A cry of triumph burst from Evan as he leaped out of the trees and raced toward the road. A babble of French, English, and Cimaroon patois filled the air as the other raiders joined him in falling on the treasure.

The bewildered pack animals halted or simply milled aimlessly on the road. Several Negro muleteers lingered, and to Evan's grim gratification, they eschewed their loyalty to their Spanish masters, showing the raiders where the more valuable treasure was stashed and praising the Cimaroons for taking revenge.

A few stubborn soldiers made a stand. One of them wheeled his mount and charged, sword swinging and lips peeled back in a wrathful grin. He was bearing down on Rico. The Cimaroon threw his spear and ran, casting about frantically for another weapon. A killer instinct turned Evan's heart to stone, for he had seen the man before. He had been among the soldiers who had tormented Casilda on the day of her death. Drawing his own sword, he rushed at the Spaniard. Rico dodged out of the way and skidded for cover behind a wagon.

Le Testu, his épée glittering in the rising sun, ran forward and hamstrung the horse. The squealing mount crumpled, but its rider leaped clear. Even as he landed, he grabbed a loaded harquebus from a fellow soldier and discharged it.

With a look of disbelief on his face, the Frenchman clutched at his stomach and staggered back.

His temper aflame, Evan faced the Spaniard.

The soldier's bloody sword whined through the air. Droplets of Le Testu's blood sprayed Evan's face. The sharp, rusty taste of it seared him with hatred.

He ducked beneath the slashing blade, then jumped over the next one. He was not the Spaniard's equal in swordplay, but his fury purged him of fear or hesitancy.

He put the full force of his rage into his next lunge. For a split second, flesh and muscle and bone resisted. Then Evan's blade slid home, just beneath the man's rib cage.

The Spaniard's eyes bugged out. Incredibly, he still stood, the blood pulsing from his wound, his eyes hardening with sudden clarity.

"You!" he gasped out.

"I didn't think you'd recognized me."

"You . . . you're English!"

"Welsh. And you can take that thought to hell with you." Evan placed his foot on the man's chest, tugged his sword free, and walked away.

The battle had been won in only minutes. A dozen Spaniards and one Cimaroon lay dead. Le Testu and two others had been wounded.

Drake set about organizing the taking of the treasure. Men fell upon saddlebags, sacks, and wagons, crowing with triumph has they brought forth great bars of silver and gold.

Evan looked on with a curious detachment. The battle had cleansed the rage from him, and he could summon no greed for the treasure.

"Odd, isn't it?" asked Drake, coming to stand with him. "For four years we have fought for this moment. Now that it's here . . ."

He let his voice trail off, but Evan understood. Their labors had borne fruit. Their dreams had reached culmination. Once a dream was attained, then what?

"I'd best be about finding the girl," Evan said.

"Not now," Drake said, raising his voice above the tolling of the town bell. "The whole city's up in arms. We'd best make haste while we can."

Evan nodded. In truth, the battle had sickened him, and he did not relish the thought of stealing into town after Annie. "I'll see to the wounded."

There was more treasure than the raiders could carry off. "My bad knee aches," Denton declared. "It always does when a storm's about to break."

As if to confirm his predictions, birds whirred away out of sight and a fresh wind blew, turning up the undersides of the leaves. The raiders buried the silver in the forest. Later, they would retrieve the bars. Each man took as much gold as his strength could bear. Upon hearing foot soldiers and horsemen thundering up from the city, Drake gave the order to flee.

"Can you walk?" Evan asked Le Testu.

"No. Leave me." The urbane Frenchman, his face the color of clay, spoke with effort.

Evan forced a grin as the Spanish army drew closer. "A Welshman would never abandon a comrade-in-arms. Rico!"

The Cimaroon, straining beneath a sack on his back, came to help. Between them, they lifted Le Testu and staggered toward the forest. Just as the thick green darkness enveloped them, the vanguard of the Spanish contingent burst onto the road.

They ducked beneath the canopy of leaves and kept walking. "Think they saw us?" Evan asked.

"I don't know." Rico quickened his pace. "Hurry!"

When they had gone perhaps a mile, the skies opened and the wind ripped at the treetops.

"A gale," Evan said through clenched teeth. "Just what we need."

Le Testu moaned softly. The blood seemed to flow faster from his wound.

"He cannot go on." Rico stopped walking.

"What the devil would you have me do?" Evan demanded.

"A true friend would end his life now—quickly and cleanly."

"No." Evan's throat felt tight. "Look, we'll hide him by the river and come back for him in a pinnace."

"He'll not last the night," Rico warned.

Evan was already dragging Le Testu into the shelter of a broad-leafed palm.

"Heed what the savage said," the Frenchman gasped out. "The wound is mortal."

Tight-lipped, Evan put a water flask and dagger beside Le Testu. "If it please God, my friend, and even if it doesn't, I'll come back for you."

Le Testu attempted a smile. "Ah, so young. So fierce. Take care what vows you make, my friend. For you are the type who will keep them—even when you would do better to break them."

The raiders stood in a line at the bank of the river.

"The pinnaces are gone," John Oxenham said, fingering his wiry beard. His shoulders sagged beneath the weight of the gold bars he carried, and an air of melancholy pulled at his mouth.

Heads nodded in bleak acceptance of the catastrophe.

The river, overflowing its banks in the aftermath of the gale, churned with huge logs and uprooted trees.

"They've been captured," Oxenham added glumly.

Drake's temper snapped. "Sir, they have not!" His arm shot out, and he grasped Oxenham by the sodden front of his shirt. "They were swept downriver by the gale, I tell you, and any man who dares to say otherwise will answer to me."

Oxenham jerked away, his own temper sprung. "Damn it, Francis, what can it matter whether they were swept away or seized? Either way, we're stranded. The Spaniards will put a patrol out to sea, and others will come searching by land."

Mutters of discontent rippled through the ranks of men.

"We'll get ourselves downriver and meet the pinnaces," Drake said.

"How?" Oxenham demanded, sweeping his arm at the violently foaming current.

"Aye, how, Captain?" a few others echoed.

Evan's nerves flared with the tension of the moment. Drake was hovering on the brink of defeat—again. Unwilling to let doubts hurl them into failure, he strode down the riverbank and plunged out into the rushing brown water. The current dragged at him, and the mud sucked at his boots, but he gritted his teeth and reached for a broken log. Le Testu lay wounded a mile back, and every moment brought the gallant Frenchman closer to death.

"What the devil are you doing?" Oxenham demanded.

Without hesitation, Drake struck out after Evan. Unlike Oxenham, he needed no explanation. Together, he and Evan grabbed a large floating log and dragged it toward the bank. "Building a raft," Drake shouted, his anger gone.

An hour later, on a lashed-together raft with a sail fashioned of biscuit sacking, Evan and Drake pushed out into the swift water. Drake turned to the grim-faced men on the bank. "My masters, I swear to you, by one means or another, and if I have to fight every Spaniard in the empire, I will come back for you."

His words reminded Evan of Le Testu's caution. *Take care what vows you make, my friend.*

Francis, too, was the type to keep them.

For hours they sailed downriver, as night turned into day

again. The heat parched their throats and the sun seared their skin. At last they reached the mouth of the river, drove the craft onto the bank, and stumbled ashore.

"We should work our way eastward," Drake croaked through his dry, split lips. "Aye, toward the anchorage of our frigate. Once we find it, you and I will steal into the city and find the girl again."

The mention of Annie enclosed Evan in a sense of guilt. She had endured months of captivity; by her own resources she had escaped. Who was he to change the course of her life? Suddenly he wanted to be back in Wales, putting his share of the booty to good use. Owen Perrott would take more than his due, but at least the treasure would sate his greed for awhile.

And yet the prospect of never seeing Annie again created a hollowness inside Evan, an ache that reminded him of the pain of losing Casilda.

A sound whispered from the thick tangle of brush that fringed the shore. Flinging off his bleak thoughts, Evan grasped his dagger and turned toward the noise. He froze when he heard the ominous snap of a musket hammer.

Out of the woods stepped a slim Spanish warrior, head encased in a crested helm with visor closed, chest armored by a gleaming breastplate. The round little eye of the musket stared coldly at them.

"He'll only be able to get off one shot," Evan whispered. "Let him take me, for it's you the men depend on." He stepped in front of Drake to shield him.

The soldier advanced. His silence was more chilling than a war cry. Evan heard only the crunch of boots on sand, the faint creak of armor joints.

"Step aside, Evan," Drake said. "Don't sacrifice yourself for my sake."

Evan stood his ground. "If you die, so does the enterprise."

"And if you die," Drake countered, "Carew will strangle in the grip of Owen Perrott."

The soldier stopped about ten paces from Evan. Reaching up, he lifted off the helm and dropped it.

A cascade of red-gold hair flew like a banner on the wind. Evan's jaw dropped. *"Annie?"* He took a step forward.

Her grip tightened on the musket. "Stay where you are. Captain Drake, step out where I can see you. And put down your weapons."

Stunned, they obeyed. Evan's tension erupted into anger. "Well? Are you going to march us back to Nombre de Dios so they can roast us on the fires of the Inquisition?"

"Don't give her any ideas," Drake muttered.

She took another step forward. A strange, cold fire glinted in her eyes. For a moment, the look was so eerily reminiscent of Queen Elizabeth that Evan shivered.

"How did you find us?" he asked.

A short, humorless laugh escaped her. "Is this not the place of rendezvous you chose? The crew spoke freely of it."

A sinking feeling weighted Evan's gut. They had grown so accustomed to Annie's presence that they had long since stopped guarding their tongues in her presence.

"I have heard much of the superiority of English honor," she said. Keeping her gun trained on her quarry, she stooped and retrieved Evan's dagger from the sand. "Is it true?"

"What do you think?" Evan asked.

"Let's see." She pointed the dagger at his chest. "You disguised yourself as a Spaniard and stole the secrets of the treasure train from my guardian's offices. You supped at Rodrigo's table, partook of his goodwill, and threatened to kill me. If that's an example of English honor, then I find much to doubt."

"He's Welsh," Drake said hastily. "Everyone knows Welshmen are cheats."

Evan rolled his eyes toward his friend. "So much for loyalty, eh, Francis? Sometimes you do get on my nerves."

"Sorry." Drake cleared his throat. "Miss, I spoke out of turn. I tend to babble when I find myself at the wrong end of a musket. What I mean to say is, all English, and Welsh as well, are men of honor. If Evan practiced deception, he acted out of loyalty to his country. He is a man of his word."

"And you?" she asked.

Evan could not suppress a surge of admiration for her. She had more physical courage than most men he knew, yet never had she looked so womanly to him. Her hose-clad legs seemed endless, her loose hair a copper-bright halo around her fiercely beautiful face.

Drake bowed stiffly. "By all that I am, Annie Blythe, and by all that God made me, I never break a vow."

"Because you never make them?"

Drake's hand touched the pouch tied at his waist. The bag bulged with gold jewelry and precious stones from the plundered mule train. "I do. But not often, and never lightly."

"I see." Her still-cold gaze slipped over them. "What of blood oaths?"

"A blood oath, once made, is unbreakable," said Evan.

"Captain Drake?"

"It's as Evan says."

She hesitated, holding them with her disconcerting stare. "Very well," she said, "hold out your hands. Palms up."

Evan and Drake exchanged a dubious glance.

She pressed the muzzle of the musket even closer. "Do it!"

They obeyed. Annie Blythe struck so swiftly that Evan felt no pain until blood oozed from the dagger wound she had inflicted on his palm.

Then she applied the blade to Francis. He drew in his breath with a hiss.

With an air of satisfaction, Annie raised her chin. Her voice flat and unrepentant, she said, "I want you to make this blood oath in the name of Saint George, England, Wales, and Elizabeth Tudor."

"It is done," Drake said. Growing ever more curious about her purpose, Evan nodded his accord.

"You will swear that, no matter what occurs, you will never reveal my true identity to a single soul."

Evan spread his fingers and watched his blood drip into the sand. What the devil was she about?

"Swear it!" she ordered.

Panic flashed in Drake's eyes. His quest had been to find her; success would assure his future. "Miss, we—"

"It is done," said Evan, and reluctantly Drake echoed him.

"Fine," she said briskly. "When we get to England, you'll find me a discreet place from which to observe my aunt. I'll decide when and if to approach her. But no one there must ever know who I am."

Her meaning took Evan's breath away. "You're coming to England with us?"

"Yes, but on *my* terms, not as some pirate's captive masquerading as your whore."

Evan blinked. Beneath her hard, brave words, he detected real pain. He had hurt her. Guilt welled from him like blood from the cut on his palm.

"Annie, I never meant—"

"Swear it!"

"It is done," they said in unison. Once again, Le Testu's words haunted Evan. *Take care what vows you make. . . .* Questions burned in Evan's mind, but he stilled them. She was coming to England with them. For now, that was enough.

She dropped the dagger, shouldered the musket, and struck out eastward. "I suppose you're looking for your pinnaces," she said over her shoulder.

Evan and Drake retrieved their weapons and hurried after her.

With an air of smugness, she pointed. "They're just past that headland, waiting for you."

Moments later, the three of them clambered aboard. The men's eyes widened at the sight of Annie, but no one spoke. Evan knew he and Drake looked the picture of defeat— empty-handed and sunburned, their clothes stiff with salt, their hair matted and beards overgrown.

An imp of mischief seized Drake. He put on his most sober expression and toyed with the strings of his pouch.

"There were no other survivors but you?" Denton asked hesitantly.

Only Evan knew the gleam in Drake's eye was not a tear. "Well," the admiral said. "Well, my masters." Blowing out a dramatic sigh, Drake pulled out a huge, gold quoit and tossed the ring to Denton.

Cautious joy bloomed on the faces of the men.

Drake threw back his head. His full-throated laughter seemed to ring for miles.

"My masters!" he shouted. "Our voyage is made!"

CHAPTER 12

Wales
1573

Annie had always thought hell to be a place of interminable heat. Now she knew better. Hell was cold. Hell was the knives of wind skirling down the strange, rugged heights of the Welsh mountains, tearing through her layers of clothes and lodging like ice daggers in her body.

Even the heat of the long-haired, sturdy pony she rode and the little gray cat riding in a sling at her waist failed to offer relief. Her hands, covered by leather gloves and woolen mittens, felt frozen around the reins.

Even more unbearable than the cold was her escort, Evan Carew. Riding along with her over the pitted track, he seemed to revel in the rugged terrain. He sat straight and proud, the color high in his cheeks, the merciless wind ruffling his black hair. Each time she looked at him, she found her gaze wandering to his lips and remembered the time he had kissed her.

That moment, tense and fraught with uncertainty, had lingered in her mind for months. Only in the most private corner of her mind would she admit that the kiss had contributed to her decision to leave Rodrigo. Evan's sudden, swift embrace had opened her awareness to a world of passion—and a desire she knew she would never find with her guardian.

"How much farther?" she asked, barely moving her stiff, chapped lips.

"Another mile or so. Round the next bend, we'll see Castle Carew, and the town's below that." He gestured at a hill gouged by caves and hollows. "When I was a boy, I used to sneak off and play up there. I must've hidden a hundred treasures in those caves."

"Treasures?" she asked.

"Bits of flint, a seashell or two. A rack of antlers sometimes." He swiveled in his saddle to gaze in pride at the two pack animals tethered by lead reins to his horse. "Now I've found myself a real treasure."

"Congratulations. I hope your travail was worthwhile."

He scowled at her flippancy. "Men paid in blood for this treasure. I'll not forget that."

She fell silent, recalling that he had befriended a Frenchman during the raid, only to discover that the wounded man had died alone in the woods. Evan's silent grief had persisted all through the voyage to England. "A pirate knows well the risks he takes," she said.

"Ah, Annie. So dour. So it's been with you since the day we swore our oath. And you've still not told me why you decided to come to England."

"I don't share my private life with brigands," she said. "My reasons are nothing to you."

"Yes, they are."

"Why?"

He shrugged. "Thanks to your conditions, I'm stuck with you for Lord knows how long."

"Stuck with me," she whispered under her breath. *Just as Rodrigo had been.* The thought came to her like an arrow shot out of the dark. It lodged in her heart, chilling her even more pitilessly than the frigid Welsh weather.

The pain swept her back over the months to the night she had returned to Rodrigo's house. How naive she had been to think he would welcome her back and declare that nothing had changed.

Even now, she recalled the feelings that had gripped her upon hearing his plan to wed her. The initial shock had given way to a brief, bright joy.

Marry Rodrigo! Her girlish heart had sung with elation . . . But then she had looked at his hard, handsome face, into his cold, angry eyes. His offer was made not out of affection but out of a sense of duty to her father. In that instant, she had known Rodrigo viewed marriage to her as a sort of death sentence.

He loved Valeria, of course. Valeria was beautiful and gentle. Valeria was a lady. But Rodrigo, ever mindful of his vow to Phillip, had been willing to put aside his love for the sake of protecting Annie.

She refused to live her life knowing her husband loved another, even as he spoke his vows to her.

She shuddered and rubbed at the numb tip of her nose. The cat purred against her stomach. She stole another glance at Evan, his wind-chapped face expressionless. His disregard hurt.

"You can always change your mind," he said. Annie was certain she heard a note of hope in his voice.

The rocky flanks of the hills created weird, hollow echoes as if he spoke down a well.

"About what?" she demanded, though she knew perfectly well what he meant.

"My vow of silence."

"No," she forced out.

"Think of it, Annie. You'd have a place at court, sleep on a bed of ermine furs, eat all the dainty sweetmeats such as royalty favor—"

"And what would you know about the tastes of royalty?" she snapped.

He drew breath quickly, and she knew her barb had dug deep. "You've a sharp tongue, Princess," he spat.

"I've a mind of my own and would thank you not to presume that I hunger for luxury."

"Then stop that infernal shivering. Unless you long for furs and a warm fire."

"I long to be away from you," she snapped.

"By God, Annie, what befell you after you escaped?" he asked, the anger gone from his voice. "What's made you so bitter?"

She knew he did not expect an answer. He had pestered her with questions all during the long weeks of the voyage to England, and the longer days of their journey to Wales.

Saddles creaked as they approached a bend in the road. The sound of hooves and harness filled the silence.

Annie caught her breath at the sight that loomed round the bend. Castle Carew, Evan had called it. The stronghold seemed to grow like a mountain of stone from the crags overlooking the sea and the tidal creeks spread out like fingers at the base.

Thick walls, machicolated at the top, surrounded a gabled inner donjon. Beautiful mullioned windows decked the front of the main building. At each corner, a slender tower pierced the colorless sky. Cruciform arrow loops made an odd juxtaposition with the great half-round oriel windows. Threads of smoke streamed from chimneys here and there. A pair of men strolled idly along the ramparts, apparently uninterested in the travelers on the road below.

A castle, she thought, strangely thrilled by the sight. She had never seen the like. The crude plaster and timber forts of New Spain bore little resemblance to the time-worn splendor of Carew.

Annie glanced at Evan, expecting to see smug pride in his face, that the place of his birth boasted such an impressive stronghold.

Instead, she was shocked to see him staring at the castle with a bitterness so vivid she could almost taste it. His face seemed frozen, his wind-burnt skin stretched taut across his cheekbones, his eyes as bright and cold as obsidian.

"Evan," he said. "What—" The wind snatched at her words. She raised her voice and spoke again, wanting to know what had brought on that look of such implacable hatred. "Why do you glare at the place as if you wish it would crumble into the sea?"

"I have my secrets, too, Princess," he muttered.

In tense silence, they passed by the castle and descended into the town. The dwellings were cottages of stone with gray thatched roofs, most of which had smoke holes instead of chimneys. In the harbor floated a number of fishing vessels and one rather grand little cog with red sails. Evan's eyes narrowed and his lips thinned, but he said nothing. Beyond the town stretched bare orchards and wind-raked fields, some of them dotted with thick-coated sheep.

As the rocky path widened to a pitted road, Annie saw a few cows and pigs shambling about, the swine rooting in the mud. A dog barked sharply in hoarse alarm.

Almost at once, doors and gates swept open, and the street filled with excited people.

"Evan!"

Within moments, Annie found herself surrounded by a throng of smiling, shouting people. They spoke in English or in strange and lyrical Welsh. She did not have to understand their words in order to grasp their meaning. She had only to see the soot-smudged face of a grinning boy or the outstretched, supplicating hands of an elderly woman to know that Evan was some sort of hero to these people.

And as for Evan . . . She looked at his face across the expanse of bobbing heads and felt a shock at the change in his expression. His eyes shone with such love and tenderness that an ache rose in her throat.

Home. Evan Carew was home with people who loved him.

Calling for quiet, he lifted his arms. The babbling subsided, and he said, "This is Annie Blythe, come to stay with us. I hope you'll honor her with a grand welcome."

Annie forgot the cold as people looked at her, craning their necks as they attempted to see into her deep hood. From her dwindling reserves of strength, she summoned a smile and lifted her hand in an awkward wave.

"Well, Evan," said a black-haired, black-eyed man. Hands reached out to propel him forward. He held his head slightly cocked, and Annie realized that he was blind. "This is a surprise. You've brought many a curiosity to Carew since you took to the sea, but never a woman."

Evan ducked his head. For the first time since Annie had met him, he looked decidedly embarrassed. He said, "Aye, well, Father, you are right. She *is* a surprise."

His father. A handsome man, aglow with pride in the towering dark rider astride his horse. Annie had never thought about Evan's family. Now, as he leaned down to embrace his father, she sensed the powerful bond of their kinship.

An older man in brown cleric's robes shouldered his way forward, his chapped red hands clasped. "Welcome back, Evan."

"Thank you, Reverend." Evan gestured at the pack animals. "I daresay this lot will last many seasons."

"You've provided for all of us, God bless you." To Annie's amazement, the cleric took command of the treasure-laden ponies and led them off.

Questions swirled in her mind. Was Evan giving away his plunder? The saddlebags contained a veritable fortune. She had nursed her bitterness for weeks by telling herself he was no better than a common pirate, driven by the lust of greed.

If he gave his treasure away, what did that make him?

Following his lead, she went to a small house in the middle of the village. His father stopped at the dooryard gate and found the bridle of Annie's pony.

"I'll help you down, miss."

Unsurprised by the hard strength of his grip at her waist, she slid from the horse. After so many days of plodding along, she no longer felt weak in the knees or sore from sitting.

"Thank you," she said.

Evan led the animals away while his father hustled Annie inside. Despite his blindness, he found his way unerringly into a tiny, dim keeping room.

"I'm Anthony Carew," he said, "and you must be freezing." A merry smile curved his mouth. "Come warm yourself by the fire."

Annie set down the gray cat and dropped her cloak on a bench. The house had a planked floor, lime-washed walls, and two windows with panes of thin-shaven horn or shell. Other than that, she saw nothing but the glowing fire. The cat curled up beside it and went to sleep.

Tears of sheer, exhausted gratitude stung her eyes. She peeled off her mittens and gloves, then stretched out her hands toward the blaze. Anthony ducked through a low doorway, and she heard the clank of iron as he put a kettle on the kitchen fire.

And then Evan was beside her, his shoulder brushing hers. "Better?" he asked.

She nodded, though her fingers and toes stung as the heat thawed her blood. "You gave away your treasure," she commented.

"Aye."

"To the whole town?"

"Since the district came under the control of Owen Perrott, their tax burdens have been heavy. The common folk of Carew have never been wealthy, but Lord Owen seeks to ingratiate himself to the Crown by sending the queen rich grants."

"Lord Owen? He lives in Castle Carew?"

"Aye."

"He's a long way from court. Why does he concern himself so with the queen?"

"Because she had his father put to death."

A new sort of chill coursed through Annie's body. "Why?"

Evan's face turned grave. "Because John Perrott was Henry Tudor's bastard."

Annie squeezed her eyes shut. "Just like—"

"Your father," Evan finished for her. A speculative gleam lit his eyes. "I suppose that makes you kin to Lord Owen. Second or third cousin, would it be?"

"Why didn't you tell me this before?"

"We've stopped telling each other anything, haven't you noticed?"

Against Annie's will, a sound of distress escaped her. Evan touched her shoulder briefly, comfortingly. "It's been a long, hard journey. Let us cry peace, Annie, at least for awhile."

She subsided into silence and watched him from the corner of her eye. The flickering firelight played over the strong lines of his face, the sturdy bulk of his body. Her initial wariness melted into bright certainty. She felt a tug of longing to be close to him, but planted her feet and resisted the urge.

"This town is the whole reason you turned pirate, isn't it?"

"A few years back, famine and plague came hand in hand to Carew. Those who survived found themselves unable to contend with the tax collectors."

"So you volunteered to seek your fortune at sea."

"Aye, the task fell to me."

"And you succeeded."

"Does it offend you, Annie, that Spanish gold pays Welsh taxes and feeds the people of Carew?"

"Of course not," she said quickly, defensively. "But is England so poor a country that a man must play the thief in order to survive?"

"This isn't England. It's Wales."

They stood in silence for a time, listening to the snap and hiss of the fire, the sounds of Anthony laying the table in the kitchen.

"Your feet are soaking wet," Evan said.

She nodded. She had managed to find a puddle out in the dooryard. "They'll dry."

He drew a round stool to the fireside. "Sit down," he said, "and take off your boots."

She sat, but her tingling fingers worked clumsily at the leather laces.

"Ah, Annie." Evan spoke her name on a sigh and knelt in front of her. He unlaced her boots and slid them off, then peeled away her woolen stockings. His large, warm hands curled around her bare feet and rubbed them slowly, infusing them with warmth.

Annie sat still, certain she would burst if she even dared to breathe. Somehow, Evan Carew made the tending of cold feet a gesture of almost sinful intimacy.

And he knew it. When he raised his face to hers, she saw desire burning in his eyes. She couldn't decide whether she wanted to flee or to fling herself into his arms.

Evan took the decision away from her. Tucking her feet against his chest, he came up on his knees and touched his mouth to hers. His lips were cool and tasted of the wind and salt air. The light brush of them against her mouth struck her like a thunderclap, raising a fierce, desperate hunger inside her.

A sound of agony escaped her as she pushed her fingers into the dark silk of his hair. His tongue moved in an oddly familiar rhythm, in and out of her mouth, and then his teeth nipped gently at her lips. She pressed forward, shocked and fascinated by the clamorous hunger inside her. His taste and scent were indefinably alluring, the tenderness of his mouth a surprise. Tentatively, she touched her tongue to his and felt a warm burst of startling intimacy.

Groaning low in his throat, Evan pulled back, his hands upon her shoulders, his teeth gritted, and a look of stark horror in his eyes.

"I'm sorry," he said, his voice low and strained. "I should not have done that."

Bereft, she wrenched herself from his grip and planted her feet on the floor. "Then why did you?"

He pressed his palms hard against his knees. "Because you tempt me, Annie. You're brave and outrageous and quick of wit. I have wanted you since the first time I kissed you."

His words sang inside her head. "Then ... why did you stop?"

A half smile crooked one corner of his mouth. "You're a princess of the blood royal, and I'm but a common Welsh corsair."

For that, she had no answer.

A sharp rap at the door startled them both. A youth in an embroidered green tunic entered the house.

Evan surged to his feet. Annie fancied she felt the temperature drop, so cold was the glare he sent to the tall, slim youth.

"I don't recall inviting you in, Kendrick," he said.

Kendrick shrugged and stomped his boots. Clods of mud sprayed the floor. "Lord Owen sent me. You're to bring your guest to the castle at once."

Evan's ears flamed with the sudden color of his temper. "Oh, aye? And what does his lordship want with me and my guest?"

Kendrick turned up his palms. "It's not a servant's place to ask why. Nor, for that matter, is it yours."

Anthony stepped to the kitchen doorway. Fear had paled his face and pulled his features taut. What was it that frightened him, Annie wondered, the summons, or Evan's reluctance to obey?

Evan, too, looked at Anthony. Though blind, the father seemed to sense his son's turmoil. A decision seemed to firm between the two men. "We'll come at once," Evan said crisply.

Wearing a pair of over-large, borrowed boots and thick woolen socks, Annie hurried to match Evan's long, angry strides across the inner ward of Castle Carew. He heard the quickness of her breathing, but was not sufficiently moved to slow his pace.

"Evan, answer me," she said. "What can the lord of Carew possibly want with us? Surely he can't know—"

"Of course not. Doubtless he means to seize his share of the treasure before it's gone." Evan knew there must be more, but did not want to embroil her in his years-old feud with Owen. He despised the fact that Owen would seize the treasure Evan had risked his life to win, yet he had no choice but to surrender the lord's portion.

"I think it has to do with that grand-looking ship in the harbor," Annie said.

Damn. Did the woman miss nothing? Evan, too, had been speculating about the cog. It was obviously the vessel of a nobleman; that alone was enough to rouse Evan's suspicions.

"Possibly."

"Tell me why the queen had his father put to death."

He stopped walking and turned to face Annie. "He was a threat to her power. To protect his own neck, Owen ingratiates himself to the Crown, but he'll never forgive the queen. So be careful around him, Annie. Guard what you say to Owen Perrott."

She caught her breath, and the fresh color drained from her cheeks. "I shall. Count on it."

They reached the great, iron-studded door to the hall. Evan put his hand on the latch. Memories rushed like storm clouds over him, reviving the old feelings of terror and frustration. With an effort of will, he beat them back, for if he submitted to the past, if he became again the lad who had lived in this castle so long ago, he would be lost.

Schooling his face into a bland expression, he held the door wide for Annie, stepped in beside her, and shut the door with a resounding thud.

She stood still, taking in the rib-vaulted ceiling, the dazzling colors of tapestries and hangings on the walls, the long tables spread with an embarrassment of food, a half dozen well-fed people eyeing them curiously.

"Come!" a resonant male voice called. Owen sat in a carved, canopied chair on a raised dais at the far end of the hall. Beside him waited a black-cloaked man who stood with his hands pushed into his sleeves and a broad-brimmed hat shadowing his face.

Annie gasped. "Is that an inquisitor?" she hissed.

"We don't have them in England." Evan could not say why, but he took Annie's hand in his. Her fingers were icy and trembling. He almost pitied the girl, who had known only the balmy warmth of the Indies. How cold she must find it here; how strange the people must seem to her.

He crushed the soft feeling of sympathy. She had forced him to swear to keep her identity secret. If she suffered, let her warm herself with thoughts of the luxury she could enjoy if she would present herself to her aunt, the queen.

As they approached the dais, Owen's face came into sharp focus. Time had been kind to Owen Perrott, the years only touching him with a gentle brush that flattered his boyish good looks. His face was the image of high Welsh nobility: fine-drawn features, an almost delicate nose and mouth decked with a well-groomed mustache. His chestnut hair was glossy and thick, framing his cold eyes, his smiling mouth.

Evan knew that face as well as his own. And he knew the sharp mind behind the pale gray eyes as he knew the pain in his own soul.

With his father dead and the power of office in his hands alone, Owen was more dangerous than ever. As dangerous as the beautiful, hooded hawk that perched on the back of his chair.

The slate-colored eyes swept over Annie, and Owen sat forward slightly. Despite his boyish looks, Owen was a man now, with a man's appetites. The hunger in his gaze was unmistakable. If Owen tried to make Annie his leman, it would be his last act on earth, for Evan knew he would kill him.

They stopped in front of the dais. Though it rubbed against the grain of his pride, Evan forced himself to sink down on one knee, then rise slowly.

Annie made a perfunctory curtsy, clearly undecided as to what, if any, deference she owed the young Welsh lord. Her hood fell back and her red-gold hair spilled out.

What Evan saw on her face was as predictable as it was disappointing. The woman had not been born who was immune to Owen's lush handsomeness, his easy charm. She stared at him in wonder, as if he were an archangel come to earth for the sole purpose of pleasing her.

Owen summoned the full force of his allure as he levered himself out of the thronelike chair. He paused to stroke the throat of the hawk, then stepped down to take Annie's hand in his.

"My lady." He lifted her hand and held it close to his smiling lips. "Word came from town that Evan Carew brought a treasure from the Indies, but I had no notion that it would be the priceless prize I see before me now."

Evan heard her soft gasp of surprised pleasure as Owen pressed a lingering kiss on her hand.

"Mistress Blythe is weary from our journey," Evan said brusquely. "What is it, my lord, that is of such urgency that you'd not grant her the time for a meal and a good night's sleep?"

"Aye, well, she's not likely to find that in your father's house, is she?" Owen lifted one eyebrow in blatant challenge.

Evan refused to pick up the gauntlet. He had endured far worse taunts from Owen. When they clashed—and he had no doubt that they would one day—Evan would not let it be over so trivial a matter. The reason would involve decades of enmity, not one snide remark.

"My lord, just what is it that you're suggesting?" he asked.

Owen lifted his fair face to the torch glow. He seemed confident that the golden light enhanced his male beauty, the burnished sheen of his hair, the whiteness of his teeth. "Why, that she stay here, as my guest."

Suspicion and resistance twisted in Evan's gut. No one was supposed to know Annie's identity. No one save he and Drake. Would Owen be so free with his hospitality if he thought Annie a mere commoner?

No. Evan knew the man too well. Owen Perrott never did anything save for his own benefit.

Evan's face went stiff, his eyes stony. "On the contrary, my lord, Mistress Blythe will stay with me."

"I think not." For the first time, the cloaked figure beside the dais spoke. He stepped forward, removing his hat. "The young lady will stay here, at Castle Carew."

Feeling like a wolf in the jaws of a trap, Evan found himself gaping at the haughty face of André Scalia.

"Am I to have no say at all in my own fate?" Annie demanded, glaring at the two men who sat with her in a private solar of Castle Carew. Evan and the man called André Scalia had brought her here. The young lord in the great hall had been more interested in collecting his share of Evan's booty from the village priest.

"I'm afraid not," André said, though no note of apology softened his words. He was truly an unusual-looking man. Old, but not elderly, his spare features marked by a severity that was more commanding than handsome. Clean, slim hands, the long fingers aglitter with golden rings. And a pair of night-black eyes that cut her like a blade.

"By what right do you keep me here?" she demanded, determined not to be intimidated.

He pressed his palms on the table. "I've no patience for games or pretense, my lady. You are the granddaughter of Henry the Eighth, and as such you will live as befits your status."

Cold horror washed over Annie. She came out of her chair and faced Evan, who sat at the end of the table. "You bastard," she hissed. "You betrayed me. You took a blood oath—"

"No," Evan shot back, talking to André. He leaned over the deep-grained surface of the table and glared into the noble, ascetic face.

Who had informed André of the truth? Annie wondered. Could Owen Perrott have found out? Or had Drake himself betrayed his sworn word?

"How is it that you have come to this bizarre conclusion about Annie?" Evan asked cautiously.

André took a long, unhurried drink of his wine. He spoke to Annie first. "The decision to seek you out was not entered into lightly," he said. "The men chosen to accomplish the task are not known to be bunglers."

Evan Carew and Francis Drake, Annie thought. Damn them and their reputation as thieves.

"I demanded anonymity as a condition of my cooperation," she said, enunciating each word.

"My lady, they did not betray you. No one else in the realm—save me—knows who you are."

"And how, pray, do you know if Evan and Francis kept their word?"

A thin smile curved his mouth like a sickle. "My chief business for the past fifty years has been intrigue. When I heard that Drake had returned with his holds full of Spanish treasure, I hastened to Plymouth. Imagine my surprise when I learned that a young woman had accompanied the adventurers home. Truly, we had all assumed the lost heir to be male, but I quickly realized who you were."

"Why did you not come forward then, in Plymouth?"

"My role is to be played in utter secrecy. Besides, when Evan and Drake started out, the matter of finding you was urgent. Now, our need is not so great. We're in no hurry to reveal you to the queen."

Annie drew herself up. "*I* will decide when—and if—I am to meet the queen."

André lifted one eyebrow. "Your show of spirit does not come amiss."

Evan paced the floor, scattering the rushes. "When we left, England and Spain were on the brink of open war. Now I gather the queen has all but bent herself in half making peace with the king of Spain."

For the first time, Annie saw a flicker of emotion in André's eyes. Raw, icy anger. Why? Would a war with Spain please him?

André's nostrils narrowed as he inhaled sharply. "Her Majesty is honor bound to keep the peace whenever possible. If conciliation with Spain is the price, so be it."

"Then the fact that we sailed in with a load of Spanish treasure is bound to upset the balance," Evan suggested. "What will the queen do? Give it back with apologies?"

André Scalia laughed, a rich, throaty sound that took Annie by surprise. "The day the queen gives back such a treasure is the day the moon turns black."

"But how will she keep it and still avoid the wrath of Spain?" Annie asked.

André paused to study her. He murmured, "You have much to learn, my dear. Elizabeth will keep the treasure by the same method she has kept her crown these past fifteen years."

"By lying, cheating, shameless manipulation," said Annie.

"And by her irresistible charm," André added. " 'Tis a more formidable weapon than legions of trained soldiers."

Evan stopped pacing to rake his hand through his hair. "Drake went to Ireland because you ordered it, didn't he?"

Annie knew the answer before André spoke. Drake had spent just one night in Plymouth with his wife. Annie remembered Mary Newman Drake with uncomfortable clarity. Timid and pale, she had regarded her bluff, flame-haired husband as if he were a stranger. She had seemed almost relieved by his sudden departure to Ireland, where he would join the Earl of Essex in putting down the rebels.

Marriage to a man of the sea was no marriage, but a sentence of interminable waiting and uncertainty. For each year of their marriage, Annie suspected Mary Drake had spent a week or less in her husband's company. It was a life no woman could possibly crave.

"I have no capacity to give orders to such as Francis Drake," said André.

"Ah, then you suggested it. A long stint in Ireland so the queen doesn't have to hang him to appease Spain."

"Aye, it would be a shame to lose such a useful man of the sea. I'd advise you to keep yourself out of sight as well, my friend. You've not gained Drake's notoriety, but some might know you."

Like Rodrigo, Annie thought. A familiar dull ache pounded in her chest as it always did when she remembered him and their last terrible night together. How cold he had been even as he had proclaimed his intent to marry her.

Now, eyeing the strange, vaguely forbidding André Scalia, she began to think she should have taken the offer.

No. Never could she marry a man who loved another, be it the sea or a woman.

"You've still not explained why you followed me here," she said. "As a female, I'm useless to you. Only a male heir can matter to the queen."

André pressed his hands together, joining them at the fingertips. "At the moment, my dear, Elizabeth's chief heir is

Mary Stuart, a Catholic loyal to France. In her mind, a monkey is preferable to stand in line for the throne."

Annie threw up her hands. "Then go find a monkey. I want no part of intrigue."

"You are part of intrigue, like it or not."

Annie opened her mouth to retort, but he held up his hand. "However, given that relations between England and Spain are stable now, and given that the queen's health is much improved, I think we can wait before presenting you to her. Although the possibility is doubtful, she might yet marry and give birth, in which case you'd be worthless."

"By God, you talk as if Annie were a chess piece on a board," Evan burst out. In two strides he crossed the room to her. Standing behind her, he gripped her shoulders. "Damn it, André, *look* at her. She's flesh and blood, a young woman with her whole life ahead of her. Will you keep her waiting like a kenneled hunting dog? Keep her shackled by eventualities that might never come to pass?"

Annie was shaken by the intensity in Evan's voice, in his touch. Was it pity, or something stronger, that brought him leaping to her defense?

André rose slowly from the table and took Annie's hands in his, drawing her from Evan's grip. André's fingers chilled her, but she forced herself to meet his eyes.

"My dear, Evan argues heatedly but unwisely on your behalf. You'll stay here at Castle Carew, to be treated as a noble guest. I, too, shall stay on as your protector and adviser. You'll live as a lady of rank. And I promise you, the moment Elizabeth needs you no longer, you'll be free to go."

Go where? Annie found herself thinking. She could not return to Rodrigo, for he must be free to make a life with Valeria. Not to Hispaniola, for the Inquisition had a long memory and would surely seize her as it had her grandparents.

"Very well," she said at last, pulling her hands from his grip. "I'll stay here for now."

"How much does Owen know?" Evan demanded.

"Nothing, save that Mistress Blythe is of gentle but obscure birth. I advanced the theory that she's fleeing an unwanted marriage, and he rather liked the role of protector."

The ache in Annie's chest took on a sharp edge, for the story struck close to the truth.

"For our purposes, she is my ward," André concluded. "And I am here to investigate the disappearance of some Crown revenues."

"What disappearance?" Evan asked.

"It seems a band of brigands keeps seizing the taxes Lord Owen sends to London. Until we apprehend the thieves, I'm to stay here. With my ward."

Evan stepped in front of her. He put his finger beneath her chin and raised her face to his. She felt a soft shock of awareness, and suddenly the ache in her chest began to burn—not for the life she had left behind, but for the feelings that coursed through her when Evan touched her.

"What say you, Annie?" he asked. "Is this arrangement agreeable to you?"

"It seems not to matter." She measured each word as she gazed into his strong, ruddy face. She could possibly convince him to take her back to his home in the village. Even as part of her yearned to go with him, another part, alert to danger, urged caution. She was drawn to this pirate, to his rough charm and unusual sense of honor. It would not do to become too familiar with him. Besides, she rather doubted that André Scalia would agree, and he seemed a man accustomed to getting his way.

"I think I shall stay," she whispered. "For now."

He dropped his hand. His face changed almost imperceptibly. His eyes hardened and grew distant. "I'll take my leave, then." He turned to André. "So help me God, if I hear even a whisper of impropriety, sir, I'll slit your throat."

André lifted one white eyebrow. "And indeed you'd be justified, sir. Mistress Blythe is a treasure. She'll come to no harm, I assure you."

Evan left, banging the door behind him. The sound echoed with such a ringing finality that Annie felt a sense of panic. She flung herself after him, racing down a dim corridor to a doorway that led out into the bailey.

She found him there, striding toward the gate, scattering a flock of chickens with heedless arrogance.

"Evan!"

He turned back. The wind ruffled his midnight hair and molded the tunic to his broad chest.

Breathless, she stopped in front of him. "You left so suddenly."

"Oh? Should I have lingered over our farewell like a love-sick swain in a penny drama?"

His anger lashed at her. "That's not what I meant, and you know it. I simply wish to know your plans. Will you stay in Carew?"

"Perhaps. Or I might join Francis in Ireland. I haven't decided yet."

"Oh." She kicked at a small gray stone. "Farewell, then. Wherever you go."

He muttered something Welsh. A curse, by the bitter sound of it. In English, he said, "I'll stay in the village for awhile. Until I'm certain André means to keep his word and Owen—" He seemed to catch himself. He closed his mouth and looked away.

"What about Lord Owen? He's a stranger to me, yet you must know him well."

"I do. Be careful of him, Annie. He's got a pretty face and a ready wit, but he's not to be trusted."

Annie pondered the edge in Evan's voice and wondered what it meant. "He seemed the perfect gentleman to me."

"So he seems to most people—especially women. But he has ambitions to raise his status in the realm, and possibly to avenge his father's death. If he finds out who you are, he will use you for his own ends."

"He wouldn't be the first," she said bitterly.

"Don't tempt him, Annie. He has a cruel streak."

"That's silly. I'd almost say you were jealous. You seem to be of an age with him. Were you friends?"

He stared at her for a long time. The wind whistled through the empty turrets and stirred the dust in the yard.

"We were not friends." Evan took a deep breath. "Yet I know him well, Annie," he said. "You see, I was his whipping boy."

CHAPTER 13

The bitter winter yielded slowly to chilly spring, and André Scalia watched his young charge with the jealous attention of a mother fox with a prized kit. Even as he stood looking out a mullioned window, he watched her reflection in the glass. She sat at a long table, idly stroking a moth-eaten gray cat with one hand and writing with the other.

In some ways, her previous life had molded her character so that she was accustomed to change. She slid into her role as André's genteel young ward as effortlessly as a bard into court, adjusting her speech and manners to match those of Owen's household.

Unlike Drake, Evan Carew had stayed in the vicinity, caring for his blind and aging father. He came to the castle from time to time, bringing grievances from the villagers. This was all a pretext, of course. Evan did not trust Owen Perrott with Annie.

Evan was making certain she lived in comfort and safety, secret though her identity remained. Yet he kept his distance, and this pleased André. A powerful attraction existed between the vagabond princess and the handsome Welshman; any fool with eyes could see that. It wouldn't do to let anything come of their tasteless melodrama of unrequited love. André was grooming Annie for a life at court and possibly the throne of England. He'd not let a common seaman ruin her for the sake of a few stolen kisses.

It would have been simple enough to bar Evan from the castle and forbid them to see each other; André was far too wise to choose that course. He knew better than anyone that the lure of the forbidden was far more compelling than commonplace familiarity.

Their host, Owen Perrott, was all too eager to ingratiate himself with one of the queen's advisers, and he proved a congenial young lord. He had convinced himself that he had been chosen to guard the virtue of a well-born young woman, and he reveled in his role as protector.

"André?"

The soft query drew him from his contemplation of a distant flock of sheep out the window. He turned back to the light-filled solar. Annie held out a freshly inked parchment.

"I'm finished," she said.

He took the page and pretended to scan her translation of Cicero. Instead, he studied her. Truly, she was enchanting. Her hair had grown long and wavy, spilling over her shoulders in a rich red-gold cascade. He had provided her with several costly coifs with which to cover her head, but she had developed a habit of losing them no matter how firmly her maid pinned them in place. He had also provided dresses, fine silk velvets and Spanish merino wools in deep jewel tones. The country woman who sewed them had little talent for fancywork, and so the gowns bore scant ornamentation save a few simple tucks and slashes. Yet the plain style suited Annie. She possessed an elusive appeal that had less to do with face and figure and more to do with the glitter of intelligence in her eyes and the sudden, rare spark of her smile. A family trait, André realized.

"You've done well with this translation," he said, always reserved in his praise for her.

"Horseshit, André."

He pursed his lips. She often tried to shock him with her seaman's language—another trait she shared with the queen, though he had not told her so. "Indeed?" he asked smoothly.

"It's an outstanding translation. Tell me you've read better."

"I have."

"Oh?" She slid one eyebrow upward. "By whom?"

"By the queen."

Annie sniffed. "You're dazzled by her, just like those other men who bow and scrape to her—Leicester and Hatton and Lord Burgh—"

"You're not to repeat court gossip, Annie. I've told you that before."

"What else is there to do here?" she demanded, planting her elbows on the table and scowling. "The only interesting thing that happens in this hellishly cold place is that couriers sail in with news from time to time. And I daresay you listen as avidly as anyone."

André did, but not for the sake of titillation. He wanted to keep his finger on the pulse of the realm by probing the nuances that underlay the gossip. His mind hungered for the court, but he dared not return yet. Having told the queen only that he had come to Wales to investigate the mysterious disappearances of Crown revenues en route to London, he had gained her permission for a prolonged absence.

"Did Elizabeth ever interpret Ovid?" Annie asked.

"No."

"Then I shall."

André suppressed an indulgent smile. Though he dared not show it, he was enchanted by his lively pupil's aptitude, her competitive spirit, her sprightly mind, and her inexhaustible curiosity. She was Elizabeth without the hard edges, without the years of betrayal, of living in fear for her life, of being in constant view of the public eye. Looking into Annie's earnest face, he realized she already possessed the seeds of greatness. If he succeeded in bringing them to fruition, she would make a magnificent queen.

"Yes," he said at last, pressing his hands on the table and leaning toward her. "You shall have Ovid, and anything else you wish." His ship, sitting in drydock now, was crammed with great works, with which he was unlocking her mind.

She frowned, studying him. "What is that badge you wear?" she asked.

André straightened quickly. His hand came up to touch the silver badge—the sole legacy from the mother he had never known. When the second Duchess of Albuquerque had exposed him as a fraud, he had been lucky to escape with that much. "'Tis nothing," he said curtly. "A mere ornament."

Annie propped her chin in her hand. "Rodrigo has a pendant with a similar device. A lion rampant, isn't it?"

A shadow of foreboding swept over André. "Rodrigo. Your former guardian?"

"Yes. He has a tapestry in the same design, too."

"It's a common enough device." André tried to brush off her comment with a wave of his hand. "In truth, I don't even remember who gave this to me."

"I see." Annie pushed back the bench and stood. "May I be excused?" she asked. "Lord Owen invited me to go hunting."

"Take a wrap, Annie, and don't stray far afield from Owen and the beaters. You still don't know your way around the country."

"I found my way across half the world, didn't I?" she asked.

Little did André know that Annie was becoming very familiar with the countryside. On the surface, she pretended to accept her station here. She truly enjoyed the lessons with André. In fact, she reveled in the freedom to pursue studies normally reserved for men of noble birth. Yet always in the back of her mind, she harbored vague yearnings and desires that made her life in the Welsh castle seem oppressive. From time to time, she dressed in plain garb and slipped out to walk the craggy hills and greening meadows, to stare out to sea and wonder where life would take her.

Owen was waiting when she came out into the yard. Bearers, beaters, and cadge boys attended him, and his favorite goshawk rode on his leather-banded wrist. A pair of sleek, short-haired dogs romped at Owen's feet.

He spied Annie, and his face broke into a boyish, heart-catching smile.

"There you are, my lady. Come, it's a grand day for the hunt."

Annie took a deep breath of the crisp air. "Aye, my lord. I'm ready."

His blue eyes darkened. "Not quite. You're missing something."

Annie checked her appearance. "You're mistaken. What's missing?"

"A smile," he said. "You can't come unless you give me one."

In spite of Evan's warning, Annie found it easy to respond to Owen's flirtation. He had never been less than mannerly toward her, and she had begun to suspect that Evan's distrust was born of the dislike a tenant harbors for his overlord. She smiled softly at Owen, dipping her head a little.

"That's better. Ah, and we can't forget this." He gestured, and the sparviter came forward, a hooded sparrow hawk on his arm. "For you," said Owen. "We've been months training her. She should be able to take partridge or even woodcock."

Excitement rose in Annie as she held out her arm. Servants fitted her with a leather cuff. A leash was passed through the jesses on the hawk's legs and secured to her wrist. The talons gripped firmly but not painfully through the thick leather. The bird felt curiously light, and a breeze ruffled the speckled features on her breast. "Thank you," Annie said, enjoying the faint click of the bells. "She's beautiful."

Leaving the castle, they went to a broad field at the edge of a forested range of hills. Far below, in a grassy cleft between the hills, she spied a small flock of sheep attended by a dark-haired man. Farther still, she saw the distant haze of the gray sea.

A brisk wind stirred the color high in Owen's cheeks. He

was such a comely man with his pretty mouth and dancing eyes. Often Annie wondered about what Evan had said: *I was his whipping boy.*

Apparently, Evan held his grudges long. Owen was shallow, easily pleased by a simple amusements, but she had seen nothing of the cruel streak Evan had warned her about.

The beaters fanned out through the tall grass, using long poles to startle the prey into flight. The dogs, too, joined in the quest, bounding far afield. Owen unhooded his goshawk, ready to give flight to the bird.

Before long, a pair of partridges sped skyward in a whir of wing beats. Calling out a Welsh command, Owen loosed his goshawk into the wind. It flew as fast and straight as an arrow aimed at the tall, sailing clouds. In moments, it achieved superior loft over one of the birds, then dived downward.

Annie held her breath as the hawk tucked the tips of its wings and struck. A high-pitched wail, like the cry of a child, pierced the air.

The partridge dropped in a tangle of feathers, close enough for Annie to hear the thud. She started forward, her feelings a mixture of dread and awe.

Owen caught her hand and squeezed lightly. "Leave it, my dear. Let the men see to it."

She kept walking, drawing him along behind her. "I just want to see. I don't intend to dress it out and roast it for supper."

High above, Owen's hawk began to kettle downward in ever-tightening circles, coming toward the austringer's feathered lure. Annie and Owen found the plump prey in the grass. It flapped its wings feebly, and its gleaming round eye seemed a window of hopeless pain.

Casually, Owen stopped and picked up the bird. With a twist of his wrist, he popped off its head and tossed it into the grass.

Annie averted her face. Owen wiped his hands on his tunic. "You dislike blood sport, then."

"Yes," she whispered.

"Ah, Annie." Guiding her by the elbow, he drew her out of

sight of the carcass. Pressing a soft kiss on her brow, he said, "You're too sweet by half."

She managed a wavering smile. "I believe you're the first person who's ever accused me of being sweet."

He touched his lips to her cheek. "Then I'm the only person who's ever truly known you."

He didn't know the first thing about her, but his warmth and friendship eased her lonely soul.

"Don't you see, Annie? It's the way of things, life's natural order. A hawk is born to hunt. To do otherwise would go against her nature."

"You've tampered with nature," she said, eyeing the hooded bird on her wrist. "You've taken away the hawk's *reason* for killing. She could survive on kitchen middens. She needn't kill something only to have you let it rot in the field."

Owen sighed. "Come and have some wine. Hawking is a time-honored sport. A sport of kings. You should learn to like it."

She glanced at him sharply. "Why do you say that?"

His expression was as open and innocent as a child's. "You're a lady of breeding," he said simply. "I'd have you learn the pleasures your peers enjoy. You spend too much time with Maestro Scalia, studying the dusty old philosophers."

Annie nodded. "I'll try to see the point of hawking."

"Good."

"Owen?" Annie took a deep breath. She should have questioned him long ago. "Is it true that Evan Carew was your whipping boy?"

Owen's pale eyes narrowed. "He told you that?"

"Is it true?"

Owen uttered a swear word in Welsh, then said, "I should have expected as much from the ingrate. He was my paid companion when we were boys, Annie. His wages kept his father from starving in lean years. Evan shared every privilege with me—the tutors, the lessons in fencing, riding, dance. Most commoners would appreciate the advantages of our association."

"And did he also share the whippings, or did you make him bear that alone?"

Silky laughter drifted from Owen. "Really, my sweet, how evil a boy do you think I was? Perhaps Evan took a beating or two for me, but he was more than amply compensated."

A shout rang across the field. In a noisy flurry of wings, a flock of birds rose. Quickly, Owen unhooded Annie's hawk and released it.

"No!" she said, but her hands grasped at empty air. The bird was already in flight, bearing hard for one of the partridges. She heard it again—the scream, the cry to heaven from a creature that had no notion of the sport of kings.

Her sparrow hawk, smaller than Owen's, failed to fell its quarry on the first strike. The wounded bird flew crookedly into the forest, heading toward the green vale where the sheep grazed.

Annie lifted her skirts and ran in the direction the bird had flown. She heard Owen call out, but she ignored him and plunged into the woods. Bracken and low hanging limbs tore at her. The green canopy of new leaves dimmed the sunlight to cool shadow. She lost sight of both the hawk and its prey, but hurried on, eager for a respite from the blood sport.

She walked downhill to the edge of the forest. Nearby, she heard a faint bleating sound and realized she had ventured near the flock of sheep.

Coming out of the woods, she found the animals grazing placidly. The shepherd was hunched over something lying in the grass.

Sunlight struck blue sparks in his curling black hair. "Evan!" Annie called, feeling a rush of pleasure so intense it took her by surprise.

He stood and turned. For a moment, an answering pleasure lit his face. Then he seemed to catch himself and frowned. "Annie. What are you doing here?"

She leaped over a small, rushing brook and held out her leather-bound wrist. "Owen's teaching me to hunt."

"I see."

"It's not to my taste. What are you doing tending sheep?"

"The shepherd is abed with the ague, so I offered to help out."

"Oh." She craned her neck to peer over his shoulder. "What's that, Evan?" Without waiting for an answer, she hurried over. And stopped short when she spied a newly dead lamb lying in the grass. "Oh." The tiny, pathetic form brought the heat of tears to her throat. "What happened?"

"It took sick. The colic, maybe." He gazed at the rough-coated ewe pacing a few feet away. The creature's udders were so bloated they brushed the ground.

"Can't you do someth— Evan!" Annie stared at the large, sharp knife that had appeared in his hand.

"Look away, Annie," he said. "You'll not want to see this."

She had just seen Owen rip the head off a still-quick bird. Surely Evan could not equal that horror.

"Look away, damn it."

"I want to see what you're about."

"Then don't expect me to hold your head while you puke."

"I won't p—" She snapped her mouth shut.

Evan picked up the dead lamb, running his hand over the soft white fleece. Then, his face as hard as stone, he made four shallow cuts around each little hoof.

"Evan," Annie said, "for God's sake, are you mad? Is this some sort of Protestant ritual, or have you turned pagan?"

He didn't answer, but deftly drew the blade around the lamb's neck. Then, slowly and carefully, he peeled back the hide, using the knife to slice through the threads of sinew. In moments, the skinned carcass lay naked, shining muscle against wind-seared grass.

Annie pressed her fingers to her lips. The dead lamb's mother grunted and swayed from side to side in discomfort.

Evan strode across the field and scooped up a tiny, bleating lamb. Murmuring in Welsh, he knelt and fitted the dead lamb's pelt over the live one. The thing stretched and fit like a knitted tunic, covering the distressed babe from neck to rump and down each spindly leg.

"This is too odd," Annie finally managed to say. "I don't understand."

He smoothed the pelt over the squirming lamb. "You will."

"I'm not sure I want to."

He tucked the strangely clad creature under his arm. "This one's an orphan. Its dam died of the bloat." He gestured at the ewe. "That one's just lost her lamb. Watch."

He approached the ewe slowly, cautiously, and set the small one in the grass near her. The lamb staggered forward on wobbly legs.

The ewe stared at it, head lowered, nose twitching.

At last Annie understood. "You're trying to get her to foster it," she whispered.

"Aye."

The ewe sniffed at the orphan, her nose nudging at the hide of her dead lamb. Lowering her head, she butted it away.

Evan straddled the ewe, holding it immobile with its neck between his legs. Taking its cue, the lamb latched on to a fleshy teat and began to suck greedily. The ewe grunted uncertainly, but the nursing lamb must have relieved her discomfort. Before long, Evan removed his legs, and the ewe stood in placid silence.

Annie breathed a sigh of relief, realizing only then that she had been holding her breath. "She's accepted him."

"I think so, aye." Evan cleaned his knife on the grass and sheathed it. Then he picked up the carcass and drew it to a pile of mown grass. He covered the body with hay and rocks.

"It's a miracle," Annie said, her rapt gaze fastened on orphan and ewe.

Evan squatted beside a trickling brook and washed his hands. "Hardly. I confused her."

"The lamb won't mind wearing that other skin?"

"Not if he's fed. In a few days, she'll recognize the scent of her own milk on the orphan, and then I'll take off the hide."

"That's a relief."

Suddenly he appeared at her side. His fingers, cold from the brook, brushed her cheek. "You're pale, Annie Blythe. I'm sorry you had to see that."

Although she stood unmoving, something within her took

a leap forward, surged toward him, seeking, searching . . . for what, she did not know.

She found herself thinking of Owen, twisting the head off a dying bird and flinging it away. And then Evan, clothing an orphan in a dead lamb's hide so that it might have a chance to live. They were two such different men; her feelings for them both were confused, unsettled.

"I'm not," she said at last, tilting her head so that her cheek fit more snugly into his hand. "I'm not at all sorry, Evan."

"I've been summoned back to court, and you're coming with me."

Round-eyed, Annie looked up from her reading of Erasmus. André's announcement came like the strike of a hawk: swift, unexpected, deadly.

She cleared her throat. "When?"

"Within the week."

"I prefer to stay here."

He lifted one thin white eyebrow. "Do you, Annie? In the past year you've mastered every skill I've taught you, read every book I brought aboard my roundship. Your speech and manners shine with the polish of years of study rather than mere months. How much longer can you be content here?"

She rose from the table and strolled across the solar, stopping to look out a tall, narrow window. Below, the fields waved with summer greenery. The village basked in the rare warmth of the sunlight. And the roundship, in dry dock at the harbor, swarmed with workers bearing buckets of tar.

"I don't know if I could be content anywhere, André," she said honestly. "I'm comfortable here. It took time, but I've come to like Wales. Something in the wildness here stirs my blood. Owen is . . . amusing at times."

"Owen." André spat the name. "A petty lord who cannot even control the thievery in his own district."

Annie blinked at the breeze that wafted in through the window. "It's happened again?" she asked idly. "Thieves took the revenues he sent to the Crown?"

"Aye, the slack-jawed fool sends excuses instead of coin to London. He flirts with death as his father did."

Annie turned to face him. "Do you suspect Owen of the theft?"

"Not even he would be stupid enough to steal money from the Crown." Frustration thrummed in his voice. André had been charged with solving the disappearance of the tax money, but in all the time he had spent in Wales, he had not found the culprits.

Annie put her elbow on the window embrasure, propped her chin on her hand, and turned to look at André. "If you've not apprehended the thieves, then you should stay until you do."

His back stiffened. "I did not come here to heed your commands, Annie Blythe."

Annie had always known that André Scalia was not a man easily mastered. His words slashed at her, but she refused to drop her gaze from his severe face. "You also came here to tutor me in the ways of statecraft, did you not? It seems to me that a servant of the queen should fulfill his duties."

"Enough!" He cut the air with his hand and leaned forward, putting his face very close to hers. "I am all that stands between you and disaster. You will do as I say." With that, he stalked across the room to the opposite window.

"And if I don't?"

"If you won't trust me, then I have no further use for you."

"Use?" She spoke harshly to disguise her hurt. "If you mean to use me, then I should demand a payment."

"My dear, you're in no position to demand anything. Keep on with your troublesome talk, and I'll see that you're returned to your guardian, Rodrigo Viscaino."

Annie caught her breath. She had told André very little of Rodrigo, only that he was a man of honor who had treated her kindly. She refused to confess the reason she had left him, the reason she could never return. "Let me stay here, André. If you don't trust Owen, then let Evan Carew find a safe place for me."

"Evan Carew!" She heard him sniff and without turning

knew his face to be lean and hard with disapproval. "It's best you avoid common rabble—"

"Aye, a commoner." She swung around then, feeling a blaze of heat in her cheeks. "Also a man responsible for saving the treasury of England from bankruptcy. You wish me to be a queen, André. How can I, if you bar me from knowing the very people of this realm?"

His thin mouth quirked with something like admiration. "You never really answered my question. Can you be content here?"

"Perhaps not," she retorted. "But court? Heirs to the throne of England—especially those with flimsy claims—have not fared well under the Tudors. Lady Jane Grey, Edward Courtenay, John Perrott—all ended their pretensions on the block. Elizabeth herself, a king's *acknowledged* daughter, was nearly put to death by her sister, Mary Tudor. Her Scottish cousin, Mary Stuart, will doubtless meet her fate in the executioner's blade. You've said so yourself."

"I wanted you to be aware of the realities of your situation," he said.

"Oh, I am. Tell me, what chance have I, Annie Blythe, my father a by-blow of King Henry, against the enemies in the Council, those who would place their own favorites before me?"

"At one time," André reminded her, "Henry's only son was Fitzroy, a bastard elevated to the Duke of Richmond. Henry did name him heir until Jane Seymour gave England a prince."

"Aye, and young Fitzroy came to a bad end as well, didn't he? They say it was consumption. Would you be surprised if it was not poison?"

"No harm will come to you, I swear it." André crossed the room and took her hand, the gesture rare and fervent for a man of his great reserve. "Elizabeth need not know you're the one she seeks. At least not straightaway. She still thinks the missing heir is—"

"Is what?"

"A boy, and she has no notion that Drake and Carew brought you to England."

"She sent them years ago, André. Surely she expects results."

"She expects nothing but the story I will give her. I'll tell her the heir lives, but has not been located."

"Will she believe that Drake and Evan, who all but stole the heart of New Spain, are incapable of finding the person she sent them after?"

"I shall make her believe it," he assured her. Strangely, Annie knew that he could. In spite of his grandfatherly appearance, André Scalia was a cold and gifted man.

"Surely you're just the least bit curious," he said.

Indeed, she had a fascination for her Tudor heritage. Perhaps, somehow, she had a sense of the blood tie that bound her to the queen. "How will you explain my presence?" she asked.

"You'll be presented as a scribe and chronicler. Many wellborn ladies serve in that capacity. You'll have the opportunity to observe and question people without drawing suspicion to yourself. And for God's sake, keep your coif on. Red hair is no great rarity, but nonetheless, you bear a faint resemblance to the queen in her younger years."

Annie glared at the coif that lay discarded on the table. "You sound as if you've planned this for months."

He lifted her hand to his lips and pressed a dry kiss to her knuckles. "For years, my lady. For years."

A serving woman helped Annie pack for the voyage. She had few possessions: the gowns and coifs André had given her, a pair of silver earrings she had never worn, some paper and books.

Unbeknownst to André, she still possessed the ring her father had given her, a token from Henry VIII to a woman he had loved many years ago.

While going through the coffer at the foot of her bed, Annie came across the falconer's cuff she had worn on her out-ing with Owen. After that first venture, she had not joined him again, but had forgotten to return the cuff.

"I should take this to the sparviter," she said, showing the cuff to the maid.

"As you wish, my lady."

Annie hastened down to the hall. To her dismay, she saw that the morning rain had turned the inner ward into a mud hole. Reluctant to soil her gown, she decided to take the cuff to Owen himself.

She had never visited his private chambers. Handsome as he was, Owen had never prodded her curiosity. She knocked at the heavy door.

"Is that you, Cuttle?" Owen called out. "I thought we agreed to wait—"

"It's me." Annie pushed open the door and stepped inside.

Owen sat at a large writing desk with a slanted top. An open wooden cask and a stack of papers lay before him. When he saw Annie, he lurched to his feet, and it seemed to her that his cheeks lost a shade of color.

He recovered quickly enough, favoring her with a charming smile. "Come in, sweetheart."

"I startled you, Owen. Forgive me."

"There's nothing to forgive." He edged around the desk and stood so that the casket was concealed from her view. His gaze swept over her, and he pressed his fist to his heart. "By God, I shall miss you, Annie. You grow more lovely with each passing day."

"I think not. Perhaps your flattery grows more facile, my lord."

"Madam, you wound me. That's no way to respond to a compliment."

Annie smiled. "I'm sorry." She walked toward the desk. "I came across this cuff while I was packing. I wanted to return it to you."

Owen pressed himself back against the desk. His movement caused the casket to slide down the angled surface, and it fell to the floor with a crash.

"Oh!" Annie dropped to her knees. "It's my fault. Let me

help y—" She broke off, staring in amazement at the wealth of jewels and gold ornaments that had spilled from the box.

With agitated movements, Owen swept the treasure into a pile. "Never mind, I'll pick it up. Just leave the cuff, Annie. I have work to do."

She picked up a pair of gold buttons and frowned at the eagle insignia embossed on them. "This is the emblem of the viceroy of New Spain," she said. Spying a few more matching buttons, she picked them up as well.

"His loss," Owen said brusquely.

"Is this your share of the treasure Evan brought, then?"

"Aye."

"I thought you had to send most of it to London."

He took the buttons from her and tossed them into the box. "Indeed. But do you think I'd be fool enough to send it now, while the roads are crawling with brigands?"

"I suppose not." Annie stood. "André could take them in the roundship."

Owen closed the box with a snap. "I'd sooner trust this treasure to a pirate."

"It was just a thought."

He straightened and pressed his hands on her shoulders. "A lady as beautiful as you does not need to think, Annie."

She rolled her eyes. "Oh? Then what do I need to do, Owen?"

"This." Before she could escape, he bent and kissed her, his lips pressing hard, his fingers gripping her upper arms. His scent of ambergris was thick, a corruption in the air.

Annie reacted without thought, pushing against his chest to extricate herself from his embrace. High color stood out in his cheeks, and his eyes shone. "Annie—"

"Owen, I'd best get back to my packing." He reached for her hand but she sped away. As she fled to her chambers, she felt grateful. Owen had finally given her a reason to wish to leave Wales.

Annie found Evan at the harbor the evening before her departure. Handsome and swarthy, his legs planted wide in a pirate's stance, he gazed out at the roundship, now launched and ready to sail.

"Evan."

As he faced her, the sea breeze snatched at his long black hair, streaming through the waves like the caress of a lover's hand.

"You're leaving," he stated.

"Yes. I came to say good-bye."

He diverted his gaze to the harbor. "I suppose it's time."

He started to walk, his long strides carrying him down a path that curved beneath a jutting cliff. Uninvited, Annie lifted her skirts and followed. She was breathless by the time they descended to a lonely, windswept strand surrounded by great rearing crags and stands of rock.

He stopped and turned to her, his dark eyes deep and probing, his hair a midnight mane tossed by the breeze. A curious tension seemed to hold him stiff. His face was as hard as the stone that rose from the seething surf.

"It's time?" Annie asked, pressing her hand to the ache in her chest. "Is that all you have to say to me?"

"Damn it, Annie!" he burst out. "What do you want me to do? Wish you godspeed and tell you I'll miss you? Recommend a London dressmaker?"

She flexed her fingers in the chill air. "I don't know. It just seems that, after all we've been to each other, you'd make a bit more of our parting."

"More?" In two strides, he stood in front of her, taking her shoulders in a grip just shy of hurtful. "What more do you want, Princess?"

She stared at his face, his throat, browned by wind and sun. "I've never known what I want from you, Evan. Sometimes you seem to care for me. Other times you push me away as if I were a stranger."

He gave truth to her words by letting her go so abruptly that she swayed. "You have no right, and certainly no reason, to be in my life anymore."

She flung up her chin. "How dare you? *You* forced me to

live among thieves while you plundered the riches of my homeland. *You* brought me here, Evan! *You*—"

"So I'm responsible for you?" he demanded.

"No. André is."

"And what of you, Princess?" he asked softly. "Wasn't it you who pointed a musket at my heart and forced me to bring you here?"

"Thanks to you, I had no choice."

His face softened, then took on a tortured look that caught at her heart. "Ah, Annie. I could wish—"

"No." The anger rushed out of her on an expelled breath. "What's done is done, Evan. I am leaving with André, and I'd prefer to part as friends. Will you stay on in Wales?"

He made a sweeping gesture at the churning gray sea. "My life is there. The sea is my mistress."

"You'll play the pirate again?"

"When the time comes."

"I'll miss—"

"No!" He pressed his fingers to her mouth. "Don't say it, Annie. You don't mean it, and I don't want to hear it."

She pushed his hand away. "But—"

"But nothing. Have you said farewell to Owen yet?"

"Yes. What does that have to do with you and me?"

"I told you not to trust him. Yet I see you, day after day, riding out with him, laughing with him, falling prey to his fatal charm."

Her cheeks flushed, and her anger renewed itself. "I've had little enough to amuse me in this place. Owen is pretty to look at and is reasonably well-spoken. He's given me no cause for distrust." She remembered the casket of jewels, but discarded her suspicions. It was not her affair.

"Not yet, he hasn't." Evan stabbed the air with his finger. "He'll find out about you someday. He'll learn of your ties to the monarchy, and he'll use you, Annie."

"He'll not find me a willing participant in any treachery he might practice," she retorted. She paced up and down the bank, her feet kicking up the sand. "You still see me as a naive girl, Evan. I'm a woman grown, trained by one of the best minds of the age."

A bitter smile twisted his mouth. "Ah. The learned André Scalia. So you've been playing Arthur to his Merlin."

"He's been teaching me the principles of kingship."

"Do you think he cares about you, Annie?"

She stopped pacing. "Why wouldn't he?"

"He can't. The man has no heart. Nothing but ambition. He cares only about himself. He wants you in line for the throne in order to save his own skin, for he knows his head will roll if Elizabeth is succeeded by one of her Catholic Stuart cousins."

"You're so angry, Evan," she said. "I don't know why. When you brought me here, you knew I'd eventually find my way to Elizabeth's court. Now that my departure is imminent, you act as if you don't want me to go."

Something stark and painful shone on his face. He pivoted sharply away from her. "My opinion doesn't matter."

She stepped behind him, close enough to smell the sea breeze in his hair and the warm leathery scent of his jerkin. "It matters to me, Evan. When I'm away, I don't want to remember you as you are now, angry and distant, not even able to look at me."

"What do you want to remember, Annie?" he asked without turning.

"The way your eyes light up when you smile. The joy on your face when you unite an orphaned lamb with a new mother. The sound of your laughter, and—"

"Stop!" He swung around, and she found herself eye to eye, nose to nose with him. "I'm not some performing monkey, Annie."

"And I'm not some chess piece to be moved about against my will." Drawing upon her last reserves of strength, she said, "Good-bye, Evan. I'm sorry we can't have a more amiable parting."

She left him then, striking off across the bank where the path wound toward the village. Damn him! He set a torch to her emotions, and none of André's training had given her the means to douse the fire.

When she heard his footsteps crunching on the pebbled beach, she refused to acknowledge him. She merely quickened her pace.

An iron vise closed around her arm. She cried out as he spun her around, but fell quiet when she saw the look of anguish on his face.

"I love you, Annie Blythe," he said.

Her mouth dropped open. His hand came up gently beneath her chin and closed it. A slow warmth crept over her, and she saw nothing but his intent, tormented face and heard nothing save his words echoing in her mind and in her heart.

I love you, Annie Blythe.

A half smile curved his lips. "I always wondered what it would take to strike you silent."

"This is a jest," she said, unable to speak above a whisper. "You mock me, Evan."

"No. It's fate that mocks me. I never wanted to love you, Annie. It's futile, impossible, unfair to us both. But you . . . you took my heart by surprise, from the first moment I saw you on the island at San Juan."

"I did?" She trembled from the chill wind and from the terrible certainty growing within her. The feeling crystallized, and she realized the truth that rang in her heart. "I love you, too, Evan."

He caught his breath. "God help us both, then."

"What are we going to do?"

"I think we should start with a kiss."

"Yes," she whispered, her hands pressing his chest and then sliding upward, winding around his neck. "Yes, *please . . .*"

His mouth closed over hers, tenderly, slowly. She tasted the salt air on his lips and a warm sweetness she could not name. Her eyes drifted shut and she made a small, yearning sound in her throat. A tingling started in her breasts and between her legs. Filled with awe at the power of his touch, she came to life like a dreamer awakening from a long sleep.

His hair was warm silk, the strands winding around her fingers as she strained closer yet. He made a sound that she could only liken to the feral growl of a jungle cat. His hands caressed her shoulders and back, molding the shape of her body as if he were blind and had no other way to see how she was made.

He pressed the tops of her shoulders, and she sank willingly, eagerly to the damp, coarse sand. His hand found her breasts; his mouth moved down her throat, his tongue leaving a trail of fire in its wake.

Then, suddenly, the warmth—and Evan—were gone. She opened her eyes to find him on his knees, staring at her.

"What's wrong?" she asked, sitting back on her heels and peering at him through a fog of passion.

"I want to make love to you, Annie."

She laid her hand on his cheek. "I wish you would."

His fingers furrowed into the sand. "What sort of teaching did you learn as Rodrigo's ward?" he asked, pulling away from her. "Did he not tell you that love outside marriage is a sin?"

"I suppose he did." She brushed the sand from his hand and covered it with hers. "If God is just," she said fervently, "then He will not condemn me for loving you, Evan."

He snatched his hand away. "You're a royal princess. Your marriage will be a dynastic event governed by treaties. Not a tumble in the sand with a common Welshman."

"Don't coarsen what we feel for each other, Evan."

"It *is* coarse," he said. "And dangerous as well."

"I'm not afraid of loving you."

"Oh no? Think of Guildford Dudley. His head tumbled from the block because he had no fear of loving Jane Grey."

To Annie's horror, tears gathered in her eyes.

Evan muttered a curse and cradled her head against his chest. "We can't change who we are or the way the world works, *cariad*." The Welsh endearment fell softly from his lips.

"Why can't we?" she asked, her words muffled by his jerkin.

"We are just two people. Annie, I never should have told you what was in my heart. I thought telling you the truth would heal the hurt I'd caused you. Instead it brings a new kind of pain. One that could prove more deadly."

"Why must we hurt each other?" She placed her hands upon his cheeks and kissed him softly on the mouth. "Can't we love each other wherever, whenever we can?"

"I won't risk getting you with child. The rigors of childbirth aside, an unwed mother at court is a scandal the queen won't tolerate."

"Then I won't go to court. I'll stay here with you."

Evan shook his head. "I'd be dead within a week; André would see to that. But most of all, Annie, we must think of your future. I have nothing to offer you save a share in a pirate's spoils taken at unreliable intervals."

"You're wrong." The tears spilled freely now. "You've given me a gift far richer than a kingdom of silver and gold."

"Aye, and it's because I love you that I must let you go, *cariad*." His voice shook as he bent to kiss her—not tenderly this time, not slowly. His embrace was as hard and swift as a knife hand delivering the coup de grace, and her soul cried out in pain.

CHAPTER 14

Windsor Castle
1577

Queen Elizabeth's thin shoulders shook. A wheezing gasp escaped her, then crescendoed into a bark of laughter. The broadsheet rattled in her hands.

Annie stood at the foot of the dais, her hands clasped together, her teeth worrying her lower lip. "Lord Burghley said you'd be wroth with me over the lampoon, madam."

The queen's gray eyes danced. She handed the paper to the Earl of Leicester, who stood at his usual place by her side. "Read it, Robbie, and tell me if I should be wroth with this young scribbler."

Annie held her breath as Leicester perused her writing. The steady conversational din of advisers, jurists, pages, and ladies mingled with the lively music from the minstrels' gallery at the far end of the audience chamber.

Robert Dudley, Lord Leicester, chuckled, his eyes alight with interest, his face flushed with wine as he read Annie's latest diatribe. "The 'miracle monger' in the story—he can be none other than Duke Francis of Guise," he commented.

Annie glanced nervously at the French ambassador, who

stood some feet away, glowering at her. She wondered if her biting farce about the massacre on St. Bartholomew's Eve struck too hard at French pride. Yet, after hearing the account from a Huguenot who had escaped the slaughter five years before, she had felt compelled to speak her mind.

"The puppet is Charles the Ninth, no doubt," Leicester murmured. "And, of course, the 'bag of hip and tit' working the strings is his own queen mother, Catherine d'Medici."

With a soft hiss of outrage, the French ambassador stalked from the chamber without pausing to beg leave.

"What think you, Robbie?" Elizabeth asked, smiling coldly at the retreating Frenchman.

"Mistress Blythe has a biting wit, a wicked sense of the irreverent."

Elizabeth's plucked eyebrows lifted. "Perhaps that's why I like her. God's teeth, Anne, I don't know where André found you, but you've been an asset to the court these three years past."

Annie dipped her knees in deference. Her stiff court gown brushed the stone floor, and the veiling of her coif fell forward. Heeding André's warning, she always concealed her hair beneath a coif. "Thank you, madam. It is a privilege to serve you."

"Your lampoon of the Catholics has sharp teeth," Elizabeth observed. "Tell me, have you a particular contempt for the papists?"

The question flung Annie back across the years. She saw again the jungle of Hispaniola engulfing the once-prosperous villa of Gabriella and Willam Blythe. She pictured the soldiers of Christ dragging her grandparents to the stake, the flames of hatred rising around the two sweetest, most gentle people she had ever known.

"Aye, madam," she admitted. "I trow that I do, and may God forgive me."

"You needn't fear the wrath of a merciful God," said Elizabeth. "In my view, one's faith is a private matter between an individual and the Almighty. That ponderous d'Medici baggage might shed her people's blood in God's name, but as for me—" She broke off and fixed her steely stare on the archbishop of Canterbury. "I'll make no windows into a man's soul."

Annie slowly released her breath. What a strange, wondrous, and liberating notion. The queen would not tolerate a clergy that policed everyone's beliefs. Secret pride rose up in Annie. Though she stood in awe and fear of her kinswoman, she had come to know Elizabeth as a fair-minded, brilliant ruler with a will of tempered steel.

Elizabeth dismissed her with a wave and a gold coin, and Annie moved back into the crowd of courtiers. She had learned much over the past three years. Court was dangerous, yet exciting and vibrant, loud and frenzied, and always dominated by Elizabeth herself.

Three years . . . had it really been that long since Evan had taken her in his arms and told her he loved her? Since she had kissed him with all the fervor of new passion? She dreamed of him still, whether awake or sleeping; it mattered not. Hardly a moment passed when she did not feel the emptiness of his absence.

Taking a cup of lamb's wool from a passing servitor, Annie sipped the warm, creamy apple drink. She studied the throng of gentlemen in their padded doublets and blousy, slashed pantaloons, the women clad in silk, their heads held high above starched ruffs, the black-robed jurists gathered around a table and gorging themselves on malmsey and sweetmeats. Elizabeth's personal stamp, her favored modes of speech, entertainment, and food, permeated the entire fabric of the court.

". . . ready for another shot at Spain," someone said, close behind Annie.

Very casually, she reached up and tucked her coif behind her ear. Over the years, she had perfected her method of listening in on conversations.

"You think so, Kit?"

"Oh, aye," said Sir Christopher Hatton, captain of the guard. "I'd wager my Bristol fleet on it. King Philip just made a particularly vicious assault on the Dutch Protestants."

"The queen's been trying to stay out of the conflict in the Netherlands."

Turning slightly, Annie saw that Hatton's companion was Lord Admiral Lincoln, a stout, apple-cheeked man. Sashes crisscrossed his barrel chest, and the ribbons of honor gave him the look of a roundship under sail.

Hatton touched the golden badge of his crest, which depicted a stag or hind. "Mark you, my lord, she'll plot everything short of war in order to curtail the Spanish."

"More privateering?" Lincoln asked. "The channel's all but fished out, I'd say."

"Aye, the channel is."

"I see. It's to be New Spain, then?"

It was all Annie could do to hold her cup steady as she strained to hear while pretending to watch a sixsome reel taking place in the middle of the floor.

". . . considerable boldness to undertake the endeavor," Hatton was saying. "The treasure fleets now sail with an escort of armed guardships. But think, my dear lord. They use escorts on the route from Nombre de Dios to Spain. 'Tis my belief that Drake will aim for an unguarded fleet."

The two moved away to join a group of petitioners and councillors. Annie stood still, her heart thundering in her ears. *Drake.* Drake was going to undertake another expedition. All but forgotten since his last voyage, he had whiled away the years in Ireland.

Now he was coming back.

And Annie knew, she *knew* with a bittersweet, soul-tearing certainty, that Evan would come with him.

For three miserable years, Evan had not been able to get Annie out of his mind.

He saw her everywhere. The autumn leaves in the high hills glowed with the color of her hair. The sea, with the rare winter sunlight reflecting off the surface, matched her eyes precisely. He heard her laughter on the wind, smelled her scent in the spring blossoms, remembered the warm ivory texture of her skin. And sometimes, deep within his dreams, he could taste her lips.

Ah, how sweet she had been that day so long ago, when she had kissed him and clung to him and wept with the pain and wonder of new love.

Loneliness seared him, its burn as deep as a brand. After losing Casilda, Evan had vowed never to love again.

Yet Annie Blythe was a woman to make a mockery of vows.

"Nervous?" Drake's voice broke in on Evan's thoughts.

Evan blinked as if awakening from a dream. All at once, the antechamber in Windsor Castle came into sharp focus. He saw tapestries, oil portraits, throngs of men awaiting an audience with the queen in her privy chamber.

"Should I be?" Evan asked.

"Ah, most definitely. The queen has just charged us with undertaking the most extraordinary voyage of our age. I tell you, it gives even me pause."

Evan smiled. Drake's long sojourn in Ireland had made him harder and more determined than ever. His association with the lordly Thomas Doughty, who had promised to help him better his station, had imbued him with a swaggering confidence. And yet the horrors he had seen in Ireland, the ruthless slaughter at Rathlin Island ordered by the Earl of Essex, had had a sobering effect on Francis Drake. It was a quality that could serve him well on the expedition he proposed.

"You're more than ready for this voyage, Francis."

"True. Are you?"

"Of course." Indeed, Evan had missed life under sail, the hours counted by the turn of the sandglass, his duties prescribed by the ship's manifest, his heart safe from the vagaries of emotion.

"As am I," Thomas Doughty declared in ringing tones as he strode toward them across the antechamber. His large hand clapped Drake on the back. "Didn't I tell you, my good fellow, that I'd get you an audience with Her Majesty?"

"Aye, you did, Tom, and I thank you." Drake raised an imaginary cup to his bluff, energetic sponsor.

Evan stood back a few paces. True, Doughty seemed a man of wit and competence. Yet even as a newcomer to court, Evan had heard it whispered that the great, bitter rift between Essex and Leicester, the queen's two favorites, had been induced by Doughty himself.

Though never anyone's fool, Drake had succumbed to Doughty's sly flattery. Evan waited as they exchanged plans to meet for supper. Then Doughty strode off, and Drake turned to Evan. "A most excellent gentleman," he commented. "He's coming on the expedition."

Evan felt a brief chill, but it was so quickly gone that he thought he had imagined it. "Excellent gentlemen rarely make excellent mariners, Francis."

"They will on this voyage." Drake scanned the crowded room. "Have you seen André Scalia?"

"No. I mean to find him straightaway."

"To see what became of the girl."

"Aye."

"You care for her, Evan."

"Aye."

Drake heaved a sigh. He propped his foot on a window ledge and gazed out at a garden where peacocks strolled among the mazes and arbors. "A pity. My wife and I are strangers now. There were times, in Ireland, when I was in the teeth of some skirmish, that I tried to picture her. But even when I thought death was imminent, I could not see her face. It was awkward, meeting her again in Plymouth before I came to court."

Evan wondered if awkwardness was less painful than the deep well of loneliness that had gaped inside him since he had last seen Annie. "Is Mary well?" he asked.

Drake shrugged, wincing when his ear scraped the high ruff he had insisted on wearing to his audience with the queen. "Well enough. She always was a biddable lass." He clenched his hand into a fist. "She wants a baby."

"So give her one. Or have you forgotten how?"

"You're cheeky, my master. I know the means. But, marry, the opportunities are few."

Thank God for that, thought Evan. Had Annie stayed in Carew any longer, he knew he would have given into the passion that seared him, even now, at the very thought of her.

"Come with me." André Scalia walked briskly toward them. For a moment, light from the window slanted across his austere face, and Evan felt a stab of awareness. André reminded him of someone, but who?

Then Scalia stepped close, dark-robed and intent, and Evan knew—and thanked God—that there was not another man like him on the face of the earth.

André held out his arm toward the door of the antechamber. Drake and Evan preceded him into a long, high-ceilinged corridor. André walked swiftly. The years were nothing to him. Time seemed to pass him by, leaving him as hale and spry as a man in his prime.

"For obvious reasons, we've told only our chief investors of your true objective," he said. "We'll say you're bound for Alexandria. Even the crew must believe that."

"People will speculate," said Evan.

"Let them. Most will conclude that you're off to find a Northwest Passage to India. And of course, the Spanish ambassador is already warning King Philip to brace himself for another assault on the plate fleets of Nombre de Dios."

Drake grinned. "Never would anyone imagine our true purpose."

"You're to keep it that way." André stopped in front of a thick double door. "Mr. Drake, your investors await within. Don't argue with them, and don't tell them any more than you have to."

Drake nodded. He opened the door, stepped quickly inside, and closed the door behind him.

Evan and André faced each other. Evan tried to find the words to ask about Annie, but his mouth felt as if someone had suddenly stuffed it with cotton wool.

"She's in the privy garden," said André, speaking reluctantly.

"What?"

"The privy garden. Let no one see you. And I warn you, Evan, let your judgment slip for one moment, and your head will adorn a pike."

At first Evan thought the garden was empty. Roses bloomed on trellises. Foxglove grew tall and straight in the beds that bordered the winding pebbled pathways. Yew trees, espaliered to form great, knotted arches, created shady arbors in each corner of the garden.

A slight movement caught Evan's eye. He saw a woman standing in the shadow of an arbor. She was dressed in green, an ivory coif covering her head and framing her face. Tall and slim as a willow, she lifted one hand in a slow, tentative greeting.

"Annie." Her name was a tortured whisper wrung from a throat gone suddenly dry. His feet carried him toward her. She was a vision out of a dream, and yet he knew he had never pictured her like this. For in his dreams, she was the Annie he knew, a laughing, half-grown girl, endearingly awkward, infinitely appealing.

The woman waiting beneath the arbor was a stranger. As he neared her, his tall boots crunching on the pebbles, he saw nothing but perfection. Her skin was as smooth as new snow, her figure slim and straight, her posture regally poised. Time had polished away the flaws and fulfilled the promise he had only suspected.

She was ravishing in her court dress, the bodice paned by gold braid lozenges, the sleeves fitted, the coif concealing all but a few stray tendrils of golden red hair. Her eyes had the clarity of the sea on a cloudless day.

"Evan," she said simply, with a catch in her voice.

Even her tone had changed. It had the resonance of good breeding, the echo of nobility evident even in a single word.

"I . . . didn't know if you'd want to see me," he said.

She caught her breath and pressed her hands together. He

could sense the tension in them. "For every moment of the past years," she said with a slight falter, "I have wanted nothing more than to see you again."

A rough sound of yearning escaped him. Suddenly the tension dissolved and she was in his arms, laughing and weeping, crushing herself against him as if she feared he was an apparition that would disappear on a wisp of wind.

"God, Annie, I've missed you," he said, and then he kissed her, deep and searchingly, drowning in her sweetness as a fierce hunger rose inside him.

She made soft little sobbing sounds in her throat. The bittersweet embrace lasted only moments; then she tore herself away. Somewhere in the distance, a peacock let out a mournful cry.

"Nothing has changed between us," she said, a dazed look in her eyes. Her fingers came up to touch the fullness of her lower lip. "I had hoped it would be different, and yet at the same time I knew I'd be heartsick if it were."

He touched his forehead to hers. "I never wanted to love you, Annie. But then, after a while, I never wanted to stop."

She stepped away and looked from side to side. "We shouldn't be seen together. This is too public a place."

Bleakness washed over him. "It will always be so for us, Annie. We must forever love in secret."

"It's better than not loving at all," she said.

Unexpectedly, her statement summoned a bittersweet memory of Casilda. The women were oddly alike, two sides of the same coin. Casilda, feral and proud and independent. Annie, cultured and refined, yet every inch as strong as the Cimaroon woman.

"Evan, I would take you in my arms before the queen herself," she said, "but I fear what would happen to you."

"Then the queen knows who you are?"

She shook her head. "André made excuses, told her about the arrests at Gema del Mar. She believes the Tudor heir to be lost somewhere in the islands. She worries less about the succession these days, for her health is improved and she seems to have many years ahead of her." Annie stared down at the pebbled walkway. "But she's fond of me. She'd not allow me to leave the court. Nor does she tolerate love affairs among her courtiers."

He traced the line of her jaw. " 'Tis a bitter business, being queen."

She caught his hand and pressed her lips to his palm. "Aye."

"If you continue to stay here, you could be found out and drawn into the succession."

"Aye," she said again, dropping his hand. "The possibility is remote, but 'tis true."

He looked intently into her eyes. He saw implacability there, and strength of purpose. "Do you wish it?"

"Where else shall I go?" she demanded. "With you?"

"You know that's impossible. Must we argue, *cariad*?"

"No." She squeezed his hand. "How is your father?"

"Well enough."

"And Owen?"

Evan shrugged. "I've managed to stay clear of him. Each year, he plans to come to court, but the queen has yet to summon him. Do you like it here, Annie?"

"I suppose I do. The summer progresses to remote parts of the realm are arduous, but I never lack for company." She shivered as a breeze stirred her coif. "I know of no other place I can live my life, Evan."

Then live it with me. His soul screamed the words he dared not utter. He was about to embark upon a voyage from which he might never return. He had no right to forge a bond with her, to leave her to endless waiting and wondering, like the sad and lonely Mary Newman Drake.

"Evan?" She touched his sleeve, her fingers closing in a compelling grip. "What are you thinking?"

He released a long, heartfelt sigh. "I'm thinking how hard it is to say good-bye to you. As many times as we part, it never gets easier."

She blinked, and he saw the sheen of tears in her eyes. An ache of longing throbbed inside him.

"Come with me, Evan." She turned toward a gate that led down to the river.

"Where are we going?"

She opened the gate and led him to a waiting barge. "To give each other a proper greeting. And then a proper farewell."

An hour later, a wherry brought them down the Thames to a small, private residence. The house was dark and chilly, and no servant greeted them. The smells of a stale hearth fire and candle wax hung in the close air.

Annie hastened to a window and opened the shutters. The main room was small, furnished with a table and two benches beside the hearth, and a cupboard by the window. To one side, a short gallery opened to a kitchen larder. A ladder against one wall led up to a loft.

"What is this place?" Evan asked.

"It belongs to André. He uses it but little, for his tastes run to the opulent, and he prefers London proper."

"He gave you permission to come here?"

An impish smiled curved her mouth. "Evan, I cannot so much as belch without permission. But that's never stopped me from doing as I please."

"You won't be missed at Windsor?"

She shrugged. "Perhaps. I don't care, Evan. Not tonight."

Her determination to be alone with him seized him with desire. Suppressing it, he laid a fire of a more practical kind. In the kitchen she found wine, a large cheese, and a supply of raisins and nuts and salty black olives from Italy. She laid the table with care, then seated herself on one of the benches.

Evan took a bracing gulp of wine.

Annie sipped hers. "I'm not hungry."

"Nor am I." He rose slowly from the table, reached down, and removed her coif. "God's teeth," he whispered as a river of red-gold locks spilled down her back. "Your hair has grown." He took her hands, drew her to her feet, and buried his face in her hair. She smelled of attar of roses. The glorious flow of coppery curls had the texture of silken thread. "Ah, Annie," he said on a sigh. "Loving you is hopeless."

She pulled back, her direct gaze probing his face. "How can there be no hope where there is love?"

He bent and pressed his lips to her brow. "You know why, *cariad.*"

"Do you think I've not considered the consequences of lying with you?" She reached behind her and caught at the back laces of her bodice. "If I do not let myself love you . . ." The strings loosened, and the bodice fell forward. "*That* is true hopelessness."

A desperate groan escaped him. Winnowing his fingers into her hair, he caught her head between his hands and kissed her hard, unleashing the passion that had haunted him for years. He knew they toyed with the destiny of a nation, but he cared even less than she did.

He unhooked her sleeves and dropped them to the floor with the bodice. Her skirts joined the pile, and she stood before him in only her shift.

The garment was sheer, made of virginal white lawn, embroidered at the neckline with white silk thread. Annie looked vulnerable, heartbreakingly young. Her small breasts thrust against the gossamer fabric, the nipples taut and rosy. Her hair tumbled fully to her waist, and he was glad she kept it covered by a coif. He was jealous of her beauty, and he clung to the idea that Annie, in her shift, with her glorious hair unbound, was a sight reserved for him and him alone.

He took her hand lightly and held it up as if to lead her in a dance. "Let us go to the loft."

Her cheeks flushed with shyness, she nodded and climbed up the ladder. The wine in hand, he joined her. There, a soft pallet covered with thick bedrobes awaited them. Fire glow from the hearth flickered through the rafters.

The roof was low, and they were obliged to kneel on the pallet in the small, close area. Evan swore under his breath.

"What's wrong?" she asked.

"This place. We should be in an elegant bower or a chamber in a great castle," he said. "You were not made to be loved in a loft."

"It matters not," she said stubbornly.

Evan kissed her gratefully, then shed his doublet, his knee boots and hose and breeches. His loose shirt hung to his thighs.

She gazed at him expectantly. A sense of trepidation fell over him, and with a trembling hand he plucked at the laces of her shift. Nestled between her breasts was a gold ring on a leather string.

Evan took the ring in his hand. A smooth cabochon ruby gleamed in the fire glow. He read the words inscribed around the jewel, and his heart skipped a beat. "This belonged to King Henry?"

"Yes. He gave it to my grandmother, Doña Gabriella, and it has passed to me." Annie took the ring and let it drop against her chest. "Don't worry, Evan. I keep it hidden."

She lifted her face for a kiss, but he held back. "God's sweet son," he whispered. "You're a king's granddaughter. This is treason."

"Only if we're found out. Please, Evan . . ." She brushed the shift off her shoulders. The garment drifted down to pool like a cloud around her.

Her flesh was warm ivory shaped by a delicate musculature. Her nipples were coral pink and contracted tightly— from the chill or from anticipation, he couldn't tell.

Flinging off all his misgivings, Evan pressed his hands to her breasts. The softness and warmth of her skin sent a jolt of agonizing heat to his loins.

"My God, Annie," he whispered. "Your beauty humbles me."

A smile curved her lips. "It's your love that makes me beautiful to you." She reached for the hem of his shirt. The brush of her hands on his thighs kindled the fire in him. And yet at the same time he felt a sudden coldness, a hesitancy.

He took her hands in his. "Annie, you'd best let me keep

my shirt on. No measure of your admiration can make me beautiful, and I'd not offend you at such a time."

Anger glinted in her eyes. "You think my love so shallow that I should fear to look upon you?"

She loved him. He saw it shining in her eyes, and deep inside him stirred the knowledge that loving her was an act of trust.

"I am . . . marked. Scarred," he said.

"Scarred or not, you're beautiful to my eyes." She drew his loose shirt over his head and slid her arms around him. When her hands encountered the ridges and taut, shiny-smooth flesh of his back, she caught her breath.

"Who did this to you? Was it Owen?"

He nodded.

"Jesu, my love." Her voice thickened with tears. "I never understood what being a whipping boy meant. I asked Owen about it, and he gave me to believe you were simply his boyhood companion, sharing in his lessons."

"So I was. But the punishments were mine alone to bear."

A tear slid down her cheek. "God above, Evan! How could your father allow a little boy to serve in such a capacity? No lessons are worth—"

"Hush." Evan stopped the tear with his lips. "My father never knew. He thought I was merely a companion. I hid the scars."

"Why? He would not have made you stay with Owen if he'd known."

"We were penniless, Annie. We needed my wage, little as it was."

"You were just a little boy," she whispered in a voice that touched his heart. "Life shouldn't have been so cruel to you. No child should have to bear what you endured."

"It's all behind me now, my love. Would you like me to put my shirt back—" He stopped speaking and froze. She had moved behind him. Her curls brushed his back, and then her hands and lips were there, touching and tasting the ugly marks of his shame. He trembled beneath the onslaught of her acceptance, her understanding. Annie's love had the power to heal his soul.

Evan made a tortured sound and turned to take her in his arms. She lay back on the pallet, opening her legs, welcoming him.

He came to her slowly, finding her ready. She winced when he took the fragile gift of her virginity. As he did so, the thought touched him that he was claiming her most valuable asset, and yet he didn't care. If she never gave herself to another man, he would be glad.

A long sigh escaped her. "Evan. I feel as if I shall burst."

He took her mouth in a leisurely kiss. "With pain?"

Her hips tilted toward him. "With pleasure."

He began to move, feeling her lovely body warm and eager beneath him, while his own passion climbed to a high, teetering crest.

She gave a small cry of startlement, and a series of tiny convulsions seized her. Evan flung himself into the pleasure. Words of love rushed from him as the final ecstasy caught him in a grip of agonizing passion.

Annie watched the glow of the firelight reflecting on her wine cup. Evan lay still beside her, his outflung arm cradling her head, his chest rising and falling with the peaceful cadence of sleep.

She took a sip of wine, and knew she'd not sleep tonight. The intense passion of their lovemaking still sang in her veins. The knowledge that Evan loved her banished all misgivings about what they had done.

She had seen the humiliation and suffering love affairs had brought to the members of the royal court. The queen, Annie reflected, had no tolerance for the marital happiness of others. She had refused to allow Lady Katherine Grey to marry the Earl of Hertford, and when Katherine became pregnant, Elizabeth had sent her to the Tower. By an act of 1536, it became treason for members of the royal family to marry without the permission of the sovereign. Elizabeth's consent was given rarely and reluctantly.

The prospect of being discovered was daunting, and the wine cup in Annie's hand faltered, spilling over her naked breasts and stomach.

"Damn," she whispered. She set down the cup and reached for her shift to dry herself.

A strong hand closed around her wrist.

A sleepy smile curved Evan's mouth. "Allow me, *cariad*." He bent his head and drank the wine from her skin. His warm tongue moved in circles around her breasts. She cried out as his teeth toyed with her tender nipples and his fingers slipped between her thighs to stroke the sensitive flesh there. His mouth traveled downward, his kiss ultimately consuming her where she burned hottest for him.

She arched her back and burst like a blossom coming to full flower for him. And then he was inside her, turning abruptly so that she came atop him as wave after wave of sensation swamped her. His response was a subtle surge of heat, and the rapt look on his face mirrored her own passion.

As the feelings subsided, he brought her to lie down beside him. "You should not curse in bed," he said. "It awakens me with a hunger."

"Then I shall think of a new curse each day."

He kissed her, and the sweet musky taste of his lips enflamed her anew.

"Evan!"

"Hush." He laughed softly. "In time, *cariad*. Pass me the wine."

She watched his every movement in fascination. She loved the ripple of his throat as he swallowed, the shaggy waves of his hair, the slumberous look of satiation that softened his face.

"Evan," she whispered.

A lazy smile curved his mouth. "Aye?"

"I will carry this picture of you in my heart. No matter how far you go, I shall always see you the way you are now, in my arms." Her own words startled her, and she gasped. "Jesu, I did not let myself think of that."

He drained his cup, leaned down, and kissed her belly. "Of what?"

"You're leaving."

"Aye." He propped himself on one elbow. With his free hand, he mapped the curves of her throat, her breasts, her thighs, with a familiarity that thrilled her.

"It's to be the Straits of Magellan, isn't it?"

His hand stilled. "How did you guess?"

"The story of how Drake climbed a tree in the Cordillera, spied the Great South Sea, and vowed to go there one day is a court favorite."

Evan blew out his breath. "Francis has a big mouth. Then others, too, might have guessed."

"Not likely. Sebastian Cabot himself failed in his attempt to navigate the straits. Even the Lord High Admiral believes Magellan's achievement can't be duplicated.

"But you think otherwise."

"I've seen the sort of man Drake is." She kissed his hand. "I know the sort who follows him."

He sat up, drew her into his arms, and pressed her head to his chest. "Tell no one, Annie. I wish you didn't know."

She laughed. "In my years at court, I've learned to speak, yet say nothing. I guard my thoughts."

And even with the man she loved, she had her secrets. She knew, with a word, she could make him turn from Drake and stay with her. But never would she use his love for her to manipulate his life. There was in him a hunger, an impatience, a need that could only be answered by the deep, uncharted seas.

She wanted to tell him that someone had been pursuing her, rifling her chambers, giving her the eerie sensation of being watched. Prying eyes were everywhere in a court that thrived on intrigue.

She swallowed her fears. Confessing them would only subject Evan to the torture of torn loyalties. Passing between the two great oceans of the world was no easy task. He would need all his concentration, uncompromised by worries about her.

"How long will you be gone?" she asked.

"Magellan's fleet took three years to make the journey. I won't pretend we can sail faster."

Her heart sank with disappointment. "I'll wait for you, Evan."

Her naive conviction tore at Evan's heart. The chances of his returning were slim, but he refused to frighten her. If he succeeded, he'd be wealthy and worthy of her. For now, he could make no promise save one.

"I'll be back," he said. And he silently begged God not to make a liar of him.

CHAPTER 15

"Your Majesty, by my reckoning," said the Earl of Essex, preening like a prize cock at a fair, "they'll be approaching the straits within the week. Soon all the world will know of your brilliance in making England the mistress of the high seas."

From her place on a window seat, Annie shot a secret, black scowl across the Presence Chamber at Essex. He had a mouth of a size to match his puffed-out chest and had never learned the meaning of discretion.

Yet with the passing of the years, the queen had developed a special tolerance for comely men who plied her with compliments. She gave him a smile that still had the power to dazzle. "You do wish them well, don't you, my friend?"

Essex swept his plumed hat toward the floor in a bow. "Of course. How could I not? Dear Madam, you have my undying support in all your endeavors."

Annie saw through his blustering assurances. He was jealous of Drake.

"All England prays for his success," said Essex. "If he manages to—"

"My lord," Christopher Hatton broke in. "Guard your tongue. The new Spanish ambassador approaches."

Annie liked Hatton—his quick wit, his unabashed devotion to the queen, his certainty that Drake and Evan would succeed. With practiced skill, he drew Essex away from the queen.

Within moments, the Spanish ambassador's herald came forward with the queen's majordomo.

Annie froze. The majordomo spoke, but his words were a dull thud in her ears. Her gaze clung to the dark, lean man bending over the queen's proffered hand.

"Oh God, help me," she whispered and started to shrink back into the shadows, out of view of Don Iago Orozco, once an aide to the viceroy of New Spain, and the man she would forever blame for the death of her father.

It was too late. As he stepped back from the dais to address the court, he spied her. And in his eyes she saw the dark, hungry certainty that he had recognized her.

Port St. Julian
July 1578

"This is the end of traitors!" Drake hurled his words at a sky that boiled with silver-bellied clouds.

The men stared at the convulsing, headless body on the rocky ground. Some recoiled to escape the spattering of blood that jetted from the neck. The axman turned away, dropped his bloody weapon, and bent over to vomit.

A keen wind ripped through Evan's hair. He felt the sting of cold on his ears, but kept his cap clutched to his chest and his eyes fastened on the disembodied head of Thomas Doughty.

He felt no remorse. Doughty, proud and self-important, had betrayed them. Even before they had left Plymouth, he had confessed, against the express command of the queen, the true destination of the expedition to Lord Burghley.

Had he stopped at that treachery, Drake could have spared

him. Instead, Doughty had pilfered sealed goods from a captured Portuguese ship. He had claimed an admiral's authority for himself. Worst of all, he had whispered doubts into the ears of the men, urging them to revolt before Drake sailed them to their deaths.

Drake's eyes were tortured and damp as he blinked against the driving wind. "Can I believe my own words, Evan?" he asked, his voice ragged.

"You're a hard man, Francis," Evan said. "And ruthless, but only to your enemies." He scanned the crew who stood in an uneven line along the beach. "There is not a mariner among us who would call you murderer."

Drake glanced at the man who had gone to kneel beside the now-still body. "Doughty's brother is with us yet."

"Francis, the jury was unanimous in denouncing Tom as a traitor. Remember what the queen said. Of all men, Lord Treasurer Burghley should not learn the true purpose of the expedition."

" 'If anyone should pass on the information, they should lose their heads therefore,' " Drake added, quoting the queen's words.

"Thomas Doughty gave you no choice," Evan said. "Here we are in a foreign land, eating foul penguin meat and strange fish, beset by natives"—Evan glanced at the rocky cairns they had built over the bodies of two slain seamen—"and poised to enter waters of legendary treachery. Those are perils enough without the threat of mutiny."

Drake scrubbed his beard with his hands. "Aye, but should I have found some alternative? Put Tom under guard—"

"That would not have silenced him."

"—or sent him back to England—"

"You couldn't have spared any men to escort him."

Drake closed his eyes and inhaled with a shudder. "Stay with me, Evan. You are a better voice than my own conscience." He opened his eyes and looked at the seamen assembled, dumbstruck with horror, on the rocky shore: Captain Winter, Ned Bright, who had heard Doughty's schemes and denounced him, Will Hawkins, Parson Fletcher, Drake's own brother Thomas and his nephew Jack. And some fifty others—men and boys, soldiers and seamen, gentlemen and commoners.

"I must speak." Dragging his hair out of his face, he squared his shoulders. "I must preach this day myself."

He beckoned to the crew with a sweep of his arms. "The hazards of this voyage still lie ahead of us, my masters. We cannot face mortal difficulties with our loyalty in fragments. I demand an end to discord and quarreling."

Mariners eyed soldiers with distrust. Gentlemen adventurers looked upon their common counterparts with disdain.

"By the life of God, we are engaged in the same adventure!" Drake pounded his fist in his palm. "We must share the burdens equally! I must have this stomaching among seamen and gentlemen left. Henceforth, gentleman and mariner shall haul and draw without regard to station. I would know him who would refuse to set his hand to a rope . . ." Drake's fierce gaze, hooded by heavy irony, settled on the group of gentlemen. "Surely there cannot be any such here."

His sword slapping his thigh and his boots crunching over the beach, he began to pace. "All who wish to leave are free to do so. Make your way back to England in the *Marigold*." His eyes glittered with a direct challenge. "But mind you, if I find you in my way, I'll sink you to hell!"

With a brilliant, charming smile, Drake pointed his toe and bowed deeply. "What say you, my masters? Will you leave me?"

The wind skirled with brutal force across the beach. Neither hand nor voice lifted in reply.

Drake planted his hands on his hips and faced the ships' officers. "Excellent. And now, you are hereby dismissed from your posts."

Jaws dropped. Eyes widened and fists clenched.

Captain Winter nudged Captain Thomas, and as one, they stepped forward. "Here, sir," said Winter. "Your authority is complete, but you need not go so far to prove it."

Drake smiled humorlessly. "Tell me why I should not dismiss you after the sedition and near mutiny that have occurred." He waited through a few moments of wind-harried silence. "Doughty was not the only one guilty of treason. But I'm a gentleman, and I swear no more will die by the ax."

To reinforce his authority, he showed the letters and documents from his investors and finally, the queen's own bill of share.

"Any questions?" he asked archly.

The men stood silent.

"Fine. Then all that's left is to break up the storeships, reassign the men and cargoes." He turned again to the officers. "And, by the by, my good masters. You are reinstated."

A cheer went up from the men. Drake threw back his head and shouted with laughter at his own munificence.

Evan watched, agog at what his friend had accomplished. He had faced a mob of fractious, frightened men, asserted his control, and renewed their faith in him and their commitment to the enterprise.

"God's holy knees, Francis, did you learn that in Ireland?" he asked as they worked together ferrying stores to the three remaining ships.

"Aye, and from the best there is."

"And who might that be?"

"The Earl of Essex, and none other."

Essex. Evan knew, from court gossip, that the man had a pretty face, a smooth tongue, and a sharp wit, and that he used all three weapons to lay siege to the queen's affections. After Drake's display, Evan would not be surprised if the charm had worked.

"A pity Essex didn't warn you about Tom Doughty," Evan muttered.

"He did," Drake admitted, and his lips thinned in self-loathing. "So did you. But I was too damned proud to listen. Imagine me believing Doughty to be my friend." He shook his head. "I was so flattered by his attention that I failed to let myself wonder why he was drawn to me. I should have seen that he cared not a whit about me, that he wanted to seize the glory for himself."

"It's over, Francis. 'Tis best you look ahead now."

"Aye, and best I put my trust in men like you, and Dirk and Denton and good Ned Bright. Men who know their worth and the meaning of loyalty don't kindle mutiny."

Evan looked away, stricken by guilt. Was not that his very ambition, to use the voyage to raise his station and lay his newfound wealth at the feet of Annie Blythe?

"Francis, I—"

"I want you to sail on Captain Thomas's ship," Drake said.

"Of course, if you ask it of me. But Francis, there's something I should tell you."

Drake stared at him for a long moment. "Save it, Evan. There's work to be done."

In August, the *Pelican* was rechristened the *Golden Hind* in honor of Sir Christopher Hatton. Together with the *Marigold* and the *Elizabeth*, the flagship surged to the brink of the Straits of Magellan.

In homage to the queen, the topsails dipped. Evan stood on the quarterdeck of the *Marigold* with John Thomas, her captain. In silence they looked starboard at the towering cliffs. Before them loomed Tierra del Fuego, a weird, otherworldly land of seething volcanoes and sharp, snow-clad peaks.

The grim scene held a strange and terrible allure for Evan. "The end of a continent," he remarked.

Captain Thomas sneezed into his sleeve. "And a bleak end it is, too. By God, Evan, this gives me a bad feeling." He stared fixedly at the dark waters, the rearing cliffs with the surf exploding against them. "Naught but death awaits us there."

"Perhaps." Even so, Evan felt no fear. Annie had given him one night. In that one night, they had loved more than most people do in a lifetime. He was not afraid to risk his very life to win her. "Can you think of a way you'd rather die, John?"

Thomas squared his shoulders and poked his large, red nose into the wind. "No."

From the *Golden Hind* came the booming of a gun. The three ships sailed into the very teeth of the straits, into the churning waters that had made kindling of every fleet save Magellan's for the past fifty years.

During the sixteen days of the passage, the three ships experienced every danger fashioned by the hand of God: rushing tides, screaming squalls, razor-sharp rocks and shoals, hidden banks. Most pervasive and perhaps most dangerous of all, Evan knew, was the sense of utter isolation.

The land was exactly as God had created it: a stark white-and-gray world untouched by man. He had the feeling that they were the last creatures on earth. In his heart he knew that somewhere far away, people toasted their toes before cheery hearth fires. They danced and worked and made love. But that world seemed as remote as the stars. As unreachable as Annie.

They left the bitter, mysterious straits behind and celebrated with a meal of wine and awful-tasting penguin meat dripping with grease. Almost before they could breathe a sigh of relief, a gale came shrieking down from the northeast.

"We can do naught but run before it," Thomas hollered. The howling of the wind snatched at his words of helplessness. Wind-driven spume struck Evan in the face and stung like needles of ice. Days and nights blurred together as the gale drove them southward. No one spoke of it, but every man knew they were being blown wildly off course. To *Terra Australis* or some undiscovered continent, or to hell itself.

Yet Drake's plea for unity seemed to linger in the minds of the men. Mariner and gentleman worked side by side, hauling, drawing, brailing up sails and working the pumps.

On September 30, the roaring advance of the storm seized the fleet with new strength. The *Marigold* pitched like a wild horse, bucking over steeple-high waves and plunging into seemingly depthless troughs. As he stood on deck and clung to a belaying pin, Evan saw a seaman in the rigging, trying desperately to shorten sail.

"Jesu, no!" he bellowed, struggling to the quarterdeck. He moved hand over hand along the rail. The wind battered him like an unseen enemy pushing him two steps back for every three he accomplished. "For the love of God, Denton! Leave it!"

Denton clung like a fly caught in a spider's web. He had lost his cap, and his hair had frozen to the rigging. "I can't move, sir!" he called. "By all that's holy, I can't!"

Evan swore and grasped the rigging. "I'm coming after you!" He slung a coil of rope around his neck and put one arm through the loop, tying the end to a hatch cover. Grimly he ascended, all the while buffeted by the wild pitching of the ship. From the corner of his eye he saw the *Golden Hind* a few hundred yards distant.

The ratlines were encased in solid ice, and the flesh on his hands tore. Bleeding and exhausted, he reached Denton. "Here," he called, looping one end of the rope around Denton's waist. "I'll lower you with this."

"We'll both fall!" Denton shrieked.

"Aye. Just be sure you aim for the deck, not the water. The nether end's secured to a hatch cover, so you won't go far."

"I'm afraid to my soul's depths," said Denton.

The ship laboriously climbed a swell, then plunged down the other side. The sky boiled with tempest-driven clouds. Sleet pelted their faces. Hell, Evan swore, was not hot but cold. All this, he reflected bleakly, to win a pinch of spice and to tweak the beard of the king of Spain. The expedition seemed, for the first time, the very worst of foolhardy endeavors.

"Do you think I'd call you less than a man for fearing this?" Evan asked.

"You're afraid, too?"

"Aye, but if I pissed myself, my trews would freeze." Using one hand and his teeth, Evan secured the knot about Denton's waist. "Off you go, then." He pried his friend's fingers from the rigging. Slowly, Denton began his descent.

Evan was about to follow him when a massive wave smacked broadside against the hull. As the shock of the blow reverberated through the rigging, Evan clung with both hands.

The ship hove to, swinging so wildly that Evan's head

spun and his vision blurred. The rope that linked him to Denton pulled taut at his waist and shoulder. He shook his head to clear it. Huge swells girdled the ship. Dimly he could see the stern light of the *Hind* winking through the spume.

Another wave hurtled forward. Its bearded crest rose higher than the cliffs of Wales. As hard and sculpted as a gleaming wall of marble, the wave came closer and closer, its white peaks curling like a set of talons.

Evan opened his mouth to pray as the giant wave struck. *"Annie!"* he screamed.

Like a stone hurled from a sling, Evan was flung from the rigging and into the icy sea.

The queen rattled Annie's letter in irritated fashion. "This is mighty cheeky, even for you," she said.

Annie twined her fingers together and squeezed hard, but she lifted her chin and returned the queen's stare. "Aye, ma'am. But in my own fashion I write the truth. The Spanish ambassador lauds the virtues of King Philip, while I trow he is a dangerous man."

"Dangerous!" A bark of laughter erupted from Elizabeth. Beside her, Sir Christopher Hatton flinched at the sound. "King Philip is the sodding devil incarnate. And aye, I'll admit it, he's the most powerful man in Christendom, and at the moment, he's building an immense fleet, no doubt to unleash upon our very shores. But I'll not suffer you to air that opinion in my court."

Annie bobbed a curtsy. "If we keep silent about his blood pogroms, do we not then condone the burning of innocents?"

The queen glared at her. "Have I not enough to do defending the Dutch Protestants?"

"Of course." Annie held out her hand for the letter. "I shall destroy it at once."

Their hands touched as Elizabeth gave her the parchment. For the briefest of moments, a strange shock of awareness bonded them. Elizabeth's cool gray eyes clashed with Annie's. Then the moment passed and Annie stepped back.

"Why do you hate Don Iago so?" Elizabeth asked softly.

"It is almost as if you fear him, and I've never known you to fear anyone."

Because he knows me.

Heat suffused Annie's cheeks. She stared down at the hem of her dress and noticed, incongruously, a few hairs from the gray cat Evan had given her so long ago. The little animal was still her constant companion.

"Well?" the queen prompted.

Annie bit her lip. Don Iago had said nothing—yet. Years had passed between their meetings, but Annie sensed him watching her, waiting like a spider in the dark.

"Madam, he advances damaging policies—"

"He's trying to keep the peace."

"By urging you to ignore Spain's aid to Ireland? To disregard the building of an armada?" Annie shot back.

Elizabeth clutched the arms of her chair and leaned forward. "I will go to war with Spain one day. I've never denied it. But I will not let English blood be spilled over so trivial a matter as Don Iago. Is that understood?"

Before Annie could answer, a page rushed to the dais and handed a letter to Hatton. "It's urgent, sir."

Christopher Hatton tore open the parchment. As he read, the color drained from his face.

"What's amiss, Kit?" the queen demanded.

"News of the expedition." Hatton cleared his throat. Conversation around the dais stilled. "The *Elizabeth* has returned to Plymouth."

Annie's heart surged to her throat. She made a physical effort to keep herself from leaping upon Sir Christopher and snatching the letter to read for herself.

"And?" the queen prompted.

"Captain Winter, of the *Elizabeth*, was forced by storms to turn back after getting through the Straits of Magellan. The *Pelican* was rechristened the *Golden Hind* in my honor and is bound away for the Great South Sea. The *Marigold*—" His voice broke. He took out a handkerchief and mopped his brow. "She went down in the storm. There were no survivors."

A hiss of pain escaped Elizabeth. "Have you a list of the men who perished?"

Hatton nodded and read from the page. "Captain John Thomas, his marshal Hugh Stanleigh, his first officer Evan Carew . . ."

The room tilted before Annie's eyes. Thunder crashed in her ears, and she heard no more of the names. For a moment her mouth moved in silent shock. Then, of its own volition, one word burst from her: *"Evan!"*

In some part of her mind she understood that she was breaking protocol and revealing before all the court her hidden love for Evan. It didn't matter. Nothing mattered anymore.

She fled the chamber, running blinding through the halls, bursting out into the river garden. There, she sank to her knees, clutching the edge of a marble bench.

Evan was dead.

"No," she whispered, clinging to the scalloped bench as if in peril of drowning. "You can't be dead. I won't let you be dead." Images of Evan blazed through her mind. She saw him laughing down at her, taking her into his arms, kissing her long and hard. And then she saw him kneeling in front of her, cradling her face between his hands and pledging his love with the solemn devotion of a man at prayer.

"I won't let you go, Evan. I won't let you!" She realized she was screaming but could not stop herself. Grief seared her with the intensity of unholy wrath. She tore loose her coif. Her hair streamed in red-gold billows around her. She pounded the cold, smooth marble bench with her fists, and sobs ripped from her throat.

"You left my presence without permission."

Annie dragged her sleeve across her eyes. She found herself staring at a dainty pair of jeweled slippers peeking from the hem of a gold and white brocade gown. Her gaze traveled upward to the stern face of the queen.

Annie did not even attempt to rise.

"Who is Evan Carew to you?"

Unwavering loyalty surged in Annie. "He is the man I love."

The queen's mouth pinched into a tight line. With a swift motion, she sat down on the bench and seized Annie's chin between her thumb and forefinger. "He was your lover?"

"Yes." Annie took fierce pride in the admission.

The queen's hand shook but she never slackened her grip. "By the teeth of God, am I condemned to preside over a court of whores and fools?"

Annie jerked her head away. "We are as you choose to see us, madam."

"And how, my young fool, do I choose to see you?"

"Through the eyes of a woman who loves power better than she loves happiness." The words were out before Annie could stop them.

Elizabeth's blow was swift and sharp, her slim hand cracking across Annie's cheek. The salt of her tears intensified the sting.

Shocked silent by the attack, Annie glared at the woman who was her only living relative.

"Do you know why I struck you?" Elizabeth demanded.

"Because I am right?"

A soft gasp escaped the queen. Annie braced herself for another blow, but none came. Elizabeth said, "You should know better than to speak the truth to me when the truth is so ugly."

"Don't you weary of the lies, the empty flattery, the insincere compliments?"

"No." Elizabeth reached out and stroked Annie's hair. Her mood changed as swiftly as a shifting breeze, and her touch was as gentle as a mother's. "I've never seen your hair before, Annie. What a remarkable color it is."

Annie dared not move. Surely the queen could not guess their blood bond simply by the color of her hair.

Elizabeth stood abruptly. "I'm sorry Evan Carew is dead. I knew him briefly. He was a man of honor, an ornament to the realm. But he was also a commoner, completely unsuited to you. You shall marry one day if that is what you wish, but your husband must be a knight or better."

Annie pressed her hands to the hollow where her heart used to dwell. "I had much, much better than a titled lover, madam," she whispered. "And because of him, I'll never marry."

Death had Annie's face.

Her shimmering image stalked Evan. Even as he had plunged into the cold, seething sea, he had seen her with her head tipped back and her eyes sparkling with laughter. She had haunted the slow process of his drowning, flitting in and out of his flickering consciousness like a magic sprite intent on mischief.

Now she was an angel, a distant golden glimmer, more light than substance. How beautiful she was, swaying gracefully as the sunlight flirted with the shadows around her.

Evan smiled.

She made dying almost pleasant.

"Hell of a way to shirk your duties," said a smooth, sardonic voice.

Evan blinked. The golden image of Annie rippled away like a phantom bog light. In its place he saw Drake, standing with one foot crossed over the other, his beard ragged and his face burned red by sun and wind.

"Francis?" Evan's voice creaked like a little-used windlass.

"Aye." Drake dropped to the planks beside the hammock where Evan lay. "Jesu, we weren't sure you'd make it. One of the surgeons died, and the other disappeared with the *Elizabeth*. For medical comfort, we've naught but a sawbones barber."

"I thought I was dead." Shakily, Evan tried to rise. His vision swam, and his strength failed. He collapsed back onto the cotton hammock. "What happened, Francis?"

"Much. The *Elizabeth* is lost; she might have gone back through the straits to England. The *Marigold* sank. You and Denton are the only survivors."

"How the hell did we manage that?"

"Denton said you were tied together for a climb through the rigging. When you fell, you took Denton and a hatch cover with you. He managed to stay afloat on the hatch. In the midst of the storm we brought the two of you aboard the *Golden Hind*." Drake pressed his hands together, and his eyes shone with wonder. "It was one chance in a million that we saw you, plucked you out of the sea. You must have been cradled in the very hand of God."

Evan squeezed his eyes shut. John Thomas and the crew. They had been brothers, squabbling often but always united by their common enterprise. Now they were gone, their loved ones ignorant of their deaths and their bodies lost forever in the icy, forbidding world of the straits.

"It was a long night," he said weakly.

"Night?" Drake shouted with laughter. "Indeed it was long. Your ship sank days ago."

Evan's eyes flew open. "Days? I've been senseless for days?"

"Helpless as a babe, and a lot messier to tend. We've all taken turns shoving broth down your gullet and performing other unmentionable tasks."

Evan shuddered with guilty relief. He had survived. His ship had gone down, but he had survived.

"What's that wound on your face, Francis?" he asked.

Drake fingered the crescent-shaped scar on his cheek. "While you were malingering here, I took an arrow from one of the natives of Mocha Island. The Spaniards taught them well to hate bearded strangers." His brows pulled together in a scowl. "I lost my gunner in the skirmish."

"We all knew the risks, Francis. Now tell me where we've been and where we are, for I feel I've been far away."

The *Golden Hind* had breasted the long uncharted coast of Chile, moving inexorably toward the unprotected western flank of the Spanish empire. It was too much for Evan to take in at one telling, but it marked the start of his recovery. Within a week, he was on his feet. Within a fortnight, he was performing a seaman's tasks.

On the fifth of December, 1578, Evan stood, much thinner

but fully recovered, on the quarterdeck. The *Golden Hind* had dropped anchor in a bay just north of Valparaiso, a fishing village with a deep harbor. The bitter squalls of the straits lay far to the south of them. Here, the breezes blew as soft and sweet as a maiden's breath. The sea reflected the cloudless azure of the sky, and on the shore, forested hills rose up like nobles clad in emerald silk.

"What think you, Evan?" Drake asked. "Have we found paradise?"

"Paradise, once found, is no longer a paradise."

Drake cocked his head to one side. His copper-bright hair shone in the sun. "Your brush with mortality made you quite the philosopher. So you think by finding paradise, we destroy it?"

"Aye, there's the irony, Francis. For once we discover it, we rob it of those qualities that made it a paradise in the first place."

"An interesting notion, but I'll not trouble my mind with your philosophy. The Spaniards have already dug in just down the coast. If we're to invade paradise, we might as well get rich doing it. What say you, Evan?"

Evan threw back his shoulders as a sense of purpose burned away his qualms. "Let the Great Raid begin."

CHAPTER 16

Francisco Robles strummed his fingers on the rail of the merchantman. Even the easy camaraderie of his seven companions couldn't ease his boredom. The repetitious bobbing of the ship anchored at Valparaiso intensified his sullen mood.

"God, I'd hoped to find some decent sport in the town," he grumbled, uncorking another jar of wine. "It's naught but a crude fishing village of bug-eating savages."

His friend, Diego, commiserated. "The natives aren't nearly as biddable as the ones of the Caribbean. I tried to bed a wench, and the foolish bitch threw herself off a cliff."

Francisco shook his head in disgust. "They have strange ways here—" He broke off, jumping to his feet. "Sail!" he said, pointing. Gilded by the setting sun, a large ship had entered the harbor. Shields bearing the device of a golden hart or horse gleamed on the hull.

"What ship is that?" someone asked.

"Who cares?" Diego said. "It can't be anything but Spanish in these waters."

"Let's invite them aboard to share our wine," said Francisco. At his signal, a boatload of newcomers pulled across and clambered aboard. Francisco spread his arms wide in welcome.

One of the men, a stocky fellow with red hair and beard, a scarred cheek and small, hot eyes, shouted something guttural and smashed his fist into Diego's face. Frozen by astonishment, Francisco put up no defense when another man kicked him in the gut, shoved him below along with his comrades, and shut the hatch.

The captives sat in the dark while the impossible happened. English pirates—*English* pirates—helped themselves to all the gold and wine on the merchantman.

Sancho Montoya ran until a stitch in his side forced him to slow his pace. High on a hill above Valparaiso, he turned to look at the town he had just fled and prayed he would wake from the nightmare.

But from his vantage point, he saw his worst fears borne out. The devil had sent his messengers. Lutheran corsairs had arrived in the undefended empire of the west. Only black magic could have brought them here in their great man-of-war. Like an army of ants they were, marching into the abandoned town, looting the houses, seizing fruit and vegetables from gardens and storehouses, and helping themselves to the treasures of the church.

"*El Draquez,*" Sancho said, panting. It had to be. Already a fearsome legend in the Caribbean, the English raider had now visited his unholy wrath upon Valparaiso.

Sancho and his fellow townspeople were as helpless as mice staked to the ground, awaiting the strike of a hawk.

Juan Saltillo slept on the bank of the *río* Pisagua and dreamed a beautiful dream. His bundle of thirteen bars of silver, worth some four thousand ducats, had induced the pleasant reverie. After years of labor, Juan had made his fortune. The silver would allow him to retire in perpetual comfort at a hacienda near Panama. He would be served by only the most beautiful of slaves. He would eat only the daintiest of fare, and his wealth would, at last, win him the favor of Julia, the treasurer's daughter.

Juan came awake with a smile on his face. With a lazy hand, he reached for his bundle—and found nothing but trampled dirt.

Horror beat in his breast as he frantically followed a trail to the mouth of the river. He arrived in time to see a party of pirates transferring his silver—*his* silver—to a large man-of-war.

The corsairs sang an English chantey.

Eduardo Castillano wiped a gob of spittle from his cheek. "Damned beast," he muttered, jerking the halter of the lead pack animal. "Why God fashioned the llama is surely a mystery to me."

Eduardo led a string of eight foul-smelling, ill-tempered beasts. Their only virtue was that each of them carried a hundred pounds of silver.

Sweet satisfaction washed over him. His fortune was achieved—and, in his mind, half spent. First, he'd get himself to Arica and buy that dainty slave wench he'd been lusting after. Then, he'd—

"Good day, my lord!"

Eduardo nearly came out of his skin. A dark stranger had appeared out of nowhere. In seconds, a dozen others joined him.

The dark-haired man smiled congenially. "My dear lord," he said, taking the halter rope from the lead llama, "my friends and I cannot endure to see such a fine gentleman as yourself turned carrier."

Disarmed, Eduardo said, "I do appreciate your help."

Other men took charge of the rest of the beasts.

"Yes," said the leader, "we feel compelled to offer our services as drovers."

Eduardo had an uncomfortable suspicion that the strangers were laughing at him. And then, as they drove the llamas down to the shore and cheerfully embarked the silver in their boats, they laughed aloud.

February 1579

"Don Rodrigo!" Captain Juan de Anton boomed a hearty greeting. "Welcome aboard the *Cacafuego*!"

Rodrigo grinned. "The *Shitfire*?"

"*Nuestra Señora de la Concepción* is too much of a mouthful for an old mariner like myself." Anton slapped his chest. "It's good of you to join us."

Rodrigo lifted his arm in farewell to the pinnace that had ferried him and his band of musketeers out to the huge merchantman, the great glory of the South Sea. The past several days had sped by in a blur: the messenger arriving on a nearly spent horse, the frantic plea from the governor of Peru, the impossible news that *El Draquez* had sprung upon the Pacific with a vengeance.

No, not impossible. Rodrigo pinched the bridge of his nose as the weariness of his days of travel threatened to overwhelm him. Francis Drake and his dread companion, Evan Carew, had a reputation for accomplishing the impossible.

The viceroy himself had prevailed upon Rodrigo to bring a troop of mercenaries to defend the great treasure ship.

"Tell me the latest news on the pirates," Rodrigo said.

Anton swore. "Bastards last dropped anchor at Callas. At that time, the alarm hadn't reached us, so when we spied the ship, we assumed they were just another merchantman. Next thing we knew, they had cut the cables of every ship in the harbor, helped themselves to all our victuals, and sailed away."

"How did you escape?"

"By the skin of our teeth, I can tell you that. I only pray the corsairs don't overtake us before we reach Panama." He eyed the party of soldiers Rodrigo had brought aboard. "Thank God you caught up with us, Don Rodrigo. At least now we've got a fighting chance."

"What are you shipping?"

"Eighty pounds of bar gold, thirteen chests of pieces of eight, jewels, pearls, and twenty-six tons of silver. Thank God we escaped Callas before the corsairs seized it."

Rodrigo whistled between his teeth. "*Demonios!* No wonder you're worried about the pirates. This ship alone contains more wealth than the treasury at Seville."

With every stitch of sail set, the *Cacafuego* coasted northward. If only they could catch a fair wind and beat the pirates to Panama, they would find protection.

Juan de Anton seemed confident that they had eluded the Englishmen. Rodrigo remained vigilant. Drake and Carew had all but snatched Annie out from under his nose. They had plundered the coasts of Chile and Peru. Capturing a heavily laden prize like the *Cacafuego* would be a lark to them.

Unable to sleep, Rodrigo stepped over the bodies of slumbering seamen on deck and stood at the rail. As they did so often, his thoughts drifted to Annie. *Annie.* The thought of her lanced him with pain. She had seemed so agreeable to his plan to marry her. Yet he should have recognized the shock and fear in her eyes when he had put forth the scheme. She had looked like a rabbit in a trap.

Then she had fled.

Since that time, Rodrigo's life had been hell. Valeria had been his only constant, a comforting and patient presence. She loved him well. But so long as Annie was lost, Rodrigo could not return Valeria's love. He had torn apart the coast and plains and jungles of the isthmus looking for Annie, to no avail. And with a forbearance that broke his heart, Valeria waited.

Annie had been gone for six years. *Six years.* God, she would be a woman grown by now. He had called at Saint Augustine, at Hispaniola and Puerto Rico. He had scribbled frantic letters of inquiry to Spain. Upon learning that Don Iago Orozco had attained the post of ambassador to England, Rodrigo had asked the man to inquire about her, but Orozco had never responded.

Annie, for the love of God, where are you?

Her disappearance had sent him spiraling into the depths of despair. Valeria had tried to haul him out of his self-hatred, but he had resisted. How could he accept her abiding love when he was not worthy to inhale the very air she breathed?

He nearly shook with the thoughts that plagued him. Unbeknownst to Anton, Rodrigo hoped the English would find them. That was his true purpose here. To learn news of Annie.

Rodrigo threw back his head and opened his mouth in a silent scream of rage. The stars spun in a bowl above him, their brilliance almost blinding.

An orange flash on the horizon caught his eye. A needle of suspicion pricked his spine. He could not be certain, but he thought the light too unlike a star or planet. Too close to the horizon. Bobbing up and down, as if with the motion of a ship.

"Captain de Anton!" Rodrigo roared, startling the crew awake. "Summon all hands! The pirates are upon us!"

By morning, the smaller, swifter English ship bore down on them. Rodrigo stationed his musketeers along the rail, weapons primed and waiting for the English ship to move into range.

Captain Juan de Anton stared in horror at the bank of cannons glaring from the gunports of the *Golden Hind*. "Can we mount a defense?" he asked.

"We can." Rodrigo buckled on his mail coat. Holding his helm under one arm, he studied the fast-approaching ship. "But not unless you order your gunners to commence their work."

Anton tugged nervously at his collar. "Don Rodrigo, our big guns are inoperable."

"*What?*"

"We never had need of them before. Keeping the cannons primed and oiled seemed a waste of work."

Rodrigo spat an oath. "Captain, I had no idea you'd left yourself so vulnerable."

"Strike sail!" In bad Spanish, the English captain shouted the order across the water.

Anton cast a frantic look at Rodrigo. "Shall I surrender without a fight, then?"

"Strike sail!" Drake repeated, "unless you wish to go to the bottom!"

"We might let them come aboard," Rodrigo said, "but the fight won't be pretty."

Anton crossed himself. "God help me, I don't know what—"

The English guns spoke. With a noise like thunder, cannon balls and grapeshot slammed into the hull. The ship lurched like a whale in its death throes. A round of chain-shot buzzed through the mizzenmast. The huge mast crashed into the sea, dragging rigging and a few luckless mariners with it.

"Run for your lives!" a man cried. He and most of his comrades dove below, chased by a swarm of English arrows. The musketeers, too panicked to obey Rodrigo's shouted orders, followed suit.

Rodrigo and the captain found themselves facing forty English boarders. Drake wrested his helm from his head and patted Anton on the shoulder. "Captain Juan de Anton?"

Anton bowed stiffly. "Yes."

"Sir, do you surrender this ship?"

Anton eyed the deserted decks. "What's left of it."

Merriment danced in Drake's eyes. "Accept with patience, amigo, what is the usage of war. Now I fear you and Don Rodrigo will have to wait below while my prize crew gets to work."

They took Rodrigo's sword. But as they led him away, they failed to notice the razor-edged dagger hidden in his boot.

A sense of sheer exultation pervaded the Englishmen as the immense treasure was transferred, bar by precious bar, to the *Golden Hind*. Chalk ballast was jettisoned and replaced by Spanish silver.

Evan and Drake pitched in, working alongside gentlemen adventurers and common seamen. A gleam of gold temporarily blinded Evan as he passed a heavy bar to Drake. "I keep thinking my eyes deceive me, Francis. Can there truly be so much treasure in all the world?"

"A few hours ago I would have disputed it." Drake, too, seemed caught in the grip of incredulity. "Do you know, Evan, this day we have made ourselves the richest men in England. Even the lowest ship's boy will spend the rest of his days in luxury."

Provided we make it back to England. Evan didn't voice his fear, but merely nodded and continued with the work until the transfer was completed.

"The ship is ready to be given back to her crew," Evan told Drake.

"Aye, we've taken all her guns, and the mizzenmast is down, so she can't give chase." Drake nodded toward the hatch that led below decks. "You do the honors, Evan, for the Spaniards had best get to manning their pumps. I'm going to draft a letter for Juan de Anton to give to Captain Winter, should he encounter the *Elizabeth*."

The fate of the *Marigold* had been sealed beneath the icy waters of the straits. No one knew what had befallen the *Elizabeth*, though Evan suspected she had run home.

He lifted a hatch and climbed down into a dim companionway. From within a storage room, he heard the curses and grumblings of the Spaniards.

Lifting the bar and wrenching open the portal, Evan blinked into the dimness. "Captain Juan de Anton?"

"Yes." The captain's voice rang loud.

"The transfer is complete. Your ship is to be restored to you. You're free to go."

Sounds of disbelief issued from the room. Were the tables turned, Evan knew the Spaniards would have shown no mercy. He waited while the vanquished crew and soldiers filed out, their heads hung low in shame and anger. Evan felt only a hard sense of satisfaction. The Spanish had grown rich and fat on the labors of conquered peoples. They deserved no sympathy.

When the last man disappeared up the hatchway, Evan

pushed at the door. Without warning, someone gripped his throat and dragged him into the room.

Evan fell to the hard planks. A pair of knees thumped down on his chest, squeezing the breath from him. The hands left his throat, to be replaced by the cold touch of a thin blade.

"Evan Carew," said a low, furious voice. "I thought I might find you among the pirates."

Evan's mind worked feverishly. "Who are you?"

The blade kept vigil at his throat while his attacker reached up and yanked open a portal. Sunlight streamed over a severely handsome, angry face.

Evan gaped at Annie's former guardian. "Don Rodrigo?"

"Where is she?" he demanded.

"If she wanted you to know, she would have sent you a letter."

A darkness seemed to pass over Rodrigo's features. The blade pressed harder, and Evan felt a warm trickle of blood. "You're hardly in a position to play games, Señor Carew," Rodrigo snapped. "I suggest you talk, and quickly."

Evan knew Rodrigo would not kill him. Not right away, at least. "She could have stayed with you, yet she chose to join us. She never told me why, Don Rodrigo. I assume you know the answer."

Rodrigo made a strangled sound of rage in his throat. Something cold seemed to click into place behind the dark eyes of Rodrigo Viscaino. Then his anger rekindled. "Enough stalling. Tell me where Annie is, or die."

Evan drew a deep breath. "Much to my regret, I cannot betray her."

Rodrigo swore. He drew back his knife hand, preparing to deliver the coup de grace.

"She's at the court of Elizabeth!" The admission, delivered in bad Spanish, came from the doorway. "There, I've told you what you wanted to hear."

Rodrigo jumped up, crouching low to challenge the newcomer. Evan glowered at Denton, who stood with a musket aimed at Rodrigo. "I had no choice but to tell him, Evan,"

Denton said. "He was going to kill you. Shall I shoot him now, or shall we bring him before Admiral Drake?"

Evan held out his hand. Muttering an oath, Rodrigo surrendered his dagger. "Leave us," Evan said to Denton, his gaze still fastened on Rodrigo. He waited until the sound of Denton's footsteps faded, then said, "I assume you'll be going to England."

"Of course."

"She left of her own volition. What makes you think she would welcome you?"

"I—" Rodrigo's voice broke. His face flushed red, and he cleared his throat. "I expect no welcome. I just want to make sure she is well and . . . and safe."

As Evan left the plundered ship, he knew he would not regret sparing the life of the Spaniard. For one thing was certain.

Rodrigo Viscaino loved Annie, too.

Annie wove her way toward the dais where the queen sat greeting newcomers to the court. The hall in Dunfield House, the first stop on the queen's summer progress, was crowded with courtiers and servants, but Annie spied a familiar face immediately.

Owen Perrott! The years had been kind to him. His hair still held that rich gleam, and his smile was as charming and guileless as a child's. He had waited years for a summons. Now here he was, looking utterly delighted to be in the presence of the woman who had put his father to death.

"Your Majesty." His voice soft with the proper mixture of awe and deference, Owen bowed low over the queen's proffered hand.

With a wave, Elizabeth bade him rise. "My God, Perrott," she said, her voice as strong as ever, "you're prettier even than your sire was."

Those who were close enough to hear fell still. The queen had issued a direct challenge by bringing up the matter of Henry VIII's bastard son, John Perrott. All waited to see how Owen would react.

He flushed. "I only pray, madam," he said loudly, "that my judgment is better."

The perfect answer, Annie thought wryly. The queen had few defenses against a comely face and such breezy charm. True to form, Elizabeth smiled and beckoned Owen closer.

Yet even as she watched, Annie could not help remembering the scars on Evan's back, the torment he had endured for Owen's misdeeds.

Reluctant to renew her acquaintance with Owen, Annie turned away, intending to go out into the gardens for a walk.

She found Don Iago Orozco standing in her way. He plucked the cigar from his mouth and smiled coldly. "Good day, mistress," he said.

Annie could not answer him. She was staring at his black doublet. A neat row of buttons was sewn down the front of it. They were the same buttons she had spied in Owen's cache of treasure; she was certain of it.

Fear stole her breath, but she managed to sniff at Don Iago in disdain as she brushed past him. "Good day, sir." Striving for composure, she made her way to the garden and sat amid the lilacs and foxglove, and wondered how to tell the queen her new favorite might be a traitor.

Bribing his way past guards and servants, Rodrigo had stolen like a thief into the apartments of André Scalia, one of the queen's closest advisers. Evan Carew had named the man as Annie's protector, and Rodrigo had voyaged across the Ocean Sea to find him. Unwilling to risk being turned away by the powerful courtier, Rodrigo had decided to enter in stealth and wait for Scalia.

To pass the time, he perused the chamber. An impressive library lined the shelves. Cocking his head to scan the titles, Rodrigo spied the works of Foxe and Trowley. So, the man had Protestant leanings.

After browsing through the books, Rodrigo examined an astrolabe on a marble-topped table, a free-standing globe, a set of wine cups made of paper-thin glass.

Behind the door hung a long black cloak. Sunlight

streamed through the diamond panes of the window and flickered off a gleam of silver. A lion, beautifully picked out by a master artisan. Rodrigo felt a jolt of recognition. He took the ornament in his hand, rubbing his thumb over the shining surface. His other hand stole to the pendant he wore and drew it out from beneath his shirt. The insignia was the same: the silver lion of Ribera, a title attainted when Rodrigo's grand-sire, Joseph Sarmiento, had fled the Inquisition many years before.

"*Madre de Dios,*" he whispered under his breath.

André Scalia paused in the arcade that led to his apartments. A bank of rushing storm clouds obscured the sun, and the distant rumble of thunder presaged a great storm. The gust of wind through the arches of the passageway enhanced his sense of urgency, and he hurried on toward his rooms.

He hated the queen's summer progress more and more each year. The arduous, cumbersome, seemingly endless train of courtiers, outriders, escorts, and baggage vehicles offended his sense of decorum and order. Year after year the queen insisted on going out among her people, parading through towns and hamlets like a goddess dispensing favors from a gilt litter.

Worse, this time a terrible sense of unease plagued André. He was worried about Annie, who had departed London two days ahead of him. The sparkle of youth had left her eyes, snuffed out by the news that Evan Carew had perished when his ship went down near the Straits of Magellan. In Annie's place lived a brittle, hollow young woman who laughed and ate too little, and who seemed not to care that someone was stalking her.

Aye, André was certain of it now. Don Iago Orozco was an adept spy. But no one had ever bested André Scalia at intrigue. He had seen couriers coming and going by night to and from the ambassador's house. He knew there was some plot afoot, and he feared the trap would spring during the queen's progress.

It made frightening sense. At court, André was able to

watch over Annie with the secret vigilance of a hawk. On progress, she traveled with the queen's ladies, vulnerable to attack.

Outside the door to his apartments, André tucked his cache of papers and letters under his arm and put his hand to the latch. He heard a sound inside his room.

Furious, he yanked open the door.

A tall man, his shoulder-length hair streaked white at the temples, stood before him. He had a lean, sun-browned face with high cheekbones, the dark eyes slightly tilted at the corners. His mouth was firm and unsmiling.

André felt a strange, visceral shock. He did not know this man, had never seen him before, and yet an awareness seemed to leap between them.

"Yes?" André asked, showing no sign of the suspicions that boiled inside him. "What are you doing in my apartments?"

"You are André Scalia?" the man asked. A distinct Spanish accent flavored his words.

"I am. And you are ... ?"

"Don Rodrigo de Viscaino y Sarmiento." The man strode to the door and kicked it shut. "I've come a very long way to meet you."

André felt a gut-deep jolt of fear. This man had been Annie's protector. Had Annie summoned him? And for what reason?

"What is your business?" he asked. "I'm about to leave London."

"No, you're not. First you'll answer my questions about Annie Blythe."

"I shall do nothing of the sort."

"I think you will." Viscaino went to the sideboard and helped himself to a glass of wine. As he turned, he drew a silver chain from the front of his shirt. The pendant dangled slowly before André's eyes. "Does this mean anything to you?"

André felt a sharp pain in his heart, as if it had turned over. He cleared his throat. "Should it?"

"Ah." A tight, satisfied smile curved Viscaino's mouth. "At last you lose a bit of complexion. I noticed you have a badge in the same design."

"You've no business rifling my belongings." André turned away to conceal the terrible hope and dread that churned inside him. For half a century, he had waited and wondered and searched.

The years peeled away and he remembered his gilded childhood, then his disgrace. The first wife of the Duke of Albuquerque, in despair over her barrenness, had taken the newborn child of a slave woman. She told her husband that she had given birth to André during one of the duke's long absences. As the treasured son and heir to the dukedom of Albuquerque, André had learned to love luxury and power.

All that had been taken from him when the duchess died. The duke remarried, and his second wife had gloatingly denounced André as a bastard. He had been stripped of his privileges, cast out into the unforgiving streets of Naples. A sympathetic house servant had given him the bit of silver, saying it had belonged to the slave woman who had borne him. All his life he had wondered about the woman, secretly praying he would find some clue about her one day.

Now that the moment had arrived, bitter denial rose in him. "The silver lion is hardly a unique device," he told his visitor.

"Does yours have the gothic R engraved on the back?"

André squeezed his eyes shut. A clap of thunder struck, rattling the windows, and a hissing rain commenced. His head pounded, and his chest ached anew. The pendant had been his only clue to the mystery of his past. He had consulted heralds and had even stooped to soothsayers and astrologers, but he had never learned the origin of the silver lion. Years earlier he had put aside his ambition to find his family. A silversmith had set his pendant into a badge. But he had never forgotten that cryptic letter R.

His legs felt wooden as he took his cloak from a peg behind the door, unfastened the badge, and handed it to Viscaino. He held the pieces side by side. For the first time, emotion flickered in the visitor's eyes: the heated glint of excitement.

"Can we sit down?" Viscaino turned a chair backward and straddled it. "I have a story to tell you."

Viscaino's easy grace, the suppleness of his long limbs, irritated André. Though he would die before admitting it, he sometimes felt his age and resented the younger man's fitness.

"Say what you came to say. I'll stand while I listen."

Viscaino sipped his wine. "Please yourself. Unless you know otherwise, I believe we're half brothers."

André felt his insides turn to stone. *No*, he wanted to scream. All these years have passed. . . . He took a deep breath. "The notion is highly unlikely."

Viscaino folded his arms over the back of the chair. The rim of his cup dangled from his fingertips. Outside, the rain intensified, lashing the windows. "Who were your parents, sir?"

"I don't know." André had never admitted the truth to anyone, yet the stranger's gaze seemed to draw the words from him. "I was born in Naples seventy years ago, more or less. I know only that my mother was a slave in the household of the duke of Albuquerque."

Viscaino shot to his feet. The chair hit the floor, and the wine sloshed in his glass. "I think your mother was the same as my own. Paloma, a woman of the West Indies."

"A native woman? A savage?" André struggled to keep his voice from breaking.

"Yes. She is the daughter of a Spanish grandee, Joseph Sarmiento, heir to the count of Ribera. He was accused of having Jewish blood and escaped to the Indies on the first voyage of Columbus."

Shock leaped in André's chest. "There were no survivors among those who stayed in the islands."

"Our grandfather survived. He took an Indian wife, Anacaona, and Paloma is their daughter. When she was just a girl, she was taken in a slave raid. My father, Armando Viscaino, brought her back to the islands. They married, and spent many years looking for you, traveling to Spain and Naples, studying birth records in countless churches and towns. But the records of the Ribera line were destroyed when the title was attainted. Still, my parents kept searching. They tried to find the child Paloma had birthed when she was little more than a child herself."

A crushing sense of futility pressed on André. Had his path ever crossed with that of the woman called Paloma? Had she gone to Naples, then? Scoured Spain in search of him?

"They live in San Augustine, in the province of La Florida now," Viscaino added. "Happily, they've prospered there."

"They're alive?"

"Yes. She was but thirteen when she gave birth to you, André. In her fortieth year, I was born." Viscaino took a step forward. "Now tell me you're not who I think you are."

André felt the Venetian stiletto he kept secreted in his boot. He fought the urge to plunge it into Viscaino's heart. "Am I supposed to weep with gratitude that you've found me at last?" he asked in a soft, furious voice. "Here you stand, you who enjoyed the love of your parents, the privilege of their success in New Spain, and you expect joy from me?"

"I know your life couldn't have been easy."

Black hatred fouled André's heart. "Get out," he said. "Now, before I—"

A sharp knock came at the door. "My lord!"

It was André's page. "Not now, Bertram!" he snapped.

"My lord, it's urgent! Mistress Blythe—"

Like an arrow shot from a taut bow, Viscaino sprang across the room and opened the door. He hauled in the hapless page by the front of his doublet. "What about Mistress Blythe?"

Bertram cast a questioning glance at André, who held up one hand to silence him. Viscaino's violent grip proved more compelling, and the lad blurted out, "A—a message just came from Dunfield House. The queen is in a temper with Mistress Blythe. The young lady has accused a Welsh lord of stealing from the Crown, and Her Majesty took it amiss!"

Viscaino dropped the page. He swung around to face André. "I hope to hell you can ride."

"It's one of my lesser accomplishments. But I fail to see what this has to do with you."

Viscaino was already leaping down the stairs, taking them two at a time. "I'll explain on the way. Hurry, *hermano!*"

Annie sat alone in a stone-walled chamber in Dunfield House, two days' ride from London. The weather had turned foul, shifting from dismal mist to lashing rain. The darkness only served to intensify her trepidation.

This time, she had gone too far. While the queen enjoyed the lively and irreverent court chronicles Annie penned with ever-increasing sharpness, the latest diatribe against Owen Perrott, Lord of Carew, had been her downfall.

She should have realized that even with Elizabeth, some topics were forbidden. Seated on a window bench, Annie shivered and drew her knees to her chest. Now she had been banished from the royal presence and had nothing to do but await her punishment.

She should have left long ago. Yet in spite of herself, she became more and more a part of life at court. She found a dark enjoyment in the vigor of Elizabeth's power, the taste of intrigue, the satisfaction of watching the queen rule. Thanks to André's manipulation and her own wit, she had been drawn into Elizabeth's charmed, elite circle of power.

Naively, she had tested the bonds of the queen's favor . . . and lost to a Welshman with a comely face and facile tongue. The notion merely deepened the sense of emptiness that had darkened every day since she had learned of Evan's death.

Their one night together seemed only a dream. A fantasy that had never happened. A sense of unfulfilled yearning tore at her, so painful that she began to understand why the queen guarded her royal independence so fiercely. Elizabeth was wed to a cause, to her people and to their future. Unlike passion, the queen's noble purpose endured. It would never die or betray her. How could any man offer her more?

Annie traced the path of a raindrop on the windowpane. Perhaps that was the key. To let life be enough. To be an empty vessel. To devote herself to the betterment of others with no thought of her own contentment. Maybe she was more Elizabeth's niece than she thought.

The door of the chamber swung open. The lamps in the wall sconces flared with the sudden inrush of air. Annie stood, smoothing out her silk velvet overskirt.

Two tall men strode into the room. Their long cloaks and broad-brimmed hats dripped with water. Their high boots left a smattering of mud on the flagstones.

"André," she said, recognizing his quick, economic strides. She started forward, hands outstretched. "Thank God you've come. And so quickly! I thought you'd wait for the weather to calm."

"I wouldn't let him." From behind André, the other man's deep, silken voice froze Annie in her tracks.

She caught her breath as emotions exploded in her chest: shock, joy, dread, guilt ... and years-old, soul-deep affection. "Rodrigo?" Her voice broke.

He dropped his hat and cloak. For a moment he just stood there, seeming to drink in every detail of her appearance while she did the same. He stood tall and lean as ever, his hair falling in a glossy mane over his shoulders. Streaks of silver highlighted his temples, and his face, fine-boned and ruthlessly handsome, was set in an expression of cautious amazement.

"Annie," he said at last, holding out his arms. "*Por Dios*, look at you, all grown up and beautiful as the sun."

Hesitant at first, she took a step forward. Then she was in his arms, laughing and weeping against his chest.

André cleared his throat. "There's something I must attend to." His glare raked Annie. "Pray God I make headway with the queen and convince her to forgive you. I shall return within the hour."

In that hour, Annie and Rodrigo spoke of the years that had separated them. The bittersweet reunion left them both feeling awkward. She had fled with pirates rather than marry him; he had agonized for years over the deception.

"What of Valeria?" she asked.

"She lives in the villa at Nombre de Dios, still."

"You should have married her long ago, Rodrigo."

He winnowed a hand through his hair. "There was a time . . . when we both wanted marriage." Resentment burned in his eyes. "I could do nothing until I found you and secured your future."

"Don't blame your failure on me," she shot back. "By leaving, I absolved you of all responsibility for me."

"Damn it, Annie! I gave up the woman I love to keep you from being a pawn of intrigue. And here you are in the very center of it all."

"Perhaps I'm happy here."

He glanced around the room in disdain. "Oh, really? Happy with a queen who showers you with gifts one moment, then banishes you from her presence the next?"

Stung, Annie walked to the window and watched the gray, hissing rain.

"André tells me the queen doesn't know who you are," he said.

"It's better that way. Her health has been excellent. The succession is far from her mind." She turned from the window. "What is it about you and André? Why did you go to him, and why did he let you come here?"

"He's my brother."

Annie reeled with shock. Rodrigo made her sit as he explained the bizarre twists of the past. She remembered asking André about his badge long ago. He had made light of it, told her it was a meaningless bauble.

"How did you find him?" she asked.

Rodrigo hesitated. He and André had discussed the issue at length. Annie believed Evan Carew was dead. André insisted that Rodrigo keep his counsel on the matter.

Rodrigo respected his brother's caution. Months had passed since he had enountered the English pirates aboard the *Cacafuego*. In all probability they were dead by now, or would perish while attempting to cross the vast Pacific. Where was the use in raising her hopes, only to disappoint her again? Besides, Carew was a Welsh pirate, hardly worthy of Annie Blythe.

"André Scalia is a man of some fame," Rodrigo said carefully. "As the queen's adviser, he would know your whereabouts."

"Was it a happy reunion?"

"You know André better than I. What do you think?"

"He was probably offended. Shocked, but he'd die before showing it."

Rodrigo nodded. "He's bitter, for I had the love of my parents while he was left to shift for himself."

"What will you do, Rodrigo? Take him to see Paloma?"

"Nothing would bring her greater joy, but I doubt André will come to San Augustine. I pray the fact that I've located him will set her mind at ease."

"Then you do plan to go back."

"Yes." He took her by the shoulders and peered into her eyes. "God, Valeria always said you'd grow to be a beauty. She was right."

Annie stared at the floor, uncomfortable with his flattery. "I hate it that you never married her."

A rueful smile curved his mouth. "Not half so much as I."

"Then go, Rodrigo. Make haste!" Suddenly, she was desperate for his happiness. With Evan, her one chance at contentment had died. "It would please me greatly to see you settled at last."

"I'll go," he said slowly, "but only if you come with me."

Her mouth dropped open. "I cannot!" The swiftness and certainty of her reply surprised them both.

"Of course you can, goose. And you will. I'll get André to help us with the arrangements. And I've moved up in the world, *muchacha*. I came to England aboard my own ship."

She stepped away from him. The Caribbean, her colorful childhood, her adventures as Rodrigo's scribe, all seemed so distant now. With a tug of nostalgia, she recalled the balmy, flower-scented air, the star-sprayed sky, the swing of a ship at sea. Then she remembered the fanaticism that had driven men to murder natives and her grandparents, the grotesque spectacles of public burnings, the injustice of slavery.

"My life is here now, Rodrigo. I want to stay."

He smashed his fist against the stone wall. "Damn you, Annie. How can you call this cold, rainy country your home? You live and breathe at the sufferance of a bitter, aging woman. What kind of life is that?"

"A better life than New Spain offers me. Here, at least, my thoughts are my own. No one forces me to think or talk or pray after a certain fashion."

"Do you think, if you had married me, that you would have suffered such restrictions?"

She gasped at the strain of agony in his voice. "Of course not," she said. "If I had married you, Rodrigo, *you* would have suffered." She rushed forward and clutched his hands. "I belong here. Once, the bond was one of the blood. Now it is one of the heart."

"Your secret tie to the queen puts you in danger."

"I can look after myself."

"So you prefer to stay here, where your royal aunt treats you like a pet monkey, spoiling you one moment and putting you in your cage the next."

"Yes." She dropped his hands and turned away. "Damn you, yes!"

CHAPTER 17

Plymouth
26 September 1580

"Is the queen alive and well?" Drake called to the crew of the fishing boat that had cruised out of the harbor to meet the *Golden Hind*.

In an agony of apprehension, forty men and boys awaited the reply. If the answer were negative, the adventurers were as good as dead. For if Elizabeth had died without issue, and her Scots cousin had taken the throne, Mary would have them all killed for crimes against her Catholic ally, Philip of Spain.

An even more horrifying possibility gripped Evan as he saw, for the first time in nearly three years, the rocky, mist-bound shores of England. During the raging journey across the Pacific, through the gales that had chased them across the Indian Ocean to the Cape of Storms at the nether end of Africa, Evan had feared the leaking, overladen *Golden Hind* would never reach England.

But the ship had held fast, and somewhere along the Ivory Coast of Africa, he was forced to face the prospect that he would see Annie again.

Somehow, the idea frightened him more than the specter of Mary, Queen of Scots.

He felt Drake tense beside him as a fisherman raised a yellow horn to his lips. "By God's grace, Queen Elizabeth is alive and well!"

A deafening roar erupted from the Englishmen. The sky darkened with a cloud of hats flung jubilantly into the air.

Evan added both his voice and his hat to the celebration. Yet deep inside him dwelt a cold, dark fear. Three years had passed since he had set sail.

He had gone off a cocky youth drunk on the spirit of adventure and returned a sober man, matured by bitter experience. He had set out determined to plunder Spanish treasure for the glory of England and the enrichment of himself. He had seen the demise of paradise, known the icy kiss of death, felt the lust for adventure singing in his veins, and embraced the strange, soul-deep loneliness of a mariner.

He was no longer the romantic corsair who had won the heart of a vulnerable girl. With the taste of Annie still on his lips, he had fled or escaped—he wasn't sure which. With painful frequency, he recalled their night of loving. Her innocence and her pledge to wait for him still haunted his dreams.

But three long years had passed. And in that time, what in God's name had happened to Annie?

"You've turned into a beauty such as the gods would envy!"

Startled, Annie looked up from her writing desk in the chamber she shared with the queen's ladies. As the tall man strode into the room, she dropped her quill. A tiny rivulet of ink bled across the parchment.

"Lord Owen!" Since his first visit to court, she had managed to avoid him. She had waited and watched, had wondered if he truly was a traitor, or if his attempts to ingratiate himself to the queen were sincere. In the end, she had accepted the queen's forgiveness in the matter of her accusations about Owen and kept her counsel. Now, feeling trapped, she wished she had spoken again to the queen of her suspicions.

He took her hand and drew her to her feet. Dressed like a prince in a stone-studded doublet, plumed hat, and silken hose, he matched the affected handsomeness of the queen's current favorite, the Earl of Essex.

"Ah, my sweet, how enchanting you look." Smiling, he bent and brushed his lips over her cheek. "You have a smudge of ink," he whispered. "Just here."

A curious odor wafted from him. For a moment, Annie couldn't identify it; then she realized that his clothes carried the charcoal scent of tobacco smoke mingling with his tonic of ambergris. Smoking was not a popular pastime in England. In fact, she knew of only one man who partook of the habit.

Don Iago Orozco. Again, her distrust sharpened.

Rattled, Annie snatched back her hand. "What are you doing back at court, my lord?"

He seemed unable to keep himself from touching her. His hands cradled her face, thumbs skimming her cheekbones. "I've come to petition the queen," he said. "For permission to marry."

"I see." Annie wanted to escape him, but behind her was a tapestry-draped wall, and she could move no farther. "Congratulations, my lord. Whom have you chosen to wed?"

His light, long-lashed eyes glowed. "Why, you, my darling girl."

Annie caught her breath. A denial reared in her mind, but she forced herself to smile. "You jest, my lord. I have no ambition to marry anyone, and the queen holds the state of matrimony in little regard."

"Ah, but it's all arranged. I've no doubt that Her Highness will give her blessing. You see, her own secretary of state, Lord Burghley, has ordered me to wed and get an heir for Carew." He grabbed her hand again and pressed it to his chest. The padding of his doublet cushioned her fingers. "And who but you, dear Mistress Blythe, can I choose?"

Thank God, Annie thought, that Rodrigo had lingered in England, intent on convincing André to sail with him to San Augustine to see their mother, Paloma. If need be, she could count on him to help her out of Owen's mad scheme.

Rodrigo lived in André's house along the Thames. Annie avoided visiting that house, for it was there that she and Evan had made love. The place held memories that, even after three years, had the power to plunge her into a melancholy that often lasted for days.

"Well," Owen prompted. "I see I've made you all misty-eyed. We'll set the date—"

She laughed and stepped to one side, releasing herself from the entrapment of his body. "La, sir, any number of maidens would be honored by your ambition. My place is here, with the queen."

"Not for much longer, Annie." He dug into the fold of his baldric and extracted a ring. "Here's a token of my promise." He slipped it on her finger. The ring was lovely, of bright yellow gold, set with an emerald the size of her knuckle. Pearls circled the jewel, and the band was engraved with a design of exotic interlocking swirls.

Annie summoned all her willpower to keep from blurting out an accusation. She recognized this ring as part of the treasure Evan had brought to Carew. It had been among the gold Owen was to have sent to the Crown. Suddenly she knew with utter certainty that Owen, not a band of brigands, had been stealing Crown revenues. Twice he had damned himself. The gold buttons on Don Iago's doublet might have been explained away, but now this. . . .

The fool. He had given himself away. He'd not get the queen's permission to marry, but a trip to the Tower of London instead.

She forced a smile. She would not need Rodrigo's help after all. "You are too generous, my lord. I've no doubt Her Majesty will take an avid interest in your plan."

The fact that he was unimaginably wealthy had not quite struck Evan as he rode hell for leather to London. Even in his haste he had quibbled over the price of his horse. Francis had slapped him on the back and declared that they could afford to buy horses for the queen's entire honor guard.

Still, Evan did not dwell much upon the staggering transformation. Odd, since gaining riches had once been a goal that had consumed him. Now he wanted only Annie. Chilled by the wind that rushed past as he rode, he traveled without eating or sleeping—a foolish act; he had lived without her for three years, and another day or two would make little difference.

Yet he could not bow to logic where Annie was concerned. Bright as a beacon, her face shone in his mind. His feelings for her reached beyond love, he realized with a slight shiver of fear. In their years apart, his passion had burgeoned into the dangerous realm of worship.

He entered London through Temple Bar and at last got a taste of what it meant to be rich. The gateman tried to delay him, make him fill out official port of entry papers. A single gold doubloon had the man groveling at his feet and begging him to pass through with all haste.

By the time Evan reached Whitehall Palace, he was dazed from lack of sleep and food. He bribed his way past wardens and pensioners, garnering looks of confusion at the sight he made. Unshaven and unbarbered, he still wore his loose seaman's trousers and shirt. His concessions to vanity included a broad-brimmed leather hat from a friendly Malay woman, a brocaded vest from Java, and tooled-leather knee boots from the Moluccas.

The Presence Chamber, aglow with candles, was the scene of wild revelry. The bright gowns and doublets of dancers spun before his bleary eyes. The music of timbrels and viols thundered painfully in his ears. He should have stopped to eat and sleep. And probably to bathe as well.

To steady himself, Evan braced one arm against a stone column. With the other, he clutched at a thick velvet window curtain.

His fevered gaze picked out the queen at the dais. The gold

and white of her gown dazzled him. Then he saw Annie, seated on a tassled cushion at the queen's feet.

Annie. His mouth formed her name, but no sound came out. Cold, abject fear seized him. She was more beautiful than he remembered. A jeweled coif concealed her hair and framed the perfect oval of her face. Her slim white hands, decked with rings, were folded in perfect repose in her lap. She kept her head tilted attentively toward the queen and listened politely. She was the picture of the perfect court lady—poised, earnest, and unfailingly courteous.

And yet she looked as brittle and untouchable as a spunglass ornament.

Annie, what has she done to you?

Like a spider, André Scalia stood discreetly behind the dais. As Evan tried to summon the strength to step forward, the palace warden approached André and whispered into his ear. Then the two melted into the shadows.

Still unnoticed between pillar and drape, Evan searched for a glimpse of the bright, captivating girl who had given herself to him so tenderly, who had promised to wait for him, so long ago. Instead he saw a stranger, as soulless and cold as a Holbein portrait.

He willed himself to go to her, to shatter her icy façade and find the warm heart within her. Sluggishly his body obeyed his will. He put one foot in front of the other.

And then he heard a sharp hissing sound behind him, like steam escaping from a kettle. The world went black.

Each bit of gossip about Drake's triumph struck like an arrow to Annie's heart. The investors had achieved a return of fourteen hundred percent on their stake. The Crown's share alone would refit the entire navy and still leave plenty to spare.

At Whitehall, nobles and servants alike talked endlessly of Drake's daring raids, his discovery of New Albion in the domain of the Californio tribes, his visits to the Moluccas, the Philippines, the Spice Islands, Java, and the Sierra Leone.

Even the queen spoke in reverent tones. "I must confer a suitable reward on Admiral Drake," she said, thinking aloud. "He'd probably like a title, but perhaps knighthood will suffice. And I must decide how and when to bring him to court."

"No matter how discreetly you welcome him," André pointed out, "Spain is bound to be offended."

Elizabeth laughed. "Marry, Ambassador Orozco has already demanded that I return the treasure and punish the pirates." She turned to Annie. "Tell me, my dear, how shall I respond?"

Annie managed a wan smile. She had felt ill these past days, for news of Drake's return had brought the terrible grief of Evan's death rushing back at her. The fact that she had reported the treachery of Owen Perrott to the queen brought no comfort to her tortured soul.

This time, the queen had set Walsingham to spy on Owen, and now Elizabeth had suspicions of her own. Owen had fled, and even now the queen's wardens were searching for him. The possibility of true happiness was dead to Annie, but perhaps once he was found, she might take a measure of satisfaction in revenge.

"Mistress Blythe." Sir Christopher Hatton touched her sleeve. "The queen has asked you a question. How shall we respond to the Spanish demands?"

Startled, Annie dipped her head in apology. "Since Spain has already taken offense, why be discreet? Reward the admiral with all the pomp and ceremony you can muster."

"Naturally." The queen unfolded an Indian ivory fan and peeked over it at Marchaumont, the agent of her current fiancé, the Duke of Alençon. Although the Frenchman believed the match a fait accompli, Elizabeth enjoyed his gifts and favors with no intent to honor their betrothal.

"As to rewards," the queen continued, "I shall have to find something for each of my adventurers. Drake couldn't have accomplished this miracle alone. Parson Fletcher shall be given a bishop's seat. Seamen Dirk and Denton shall get their own frigate. A grant in the marches for Jack Doughty, the rabble-rouser's brother; that ought to keep him far from intrigue. And as for Evan Carew—"

Annie shot to her feet. André Scalia took in his breath on a hiss, and his face drained to the color of sun-bleached parchment.

"Evan Carew, madam?" Annie blurted out.

The queen aimed a chilly glare at André. "You said you would tell her."

"Tell me what?" Annie demanded. She clutched at the front of his cloak, oblivious to the scandalized stares of the courtiers. "Damn you, André, speak!"

"Evan Carew did not perish as Captain Winter reported. Carew and one other survived the wreck of the *Marigold*."

Annie felt as if the ground quaked beneath her. "Why did you not tell me sooner?"

André's nostrils thinned. "He has already left on another mission to the West Indies."

"No!" Annie screamed at him. "He wouldn't have left without seeing me! He—"

"Warden, if you please." Elizabeth waved her fan in annoyance. "My young friend needs to be taken to privacy."

"André!" Annie sobbed as a pair of gentlemen pensioners escorted her forcibly to the door. One of the Spanish ambassador's lackeys sidled along behind her, but she ignored him. "André, I beg you! Tell me the truth! Tell me—"

"The Tower, miss," whispered one of the pensioners between his teeth.

Annie stopped struggling. "What?"

He drew her out into the antechamber. Like a shadow, the Spaniard slid near. The sympathetic pensioner glanced at him and dropped his voice even lower. "I can't be certain it's Carew, but last week Lord André sent a stranger to the Tower."

"Thank you, sir." Annie wrenched herself from his grip. Before he could recapture her, she raced from the palace.

Her mind churned with fury and unbearable hope as she rushed alone through the dark streets of London. For years she had put her trust in André. He had been her teacher, her mentor, her confidant.

She should have known that, where the succession was concerned, he was as ruthless as a Catholic Inquisitor. Her commitment to Evan had jeopardized André's plans. She had been a fool to reveal her feelings to a man who could not understand the agonizing joy of love.

She prayed she would reach Evan in time. Prisoners of the Tower suffered grievous tortures. Nobler men than Evan Carew had endured starvation in windowless cells so tiny a man couldn't stand up. Men and women alike had been subjected to interrogation aided by branding irons, gauntlets, the rack, the Scavenger's Daughter.

"No," she whispered under her breath. "Please God, not Evan. Not Evan."

Shivering in the night air, she ran along Thames Street toward the Tower. The smell of tar and sewage blew on a cold wind from the river. The warehouse district along the muddy track of Petty Wales was haunted by shadows, the buildings hunched shoulder to shoulder, some of them spanning above the street and creating an eerie darkness.

With a shiver of fear, she realized she had never been abroad alone before. André's subtle presence—a guard, a maid, a footman—had always accompanied her whenever she ventured out.

Not this time. Not ever again.

Just as she was about to dart across Petty Wales to the Tower, four dark shapes emerged from a doorway.

"*Esta la mujer,*" one of them said.

A musty rag of hopsacking smothered Annie's scream of terror.

"Gone!" Evan's shout rang through the plaster-walled chamber in the Broad Arrow Tower. He slapped his palms on the rickety tale and leaned menacingly toward André Scalia. For a week, he had subsisted on meager prison fare, and his vision swam as he glared at the elder man. "What the hell do you mean, Annie's gone?"

"She slipped out alone and never came back. I've sent inquiries to every quarter of London and beyond."

Rage seared Evan's mind. He battled the urge to choke André. "So you came here to torture me with the news?"

André's face was as impassive as chiseled stone. "I came because I thought you might know where she went."

"Thanks to you," Evan snapped, "I don't even know what day it is."

"You know nothing of her disappearance?"

"I know you're a rotting, manipulative bastard whose schemes have finally misfired. Who the hell are you to play God with the life of an innocent woman?"

"It's a question you should have asked yourself when you first sailed off in search of Annie Blythe."

The comment had a lethal sting. Evan had been so bent on playing the hero of Carew that he had not let himself think about the ramifications of his actions. He had seen Annie as a prize to be won, not a woman with a life and a future of her own.

"The destiny of England depends on her," André said.

"You should have let her decide that for herself."

"*You* should have—"

The cell door banged open. To Evan's shock, Rodrigo Viscaino stood there. For a moment the two merely stared at each other. Annie's guardian and her lover, united only by their love for her.

Rodrigo recovered first, turning to address André. "She's been abducted. By agents of the Spanish ambassador. And a certain Welsh lord from Carew who recently suffered the disfavor of the queen."

"Owen Perrott," Evan said between his teeth. He knew it could be none other. Nightmare images of the young lord reared in his mind. He should have known Owen would find his way into the web of Spanish intrigue.

"You work quickly," said André.

"It took only a brief round of torture. Orozco's aide sang like a lark at dawn." The corner of his mouth slid up in a self-deprecating grin. "We Spaniards are so much better at meting out torture than enduring it. They're taking her to Spain—for a wedding."

Color shot to André's cheeks. *"Demonios!"*

"What wedding?" Evan demanded.

"Lord Owen means to marry her and lay claim to the throne—much as the first Tudors did in the last century."

Evan's breath left him as if someone had kicked him in the gut. "Are they already at sea?"

Rodrigo nodded. "They left in a cog from the Galley Key yesterday."

"Then there's no time to waste." He started for the door.

André planted himself in his path. "You're staying here." Two yeoman warders stepped forward and crossed their long pikestaffs to bar the door.

Evan clenched his jaw to contain his anger. "Damn you, André," he said between his teeth. "You need me."

"He's right," said Rodrigo. "Though I wish it could be otherwise, Evan is the one man who can help us. We need a crew, and one that knows what they're doing."

"What about the crew of your ship?" André asked.

"Most have signed on with other Spanish merchants, for they draw no pay while I tarry in London." Rodrigo swept his arm toward Evan. "These days, he has friends in high places."

"He's a danger to Annie," André insisted.

Rodrigo lifted an eyebrow. "And you're not?"

"Evan Carew stays here," André said.

Rodrigo's hand streaked out. He grasped André's badge. "The silver lion of Ribera, Brother. Does it mean nothing to you? It's your only legacy from the mother you never knew. She escaped cruel bondage and spent a lifetime searching for you."

Evan frowned. Was there some blood tie between these two men? He didn't care; at the moment he wanted only to be away, in pursuit of Annie.

"My heart bleeds," said André, "but I fail to see your point."

"There's a higher calling than power and intrigue. If you learn nothing else about the woman who gave you life, learn that. André, there is no honor in what you have done to Annie. But it's not too late to make amends."

Annie watched the rat with idle disinterest. Seated on a bunk with her knees drawn up to her chest, she saw it poke its sleek black head out of a coil of rope. The sharp little nose twitched, and the rat scuttled toward a bit of biscuit Annie had dropped when her appetite had failed her earlier, upon learning that the ship had headed out into the open water of the channel.

With furtive, sinuous movements, the rat snatched up the morsel, then slunk back into the shadows.

Annie glanced at the doorway. She did not know how long the man had been standing there. Nor did she care.

"The evening's entertainment is as fine as the company," she said.

With a cool smile, Owen Perrott stepped into the cabin. Despite the fact that his actions had rendered him an outlaw, he was as inhumanly handsome as ever, his burnished curls a halo around a chiseled, godlike face. "Come up on deck," he said. "The mariners will strike up a tune on their pipes and drums."

"I'll stay down here. I've no taste for the monkeyshines of your band of rebels."

Owen shrugged. "Please yourself." He stepped close to her, reached down and fingered a lock of her hair. She had lost her coif in the desperate struggle with her abductors, and her hair hung unbound and unkempt down her back.

"So soft," Owen murmured. "Like silk, it is, and the color brings to mind the brightness of new gold."

Annie wanted to slap his hand away and shrink from him, but she forced herself to stay still. Her captors had taken everything from her; all she had left was her courage—and the cursed ring she wore in her bodice.

"I wonder," Owen mused in a satin-smooth voice, "has

your lady aunt ever remarked on your resemblance to her?"

Annie drew a sharp breath. Was he bluffing? Seeking confirmation of a wild guess? "What an odd remark, since I have no living kin."

"Come, come." With unhurried grace, he sat down beside her. "You needn't pretend anymore. Don Iago has known the truth for some time."

"Don Iago is an accomplished liar. What truth do you credit him with?" She knew the answer, but wanted to be certain Owen did, too.

"That Elizabeth had an illegitimate half brother, namely Phillip Blythe of Hispaniola. That you are Phillip's daughter, and the granddaughter of Henry the Eighth." Owen smiled at her stony look. "You see? We are cousins—happily, distant enough for marriage. Don Iago discovered the connection in your father's cache of private papers."

Annie felt an inner chill. Her father's papers had been missing from the wreckage of the plantation, Gema del Mar. Now she knew for certain that Don Iago's manipulative hand had lent itself to the destruction of her grandparents' home . . . and to the murder of Will and Gabriella Blythe.

Years had passed. He had only been biding his time before he made use of the information.

"This latest outrage of Drake and Carew sealed your fate, my love. The insult to Spain was too grievous to abide, and our actions are justified." A smile curved his mouth. "And of course, your betrayal only made me easier in my conscience. You shouldn't have told the queen how I acquired my wealth. Now you force me to set aside my scruples."

Annie laughed without humor. "As if you ever had scruples."

He moved close; she could smell his scent of ambergris and sweat. She could feel the warmth of his body. It seared her like a forge, and she wanted to scream with the oppression she felt in his presence.

"If you think abducting me is adequate retribution for the treasure of the *Golden Hind*," she said, "you're sadly mistaken. For that amount of wealth, the queen would part with her very soul. I'll not be missed."

Owen leaned closer. Annie hugged her knees tighter. He reached out and, very slowly, traced a finger down her cheek, across her lips.

"At first," he said softly, "you'll not be missed. But when news of you marriage reaches the queen—"

"Marriage!" Annie's cheeks took fire. "The queen laughed in your face the first time you petitioned to marry me. Surely you know you can't return to Carew now, wife or no wife."

Owen chuckled, a dark, satiny sound that skimmed like a cold finger at the base of her spine. "You'll marry me, just as I'd planned, Annie. And the world will lie at our feet."

"You're mad."

"No. Elizabeth will die without issue. Mary of the Scots will claim the throne if Elizabeth doesn't execute her, but the Stewart queen's a silly bitch and won't hold it. With Philip of Spain's army at our back, we'll seize the crown."

"Usurping is such a simple matter to you, my lord."

"It was to Owen Tudor, was it not? You do know your history?"

She did. Owen Tudor, a Welsh squire, had married Henry V's widow, Catherine of Valois, setting in motion a succession of events that was to topple the reign of the Yorkist Plantagenets. Owen's grandson, Henry, won the crown at Bosworth Field and thus began the dynasty of the Tudors. Now Owen Perrott meant to continue the tradition.

Annie said nothing for a long time. Though it was the middle of the night, a good wind filled the sails. She could feel the tug of the taut canvas, could hear the creak of straining ropes, and the *shush* of the hull gliding through the water.

"Why must you go to Spain to make this marriage?" she asked at last.

"It will be our home until the time is right. Don Iago has secured an invitation and a safe conduct from the king." Owen touched her beneath the chin. "What beautiful children we'll have, you and I—" He leaned forward and kissed her, his lips cool and firm and commanding.

Annie wrenched herself away from him. " 'Tis a fool's errand, Owen! Can't you see that? Better men than you have tried to take Elizabeth's throne, and not one has survived the attempt."

"Better men than I?" Owen took her by the shoulders and kissed her again, grinding his mouth against hers. Just when she thought her lungs would burst from holding her breath, he pulled way. "Do you know any?"

Evan Carew, she thought, but held her tongue. Jesu, Owen was as proud as a Spanish grandee. And maybe that pride was the key, Annie thought with a spark of hope. "Surely I don't, my lord," she murmured. "It makes me wonder why you would take a woman like me for a bride."

"You've the blood of kings in your veins, dear heart. You are beautiful, cultured, honorable—"

"No!" she burst out, feeling her cheeks go red with rage. "You don't know me at all, Owen." She fixed him with the hard stare she had learned from Elizabeth. "I gave my honor away years ago," she announced.

He blinked, clearly taken aback by her fierce pronouncement. "I don't know what you mean."

"I am Evan Carew's lover," she stated, "and I consider it a distinction of the highest honor."

Owen surged to his feet. In the same motion, he struck her hard across the face. "Harlot!" As she recoiled, he grasped her arms and hauled her to her feet. "I had my own way of dealing with Evan Carew," he said in a deadly whisper. "In truth, I miss having a whipping boy. But perhaps I'll not feel the lack so much once I have you."

"Coward!" she shot back. "Will you never learn to take your punishment like a man?"

He drew his hand to strike her again, but stopped when someone pounded at the door. "What is it?" he called over his shoulder.

"My lord!" A stocky man in a striped knit cap poked his head into the cabin. Annie eyed him with contempt. The crew of the ship was composed of Catholic rebels, outlaws, and mercenaries who had sold their loyalty to Owen and Don Iago.

Owen gave a grunt of annoyance and released her. Annie let out a sigh of relief and wiped her sleeve across her mouth, for his kiss offended her more than his slap.

"Yes, Edmund? What is it?"

"A ship's been sighted, sir, and she's flashing a distress signal. Don Iago and the captain are arguing about whether or not to offer aid."

Owen spat a Welsh curse and left the cabin. Prodded by curiosity, Annie pushed her feet into her slippers and followed the men up on deck.

Several crew members had gathered at the rail to watch the small ship. Starlight and moonglow streaked the black waters of the channel and gave the distressed vessel the look of a ghost ship. Her stern lantern winked repeatedly into the night.

Standing by the binnacle lamp, Don Iago and the Welsh captain argued heatedly.

"We must give aid," the captain was saying. " 'Tis the law of the sea."

"I say we do not," Don Iago retorted in his thickly accented English. "I financed this voyage, and my word is law."

Annie stifled a snort of disgust. These rebel mariners were a gullible lot to put their trust in Don Iago.

Moving toward the stern, she gripped the rail and stared down into the inky black water. Like a penitent in confession, she silently recounted her troubles. Mad with ambition, Owen planned to marry her. Evan was in the Tower; no doubt André would find some excuse to have him put to death. Rodrigo pined for Valeria but would never be free to marry her until he knew Annie's fate.

And what of me? she wondered. Born a grandee's daughter, she had progressed to orphan, to scribe, to pirates' captive, to court lady. And, strangely, none of them was she.

The only time she truly knew herself was with Evan. Evan, whom she would never see again.

Her life lay in shambles at her feet. All she cared about and everyone she loved was lost to her.

How simple it would be, she mused, leaning out over the rail, to cast herself into the cold black water. It was said that the experience of drowning was like a beautiful and peaceful dream.

But two obstacles hampered the plan.

First, she was an excellent swimmer, and instinct alone would keep her afloat until they seized her again.

Second, she was blood kin to Elizabeth Tudor. Like it or not, Annie possessed the strength and courage of her line. King Henry had wrested control of the church from the pope. Mary had put down Protestants with the zeal of a fanatic. And Elizabeth had made herself the mightiest monarch the world had ever seen.

Annie was terrified, but she was also a Tudor.

As she moved along the upper deck rail, she nearly stumbled over a sleeping man. The common seamen had no proper quarters; they made their beds on odd patches of deck. This man looked singularly uncomfortable, his shoulder pushed against an archery screen, the knife in his belt wedged between his body and the wooden blindage.

Almost without thinking, Annie reached down and took the knife. The man muttered but did not awaken. She glanced at the men on the quarterdeck. Satisfied that no one was watching, she slid the knife into the top of her stocking.

Emboldened, she moved across the deck, disarming each sleeping man in turn until she had four knives hidden in her stockings and bodice. They were only eating utensils, but the seamen kept a good edge on them. When the men awakened, they would accuse each other, and with any luck a row would break out. Owen would accuse her, of course, but she would deal with that later.

A little dissension among the crew couldn't hurt her chances—however slim—of escape.

The captain's will prevailed. Grumbling ungraciously, Don Iago decided to send a ship's boat over to parlay with the approaching vessel. A small armed crew went out, and some time later returned with five strangers.

At least, Annie thought they were strangers . . . until she recognized Drake, Denton, Rodrigo, André . . . and Evan.

Her heart leaped to her throat. Clinging to the rail to keep from falling, she struggled across the gangway and dropped down to the main deck.

Evan spied her. A cry broke from him, and he started forward. Two men held him back while others restrained his companions.

Forcing herself to remain calm, Annie drank in the sight of Evan. His face was a map of the past three years. He looked leaner, harder, his features sharper and more wary. Yet despite the changes, she nearly lost her footing at the expression in his eyes. Neither years nor distance had dimmed the stark, honest passion that emanated from him.

"Your light o' love is fine," Owen said, looking like a fisherman who had just landed a prize catch.

Annie schooled her features into a bland expression. The cold emptiness in Owen's eyes told her Evan was as good as dead. She must make no complaint, give Owen no excuse to hasten Evan's demise.

"Actually, I'm glad you've come," Owen continued. "I always was too lenient with you, Evan. No matter how many times you were beaten in my stead, you always healed, only to lean over the whipping stool once more. Perhaps this is my chance to finish what I should have ended years ago." Owen rummaged in a cargo bin and brought forth a nine-tailed leather whip. He let the knotted ends trail along the deck. "Aye, it will be good to enlist you as my whipping boy again—only this time *I* shall wield the strap."

No! With all her will, Annie stifled a cry of denial. Her objection would only goad Owen to further cruelties.

Hands clasped behind his back, Don Iago strode up and down the deck in front of the prisoners. "You've disarmed them?" he asked a seamen.

"Of course, my lord."

Don Iago continued pacing for a moment, then stopped in

front of Drake. "Ironic, isn't it?" the Spaniard asked, un-sheathing his thin sword and touching the blade to a small white scar on Drake's cheek. Then he lowered the point to touch the medallion on Drake's chest, which depicted a globe enclosed in a ring. "*El Draquez* sailed around the world only to meet his fate in the English Channel."

"M-my lord?" Eyeing the famous medallion, a young sea-man hesitantly approached Don Iago. "Is that truly Admiral Drake?"

"It is, though he'll not bear the title long."

Despite their obligation to Don Iago, the English mariners stared in awe at Francis Drake. Already his deeds were leg-end.

Annie felt a surge of new hope. Perhaps these men of the sea would be reluctant to raise a hand to a hero.

"Stop your gawking!" Don Iago's blade glittered briefly; a nick opened beneath Drake's ear. "See, he bleeds like any man. He's a pirate and will die as one."

"We want no trouble," Rodrigo said quickly.

"It seems you're in enough trouble, amigo," Don Iago stated. "What manner of Spaniard are you, that you come in the service of England's Protestant slut?"

"I owe no loyalty to Queen Elizabeth," Rodrigo said even-ly. "We came for Annie Blythe."

"Then you came in vain," Owen stated. "She stays with me." He leveled a stare at Evan. "Her future husband."

In the dim light of the ship's lanterns, Evan's face paled perceptibly. At the same time, his eyes gleamed with a look of such hatred that Annie's heart skipped a beat. She knew then that Evan would fight to the death for her. The notion gave her no comfort.

"Look," said Rodrigo in his best English, "we'll compen-sate you for your trouble. We've brought a treas—"

"Do not listen to his babbling," André cut in, shoving his elbow into Rodrigo's ribs.

Don Iago laughed softly. "Don Rodrigo lacks your diplo-matic skill, André. Come now, you say you've brought us a treasure? Spoils from New Spain, no doubt."

"Yes," Rodrigo said desperately. "The hold of the pinnace is fair full of—"

"You Spaniards," Drake said breezily. "Always so fond of exaggeration."

"Perhaps I do overstate," Rodrigo admitted, looking sheepish. "Surely there's not more than a few chests full of doubloons aboard."

André rolled his eyes up. "There is no God," he muttered.

Annie watched her rescuers in fascination. Rodrigo was playing the lackwit, but why? And why was André allowing him to blurt out information about the treasure?

Owen heaved an elaborate sigh. "I suppose there's only one way to find out if they speak the truth." He nodded at the captain, who ordered a dozen men to lower a boat and search the pinnace.

Don Iago watched the English seamen row toward the smaller ship.

"We English do have an aptitude for taking prizes," Drake murmured, a taut smile curving his mouth.

Don Iago caught his breath. "Lower another boat. I don't trust this English crew. If there's a treasure aboard, I'll supervise the taking of it."

As four men rowed off with Don Iago, Drake lowered his head and suppressed a chuckle.

Owen's hand shot out and grasped the front of his shirt. "You dare laugh?"

Still smiling, Drake lifted his face. "Those two boats can't possibly hold all the treasure." He aimed a pained look at Evan. "Remember when we got reefed in the Celebes?"

"Aye, we had to jettison three tons of cloves and eight guns. A terrible waste, it was."

"Lower another boat," Owen said.

"My lord, we have only one more—"

"Do as I say!" Owen shouted.

Six men scurried to obey. When they had rowed into blackness, André exploded. "*Damn* you, Rodrigo! They weren't to know about the treasure."

"We brought it to trade for Annie."

"On *our* terms, not while they hold us captive."

Rodrigo sent his brother a sulky look. "Would you have me give up my life?"

Annie saw that Owen was losing patience. He was quickly and easily bored, a fact that boded ill for his future wife. With an agitated movement he picked up the cat o' nine tails again and began slapping the braided handle against his thigh.

"No!" Annie could control her fear no longer. Hurrying toward him, she said, "My lord, I don't want you to harm these men."

Owen smiled. "They give me no choice."

"Just set them free. Let them go back to their boat. Owen, I'm begging you."

He looked her up and down. "I don't see you begging, Princess."

She plunged to her knees at Owen's feet. The stolen knives pressed into her legs. Humiliation burned in her cheeks. She would not look at Evan, for his shock and disgust would shatter her. "Owen, by all that I am, I beg you—"

"You do?" He caught her chin in his hand and squeezed hard.

"Aye, I beg you. If you set them free, I'll marry you willingly and serve y—"

"Annie, no!" Rodrigo struggled in the grip of his captors. "You must not make promises."

She forced herself to ignore him. "Owen, please!"

Owen laughed with sheer delight. "I like begging, Annie. Maybe I'll wrest a few pleas from Evan as well, before the night is out."

Immediately Annie saw her mistake. She had revealed her weakness for Evan, and Owen would not hesitate to use it to his advantage. Pulling away, she lowered her head. "Forgive my outburst," she murmured.

The captain cleared his throat. "Sir, all three launches have reached the pinnace. I just saw their signal."

To Annie's shock, Evan laughed, a harsh, brittle sound.

Owen swung around. He put his face very close to Evan's. "I thought I beat all the mirth out of you years ago."

"Think again, Owen," Evan said softly.

"How can you laugh to see the woman you love on her knees in front of me?" Owen demanded.

"Oh, I wasn't laughing at that." His eyes narrowed. In the light of the binnacle lamp, they gleamed like burnished blades. "For that, I shall kill you."

"I hardly think so." Dropping the whip, Owen twisted his hand into Evan's shirt and hauled him close. "Damn you, tell me why you find your situation so amusing."

Evan shot a guileless look at André. "Shall I tell him, André?"

"Tell me what?" Owen roared, giving Evan a shake.

"About the explosives," Evan said, all innocence.

Confusion dulled Owen's eyes. Then, his face full of dread, he looked across the water at the pinnace. Annie, the captain, and the few remaining mariners followed his horror-filled gaze.

An orange blaze streaked across the pinnace from bow to stern. A muffled thud rolled like thunder over the water. And suddenly it was as if the light of day shone upon them. A fount of fire plumed into the night sky, a great blossom of deadly heat. Even from a distance, Annie felt the force of the explosion.

Owen still clutched Evan's shirt. Almost casually, Evan cocked his leg and slammed it into Owen's groin. Owen howled and fell, then dragged himself up on one elbow. "Kill them," he shrieked. "Kill them all!"

Evan stooped and grabbed the black whip. Drake, Rodrigo, Denton, and André began to struggle with their guards.

A dozen seamen swarmed across the deck toward the rebels. With satisfaction, Annie saw some of them groping in confusion for their missing knives.

Her rescuers faced the onrush bravely. None of them seemed to pause to consider that they were unarmed and hopelessly outnumbered.

Or was it hopeless?

Denton braced his hands against the rail. Like twin bolts of lightning, his legs shot out, toppling the two men charging him.

Drake dropped into a crouch in the shadow of an archery screen. A man swung down the sterncastle ladder toward him. At the last instant, Drake disengaged the screen behind him. Without the blindage to stop his momentum, the man went overboard.

With an ominous whining sound, Evan's whip snaked out at the men advancing on him. All three of them stumbled back, their faces stung by the tarred and knotted leather.

Carnival tricks would serve but once, Annie knew. Receding under the gangway, she reached beneath her skirts and produced the weapons she had stolen.

"So that's what happened to my knife," said a voice nearby. A man stepped toward her.

Fighting panic, Annie shrank back against a crate.

"Here now," said the seaman with a terrible smile. "Give us the knives, my lady."

"Evan!" Her scream echoed down the deck. At the same moment, she threw herself to the planks and loosed a handful of knives. Three blades skittered away.

Hearing her cry, Drake dove for the knives. He captured one while Evan seized another and tossed it to Denton. The third disappeared through the midships fence.

Neither André nor Rodrigo had need of eating utensils. From his boot André produced a pair of gleaming Venetian stilettos. Rodrigo helped himself to a long, sharp marlinespike. With a curse, he stabbed the man nearest him, but did not notice the one who came from behind.

"Rodrigo!" André screamed his name hoarsely. Moving like a shadow, André crossed the deck and drove a stiletto into the advancing seaman.

"I'm not certain I like being in your debt, *hermano*," Rodrigo said shakily. "But thank you all the same."

Evan tried to use the whip to clear a path to Annie. Four mariners fell upon him several yards short of her. Annie didn't pause to think when the menacing seaman swooped down on her. She thrust the blade up and out, feeling it rip into fabric and then into something that felt like a sack of grain.

The man's howl of pain had an edge of dementia. Clutching his bleeding side, he toppled like a felled tree. Annie hoisted herself up onto the gangway and raced toward the stern.

Suddenly, the numbers ceased to matter. Evan and Drake and Denton were the famed sea dogs, accustomed to fighting against overwhelming odds. Rodrigo was the grandson of the gypsy warrior Santiago; he possessed his grandsire's passion and skill in combat. He and André fought back-to-back like a deadly four-armed siege engine, taking all comers with lethal efficiency. Within moments, fallen bodies littered the decks.

When the way was clear, Evan leaped toward Annie. His foot was on the bottom step of the sterncastle ladder when Owen appeared before him.

Evan faced his old nemesis with blood lust singing in his ears. Owen used the tempered blade of his sword to sever some of the tails of the whip, yet Evan felt no fear.

He beckoned with his free hand. "Come, Owen. We've both waited a lifetime for this moment."

"Evan, be careful!" Annie started forward. Her foot caught in a coil of rope, and she fell. Wood splinters gouged her palms. Ignoring the pain, she struggled toward the men.

Like light and dark they were, Owen's bright hair silvered by moonlight and Evan's midnight mane flowing like black silk. They circled one another slowly, warily, the tension unbearable. Annie started down the ladder.

Owen's blade swung back and forth. Evan ducked under it, then jumped over it. He lashed out with the whip. The hard, knotted leather struck Owen across the face, opening a red weal in his cheek.

Owen let out a yelp of pain and covered his cheek with his hand.

"At last you feel the sting, you bastard," Evan said. He

struck again, but this time the leather coiled uselessly around a gun carriage.

Owen thrust forward with his sword. Reaching up, Evan grasped a ratline. At the last instant, he swung out of the way, kicking with his feet and catching Owen beneath the chin. From the corner of his eye, he saw Annie moving toward them. He wanted to scream at her to stay back, but stifled the impulse. His cry would only alert Owen to her presence.

The sword slashed at the ratlines. The rope came out from beneath Evan's feet. Desperately he climbed higher, grasping a wooden tackle to haul himself up. Owen jumped to the gangway in pursuit. At that moment, the severed ropes slid through the tackle and Evan fell.

With a roar of triumph, Owen backed him against a hogshead lashed to the mizzenmast. A bark of victory escaped him as he aimed his killing thrust.

The sword blade pinned Evan to the hogshead. A dark red river leaked down his side and pooled on the deck.

"No. Oh God, no!" Annie screamed, rushing toward him.

A dark shape sailed through the air toward Owen. Drake, clinging to the end of a flailing yardarm, swooped down. The short, wide blade of his knife arced toward Owen, but missed.

Evan grabbed the knife in passing. Icy satisfaction filled him as he slipped the blade under Owen's ribs.

Owen staggered back, a stunned expression on his face and a curse on his lips. His arms wheeled, grasping at air. He fell, his blank stare skyward, the quivering hilt of the knife protruding from his chest.

Sobbing, Annie went to Evan.

"Pull it out," he said, jerking his head at the sword.

"I can't. 'Twould kill you," she said in horror. His dark blood gathered under her feet.

"Just pull the damned thing out, Annie," he said, "or shall I ruin a perfectly good shirt?"

The reek of spilled wine filled her nose. At last she understood. Owen's blade had caught Evan's shirt and pierced the wine barrel. Giddy with relief, she grasped the pommel of the sword and tugged the blade free.

Evan's gaze swept the deck. The remaining mariners had surrendered, some of them on their knees, to Drake and Denton. *"Cariad,"* he said, holding out his arms to her. "Come here."

At last, after three bitter years of waiting, she fell into his embrace.

CHAPTER 18

"Well," Drake said heartily, hoisting a flagon of wine. "We've rescued the damsel, vanquished the villains, and got ourselves a sound ship. Not bad for a night's work, eh?" He passed the wine to Denton.

Rodrigo grinned. "You're an irreverent sea dog, Drake."

"I know. 'Tis why my men followed me around the world."

Denton took a swig of wine and wiped his mouth on his sleeve. "Will there be trouble? After all, we've killed a lord and the Spanish ambassador."

"In defense of our lives," André pointed out.

"I suppose," Drake said, taking back the flagon, "we'll find out when we make port."

Evan took Annie's hand and squeezed it lightly. A certain awkwardness hung between them, the shyness of three years' absence. The horror of the fight was fading with the moon. Owen had been buried at sea; the surviving mariners had submitted willingly to Drake's command, and, under Denton's stern eye, they were headed back to London.

She managed an answering smile, but weariness shadowed her eyes. Love rose inside him, a feeling as shining and new as it had been the first time he had kissed her.

He slid his arm around her waist. It felt strange to touch her at last, yet at the same time he wanted to crush her in his embrace and never let her go.

"You should rest," he said. "I believe the captain's cabin is available."

She nodded, and they walked together to the stern. He helped her up the ladder, stopping at the low door.

"I think you'll find everything you need within," he said.

She placed her hand on the latch.

Evan steeled himself. He knew she still had feelings for him, but he also knew they had both changed. They had loved briefly and fiercely. Years had passed. The flame still burned inside him, but when he looked into her eyes, he saw a stranger. A beautiful, troubled stranger.

She bit her lip. "Not everything, Evan."

"I checked the amenities myself. There is bread and wine, a supply of candles, warm furs on the bunk—"

"You're not there," she said softly.

At first he thought he had not heard her correctly. Then her meaning rang clear, and his heart soared. "*Cariad,*" he said, sweeping her into his arms. She felt as light as air, warm and soft as she tucked her head against his chest.

"Annie!" André's voice froze Evan. Like a great dark-winged bird, he appeared before them. His features were taut with disapproval. "Annie, I beg of you. Don't do this."

She tightened her arms around Evan. "I've been manipulated by you, kidnapped by Owen, had my life threatened. . . . How dare you challenge me?"

"We all suffered a shock, Annie, and clear thinking is needed. You might ruin your chances—"

"You already tried that, André." She relinquished her hold on Evan and stood. "You let me believe he had died. You would have killed him yourself had you not needed his services. You're a cold man, André. One who doesn't even care to meet his own mother!"

André caught his breath. "That is none of your affair, and I'll thank you not to speak of it. I simply believe you should think things through before you make yourself a sea dog's slut."

Evan tensed, ready to avenge the insult, but Annie spoke quickly. "I've had three years to think. A sailor's slut, or Elizabeth's heir. Either way, I make a whore of myself."

She grabbed Evan's hand and pulled him into the cabin, slamming the door in André's face.

A candle lantern hung on a peg in a rafter, bathing the room in gold and shadow. Annie pressed her back against the door. The color stood out high in her cheeks, and her breath came quickly, as if she had run a long distance. Pain haunted her eyes, and Evan felt her disillusionment, her sense of betrayal. She had cared for André, had trusted him.

Evan forced himself to keep from touching her. "Annie. Did you mean what you said?"

A fierce look came over her. "Evan, the happiest moments of my life were spent in your arms."

He reached for her. "Come here."

When she was next to him, and the womanly scent of her warmed his senses, he said, "Long ago, we found a rare magic, and not one that is easily attained. Much has happened to us both. Much has changed."

"Not my feelings for you." Lifting herself on tiptoe, she wound her arms around his neck and pressed her mouth to his.

He needed no more convincing. They had plenty to talk about, but talking could wait. He undressed her and then himself, pressing her onto the coverings and furs in the alcove bed. Her hair fanned out on the pillow, a coppery halo framing a face too impish to be termed beautiful, too interesting to be called pretty.

Though he cherished the subtlety and complexity of their first union, he joined with her swiftly this time. He knew her urgency matched his, and when he was deep inside her, he braced up on his arms and said, "When I was at sea, I dreamed of you as my princess in a gilded tower."

"I'm a flesh-and-blood woman, Evan. I need you as my lover, not a knight-errant carrying my token."

"And I did so want to be a knight."

She laughed and lifted her hips, and he began the sensual rhythm that had beat in his blood for years. A series of tiny gasps escaped her, and her hands glided down his back and buttocks, compelling him, bringing him to a state of unbearable tension. Whispering her name, Evan quickened them both to a shattering climax.

Sweat bathed their bodies, and wordlessly they clung together, sharing the wonder of their reunion and rediscovering all the reasons their love had burned so brightly for so long. Evan drifted for a time in a state of bliss, glad to lie silent with her, loath to test their new harmony.

After awhile he made love to her again, his pace leisurely as his hands and mouth worshiped every part of her and drew cries of pleasure from her lips.

As daylight slid in through the stern windows, they lay entwined, listening to the creak of the ship and the groan of the rudder as the helmsman set a course for harbor.

"André will say I've ruined you," Evan whispered, kissing the damp, silky hair at her temple.

"André will say a lot of things. I no longer trust him."

"He's guided the queen wisely for years."

"I'm not the queen."

"You're her kinswoman."

"An unfortunate accident of birth."

"Annie, I saw you, the night I was taken to the Tower. You glowed like a flame in her presence. There is something in you, a God-given sense of power. André is right about one thing—you'd make a magnificent queen."

"A reluctant one."

Yet he noticed she did not deny the possibility.

"Let's not speak of lineages any more." She folded her hands on his bare chest and rested her chin on them. "I want you to tell me everything, Evan. Where you've been, what you saw and thought and felt on your voyage."

Drake should have a woman like this, Evan thought. If

Mary had taken half an interest in his doings, they might have found contentment.

"The world is so incredibly vast, Annie. I saw terrible beauty and awesome perils, wonders such as I never dreamed of."

She listened with rapt attention as he described the hazards of the Straits of Magellan, the strange, hospitable Californios of New Albion, the endless crossing of the Pacific. The exotic Orient had been a place of decadence, violence, and incredible splendor. They took on spices, silks, and treasures from the richest ports in the world. They braved storms and calms, near-mutiny, disease and dissension.

"It was always Drake who got us through the adverse times," he said. "Francis knows well how to lead his men."

"Rodrigo's grandfather, Santiago, said much the same of Admiral Colón." She settled beside him, trailing her fingers over his chest. "You've seen the world, Evan. Now what will you do?"

He hesitated, pondering her question. Part of him felt drawn to her and her alone, yet another part hungered for adventure and action and aye, even danger. They were still strangers in many ways, and he was not certain he could make her understand.

"There are no simple choices for me. I'd be lying to you if I said I didn't long to see more, to go farther. God, there are wonders such as I never believed to exist. England seems so very small and cold to me now." He stroked her shoulder lightly.

Annie was glad he could not see her face, for tears of disappointment stung her eyes. "You're one of the richest men in England. Now that Owen is gone, the village of Carew will suffer no more. How can you go farther than around the world? You need not venture anywhere again."

"My need is as strong as ever." The stark truth escaped him even as he held her tighter.

"What of me? Of us?"

His hand fell still on her shoulder. "While we were sailing

the channel after you, Rodrigo asked much the same question."

"And how did you answer?"

"Annie, I can offer you a beautiful home, servants, and goods in abundance. Drake said the same to his wife, but it failed to make her happy."

"All she truly wants is to be with Francis, to have him at her side, to bear his children and grow old with him."

"Aye."

"I know how she feels."

"Annie, if I thought I could keep you happy, I'd marry you tomorrow."

"But you won't." Only pride held her tears in check.

"It would not be fair. Despite the fortune I made on the voyage, I am still a common Welsh mariner. You stir my blood, you set me aflame. And yet the thought of leaving you to wait for me fills me with guilt. According to Drake, the queen is beginning to build up her navy. Both Francis and I are certain to be called into service. I could be gone for months—"

"Years," she said dully.

"Aye, years. But I love you, Annie. We need not decide anything for certain today."

Gratefully she agreed. "Then love me again, Evan, and make me forget that tomorrow exists."

Annie touched her hand to her throat, even though she knew nothing could ease the ache of tears. Beneath her wrist, the ruby ring of Henry VIII pressed into her breastbone. Never had the legacy felt more burdensome.

At the London Pool, where great ships made a forest of masts, activity bustled in every quarter, but she could focus only on the two men who stood before her on the deck of a ship.

Rodrigo and André both looked grave, though excited.

A shrill whistle broke the tension. "Time to board," said Rodrigo. "We leave with the tide."

Annie nodded and forced herself to speak. "I'm glad

you're going to see your mother, André. You'll find Doña Paloma a very great lady."

He fingered the silver badge on his cloak. "But what on earth will she think of me?"

It was unprecedented, his nervousness. André Scalia had served princes and prelates with haughty, unfaltering confidence. Yet the thought of meeting his mother filled him with uncertainty.

"She'll take pride in what you've achieved, I think."

"Pride?" He narrowed his eyes in disbelief. "By my lady, what have I ever done but seek power through endless manipulation and intrigue?"

She knew he was thinking of his attempt to dispose of Evan and let her go on thinking he was dead. "Some things are more powerful than lies or ambition or pirates' treasure. Or even the royal succession."

"It's true, *hermano*," Rodrigo said, clasping André on the shoulder. "What was it that drove you to defend my life on the deck of that ship? Surely not ambition, eh?"

The boatswain's whistle sounded again. Annie took a step toward the ramp leading to the quay. At the bottom, Evan and Drake waited.

"I'd best go," she said, watching Rodrigo and André through a blur of tears.

Rodrigo caught her in his arms. For a moment, she was a child again, and he her bluff, laughing guardian, protective and a little confused by her. She remembered all they had shared, from the wonder of her first lost tooth to the terror of her first monthly bleeding. It seemed he had always been there, and only now, in adulthood, did she understand all he had given up in order to care for his best friend's daughter.

"Rodrigo," she whispered, "you've sacrificed so many years of your life for me."

"I would give them all again," he said in a low, rough voice. He pressed his lips to her brow. "You're a rare and infuriating young woman, Annie Blythe, and I'll not regret a moment I spent with you, scolding you, worrying about you. Or loving you."

"Or cursing the day I was born?"

"Ah, Annie." He held her away from him. "I thought you'd like to know—before we go to San Augustine, we'll be calling at Nombre de Dios."

Her heart lifted. "For Valeria?"

He nodded. "I want my parents to meet my new wife."

She hugged him hard. "It's about time, Don Rodrigo." Then she turned to André. "There are things I can thank you for," she said in a conciliatory tone. "You were my teacher and my protector. I suspect you did a great many things for me that I don't know about."

"You've a generous heart, Annie Blythe," he said. "I could wish—"

She snatched at his hand. "Don't wish, André. England will go on without you. And, though it's hard to imagine, England will go on without Elizabeth one day. Be at peace in your heart."

"I think I can do that now." He brushed his lips over her cheek. The whistle sounded a third time.

Annie could no longer hold back her sobs. Flinging her arms around both of them, she said, "I will not say good-bye. I will not!"

"Then don't." Rodrigo's eyes were suspiciously bright. "After all, *muchacha*, I've always known how fond you are of sea voyages."

She rushed down the quay without looking back.

Evan and Drake exchanged a glance of cold, abject fear. The letter in Drake's hand rattled in the wind off the river.

"What can it mean?" Evan asked.

"I'm almost afraid to find out," Drake said.

Evan watched the royal messenger who had delivered the note ride off on a liveried palfrey. "How the devil did he know to find us here? We told no one we were going after Don Iago's ship last night."

"Add it to our muster roll of worries," Drake said. "I wonder if we could get away with ignoring this. Just sail off toward the horizon. The world's a big place."

Memories of making love to Annie haunted Evan's mind, and yet Drake's words awakened a familiar restlessness. He felt strange, knowing that their successful circumnavigation had stripped away some of the secrets of the earth. And yet a whole realm of mysteries had opened for them anew, tantalizing as the cliffs of New Albion half a world away.

He looked at the ship Rodrigo and André would sail to the Indies, and for a moment he forgot the dire message clutched in Drake's hand. Peculiar, how they had all come full circle: from bitter enemies to friends united in their love for Annie. Perhaps the world of emotions was as vast and unfathomable as the physical world.

As he watched, Annie flung her arms around Rodrigo and André. Evan could almost feel her pain as she clung to them one last time.

"You look a bit glum for a man who's just been reunited with the woman he loves," Drake said.

And what a reunion it had been. Just the memory of Annie's silken limbs twined around his, her soft sighs gusting in his ear, made him glad he had risked life and limb to win her heart.

Yet physical joy was one thing. Emotionally, they had grown apart, their loyalties and priorities divided and uncertain.

"Three years is a long time," Evan said simply. "Tell me, Francis, when you saw Mary again, did you feel you saw a stranger?"

A bittersweet smile pulled at Drake's lips. "Evan, if I lived with that woman every minute of every day, I'd still think her a stranger." He blew out his breath. "I did the poor girl no favor when I married her. Even now that I've made her one of the richest women in England, I cannot purchase a love that never existed in the first place."

His words sent a chill through Evan. Was he like Drake in that, unable to find contentment even with a woman he adored more than life itself?

He glanced again at the letter. Perhaps the point was moot. By the morrow, he might be dead.

Annie rushed down the gangplank, her cheeks shining with tears. "They're off, then."

Evan kissed her forehead. "Are you all right?"

She nodded, then took out a handkerchief and dried her face. "I feel as if I closed the door on my childhood." The letter caught her eye. Her gaze riveted on the seal stamped into the wax. "Francis? What is it?"

Drake took a long, deep breath, then expelled it slowly. Dread pounded in Evan's ears.

"A royal summons," said Drake. "I fear the queen is in a rage about our escapade with Owen Perrott and Don Iago."

CHAPTER 19

Gripped by worries for Evan and Drake, Annie stood among the queen's ladies on the deck of the *Golden Hind*. Strange to think that this narrow-waisted vessel had been Evan's home for years. Now, scrubbed and careened, the ship was festooned for ceremony. Silk bunting flew from the masts and yardarms, and great painted shields flanked the hull. The whole town of Deptford had come out to the port to watch the spectacle. Time and time again, Annie heard a wonder-filled voice saying, "Yonder is the bark that hath sailed round the world."

Moments before sunset, a blare of trumpets signaled the arrival of the queen. Wearing the diamond-and-emerald encrusted crown Drake had commissioned for her from the stolen treasure, Elizabeth boarded the ship.

Together with the ladies, Annie sank into an obeisance. She felt stiff and cold, unbearably apprehensive about the meaning of the royal summons. Had the queen found out about the exploits of Evan and Drake in the channel? Rescue mission or not, they had caused the deaths of a Welsh lord and a Spanish grandee, no small insult to Spain.

Marchaumont, an agent of the Duke of Alençon, attended the queen with considerable Gallic pomp. Elizabeth had consented to a betrothal with the French king's son, and the poor sod actually believed she would marry him one day.

Annie knew better, and her certainty was borne out a moment later. Just as the queen passed her, one of her purple and gold garters came loose and trailed onto the deck.

Some of the ladies gasped in sympathetic embarrassment. As smooth as aged wine, Marchaumont swept up the token. "Your Highness, I beg you leave to send this prize to my master. Your much-beloved Alençon would treasure it always."

Mischief gleamed in Elizabeth's eyes. "What say you, Mistress Blythe?" she asked, motioning Annie up from her curtsy. "Shall I award this prize to my suitor?"

Annie hesitated. Elizabeth was testing her, as she often did. Sending so intimate a token to Alençon would strongly encourage his suit, yet withholding it could put a stop to his costly gifts and flattering missives of devotion.

"In truth, madam, it would be a remarkable gesture," Annie said carefully.

The light in the queen's eyes dimmed in disapproval. Quickly, Annie added, "But without the garter, you'd have nothing to keep up your stocking!"

Elizabeth's face reddened, and Annie braced herself for a storm of royal rage. Instead, the queen grabbed the garter from Marchaumont, then threw back her head and guffawed. "Quite so, my clever poppet. Quite so." With elaborate care, she lifted the hem of her gown, extended the royal leg, and tied the garter back on.

Annie allowed herself a small breath of relief. The queen seated herself upon a U-shaped stool with gilt arms. Behind her, the sun lowered slowly toward the horizon. Near her stood Sir Christopher Hatton, Robert Dudley, and her white-haired secretary of state, William Cecil, Lord Burghley. At her side was the Frenchman Marchaumont, his prominent nose sniffing the breeze like a hound on the hunt.

"Please," Annie whispered to Lady Charlotte Mayhew. "What is Her Majesty's intent?"

Lady Mayhew's eyes narrowed. "I thought she told you everything. Though I trow you did provide a suitable answer regarding the garter."

Annie had already forgotten the incident. "I know only that the officers and crew of the *Golden Hind* have been summoned. For what purpose, I have no idea."

"Nor do we." Lady Mayhew tucked a finger into her starched ruff and discreetly scratched her neck. "Damnable collars," she muttered, then said, "Perhaps the queen has decided we're not ready for a war with Spain, so she'll execute the pirates to make an example of them. And didn't Drake execute Mr. Doughty during the voyage? Perhaps he'll be made to answer for that."

"The queen was elated with their accomplishment and has put aside the complaints of Doughty's brother," Annie said, desperate to drive away her fears.

"Of course she was, and she wouldn't give up the bullion even at the point of a sword. If she has to placate the king of Spain, she'd rather do it with a pirate's blood than gold." Lady Mayhew tapped her slippered foot. "And then, of course, there's the disaster you caused. The Spanish ambassador's chief aide is dead."

Annie cast her eyes down. "He broke the law, as did Owen Perrott."

"Not everyone sees it that way."

"Not even the queen?"

"I'll tell you what she sees, you little fool. She sees her favorite lady all calf-eyed over a Welsh pirate!"

"I beg your pardon. A Welsh hero." Despite her brave words, Annie suppressed a shiver. Would Elizabeth accomplish what even André Scalia could not? It would not be the first time she had used her power to break up a pair of lovers.

A drum beat broke in on her troubled thoughts. Up the gangplank came the crew of the *Golden Hind*. All wore colorful new hose, trousers, and doublets, their hair combed and beards trimmed.

Drake led the procession, carrying a gleaming silver casket. Yet another gift, no doubt, to temper the queen's ire.

Behind Drake came Evan. Annie's breath caught, and it took all her willpower to keep from running to him. The breeze lifted his long dark hair over his shoulders. His face was grave. He looked neither right nor left. They stopped in front of the queen and knelt. Drake placed the casket at her feet.

Elizabeth stood. "You have committed one of the most magnificent acts in maritime history," she stated. "It surprises me not at all that God chose an Englishman to circle the globe."

Drake nodded solemnly. Annie could not hear his murmured words.

Though advancing in years, Elizabeth still had the voice of a young, strong woman, and her words rang clear. "You committed deeds of piracy against the empire of my brother, Philip of Spain."

Reaching behind her, she drew out a gleaming sword and handed it to Marchaumont. "King Philip demands that I strike off the heads of the pirates. I think it fitting that France join me in giving the accolades."

"No!" Annie started forward.

Lady Mayhew gripped her arm. "Be still! You'll have her wrath on us all!"

The sword came up. Annie held her breath. The blade descended, tracing a sunstruck arc in the golden sky above the heads of Evan and Drake.

Annie whimpered and shielded her eyes.

"For your service," the queen intoned, "I dub thee Sir Francis Drake, knight of the realm and master pirate of the unknown world." A familiar, enchanting guile colored the queen's words.

Incredulous, Annie peeked through her fingers. The flat of the blade touched Drake on each shoulder.

"And Sir Evan Carew." The blade touched him as well.

"You see," Elizabeth pointed out, "I never bestow knighthood cheaply. You men have brought me a kingdom of gold."

"Thank you, Jesus," Annie whispered. She nearly melted to the planks with relief. Then a fierce pride glowed inside her. Whatever else they had done, Evan and Drake had achieved their fame through courage and commitment, their fearless hunger for adventure.

As they stood, a great cheer went up. A group of musicians began to play their pipes and drums, and the deck swarmed with reveling mariners and dignitaries. Annie craned her neck to catch a glimpse of Evan, but a throng of well-wishers quickly surrounded him.

"A fine ending," Lady Mayhew remarked, speaking loudly over the din.

" 'Tis only the beginning," Annie said, and a lump rose in her throat. Evan would always be a knight of the high seas, destined to seek adventure and carry the banner of the queen to all corners of the world.

What of me, Evan? she wondered, her eyes burning. On unsteady feet, she made her way along the rail.

A sudden decision rocked her entire being. As she edged forward, she untied the leather string around her neck and took the ruby ring of Henry VIII in her hand.

The sounds of celebration faded around her as she pondered her future. Could Evan want her now? He stood at the pinnacle of his success; she could offer him nothing but love to compete with the glory of knighthood and a gilded career at sea.

A footstep behind her disturbed her thoughts. She turned, the ring clutched in her suddenly cold hands. "Madam!"

Stone-faced, Elizabeth grasped Annie's wrist and pried open her fingers. The ruby ring lay in her palm. The queen drew a quick breath. Her eyes narrowed in the twilight. "It is you, isn't it?"

Annie stared down at the gently shifting deck. It was over. All the pretense, all the hiding, the whole dangerous game she had played for years. What a fool she had been to imagine herself Elizabeth's superior on the perilous field of intrigue and deception.

She forced herself to look up, to hold that burning gaze. "Yes, ma'am," she said in a clear, steady voice.

"I always thought the lost heir was a boy."

Annie could think of no answer. The sounds of revelry swelled around her, beating like a pulse in her ears.

"I could have you killed for your deception," Elizabeth said. "I've executed men for lesser crimes." Her long, slender fingers tightened around Annie's wrist, and for a moment she studied the age-smoothed ring of her long-dead father. "Or," the queen went on, "I could subject you to an even greater curse: I could give you the crown of England."

Annie gasped. The queen's intense regard held her spellbound. She knew better than to plead; nothing so incensed the queen as groveling.

Elizabeth's gaze searched Annie's face, and she seemed to soften at what she saw in her niece's eyes. Letting go of Annie's arm, she made a dismissive gesture. Suddenly her expression held tenderness, respect, and deep, heartfelt regrets.

"Go now," she murmured, stepping back. "Go in peace. I swear I'll outlive Mary Stewart, and train up her son James to be king after me." She tapped her bejeweled hand upon the rail. "Something must be done with Castle Carew, since that young reaver came to such a bad end. Aye, I should put a responsible man in charge." The old impish gleam returned to the queen's eyes. "A knight or better, don't you think, my dear?"

Stunned, Annie managed a formal curtsy.

Elizabeth struck the rail harder. "Well, this is a rare sight. My own kinswoman gape-mouthed like a haddock, speechless for once in her life!"

Annie's heart soared, and the blood rushed in a loud, triumphant, and incredulous rhythm through her body. The queen was setting her free. She thought of Evan, of the places they would go, the adventures they would have.

Her fingers closed around the ring. Her gaze never leaving

Elizabeth's face, she held her hand over the open water. Then she opened her fingers and the ring fell, the gold flashing bright upon the water, then sinking out of sight.

Elizabeth sniffed. "At least you'll always know where the cursed thing is."

"God bless Your Grace," Annie managed to whisper. She rose to kiss the queen's cheek, then turned to go.

"Annie!"

She turned back, dreading that the queen had changed her mind. "Yes, Your Grace?"

"Be content, Annie. That is all I ask of you now."

"I shall be, Your Grace." Lifting her skirts, Annie rushed down the decks, the crowd passing in a blur. She came to the waist of the ship amid a group of seamen.

"Evan!" she called, fighting her way to him. A pair of laughing mariners caught her and bodily passed her along the deck. Then strong arms reached for her, and she found herself in Evan's embrace.

"My love," she said, "it is over. The queen knows my secret, and she gave me my freedom."

Cautious joy shone in his night-dark eyes. "Truly? No conditions?"

"None, save that I be content." She cradled his cheek in her hand. "I can't do that without you, Evan."

He took her hand and held it against his heart. "You'd leave court? Leave England?"

"I might not have to. The queen means to bestow Castle Carew on you."

"I? Lord of Carew?"

" 'Tis what she promised. What say you, my darling?" Annie bit her lip. "I know you favor venturing asea, and surely you could from time to time—"

"Hush." A heart-catching smile curved his mouth. "I'd say I cannot be a proper lord without a proper lady." He kissed her briefly, lightly, and the touch of his lips promised tenderness, and adventure, and a future bright with hope. "Marry me, Annie."

"Yes! Oh, yes!" she shouted, laughing and covering his startled face with kisses. "Everything is going to be fine—better than I ever dared to dream."

"Cariad," he said, holding her tight against his chest and smiling with sweet irony as he recalled the perils they had survived. "Didn't we always know that?"

BESTSELLERS FROM TOR

Buy them at your local bookstore or use this handy coupon:
Clip and mail this page with your order.

Publishers Book and Audio Mailing Service
P.O. Box 120159, Staten Island, NY 10312-0004

Please send me the book(s) I have checked above. I am enclosing $ _____
(Please add $1.25 for the first book, and $.25 for each additional book to cover postage and handling.
Send check or money order only—no CODs.)

Name _____
Address _____
City _____ State/Zip _____
Please allow six weeks for delivery. Prices subject to change without notice.

READ TOR CLASSICS